Untreed
Reads

Leah's Journey
By Gloria Goldreich

Cover Design by Ginny Glass

ISBN-13: 978-1-61187-801-1

Also available in ebook format.
Previously published in print, 1978.

Published by Untreed Reads, LLC
506 Kansas Street, San Francisco, CA 94107
www.untreedreads.com

Printed in the United States of America.

For Sheldon Horowitz

CONTENTS

Russia
1919
1

Although the morning sun blazed across the fields, turning the newly blossoming wheat a dull gold, it was cool in the attic and the tall girl who stood naked beneath the beams shivered. Stooping slightly, she looked at herself in the long mirror, its frame shrouded in dust and its glass cloudy despite the fact that she had wiped it with a damp cloth only minutes before. It was the mirror which had brought Leah Adler up to the attic this morning and she smiled at her reflection as she had smiled months before at Yaakov, her young husband, when she saw him for the first time at the meeting of Social Zionists which her brother Moshe had chaired. It was a smile of shy recognition, of tentative invitation, of sweet promise. Just as she had offered it to the serious, red-haired youth whose eyes had darted with nervous excitement from her face to the speaker's rostrum, she offered it now to her own image. It was, after all, the first time in her life that she was seeing herself completely unclothed and she lowered her eyes to greet the young woman who stared back at her.

Her reflection pleased her and she smiled more widely to show her strong white teeth and the small half-dimple that twinkled at the corner of her mouth. Her sister Malcha, small and round, had always told Leah that her mouth was too wide—but Leah had never thought so and did not think so now. One did not want a small thin mouth when the nose was just a bit too prominent and the dark eyes so widely set. There was a seed of sororal malice in Malcha's observation, Leah knew, but she was too happy to resent her older sister and thought of her instead with pity. Malcha, after all, had submitted to all the things Leah had fought. She had remained at home in the tiny *shtetl* town of Partseva, dutifully imitating their mother. She worked in the kitchen, weeded the small garden that grew behind the house, and sat behind the counter of the small dusty shop where their mother stocked rolls of dull gabardine and faded cottons which the village women bought to fashion into coats and dresses. Quiet, patient Malcha had adhered to the marriage contract which their father had signed on her behalf when she was only a toddler. The bridegroom, Shimon, betrothed before he could talk, was the son of a kinsman from a distant village.

Leah remembered how Malcha had stood beneath the wedding canopy, a worn prayer shawl held aloft by four relatives, her long hair brushed loose about her shoulders so that it fell like a shawl of shining dark velvet across the white dress. Malcha had shivered suddenly as the rabbi intoned the marriage prayer and proffered the ritual glass of wine—Leah wondered if that sudden tremor was because of the cool of the late afternoon or whether her sister had submitted briefly and reluctantly to a sudden seizure of fear. Malcha had, after all, seen her groom for the first time that afternoon and with each word that the rabbi uttered her life grew more intricately knotted with that of the slender young stranger who did not raise his eyes from the ground throughout the ceremony. When Malcha reached to drink from the marriage cup Leah saw that her sister's hand was trembling and her own fingers shook in sympathy and protest.

But afterward, at the wedding party, Malcha had danced with wild joy, even tossing off her white slippers to join her sister and her mother in a whirling circle dance that concluded with the three of them laughing wildly and panting for breath. The other women of the village circled about them joyously chanting, "Greeting to the bride—luck to the bridegroom!"

Malcha had even been calm when her hair was cut according to orthodox ritual and the rich thick lengths of black hair clotted the grass at her feet. Leah had cried then and touched her own dark braid protectively, vowing silently that she would never cut her hair and wear a marriage wig.

And she had not, she thought proudly, on this sun-licked morning. Touching the dark coronet of braids that crowned her head, she thought of how Yaakov loved to loosen the dark coils of hair and wind them about his thin freckled fingers. Impulsively, she ripped the pins out of her hair and undid the braids, allowing the hair to flow loosely about her bare shoulders as her sister's had flowed across her wedding dress. She bent even lower to see her full form in the mirror and she smiled as a sudden shadow sent a shaft of darkness across the pale skin of her stomach and at the dappled patterns the leaves of the Lombardy tree that grew just outside the attic window made across her young breasts. The rose-tipped nipples jutted out of the leafy shadows like small unripe fruit and she touched each gently, marveling at their tenderness and their secret.

She stood to her full height now, shook her hair out, and executed the delicate, intricate steps of a folk dance she had learned at the Socialist meetinghouse. The boards of the attic floor were pleasantly rough beneath her bare feet and she hummed softly, swaying and turning in the mirror, no longer chilled, her blood warmed by her own movements, the remembered music, and the thought of the gentle pressure of Yaakov's arms and the thrust and force of his strong young body. The warmth vindicated her. She had been right, after all, to resist her parents' pleas that she emulate Malcha and remain in Partseva, peeling potatoes, unrolling yard goods, and waiting for the day when her own crown of dark hair would be shorn and she would become the wife of a man whose face she did not know.

She never knew where she found the strength to fight their threats and ignore their tears and entreaties, to leave the closeness of Partseva for the broader life and streets of Odessa, just as she had run from the closeness of the kitchen to the freedom of the sweet-smelling broad fields when she was a little girl. Always, she had struggled toward wide expanses, uncharted landscapes, and her mother had often told her that in the days when small girls played house beneath the kitchen table, Leah had climbed a low-slung apple tree and erected her imaginary domicile among its heavy sheltering branches, choosing the sky for her ceiling and the fruit-laden boughs for her floor.

Of course, in Odessa, she had her brother Moshe's support and the knowledge that he had broken out of the ruthless cycle of *shtetl* existence years before. She had lived with Moshe and his wife Henia, a gentle fair-haired girl, the granddaughter of a renowned rabbi who had left the mystique of Hasidism for the "practical dream" of Zionism. Henia and Moshe had arranged for her to study at a small academy for Jewish girls and found work for her as assistant to a seamstress. And it was Moshe who had traveled back to Partseva and engineered a tenuous domestic peace treaty so that Leah's parents came to forgive what they could not forget. They had even come to her wedding in Odessa, satisfied that the ceremony was conducted according to orthodox tradition, even though the bride did not cut her hair and refused to wear her sister's white wedding dress, choosing instead the full blue skirt and wide-sleeved embroidered white blouse, the festive costume of the young Socialist.

Remembering her wedding, Leah moved closer to the mirror, still lightly dancing, but exchanging her smile for a serious gaze which she practiced with such solemn concentration that her own seriousness made her laugh. But something she saw in the mirror caused the laugh to turn into a sudden gasp of fear and she whirled around, her heart beating wildly, her hands trembling. The delicate green leaves of the Lombardy tree were trapped in an enclosure of flame and the sky beyond blazed with the ominous molten gold of a fire that was not born of sunlight.

She pulled on her dress and dashed to the window, kneeling so that she might see better. The small neighboring house, the home of Zvi Goldenberg, a miller and Torah scholar, had turned into a cone of spewing flames. The fire licked its way skyward, its fierce orange tongues vanquishing the gentle golden rays of August sunlight. From her attic window, Leah saw two figures hurry from the burning house, clutching sacks from which bright sparks of fire danced and crackled. As the men drew closer, she leaned down to call to them but remained silent, her voice strangled in her throat. The running men were peasant farmers and she recognized the taller of the two as a man for whom Yaakov had composed a letter of complaint against the vicious raids of Marshall Grigoriev's soldiers. The man could neither read nor write and Yaakov had guided his hand so that he could form his signature. These men, she knew, had no business in or near Zvi Goldenberg's house. Their presence there could mean only one thing.

Leah willed herself to calm, possessed by certain awareness of what had happened. She listened as a child's distant scream ripped through the fiery sky and died before it had reached full pitch. She recognized the scream as she recognized the flames, as though her knowledge of them had long been buried within her, a secret vein of terror to be mined at just such a time of fire and fear. She remembered her mother's weary voice, telling stories of a wintry evening—tales of burning villages and screaming children, of men running through panic-ridden streets, clutching at facial holes that had been eyes, now bloodied pools, shouting out the names of wives and children, while the keening voices of women rose and fell and rose again. Her mother had been orphaned in such a pogrom and her father's father had lost his eyes on the bloody streets of Kishinev.

But that had been before the Revolution, Leah thought, willing herself to reason, to clarity of thought. She and Yaakov were building their lives in the new Russia, where justice and equality would erase ancient hatreds. The thought of her husband spurred her to action and she darted downstairs, her long hair still undone, flowing wildly about her shoulders.

Yaakov was safe, she assured herself. He was in Odessa where he was known and respected as Secretary of the Young Socialist League. He had, in fact, traveled there at the urgent request of a party leader to help draft a manifesto against the raids of the soldiers returning from the Czar's war who roamed the countryside, pillaging from farms, setting random fires, raping women, and harassing children. She had heard that some of these men chanted the ancient slogans of anti-Semitism—"Strike at the Jews and save Russia!", "Kill the Jews for the sake of the land!"—but like Yaakov, she felt they mouthed the words without really understanding the sentiment. They were like children who shouted spiteful names at each other, names they neither understood nor meant. One had to sympathize with these displaced peasants who had been exploited by a corrupt aristocracy. Their clothing was torn and their beards and hair were full of the nettles of their hillside beds. They had not yet been educated into the new philosophy and were trapped by their ignorance and their ancient prejudices.

Standing in the kitchen and watching the flames leap in a fiery dance from the miller's house, she wooed herself into a calm by repeating this catechism of political faith. If there had been any danger, Yaakov would never have left her alone like this, in the countryside at his parents' home, particularly not at a time when she had been feeling weak and light-headed in the morning, her empty stomach stirring uneasily so that she had to dash suddenly for the bucket to relieve the nausea. She thought that she might be pregnant but she had not yet missed a period. Although they had been married only seven months and she knew Yaakov was not ready for children, the thought of life growing within her was intriguing; even now, with the fear still pounding against her heart, she touched her abdomen lightly, protectively.

The child's scream moments before—it must have been Zvi Goldenberg's little girl, a toddler who often sat in fields of wild flowers singing softly to herself. The child might be trapped in the burning house, she thought, and she flung open the door, angry with herself because she had delayed so long and even more angry because she knew her delay was rooted in her fear.

Fear was familiar to her. It clung to all Jewish children like a stubborn shadow woven of tales of terror and pinned to them by muted memories of death and destruction. She struggled against it as she stepped outside and felt the grass crunch beneath her bare feet and the gentle stroke of a soft breeze against her unbuttoned back. The air was thick with smoke and her eyes teared against the acrid ashen odor. A crow circled above her and settled itself on a branch of the Lombardy tree, cawing a harsh chant of warning to its mate in a distant wheat field.

"Yaakov!" she shouted in wild hope. She had seen a figure weaving toward her through the thick dark air and for a moment she had caught sight of a familiar mass of bright red hair.

Of course, Yaakov had heard about the fire, or perhaps had even seen it from the outskirts of the village, and hurried back for her. She ran toward the approaching figure, her arms outstretched. She reeled backward in surprise, almost falling, when she was seized in a rough grasp and a voice she recognized but could not place sneered, "So it's young Adler's new bride. Why are you barefoot, bride girl, when all Jewish women have shoes?"

His fingers kneaded the soft flesh of her arms and she wrenched away from his clutch, summoning up strength she had not known she possessed, causing her to fall backward against the Lombardy tree. The marks of the man's fingers against her skin were like searing welts and she pressed herself against the fortress of bark, wondering whether it would be best to dash for the house and bolt the door or try to run across the fields toward the town. Her thoughts, tumbling over each other in bursts of fear and indecision, were interrupted by a deafening crash and showers of bright orange sparks soaring skyward like rockets of fiery flowers.

"Aha, the center beam has gone. The house is down," the man said calmly as though he were a contractor analyzing some structural mystery. There was no satisfaction in his voice, only an insouciant calm. He moved toward her, his step and eyes holding her prisoner, impaling her against that tree under whose branches she and her young husband had so often laughed and kissed.

"But the child," she cried, "what of the child?" How dark the small girl's eyes had been, as she played among the blue flowers that bowed and waved in the summer wind.

"Oh, the kids got out the back door and ran for the town. The miller and his wife too. But there'll be trouble there too for them. There's trouble all over Odessa today."

"Why today?" she asked, her voice controlled, disguised with a calm she did not feel. She knew she could not outrun him across fields he had known since childhood and she knew too that to escape to the house—if it could be done at all—was no escape at all but simply a reprieve until he broke the door down or tossed a flaming torch against the fragile wooden structure. Her only hope lay in conversation, in leading him through the wasteland of irrational hatred to the calm plateau of reason. They can all be reached, Yaakov had said often. They only need to understand. Leah girded herself now with her husband's faith and struggled to reach with words the man who made no move toward her but stood sniffing the smoke-filled air. He laughed harshly before answering her and his voice was rough with fury.

"It's August, bride girl. The crops are burning in the fields and what the sun doesn't eat Grigoriev's men steal. Hungry men cannot sleep. Their wives walk barefoot and their children's mouths are dry. Others take what belongs to us. Others."

"But whose fault is that? What good will setting fires and killing people do for your wives and children? The thing to do is to work. We must build irrigation ditches, learn new ways of planting, share the harvests and timberlands." All the theories she had heard expounded at countless meetings shot out at him in verbal bullets which he fended easily with another brutal burst of laughter.

"We cannot wait for your ditches and your collectives. We need food and clothing now. We will take what we are not given. We need other things too, bride girl. Other things that we do not put in cupboards or larders."

He laughed fiercely now and started toward her, roaring with amusement as she skirted about the tree, using its wide trunk as a shield so that it seemed they were engaged in a child's game of tag, trapped in a leafy enclosure of shade from which they could not move for fear of losing.

The bark scraped her legs and she ran even faster, waiting to dash from the tree and take her chances across the field but, bored with the game, he seized her skirt and held her fast, pinning her arms behind her back and trapping her legs within his own.

"What do you want, Petrovich?" she shouted, for she had recognized him at last, knowing him through his wild burst of laughter as a foreman of the timber lock which her father-in-law managed. He had laughed that way with Yaakov's father one evening as he drank a glass of schnaps offered to celebrate Yaakov's marriage. He was a tall man, redheaded like Yaakov, his arms and chest billowing with muscles raised through years of battling the woodlands with great strokes of the steel ax that hung from his belt. She caught sight of her own face in the shining metal, and the face that had pleased her in the attic mirror was now a mask of fear so that she closed her eyes, terrified at her own image.

"You know what I want, bride girl. Of course you know what I want."

He flung her to the ground, still holding her arms and legs immobile and laughing as she spat into his face and bit the heavy features he thrust against her mouth.

"Yaakov!" she screamed wildly, "Papa! Oh God!"

He ripped her skirt in one sharp sure movement and thrust himself against her, forcing himself into the resistant narrowness of her body, thrusting upward against her while she writhed and screamed, fighting his weight and force. The last thing she remembered before sinking into a darkness of mind and numbness of feeling was biting fiercely at the hand he held over her mouth. When she drifted from that darkness into a shadowy wakefulness, a sliver of pink flesh clung to her teeth and she spat it out and covered it with her own vomit. The fire had died and the mound of charred wood and ashes rose from the earth like a gentle grave.

*

A month later Leah sat in her brother Moshe's flat, slowly pulling a needle and thread through a gaping rip in a blue cambric shirt and absently listening to the rise and fall of the voices around her. She had mended that shirt almost a dozen times but each time something about her work had displeased her—the stitches were too small or uneven, the mended fabric bulged where it should have remained flat, the thread was of the wrong shade. The shirt had belonged to her husband Yaakov and had been peeled from his body by Moshe who had thought his brother-in-law might still be alive when he was found on an Odessa street, his head shattered and a farmer's gleaning tool stuck in his chest. Moshe had ripped the shirt to probe for life in the heart that had stopped beating hours before, and Leah worked now to repair it as though the fabric made whole would mysteriously restore her husband to her.

She rethreaded the needle, but her eyes had grown tired in the dim light of the paraffin lamp and she put her work aside and looked about the room as though startled to find herself there, surprised that she was in fact alive and that the words of those about her had any meaning.

Moshe sat on the low cot which Henia had covered with a bright woven cloth. Next to him David Goldfeder, who had also come to Odessa from Partseva, slowly sorted a pile of papers, arranging them on a wooden plank that served as desk and table. Moshe and Henia had lived in the Odessa apartment for five years but they had never furnished their rooms, thinking their stay temporary. Their future lay to the south, in the ancient land of Palestine which they referred to only as Zion. They did not want to encumber themselves with possessions which they would not be able to take to the small settlement in the Huleh valley they hoped to make their home. They knew that there they would live in a tent mounted on planks against the encroaching dampness of the swamp and that all their energies would be needed to struggle with that swamp. Only that day Moshe had had a letter from a comrade in Palestine telling him of the death of yet another pioneer who had succumbed to malaria carried by the mosquitoes that infested the stagnant waters.

"It's a terrible thing about Rackman," Moshe said now. "He was so full of hope."

"What else do we have to be full of?" David Goldfeder asked and Leah saw that his hands trembled slightly so that the papers he held fluttered like forlorn white flags.

David Goldfeder's brother Aaron had been killed in the pogrom and also his fiancée, tiny Chana Rivka, who had written long manifestos on social justice in metered rhyme and traveled the countryside lecturing peasant women on concepts of hygiene and nutrition. She had died trying to save two small girls who were being taunted by a group of marauders who tossed the youngsters up into the air, passing the terrified children from one to the other as though they were balls, laughing as a child dropped and a small bone cracked. In the end they had killed Chana Rivka and the body of one of the children had been crushed beneath the wheels of a passing lorry. The surviving child, a thin dark-haired girl, hobbled about the streets of the town, using a crutch constructed of a red-painted table leg. The child did not speak but when an adult approached she would scream wildly and hover in the shadow of a doorway. When Leah, during one of her rare excursions from Moshe's house, had passed the small girl the child had followed after her, hopping in the protection of Leah's shadow, as a lame animal will often follow another maimed creature as though shared misery assured protection.

"We must be full of plans," Henia said, answering David Goldfeder's question. "Hope is a luxury. We must decide what to do. One thing is certain. We cannot stay here. Russia will be a graveyard for Jews."

"Why only Russia?" Moshe interjected. "All of Europe will be a graveyard for Jews. They will need only a few years to recover from the Great War and then they will turn around and begin. Already in Germany they are saying that it was the Jews who made the Kaiser lose the war. No, Palestine, Zion, is the only answer, the only place for plans, the only place for hope."

"And when do you leave?" David asked. "I hear that the Rothschild family has offered money to help at least one thousand more immigrants."

"He doesn't want the Russian Jews coming into France and Germany," Moshe said, laughing, but his gaze was heavy. He and Henia looked at each other and then each darted a nervous glance across the room where Leah had resumed her sewing.

In the dimly lit room she seemed more like an old woman than the beautiful teen-aged girl who only a month before had danced naked before an attic window and watched leafy shadows move across her bare breasts. She sat erect, her long dark hair knotted into a severe bun, her large dark eyes staring from a face whose pale skin was stretched too tightly across the fine bones. She wore the same black dress she had worn to her husband's funeral and her fingers moved now and again to touch the symbolic tear the rabbi had made in her mourning garment at the burial. She had worn that dress to all the other funerals held during that week when the streets of the Jewish quarter of Odessa rang with the moans of the dying and the wild grief of the mourners.

Leah had watched, dry-eyed, at Yaakov's funeral, as the pine box slid into the shallow grave. The coffin had rattled lightly as the stones and earth within it slid about. Yaakov had been killed on a cobbled street, his head bludgeoned so that the cranium had crumbled and the spongy white mass of brains had littered the bloody stones. The members of the burial society had carefully scraped up that mass of decaying detritus that had been the mind and thoughts of the young Socialist and placed it in the coffin. They had even dislodged the cobblestones stained with his blood and the earth around that had been drenched with it. According to Jewish law it was essential that the corpse be laid to rest with every particle of the body that could be salvaged, and so the stones and earth had been placed in the coffin on which the widowed bride dropped a handful of graying earth that crumbled beneath her trembling fingers.

Leah had observed the seven days of mourning at her brother's home, refusing to return to her in-laws' house where they mourned Yaakov using the same mourning benches upon which they had sat shiva for his brother, killed only two years before in the Czar's army.

The Czar was gone now but still Jews sat in mourning for their young men, Leah's father-in-law observed as Yaakov's Socialist friends came to comfort him.

"You should sit shiva with Yaakov's family," Leah's father had urged, but the girl had cried out in wild protest and they were afraid to insist.

Moshe and Henia did not know what had happened to Leah during that first morning when the pogrom began. She had come running into their apartment, her legs scratched and scarred by her journey across the fields, her hair tangled and loose, and a small network of scratches etched across her cheek. She wore a dark winter dress and brambles and nettles clung to the sweat-stained wool.

"Leah, what happened? Are you hurt?" Henia had cried but Leah had not answered. She had instead remained at the window, hour after hour, moving her lips soundlessly, searching the street for a sign of Yaakov.

He was dead even as she stood at the window, but she did not relax her vigil until Moshe came home, carrying the blue cambric shirt, his face collapsed with grief and loss. She held the shirt against her cheek and when she fell asleep at last, she cradled it in her arms and the pale blue turned dark with the tears that would not stop falling even as she slept.

"I don't know when we will go to Palestine, David," Moshe said. "But it must be soon. Henia does not want to spend another winter in Odessa."

"No, that's not true," Henia said. "The truth is I don't want to spend another day in Odessa."

They all laughed but their laughter was dry and cracked, a humor born not of joy but of bitterness. Even Leah smiled slightly, but almost at once her fingers found the tear in the mourning garment and the smile faded as she stroked the severed fabric.

"And what will you do, Leah?" David Goldfeder asked, assembling his papers in a cardboard portfolio. "Will you go to Palestine too?" He was a thin man who worked quickly, his pale-gray eyes fixed on the job at hand, his mouth set in a thin line of concentration. Because he was in mourning for his brother and Chana Rivka, he had neither shaved nor cut his hair for a month and Leah noticed for the first time how thick and dark his hair grew, making his thin face and light eyes seem even paler in contrast. She had known him in Partseva and knew that he was always the older boy who concerned himself with younger children, marshaling them for games, telling them stories, keeping pace with the smallest during hikes across the field. A hurt animal was always brought to David Goldfeder, and women came to him often and placed their worries before him. With gentle talk he sorted out their fear and grief, just as he had sorted the papers that he now gathered together in his worn folder.

Again Moshe and Henia glanced quickly at each other and then at Leah. Clearly, it was a question they had wanted to ask her but were unwilling to. There are defined borders to the territory of grief and they did not want to trespass.

"What are those papers you are working on, David?" Henia asked as Leah remained silent, staring straight ahead.

"Affidavits. Affidavits that our society has obtained from Jews in America. These papers will make it possible for some of our people to settle there. It's a new world over there across the ocean. A new society. A new philosophy of life."

"All worlds are the same," Moshe said. "There was a new philosophy here in Russia. Ah, yes. The brotherhood of man under the fatherhood of communism. But it would seem that the brotherhood is an exclusive one and Jews are not invited into the fraternity. In your United States there is the brotherhood of democracy, but such noble sentiments will do nothing to prevent pogroms there. The only answer is Palestine, Zion. The only answer is to build our own state, establish our own society, protect ourselves."

"And when the Arabs of Palestine attack your settlements, your state, your society, what will you call that?" David asked. "Ah, you will not call it a pogrom because pogroms belong to the old world, to the Diaspora. You will have another name for such attacks, but it will be the same thing. Jewish blood will be shed. Jewish children will die. Jewish lives will be in constant danger and the British will not care just as the Czar did not care and the Comintern did not care. Would I grieve less for my Chana Rivka or my brother Aaron if they had died at the hands of an Arab instead of at the hands of drunken Russians?"

"Stop!" Leah shouted and paused for a moment as though surprised at the harshness of her voice. "Please." Her tone was soft now, falling almost into a whisper. "Stop all this talk of killing. Please. No more. No more." She drew the needle fiercely through the blue cambric and cried out in pain as it pierced her finger and a tear-shaped drop of blood fell on the collar of Yaakov's shirt. She threw the garment aside and ran from the house, slamming the door behind her.

The three remaining in the room stared at each other and at the door.

"Go talk to her, David," Henia said. "You were so fond of each other as children. You always understood her."

"Yes, I remember," David said thoughtfully. "I will talk to her. But in a while. Let her be alone now. It will be all right. You'll see. It will be all right." He repeated the phrase with practiced ease, not thinking about its reality but offering it as comfort to himself and to those who waited for placebos of reassurance. "Believe me, it will be all right," he said again flatly and turned to a few forgotten papers, absently fingering the thin documents of hope.

*

A light mist drifted up to the streets of the Jewish quarter from the harbor and Leah felt it settle coolly on her face and dampen her hair. The familiar salt smell was pleasant and she opened her dress slightly at the throat and let the moist air settle on her skin. Her pleasure at the evening cool surprised her. She had thought herself numb to all feeling, relieved of sensation. She was a newcomer to the landscape of grief and did not know how to sift through the sands of sorrow and grab small footholds of life, grains that could be fashioned into strength. The events of the past month had paralyzed Leah with the ferocity of their impact, their terrible finality, and she had burrowed deeper and deeper into a cavern of fear. She had retreated into the shelter of Moshe's home, taking refuge there just like the small crippled girl who huddled in shadowy doorways. She could not stay there forever, she knew, and the time was coming when she would have to make a decision.

She was certain now, not with joy but with terror, that she was pregnant. There was no longer any need to count the weeks since her last menstrual flow or to touch her breasts, now grown full and tender. The child within her was growing and in a few more months it would stir with life. And soon too, her condition would become obvious and her secret would be common knowledge.

She knew there were those who might seize strands of hope from her pregnancy and the birth of her child. A life had been taken, they would say, but one had been given, blessed be the name of the Lord who fathered the fatherless. An infant had been named in the synagogue just after the pogrom had at last been squelched by government forces. The aged rabbi who during his years of service in Odessa had intoned the Kaddish, the prayer for the dead, for more Jewish souls than he could remember, had lifted the newborn baby high for the entire congregation to see. It was a girl and its mother's cries of labor had mingled with the screaming of dying children and the moaning of bereaved men and women. The child had been born on a night when the town blazed with fire and shards of broken glass littered the cobbled streets so that the horses of the funeral carts kicked wildly and would not pass through. But the newborn was a healthy baby, weighing almost ten pounds, and the assembled congregation smiled as the infant stretched luxuriously and purred through dreamless sleep.

"The parents of the child name her Tikva—hope," the rabbi told the worshipers. "Her birth and her name are a message for all of us. Where there is death there is also life. We dare not despair. We go on. We bring forth new children to take up our faith and we entrust them to God's care because in His mercy He shall see that Israel will endure, that new generations will rise up."

Leah, sitting in a rear pew, leaned forward with the other women, as they lifted the thick gauze curtain that separated them from the men so that they could see the child. They murmured softly, with satisfaction, as the strong baby kicked away its swaddling and they smiled when the young father, wrapped in his prayer shawl, carried his child down from the pulpit.

It would be said of Leah's child, also, that the new birth marked the continuity of the generations, that Yaakov's child was an obscure compensation for Yaakov's death, that it would provide comfort for her, grant her a gain against the magnitude of her loss. But what would happen to their emotional bookkeeping if she were to announce that it was possible that the child that clung so tenaciously to her womb was not of her dead husband's seed, that it might have been conceived through struggle and hatred? She had thought she was pregnant in the innocence of that August morning but it had been too soon to know. In moments of calm she assured herself that the child was Yaakov's, born of their tenderness, but the stormy moods of uncertainty tore into that calm, forcing her to recognize that she might have been impregnated by the redheaded woodsman whose laugh was tinged with fury and whose eyes had burned with hatred.

It had taken her weeks to organize her thoughts, to recognize the consequences of that anguished struggle. Even in the blind hours that followed Petrovich's attack, when she had at last struggled to her feet, removed the ripped dress, remembering to shred the fabric even more and to consign it to the rag pile, she had thrust all thought from her mind. She had washed herself over and over, using a coarse sponge and rubbing the lower part of her body with such fierce strength that for weeks afterward it remained red and raw. She had put on a winter dress, thinking of the thick material as a shield, and run through field and thicket to Moshe's home in the town. There, she had shrugged away all questions knowing the danger that lay in answering them.

Other women had been raped during the pogrom and each day Henia brought her a new tale of sexual violence and violation.

"Goldstein's daughter. Only sixteen years old. They say she has not spoken since the attack. And Eisenberg's wife. A pregnant woman with a suckling at her breast. God help them. God help the daughters of Israel."

At such moments Henia forgot her Zionist zeal and became again the daughter of a Hasidic rabbi. She swayed in silent prayer and her tear-filled eyes turned heavenward.

There was no shame, Leah knew, attached to the violation of innocent, powerless women and it was not out of shame that Leah maintained her silence but out of the terrible doubt that haunted her. For a while she had hoped that her menstrual flow would begin but now she recognized at last that it would not. It was probable that the child she carried was Yaakov's but there was a chance that it was not. To tell of Petrovich's attack would mean planting the seeds of doubt in other minds as well and the child would grow up in this shadow of communal uncertainty. And so the teasing half-knowledge remained hers alone and she hoarded her secret like an emotional miser, shrouding it in silence.

She would have to make plans for herself and for the child and she knew she must come to a decision soon. Moshe and Henia were eager to embark for Palestine and join their friends who were building a kibbutz, a communal settlement in the Huleh valley. They were delaying their departure, she knew, until she was better able to cope with her grief and order her life. They had urged her to join them but the thought of Palestine terrified her as did any mention of violence. The Arabs did not welcome the Jewish settlers and were mobilizing against them. Only the previous week there had been a newspaper account about the burning of a Jewish settlement in the Galilee, and she had thought again of the miller's house and the orange flames of death that had rocketed from the thatched roof. She never again wanted to watch helplessly while the fires of hatred blazed.

Her parents were staying in Russia although every day more and more Jews from Partseva came to bid them good-bye. Most of them were leaving the *shtetl* for the United States and Canada, a few for Palestine, and others were sailing to England and Australia. One family had even opted for New Zealand amid considerable speculation about whether kosher food was obtainable in Auckland.

The Jews of Russia were on the move, practicing their ancient skill of tying intricate knots around clumsy bundles and trunks and suitcases that seldom closed properly. Huge cartons were anchored together with lengths of cord and rope and finally strapped with broad strips of leather. Pots and pans clattered as they were linked together on a chain of rope. They would be needed to prepare meals during the journey and some worried housewives attached them like a belt to their aprons.

Families were split asunder as one brother chose Palestine and the other set sail for New York. Husbands left their wives, planning to work for several years in the new world and earn the dollars that would purchase tickets and passports for the families left behind. Each day processions of horse-drawn wagons clogged the streets of Odessa that led to the seaport. There old men kissed their sons good-bye, urging them to remain good and faithful Jews. Brothers embraced with desperate finality and left each other without looking back. Children waved frantically to fathers they would not see again for years, and old women pulled their shawls tightly over their heads and walked slowly back to houses grown silent and empty.

Leah's brother-in-law, Shimon Hartstein, had left for America the week before. He estimated that it would take him two years to send for Malcha and the children.

"Stay with us in Partseva, Leah," her parents had urged, but the thought of returning to the small town filled her with dread. To return to Partseva would be to step backward, to surrender the advances she had made, to suspend a journey which she knew must lead away from that village which smelled of the past and was rooted in resignation. She could, of course, stay in Odessa and live on in Moshe and Henia's flat. Yaakov's parents had been generous to her and she knew they would continue to offer her money, especially when they learned of her pregnancy. She was an accomplished seamstress, she could tutor schoolchildren, and she had friends and acquaintances in Odessa. Some of Yaakov's friends from the Socialist League had come to see her during the seven days of mourning and offered her reassurances and sympathy. But she knew that most of them had not come forward and the knowledge angered her. Still, she liked the small city with its cobbled streets and low-storied stone buildings. It throbbed with activity and life. Ideas flourished, presses rolled, urgent discussions took place in book-filled parlors. And the city held many memories for her, memories of her brief courtship and even briefer marriage.

Leah paused now in her walk, stopping at the entry of a small municipal park. She and Yaakov had often sat on the stone benches here, listening to the music of the twin violinists who played at the café across the way. But tonight only one violin filled the air with aching melodies that were lost in the rustling of the leaves. Had the other brother decided to leave Odessa, leaving his twin to play on mournfully alone? The park was empty except for a woman who sat on a low stone bench surrounded by canvas shopping bags and clumsily laden straw market baskets. The woman was reading from a Hebrew book and Leah, glancing quickly at the volume as she passed, saw that it was the Book of Psalms. Above the strains of the violin the woman's monotonous voice echoed through the empty park.

"The sorrows of death compassed me and the pains of hell got hold upon me. I found trouble and sorrow. Sorrow and trouble."

Leah recognized the woman as Bryna Markevich and her heart turned in pity. Bryna Markevich had been a young bride, like Leah herself, during the terrible pogroms of 1903. Her husband, a prosperous young businessman, had been among those Jews apprehended during train journeys whose naked bodies were found weeks later, lying at the side of the tracks. Peasants and Cossacks, wearing the dark business suits and gold watches of the murdered Jews, brazenly walked the streets of Odessa, boasting of their murderous exploits. A widow would pass a man wearing her dead husband's suit and collapse in anguish but no one turned to the authorities, knowing that it would do no good. Bryna Markevich's husband had boarded the train at a distant city but he had never reached Odessa. His wallet had been discovered on a road and his watch had turned up at a pawnshop, but the young Jew had disappeared. Years later, during excavations for a new track line, a skeleton was unearthed and after much consideration, the shining pile of bones to which ragged scraps of flesh still hung was buried in the grave of the young Jewish businessman.

But Bryna Markevich did not go to the funeral. For sixteen years she had haunted the train station waiting for a train that would never arrive. During the winter she slept in the waiting room, constantly asking the attendants, who had grown weary of ousting her, when the express from the provinces was due. During the summer months she slept in the park, jerking herself into wakefulness and hurrying to the station as though fearful that the long-awaited train might have arrived while she slept.

Leah felt in her pocket for a half-ruble note and dropped it into the overflowing shopping basket, but the madwoman did not look up.

Leah shivered, chilled by a prescient wind, by the foreknowledge of what could happen if she were not moved to action. She had been seized by such knowledge at her sister Malcha's wedding when she had resolved to leave Partseva and fight for her own fate. Now again, she felt the ghosts of the future hover about her and knew she must struggle against them.

"This is what happens," she thought, "if you stay behind, if you remain entangled in the net of sorrow."

She suddenly remembered another line from the Book of Psalms and repeated it aloud.

"I will walk before the Lord in the land of the living," she said in a clear strong voice—and for the first time since that August morning of terror her life was pierced by the brightness of hope.

"Leah!" Her name was spoken in a breathless tone, as though the speaker had been hurrying and slightly frightened.

She turned in surprise and saw David Goldfeder rushing toward her.

"Leah, where have you been? I've been looking all over Odessa. Even down at the pier. Henia and Moshe were worried."

"Just walking," she said.

"But now you're tired?" David asked and found his answer in her pale face where sharp lines of fatigue were etched about her large dark eyes.

"Yes, I'm tired," she admitted.

"Then let's sit and talk."

David Goldfeder took her hand, surprised at its weightlessness as it lay passively in his own, and led her to a bench. From where they sat she could see Bryna Markevich suddenly set aside her prayer book, arrange her packages, and then carefully comb her hair and apply liberal amounts of rouge to her sunken cheeks. A railway train hooted in the distance and the woman hurried toward the station to search among the arriving passengers for the husband who had left Odessa so many years ago.

"Have you thought about what you will do when Moshe and Henia leave for Palestine?" he asked. "Perhaps you would want to join them? They would like that."

"I know," she said. "But I don't want to go with them."

"You don't want to return to your parents' house?"

"No."

"And you cannot want to stay in Odessa." He offered the last statement with flat certainty. Like Yaakov and Leah, he and Chana Rivka had met in Odessa. Each cobblestoned street rang with memories. The sound of the evening breeze, stirring through the scrub pines that rimmed the port, reminded him of long evening walks when Chana Rivka's small hand lay in his and they strolled in silence, thinking the same thoughts, planning the same plans. Sometimes, during such a walk, they would pass Yaakov and Leah; the tall, slender redheaded groom always linked arms with his dark-haired bride whose gentle laughter rippled through the evening quiet. Now, as he walked alone through the streets of Odessa, David Goldfeder felt himself half a person and the enormity of his loss pounded against him as he went alone through the streets and courtyards they had once passed through together. He turned to Leah and saw in her downturned glance an affirmation of his own feelings.

"No. I don't want to stay in Odessa," she said at last.

"Then come to America. Come with me. I have passage for two. All the papers are ready. Chana Rivka and I were almost ready to leave. I am all prepared." He spoke softly, but she sensed the desperate urgency in his tone and she saw that his hands were knotted into fists which he clenched and unclenched as though fighting a silent battle against the encroaching despair.

"What exactly are you suggesting, David?" she asked gently.

"I'm suggesting that we marry. That you go to America with me as my wife. You've lost Yaakov and I have lost Chana Rivka. We are both alone and lonely. We need each other. We have always gotten along well, even when we were children in Partseva. I think it would be a wise thing for us to do. Believe me, Leah, I have given it much thought. We will be good for each other."

He sat up straight now, his hands at last motionless on his lap. He did not move to touch her, but stared straight ahead as though gathering strength after the effort of his speech.

Leah too sat quietly, thinking about David Goldfeder, gathering all she knew about him and piecing the facts together like the scattered parts of a jigsaw puzzle. She knew of his kindness and gentleness and she remembered now how he had been one of the brighter students at the Hebrew school. The rabbi had wanted him to go to the great yeshiva at Ger, but David had refused and left his father's home in much the same manner that Leah had left her own family. He had wanted to study medicine, to become a doctor, and the elders of the village had laughed at the idea. Jewish boys were not allowed to pursue medical studies in Russia and there was no money available to send him to France or Italy, where some of the richer families sent their children. He had found work in Odessa and like Yaakov he had been caught up in the dream of a new system of equality. She had often seen him at meetings, sitting next to his small fiancée and taking copious notes. But unlike Yaakov's, his belief in the new philosophy had not been implicit. His questions had been piercing and troubled, and finally he had stopped coming to meetings and there were those who had been disappointed to learn that he and Chana Rivka planned to emigrate to America.

"I am pregnant, David," Leah said at last. She uttered the words flatly and searched his face to see what impact they had made, but he sat expressionless in the darkness.

"All right," he said finally, as though her statement had settled something that had hung in abeyance. "We are fortunate. The child will be born in America. In the land of the living."

She started at his choice of words and looked up. The pale evening light had vanished and with the darkness the first stars had become visible. David's eyes followed her and together they sat quietly and gazed at the vast blackness of the sky strewn with starry silvern shards.

"Yes, David, we will marry," she said and lightly placed her hand on his, then withdrew it. Slowly, in silence, not touching, they made their way back to her brother's home to arrange for their marriage.

The Lower East Side
1925
2

Aaron Goldfeder sat beneath the kitchen table, meticulously sorting worn wooden clothespins into mysterious patterns which he arranged and rearranged as the sunlight shifted. Now two pins shaped like a T lay in a pale shaft of light. A shadow pierced the arrangement and the child plucked the pins up and set them next to a scarred table leg where the sunlight fell in a small circular pool of brightness. The sun, entering the kitchen window at a curious angle, defied the narrow panes that were covered with coal soot minutes after they had been scrubbed clean, and turned Aaron's bright hair into a coppery crown of flaming curls. Solemnly now, he abandoned the game of patterns and began a new enterprise. He arranged four of his clothespins against the table's legs and sitting before them, he addressed them sternly, issuing a series of commands in strangely compounded scraps of simple Yiddish and simpler English.

"Du, Mottel, stand like a mensch," he told the clothespin nearest him. "Du bist a Yankee soldier."

The two women working at the table above him listened to him and smiled.

"How nice he plays, Leah. You're lucky he's not a wild thing, like my Joshua. Aaron's such a quiet boy, such a good boy."

Sarah Ellenberg's voice was sorrowful, wistful, as though Aaron's goodness reflected sadly on her own small son, a cheerful gamin who at the age of six was familiar to every pushcart peddler on Hester Street. Joshua Ellenberg, his cap askew and his knickers flapping, dashed between the wheels of their carts, begging scraps of merchandise, running to fetch water in tin cups from the public fountains on Monroe Street or pickles and slices of herring from the huge wooden barrels that blocked the entryway of every small grocery. The peddlers rewarded him with bright strips of fabric or copper pennies worn thin and dull. They were not surprised when Joshua set up business himself, wheeling a small cart he had crafted out of old crates and the wheels of a discarded baby carriage. The cart was loaded with their debris and the smallest peddler on Hester Street had the loudest voice.

"Buy! Buy! You can't get cheaper anywhere. From me only the best. Only the cheapest. Bargains only!"

"That's some boy. He'll be another Straus. The head of a department store," the admiring street merchants told Sarah Ellenberg, but Joshua's mother turned sorrowful eyes on her son and knotted his earnings into the corner of a handkerchief which she stuffed into the knee of her cotton stocking. She sat now with Aaron's mother, softly grieving that Joshua was not seated safely below the kitchen table with Aaron playing soldier with a basket of clothespins.

"Yes, Aaron's a good boy," Leah Goldfeder agreed. She continued to knead dough for the Sabbath loaves and the table shook beneath her strenuous effort. Aaron's clothespin soldiers collapsed and he gathered them together and emerged, defeated, from his fort, stealing a shy look at his mother as he left the room.

How beautiful his mother looked, he thought, and felt in his pocket for the piece of coal that exactly matched his mother's hair.

In the public library on East Broadway, the thin blonde lady who ran the story hour had read the children a tale of a princess who had slept for a thousand years and had shown them a picture of the beautiful raven-haired girl.

"Just like my Mama," small Aaron cried and the librarian had motioned him to silence and smiled secretly to herself. She knew the mothers of the children who came to her library. They were stout worried women who wore their dull hair twisted into shapeless buns which they covered with kerchiefs because of some weird religious Jewish injunction about married women covering their hair. Their plain cotton housedresses glistened with spots of cooking grease and their thick cotton stockings were wadded about their knees. How could the mother of this auburn-haired little boy (he was quite cute, she admitted, and it was odd to find hair of that color among the dark Jewish children of that neighborhood) resemble the Sleeping Beauty? In library school she had always imagined herself sitting in a bright sunlit room, reading to children dressed in starched gingham who asked clever questions and admired her greatly. She had not then anticipated a depression which made children's librarians expendable, and she was glad to had found this post where the Borough of Manhattan began. And truly, some of the children were charming, especially this small bright-haired boy whose name tag, cut in the shape of a turkey from bright orange construction paper, announced him as Aaron Goldfeder.

When Aaron's mother came to call for him, the librarian had to admit that the child was right. Something about the young mother was indeed reminiscent of the artist's drawing. Perhaps it was her dark hair, the coal-black braids fashioned into an intricate crown—or the high pale brow and dark eyes, sad and watchful. The librarian had taken careful note of the woman's hands. She had seen that the skin was red and roughened, cluttered with small bruises where knives and chopping implements had slipped. There was the pale scar of a burn, doubtless a memento of the day a cauldron of boiling water for laundering had tipped over on an unsteady kitchen table. But Mrs. Goldfeder's fingers were long and tapered and the nails were beautifully shaped. Women notice such things about each other and because of those hands the librarian had spoken softly to Aaron's mother, had offered her some books to take home, and had told her what a good and quiet boy Aaron was.

Aaron, as he left the kitchen, also glanced at his mother's hands. Small golden clots of dough clung to her fingers and he wanted her to hold them out to him and let him lick the moist sweet challah dough as she sometimes allowed small Rebecca to do. But his mother continued her work, never noticing that he no longer played at her feet, and he left the doorway and moved on through the dark hall shadowed by a familiar sadness he did not understand.

"Yes, Aaron is a very good boy," Sarah Ellenberg continued. "And his hair is so beautiful. Yaakov's hair. Ah, how I remember poor Yaakov."

Leah looked at the woman who sat across the table from her, methodically decimating walnuts so that the small nutmeats were spread before her on the bare tabletop like a jagged relief map on which the discarded shells formed an uneasy mountain. Leah and Sarah had been students together in Odessa and Sarah had come from the same small village as Yaakov. She had known Leah's first husband from childhood and surely, because her father too had managed timberlands, she had known the woodsman Petrovich. Someday, Leah thought, she would mention his name to Sarah, some day when Aaron played in the sunlight and his curls blazed like flaming flowers of the kind that had burned in distant blaze in the distant land of her birth.

"Do you remember the forest worker, Petrovich?" she would ask. "Isn't Aaron's hair very like his?"

But, of course, she knew she would never do that. She had guarded her secret with grim strength for five years and she would not surrender it to Sarah's greedy ears. Her friend's appetite for gossip and conjecture was insatiable. She knew of desertions before they took place and could recount the illnesses plaguing families, anticipating deaths before they occurred. She shared her news with cheerful generosity, carrying each item to Leah, whose lack of interest perversely encouraged her.

"Leahle, could I ask you something," Sarah continued, and did not wait for an answer but blurted out the question as Leah had known she would. "Why did you name the boy Aaron? Why didn't you give him Yaakov's name?"

"Would it be fair to David to have Yaakov's name always in the house? Remember, David and I had to start a new life together. We didn't want to carry too much sorrow with us. And then David's brother Aaron had also died in the pogrom, with no family at all. It seemed right to give the child Aaron's name." The answer sprang with easy readiness from Leah's lips. She had, after all, rehearsed it so many times, justified it so often, that occasionally she even believed it herself.

She remembered the first time she had offered the name, moments after the child's birth. David had come to the room where she lay heavy with exhaustion, the bedclothes soaked with her sweat. He had walked softly, as though fearful that even the cushioned tread of his rubber soles might disturb her.

The labor had been long and difficult and twice the midwife had despaired of a normal delivery and urged David to go for the doctor. But Leah, her face streaming with perspiration, her lips caked with blood where she had bitten through them in pain and anguish, had restrained them. The unborn child thrust against her in frenzied terror and she writhed against his attacks, locked in mortal conflict with the tiny form that had grown within her womb. Her fingers curled desperately about the posts of the brass bed, grasping for support against the urgent spasms of the infant who thrust his way downward, seeking the air and light of her body's entry. Only once before had she engaged in such fierce combat, such urgent resistance, and in her pain the bedpost seemed to take the shape of the weathered Lombardy tree to which she had clung on that day she could not forget.

"You must help the baby. Bear down! Bear down!" the midwife had shouted. "Do you want the child to die?"

The midwife was a small bewigged woman who had herself borne a dozen children and delivered scores of others. She was stoical toward the cries of laboring women and viewed their sweat and vomit, their tears and blood, as unimportant appendages to the giving of life. But she had never before assisted a woman who fought her own screams and braced her body against the onslaught of the struggling infant, refusing to help speed the birth.

In the end they had not sent for the doctor and the child had forced himself out, his lungs screaming for air. He was a large infant whose bright hair shone through the gluey mucus that coated his emerging head and his pale limbs had thrashed in bewilderment. The midwife washed and swaddled him, feeling her weariness fade and her heart grow lighter at the sight of the bright-haired boy whose wails made the women in the house smile and the men to glance away from each other in pleased embarrassment. But when she brought the child to Leah the dark-haired young mother had only glanced wearily at the tiny bundle that was her son and turned her face away, her eyes bright with tears. The midwife was not surprised when no milk sprang from the new mother's breasts and a wet nurse had to be brought to nourish the child.

"What shall we name the child then, Leah?" David had asked and it was then that she suggested his brother's name, offering it as a gift he could not refuse. A child had already been named for Yaakov, she pointed out. Her brother Moshe, living now in a communal settlement in the Galilee, had given his firstborn child the name of the young brother-in-law whose dead body he had cradled on an Odessa street.

"Yes, I can see why you would not call him Yaakov," Sarah Ellenberg said. But she remained quiet for a moment thinking that it was doubly strange, then, that when Rebecca was born they had named her for Chana Rivka, David's first betrothed who lay buried in the Jewish cemetery of Odessa.

Sarah changed the subject quickly now and talked of poor Yetta Moskowitz from across the hall, whose husband had disappeared. There were four children and one on the way, too much perhaps for the stoop-shouldered, weak-eyed fur nailer who went off one morning carrying his lunch wrapped in newspaper and never returned. The police had been summoned, and a bored, ruddy-faced Irishman had sat taking notes, licking his pencil laboriously as the deserted woman spoke in Yiddish while a teen-aged girl translated into English. Both officer and translator were bored. They had heard the same story too often, and where, in all these United

States, could they look for Pincas Moskowitz? Still, they did their jobs and muttered feeble encouragement to the woman, who rested her swollen hands on her stomach and swayed perilously from side to side.

Leah had drawn up a small advertisement for Yetta, which she placed in the Yiddish papers' classified column, where dozens of other such notices appeared with disturbing regularity: "Velvel Greenberg of Lodz. Contact wife Hinda. Moshe is sick." "Information sought on the whereabouts of Chaim Lemberg of Attorney Street. Family in dire straits." "Zanvel Greenberg please come home."

"You know, in Russia and in Poland, life was very hard. Not enough to eat, sickness, pogroms. Yet this did not happen. Men stayed with their families. Why should it be happening here?" Sarah asked.

"Over there—where could they have gone?" Leah asked, surprised at the harshness of her tone. She was relieved when, at that moment, Rebecca woke from her nap and filled the flat with a combination of crying and prattling that sounded to Leah like the language of the angels.

"Sarah, please put on the water for the soup," Leah said and rushed down the long narrow corridor of the railroad flat to the tiny windowless room where Rebecca sat up in her crib.

Leah's heart always caught at the sight of her daughter. Rebecca had been conceived on the night of the Day of Atonement, in a velvet darkness soft with peace and gentleness. Leah could fix the exact time of conception because she and David seldom slept together as man and wife. Their marriage was lived in muted harmony and might have been the partnership of a gentle brother and sister. Their lovemaking was rare and always quiet, tentative, as though passion might shatter the delicate equilibrium of their life together.

Sometimes Leah, lying in the darkness of a sleepless night, felt David's eyes upon her and sensed the flutter of unarticulated questions float across the silent air as her husband's hands clenched and unclenched in the pain of loneliness and desire. Sometimes, then, her own need to be touched broke across her with frightening fierceness and she would roll into the arms of the gentle, soft-spoken man who had offered himself as her husband but had never presumed to proclaim himself her lover. They soothed each other's bodies then, their flesh coming together beneath the tent of coarse cambric sheet as though the protection of the fabric were necessary to them. Leah remembered, at such moments, how she and Yaakov had always lain across the bed, their naked bodies open to each other, welcoming touch and tenderness, soaring on waves of breathless passion. She and David concealed their bodies from each other, offering each other solace and compassion but never eagerness or spontaneity.

But on that night of the Day of Atonement, the second such day they had observed in America, as they lay in the soft darkness, David had moaned softly, as though the day of fasting and prayer had released a secret sorrow.

"Leah," he said quietly, his arms rigid at his side, "I want a family, another child. I do not want Aaron to be alone. I do not want to feel so alone. It's too hard." His voice broke then and she pushed off the coverlet and drew closer to him, meaning to comfort him as she sometimes comforted Aaron when he woke from sleep trembling with wild terror.

But he would not have her caress and instead removed her nightgown, kissing and fondling her, his breath growing strong with a desire that ignited her own. They made love that night without the protection of covering and slept at last, exhausted, in each other's arms.

And small Rebecca, born of that coming together, was a gentle child who placidly sucked at her mother's breast (because for this child Leah's milk flowed rich and plentiful) and slept easily with measured breath while her brother, in his trundle bed, thrashed against mysterious nocturnal demons, ground his teeth, and woke in the night shivering with a dread that only David could control.

Rebecca had her mother's thick dark hair, which Leah patiently formed into curls with a narrow damp comb, and David's thoughtful gray eyes. She was a child who cherished tiny objects and her brother Aaron had fashioned for her a crib made of half a walnut, in which he had placed a small pebble with hair of grass which Rebecca called Shaindel. It was to that doll, created out of a pebble, that Rebecca crooned softly at night until she fell into her deep and peaceful sleep.

She held her walnut now and called her brother's name.

"Aaron—A-a-ron," she called happily as Leah diapered her and spread cornstarch across the dimpled pinkness of her backside. Gently she bent and kissed the child's exposed skin, the white powder streaking her own cheek.

"Is Rebecca awake?" Aaron asked.

He stood in the doorway, keeping his distance from his mother as he always did, and she in turn, inexplicably angry that he had found her bent like this over the child, answered shortly, "Yes. Take her and play somewhere. I must get dinner. We light Shabbat candles early tonight."

But she remained still as the children left the room and walked down the dark narrow corridor that linked all the rooms of the large flat.

Why was it, Leah wondered wearily, that Aaron was so calm and quiet during the day and seized with violence when trapped by sleep? The thought, worrisome and painful, stung Leah with a sharp grief and she buried it, hurrying off to begin cooking dinner before the boarders arrived. They would all eat together that night because it was a Friday, the eve of the Sabbath and the only night of the week on which David Goldfeder did not travel the subway up to 137th Street where the City College of New York had been built between the curves of coarsely textured hills.

Leah and Sarah lit candles together in the half-light of the late afternoon. The children watched them from a corner of the room where they played among the straw brooms and feather dusters. Joshua Ellenberg had brought home a small heap of rags which he was laboriously sorting with Aaron's help. Among his cloth treasures he found a small scrap of bright red velvet which he gave to Rebecca, who delightedly turned it into a covering for her walnut crib.

"Here, Becca, let me show you how to fold it," Aaron said and carefully rearranged the fabric.

Leah completed the blessing of the candles, but held her hands before her eyes a moment longer and watched the children through the shadowed lines of flame that danced between her fingers. How gentle Aaron looked in the glow of candlelight and how like Yaakov's his tone had been when he offered to help his sister. At moments like this she was certain that he was Yaakov's child, but then harsh doubt unsettled her. She could not be sure. She would never be sure. She lowered her hands and sighed, the long escaping breath accompanying Sarah Ellenberg's whispered prayer.

"Good Shabbos," Leah said, smiling at her friend, and the two women kissed in quiet acknowledgment of all that they shared.

"Soon, soon, I pray I'll light candles at my own table. Soon, I wouldn't be a boarder by you," Sarah said as though continuing a discussion abruptly interrupted.

"Sarah, you know we are glad to have you. Without boarders how could we manage? David wouldn't be able to go to the night classes. He'd have to work at another job," Leah replied, as she had so many times before in the years during which the Ellenbergs had lived with them as paying guests.

Leah sank into an armchair in a corner of the room that served all of them as a combined living room and dining room. It was the only piece of upholstered furniture in the room and had been purchased by her brother-in-law Shimon Hartstein from a family facing eviction.

"A good buy," Shimon said proudly, stroking the tufted peacock-blue satin of the chair. "Certainly worth six dollars. I'm starting to collect a few things for when Malcha comes."

"And when will that be?" Leah asked.

It was five years since Shimon had left Russia. Leah remembered standing with her sister and the two small children on the Odessa dock with Malcha's fingers digging deep into her arm and her head, always too small for the heavy fringed marriage wig, bobbing wildly under its weight.

"When will I see him again? When will the children see their father?" she had mourned.

"Soon. Soon he'll send for you," Leah had assured her.

And it was true that Shimon, who had moved in with Leah and David as soon as they arrived in America, talked constantly of sending for his wife and children. He was saving. He was surveying business opportunities. He was getting a feel for the new land. Each week as he handed Leah the three one-dollar bills which covered his room and board, each bill crisp and fresh because Shimon Hartstein loved new money and always stood on line at the bank on payday asking for newly minted bills, he would repeat, "Now I'm a week closer to bringing my wife and children over."

"They'd better come while they can still recognize you," Leah replied dryly on the day he shaved his beard and flowing ear-locks. He had long since discarded his gabardine coat and high skullcap, and Leah had difficulty recognizing her clean-shaven, robust boarder as the shy young bridegroom who had stood with Malcha, his eyes downcast, beneath the wedding canopy.

He entered the room now, perfunctorily kissing the mezuzah on the doorpost, and bent to scoop Rebecca up in his arms. He was a good-looking man with thick dark hair and shrewd, narrow brown eyes. In recent years he had put on weight and small jolly jowls had formed below his cheeks. The new strength of his body pleased him and he went regularly to the public showers on Monroe Street. Twice a week he went to the Irvington Settlement House and played basketball in the gym, describing the game with gleeful incredulity.

"From the wall they hang a hoop and the game is to jump up high and throw a ball through it. Sounds meshuga, crazy, but it's fun."

He was a man who had spent his boyhood hunched over the study tables of one-room Hebrew schools and shadowed Talmudic academies. It was only in the years of his young manhood that he discovered the joys and freedom of play. Leah did not begrudge him his new life but she worried about her sister in Russia.

Malcha's letters were simple, written for her by the village scribe, but Leah read into the shy, short sentences her sister's impatience and loneliness.

"Yankele started cheder. Chana helps me bake on Fridays. Will their father recognize them?" Malcha wrote and Leah would then prod Shimon to bring his family over.

"Good Shabbos, Leah," he said and bent to kiss his sister-in-law. He strutted proudly across the room in a new navy-blue suit with a vest and presented each child with a bright red lollipop.

"Not before dinner," Sarah Ellenberg cautioned her son, but she had no cause for worry. Joshua had thrust his lollipop beneath his assortment of rags and Leah knew he would sell it at the first opportunity on Sunday morning. Her own children had stripped the cellophane off and were licking the sweet with wide-eyed delight.

"Aaron, do we eat candy before dinner?" Leah asked harshly.

"Rebecca's eating hers too," the boy protested.

"She's only a baby," Leah replied, doubly angered because she knew she was wrong to have singled out only Aaron for reproof. Still there was no time to patch things up because the staircase echoed with the sound of the boarders' tired footsteps as they trudged up the many flights.

She rushed to the kitchen to make sure there was enough hot water for everyone, ladling it into porcelain bowls which each boarder in turn carried into the common bathroom. Leah and David considered themselves lucky to have found a flat with a self-contained bathroom, and the boarders were happy to pay an extra twenty-five cents a week instead of having to use the hall bathroom, which always exuded a stench of ammonia. Occasional complaints about the inaccessibility of the bathroom were met with Shimon Hartstein's account of the outside facilities he had been forced to use during his first year in America.

"This here is luxury," he would proclaim and banish the complainer.

When they were all finally assembled at the long table, David Goldfeder arrived, breathless and apologetic about his lateness.

"There was a line at the library," he explained.

His arms were loaded with books and Leah thought that she had never seen him look so tired. Just as Shimon had put on weight since coming to America, David Goldfeder had become thinner and paler. He had, since their arrival, lived a double life, dividing his time between work and study and applying full strength to both tasks. For ten hours a day he worked in a large flat which an enterprising tailor had turned into a factory to produce men's pants. A cutter worked in what had once been the dining room and passed up the sliced heaps of fabric to the men in the living room who stitched seams and passed them on to other workers who sewed belts and cuffs. David worked in the kitchen, pressing the finished garment with the heavy steel irons that were kept burning hot on the stove. He had chosen pressing, which paid even less than the other jobs, because it required the least amount of concentration. Using his fingers for guides against creases, he automatically passed a heavy iron over the fabric and kept a textbook always open on the ironing board. While his arm moved agonizingly up and down the thick materials, his eyes followed the printed page, memorizing irregular French verbs, geometric axioms, basic biological principles. He read slowly in a language that was not his own.

"Goldfeder, you're meshuga. What will it get you? A lot of burned garments," his fellow workers jeered, but David shrugged indifferently and turned back to his books.

In five years he had never burned a garment, although an ugly mound of shriveled skin on his arm marked the spot where an iron had seared his flesh, burning him so deeply that for hours afterward the room stank with the odor of scorching meat. He remembered always the text he had been reading that day, which so distracted him from his usual caution. It was Sigmund Freud's essay on the nature of the subconscious.

"Did you get me a picture book, Papa?" Aaron asked now and David smiled. "Of course. When did I forget you?"

He encircled the boy in an embrace and Leah thought, with an odd mixture of relief and annoyance, that David sometimes paid more attention to Aaron than to Rebecca, his own child.

David did not kiss Leah but touched her lightly on the shoulder, his fingers gently fondling the soft gray wool of the dress she always wore for the Sabbath meal. She had designed and made the dress herself, and sewn a scarf for it, piecing together brightly colored scraps of taffeta from Joshua Ellenberg's discards.

"Let us eat," she said and David softly intoned the blessing over the wine and the braided Sabbath loaves, slicing the golden bread, still warm from the oven, and passing the plate around the table.

The three young women boarders, who shared a small corner bedroom, each broke off a tiny piece and ate with such delicacy that Leah smiled. They were all attending an etiquette class at the Irvington Settlement House, taught by a German Jewish woman who arrived each week in a chauffeur-driven car and gave elegant directions on how to walk and sit. Since Bryna, Pearl, and Masha had enrolled in the class the Goldfeder flat rang with courtesy.

"I beg your pardon," they sang to each other at every opportunity. "Would you be so kind to excuse me?" "I would so appreciate if you could hurry in the bathroom." Masha, who was the prize student, even used the word lavatory, but still it was better than the pounding and shouting often heard at the door of the hall toilet, and they were all good girls.

Blond Bryna, a bookkeeper, was engaged to a furrier who had given her a tiny fox collar with the animal's head attached to it, and when she left the flat each evening, the bright dead eyes stared accusingly at them. Pearl worked in a pencil factory and Masha ran the buttonhole machine in the factory where Shimon Hartstein worked as a cutter.

Occasionally when Masha and Shimon arrived home together they would be deep in conversation, and they shared a repertoire of secret jokes.

"Who's this?" Shimon would chortle suddenly, as they sat about during an evening. He would mince about the room on his toes, twitching his behind with surprising skill. He was an accomplished pantomimist, a talent he seemed to have discovered when he shaved his beard. Masha would then collapse with laughter and offer the name of a fellow worker and they would both clap with delight at their shared cleverness. On other evenings, Masha tried to teach Shimon some of the dance steps she had learned at the dancing academy she and Pearl frequented. Laughing, she pulled him across the room while Joshua Ellenberg hummed the music and Leah watched, thinking of her sister Malcha alone in Russia.

"East Side, West Side," Joshua sang while Leah wondered whether it would not be better if Masha found another flat to board in.

Across the table from Masha sat Label Katz, a hatter who shared his room with shy, thin Morris Morgenstern who had recently taken the lease of a small trimming store on Orchard Street. Morris Morgenstern spent his evenings making endless lists of figures, adding, subtracting, and then passionately crumbling his calculations and beginning again. He was saving to bring his parents over from Poland. He had already paid the passage of his brother's entire family and once he had made arrangements for his parents he would be free to think of a wife and family.

"After all, I'm not an old man. Is forty-eight old?" he had asked Leah shyly.

The last group at the table was the Ellenberg family. Sam Ellenberg was two inches shorter than his wife, a fact which he considered a great joke. He delighted in pushing his porky little body next to her and laboriously stretching himself upward. His red face, the features almost lost amid the flesh, and his multitude of chins trembled as he laughed uproariously. Aaron Goldfeder was fascinated by Joshua's father and often spent an entire meal staring at him. This was because Sam Ellenberg had only one ear. A neat flap of pale skin had been sewn into a patch where the other ear should have been, and although Sam's face was always florid with wine and humor, the pallid fold of dermal covering never changed color. The ear had been removed in Russia, when Sam was seven years old, as a protective measure against the Czar's conscription of small Jewish boys into the imperial army. Aaron could not understand two things in Sam's recounting of this incident. First, he could not understand why anyone would not want to go into an army and do brave things for his country. Secondly, he could not understand how anyone would opt to lose a perfectly good ear. Nervously he put his hands to his own ears and saw his father wink at him as though he knew exactly what Aaron was thinking.

Leah and Sarah moved swiftly about the table serving the meal. Only when all the plates were full did they themselves sit down to eat.

"Delicious as usual, Leah," Shimon said and sucked noisily at a chicken bone.

Pearl and Bryna stared at him disapprovingly and delicately dissected the meat on their bones, but Masha defiantly whistled through her own wishbone and kicked Shimon under the table, a movement which Leah noticed.

"Oh, in my family my sister Malcha, Shimon's wife, is the best cook. Remember her borscht, Shimon, and her schav. You know she used to go out to the fields and pick the sorrel grass herself, she was so particular," Leah said, smiling innocently at her brother-in-law.

She did not look up from her plate but knew that David was staring at her, his lips curled in amusement. Like Aaron, she felt that David always seemed to know what she was feeling, but unlike her son she took no pleasure in the knowledge. Her husband's prescience made her uneasy and her eyes avoided his gaze. She was relieved when Morris Morgenstern took up a new conversation.

"Does your sister also sew so beautifully, like you?" he asked. "Tell me, Mrs. Goldfeder, where did you get the pattern for that dress? Such a pattern I don't have in my store."

"The pattern I made up," Leah replied. "I had the idea and cut the pattern from newspaper."

It did not seem a great accomplishment to her and she was surprised by the gasps of admiration from Bryna, Pearl, and Masha. Only Sarah Ellenberg was not surprised.

"Leah always made her own clothes that way. I remember like yesterday the full skirt she made for her wedding to Yaakov. For months afterward every bride in Odessa had to have a skirt like Leah Adler's," Sarah said, stumbling over the last words because a tense silence had fallen over the room.

Everyone there knew that Leah had been married before and that David Goldfeder was not Aaron's father, but Sarah's words disturbed them and they felt uneasy, as though a lingering ghost had suddenly wafted over the crowded room and hovered above the cluttered table. All of them had come from Eastern Europe, fleeing poverty and pogroms. They had all heard the screams, seen the flames, felt the hunger, and shivered in fear and uncertainty. Death and loss haunted each of them, and in the darkness of their rooms on Eldridge Street they were visited by the faces of parents they would never see again, brothers and sisters lost and dead, friends wandering in South America or pitting themselves against the swamps of the Galilee.

Pretty Masha, her hair clustered into a castle of ringlets topped by a velvet comb, flirting now with Shimon Hartstein whose wife and children awaited an unwritten letter, had been betrothed to a young merchant killed in a pogrom. Label Katz, the sad-eyed hatter, had once had a wife who also set the Sabbath table with snowy cloth and watched the lateral lines of flame streak out against silver cups and golden Sabbath loaves. He had found her one night lying across the kitchen floor, her dress pulled up above her head, the breath forced from her body by fingers so harsh that their purple impressions hardened and were frozen into the woman's death-stretched flesh. He never knew whether she had been raped before or after she had been strangled although he prayed it had been after.

The mention of Leah's first marriage released these troubled memories and in the silence that settled on the room, small Rebecca suddenly began to cry. The child's sobs released them and as David Goldfeder cradled his daughter, new wisps of conversation rose. Joshua Ellenberg told them that the woman who sold chestnuts on Pitt Street had given him some scraps of satin.

"I saved some for you, Mrs. Goldfeder, to make a scarf like that one. You know, if you made enough of them, I could sell them for you." His high squeaky voice was rich with street wisdom and Leah sometimes thought he was a midget businessman and not a child only a year older than Aaron.

"The scarf you also made yourself," Morris Morgenstern asked, with professional interest. He had been looking at the gay ascot, with its brilliant rainbow colors, and had noted the expert stitching and how well the different materials had been placed to form an unusual and striking pattern. "You have a good hand and a good eye, Leah Goldfeder. You should do something more with such talent."

"You know what you ought to do," Pearl suggested. "You ought to come down to the Irvington Settlement House with us and take a design course. There's a wonderful teacher there—Mr. Ferguson. I have a friend of mine who took a class with him and she says he's just marvelous."

"Ach, she doesn't need a course," Sarah Ellenberg retorted. "Leah could teach such a course. Besides, isn't one student already enough in the Goldfeder family?"

They all turned to look at David, who calmly spread honey across his challah. Although they asserted to each other that David Goldfeder's undertaking was a madness—who had ever heard of a greenhorn first studying English, getting a high school diploma, and then getting admitted to the night school at the City College? But their landlord had done just that and they were secretly proud of him, awed by his energy and achievement. Furtively, they stared at the books and notebooks he brought home—Morris Morgenstern, who had studied briefly for the law, touched them sometimes, as though they were magic talismans—and during the rare hours David spent in the apartment, they always contrived to give him the seat where the light was strongest.

"I think it's a good idea," David said thoughtfully. "Why not? What do you think, Leah? It's time you went from this apartment a little."

"I don't know," she replied and began to dish out the compote. Even as she was negative she knew that she wanted to walk through the doors of the settlement house, to hear the sounds of young people talking and laughing, to sniff the odors of chalk and paint and feel the electricity of learning. She felt again a stirring of the excitement that had spurred her from her parents' village to the academy in Odessa. Of course, she must do something, study something. She was, after all, only twenty-three. Sarah was always on hand to look after the children.

Leah looked at David who calmly ate the compote as he read from a propped-up text, his mind riveted to a problem his professor had discussed that day dealing with Freud's analysis of the root of involuntary action. How good David was, Leah thought, and how he always seemed to sense what she wanted, what she needed. But when he passed her chair and lightly touched her hair, an imperceptible shiver escaped her and he moved quickly on and went to sit with Shimon Hartstein, Morris Morgenstern, and Label Katz, who were angrily arguing against Sam Ellenberg that David Dubinsky and his ideas of trade unionism would mean the ruination of small manufacturers.

On Monday, Leah decided, she would go to the Irvington Settlement House and make inquiries. The determined thought pleased her and she hummed softly as she cleared the table. Aaron got up to help her and when he nuzzled shyly against her she bent and planted a soft kiss on the bright coppery crown of her child's hair.

3

Charles Ferguson stood at the window of his studio on the second floor of the Irvington Settlement House and watched the street below. His fingers were wrapped around a stump of charcoal which he idly moved across the thick white page of the drawing pad he had balanced on the windowsill. Small figures slowly crawled into life on the sheet of paper and now and then the young artist glanced away from the window to see whether his fingers had been faithful to his eyes. Critically, almost harshly, he stared at his work, and slowly corrected it. Using his fingers, he blurred and brushed the figure of the old Jew pushing a wheelbarrow through the streets, hoping that the newly imposed shadow would imply the sense of urgent movement that characterized the old man's painful progress.

Everyone on the street below was hurrying because it was three o'clock on a wintry Friday afternoon and only an hour or so remained before the Sabbath hush would steal across the teeming, busy streets of New York's lower east side. Bearded rabbis, their earlocks still damp from their Friday afternoon ritual immersion, hurried homeward, thin white towels tucked beneath their black gabardine caftans. Women dashed by, huddled within thick shawls, clutching straw market baskets. These were the poorest housewives, who waited until the shops were ready to close so that they might buy their food at half-price.

He watched one plump little woman rush from stall to stall. She wore a man's heavy dark overcoat and her head was covered with a bright-red wool scarf. With the eagerness of a child finding a new toy, she plucked up a large cabbage and tossed it, with surprising skill, into her basket. Now she cajoled the aged fish merchant who leaned against his cart, his beard and once-white apron flecked with scales and blood, a narrow fishbone gleaming on the visor of his work cap. The woman pirouetted before him. She pointed to her cabbage and, digging into her basket, held up a bunch of scrawny baby carrots. With flying fingers and dancing vegetables, she demonstrated the dinner she could cook if only she had one fish head. The fishmonger looked up at the darkening sky and down into the slimy confines of his cart. Shrugging finally, he removed a thick glove, plunged his hand in, and held up a grinning carp head. He wrapped it in sheets of newspaper so thin they were soon stained with blood, but the small woman hugged the package with joy and held out some coins. The merchant ignored her outstretched hand and bent to hoist his cart. Slowly, bent almost double, he trudged on down Bayard Street and the woman arranged her purchases and hurried triumphantly home.

Charles Ferguson's charcoal stub had swept furiously across his pad during these transactions and he looked down at the series of swift drawings. The one of the old woman plucking up the cabbage was not too bad and he added a line for emphasis and a smudge of shadow to hint at the mood of the darkening day. He was dissatisfied with the drawing of the fishmonger but he liked the outline of the cart, and he bent close to his work to add some small detail, sketching in the sheath of Yiddish newspapers draped over a wire hanger which the man used to wrap the ice-caked pike and carp and the small slivers of herring which the children carried home in cornucopias of newsprint. As he worked he glanced unnecessarily at his watch. He could tell by the noise in the corridors that it was almost three-fifteen and within minutes the low muted gong would sound and he would begin teaching his last class of the week.

His students were already assembling their equipment on the long, low worktables. Sheets of paper were clipped into place on drawing pads and pencils, rulers, and erasers were neatly ranged in slots on the table. One or two students were absorbed in erasing the previous week's work so that the sheet of paper could be used again. Those who could afford them were setting up their colors, small precious jars of tempera purchased at a Greenwich Village shop where Charles Ferguson had made a special arrangement with the proprietor. The settlement house students walked the two-mile distance and were sold their supplies at a substantial discount, which Charles Ferguson later covered.

He walked up to the lectern now, glanced at his notes and then across the room. Automatically his eyes rested at the empty worktable in the second row where Leah Goldfeder usually sat. She was not here today. He understood her absence but, like so many things at this shadowed hour, it saddened him. She had explained, when he urged her to register for this class, that it was given at a very difficult hour for her. Friday afternoon was the busiest time of her week. She had to shop and prepare dinner for a houseful of boarders and make certain the laundry was up to date because no work could be done on the Sabbath.

Still, Ferguson had persisted. This might be the last year the course would be given. He was planning to return to Illinois—a plan he continued to diagram year after year so that the battered trunk in his Bleecker Street apartment remained perennially open. One week feeling restless, he would pack; the next, angry or despairing, he tossed his possessions out. Occasionally, particularly in the spring when small boys skittered down the sun-spattered streets on improvised skateboards and the chestnut trees in Washington Square burst into bloom, he closed it and covered it with a Mexican serape.

It had occurred to him that the reason he was so drawn to the people of the lower east side was because he too was a refugee, fleeing the calm stretches of fertile plains, the endless rural skyscapes, the farmlands with their fields ranged with geometric neatness, the houses and silos as trim as the small buildings carved for children's play. Just as Leah had fled the sameness, the repetitious life cycle of the village of her birth, so had Charles Ferguson fled his rural fate for the studios of the city. He had studied at Chicago's Art Institute, becoming familiar with terms like perspective and composition, and then he had come to New York, a tall blond man with a wisp of pale moustache, magic in his fingers, and uncertainty in his heart.

He had gone first to the Art Students League and stood before huge canvases splashed with light by the vast skylights. He struggled with thick brushes and plump tubes of oils that bled their rainbow hues across his palette, but on the canvas the bright colors froze and the uncertainty in his heart grew. He began to suspect that he had been cursed with talent but not blessed with a great gift. He found the job at the Irvington Settlement House, thinking of it at first as an economic necessity—his teaching would make his own studies possible. But soon he was spending more and more time on the east side and fewer hours on Fifty-seventh Street. He taught graphics and design, elementary drawing and oils. He offered lectures on art history and sat for hours over his students' portfolios making comments, worrying, conferring.

His students came mostly at night, tired men and women, their backs habitually bent low in the habit of their work over sewing machines and ironing boards. But a new vitality gripped them in Charles Ferguson's classroom and even those with little or no talent sparked with interest as the tall blond man who spoke in the flat tones of the Midwest shared with them the secrets of his craft—for that was how, in defeat, he had come to think of his talent.

Among these eager apprentices, he found talent of one sort or another. There was Theresa Mercuriotti, a bright-eyed young Italian woman who worked in a powder puff factory. Under Ferguson's guidance she had learned to draw flowers so well that she soon started a small enterprise for herself, painting bouquets across china plates; when she married she and her husband opened a small shop where Theresa's plates dominated the window with their bright offerings of rosebuds laced with baby's breath and buttercups sleeping amid beds of fern. And there had been Faivel Goldstein, a stoop-shouldered Talmudist who had stayed after class one day and shown Ferguson his drawings of insects. Intricate spiders danced across thin sheets of tissue paper, crickets leaped upward in bold strokes of India ink, and graceful butterflies flew low across Yiddish circulars. Faivel was a fabric designer now and his delicately executed drawings appeared on men's cravats and women's stoles.

Each year, at Christmas, he sent Ferguson a heavy silk scarf emblazoned with his small patterned creatures.

But it was not until Leah Goldfeder had entered his class, a year ago, that Charles Ferguson felt the surge of excitement peculiar to teachers who suddenly encounter a student of unexpected, unpredictable talent.

Leah, her thick dark hair coiled about in a glossy bun, her brow high and pale, reminded Ferguson of a Velasquez queen he had studied in a Madrid museum. She registered first for a class in geometric design and he saw at once that although she had had no training, there was a natural sophistication and ease to her compositions. While the other students struggled to order simple triangles and circles, her convex octagons formed graceful pyramids and her quick fingers shaped riots of concentric circles. He worked closely with her, lending her his own colors because he saw, from the careful mending of her cotton stockings and the frayed sleeve of her worn coat, that she could not afford supplies.

The following semester she took his class in composition and drawing, always rushing in just a bit late and hurrying apologetically to her seat. In the neighboring room the settlement house chorus met, and their high sweet voices, struggling to sing English words they barely understood, drifted over the transom into the studio. Leah hummed as she worked, and once when the chorus director gave Ferguson tickets to a concert he offered them to her. She blushed with pleasure and surprise but shook her head.

"I am sorry but my husband David goes to school every night and I would have no one to go with."

"Every night?" he asked in surprise.

"Yes. To the City College. He already finished the high school courses. He studies very hard."

"Then perhaps you'll go to the concert with me. Your husband would not object?"

"Object? Be against? No," she replied calmly and again he struggled to conceal his surprise. He knew that she practiced traditional Orthodoxy and he had lived among the Jews of the east side long enough to know that their religion was very rigid regarding social and sexual mores. He had seen men cross the street to avoid walking next to strange women and he knew that Orthodox women covered their hair lest they seem attractive to men other than their husbands. Yet Leah Goldfeder had, without hesitation, agreed to go to a concert at Carnegie Hall with him, a single man and a Gentile. Of course, his tall dark-haired student did not cover her hair (today she wore it in a loosely twisted bun and he found himself sketching the loosely wound coils and wondering how they would look brushed loose against her regally held back) and it was unusual that her husband was studying at City College. The Goldfeders appeared to be an extraordinary couple and his curiosity about Leah mounted. He arranged to meet her on the evening of the concert on the steps of Carnegie Hall.

Charles Ferguson's invitation marked the first time Leah had traveled the subway beyond Fourteenth Street. She had lived in New York for five years but her life in the largest city in the United States had been confined to the crowded streets near her home where she did her marketing, took her children to the free clinic, went to the settlement house and the synagogue. Occasionally she and David went to the Yiddish theater on Second Avenue but that too was within walking distance of her home. Only once had she gone as far as S. Klein's imposing emporium on Fourteenth Street, with the enterprising Sarah Ellenberg.

Leah sat in the dimly lit subway car and studied the faces of fellow passengers. Students sat on the wicker seats with notebooks spread across their laps. The books danced skittishly as the train jerked to a sudden stop but the students read on, their concentration unbroken. So David must sit night after night, Leah thought. The speeding subway was his study hall too, and he had that rare capacity to remain immersed in his books, undisturbed by movement, children's play, or men's arguments. In one corner a group of Italian men argued vociferously until the debate suddenly became a joke and they laughed with such good feeling that even the engrossed students looked up, blinked, and smiled before returning to their books.

A beautiful young black girl sat across the aisle from Leah calmly applying makeup. Leah watched with fascination as the girl, with the care and precision of an artist, brushed her face with a tawny powder puff and etched new coats of redness around her full lips. Leah herself had never worn makeup but now she felt pale and colorless. She bit her lips and pinched her cheeks, glad that she had worn her brightly colored scarf. Twice she opened the leather purse, borrowed from Masha, and checked the small handkerchief into which she had knotted three nickels.

"Make sure you have the money safe. New York is not a *shtetl.* New York is a big city," David had said. But he was pleased that she was going to the concert. It was hard on her, spending so many nights alone while he studied.

Leah did not remember the music that was played that night in the cavernous concert hall, but she never forgot the gowns of the women who sat in the orchestra below their balcony seats. She observed the simple lines in which the elegant dresses had been cut and took careful note of the materials—the deep richness of red velvet, the iridescent gleam of blue satin, the gentle jewel-like tones of emerald green silks and topaz yellow brocades. The beautifully gowned women, their jewels resting against creamy skin, sitting in their green velvet chairs, were like graceful flowers blazing in a distant field.

During intermission, she watched them rise and wave to each other, their stoles draped across their shoulders, fur capes carelessly balanced on their arms. Her fingers ached to touch the fabric of their dresses, to shape the luxurious red velvet not into a ball gown but into a simple afternoon dress. Deftly, in her mind's eye, she borrowed white satin from another gown and fashioned collar and cuffs for her red velvet creation.

Charles Ferguson watched as her eyes grew brighter and the color in her cheeks rose.

"Wasn't the Haydn lovely?" he asked as they rode the subway downtown.

"The music was marvelous. But ah, the gowns. The colors. How wonderful," she breathed and they rode the rest of the way home in a comfortable silence.

He had walked her to her apartment house and as she thanked him, standing in that street which even at that late hour throbbed with activity and noise—a group of girls sat singing on the tenement steps, children cried, an angry shout lashed the air—a man approached them. He was laden with books, and walked slowly as though each step were an effort.

"David," Leah cried and introduced her husband to Charles Ferguson. The trained artist marked the man's deep searching eyes, the strength written across the exhausted face, and the quick flash of intelligence when Charles spoke of the music they had heard.

"Haydn," David said musingly. "Wonderful. Only today I heard the Creation. In the factory we keep the radio on all day to the classical music stations. Imagine this country—to be able all day to listen to classical music."

Charles Ferguson thought of the rows of men bent over sewing machines and cutting tables, skullcaps on their heads although they worked stripped to their undershirts in the hot crowded lofts, while Haydn's crescendoes whirled about them. Some factories, he had heard, hired high school students who read novels as the men worked. The workers paid these readers themselves from their small salaries. Some day, the art teacher thought, he would like to paint a room full of such men.

"Will you come in for a glass of tea?" David asked but Charles Ferguson declined, accepting instead an invitation to a Friday evening meal.

He had, since that night, spent several evenings in the crowded Goldfeder apartment among their children and boarders. In his sketchbook there was a series of drawings of pert, dark-haired Rebecca and quiet Aaron with his crown of copper-colored curls casting a shadow across the pages of his ever-present books. Charles thought it strange that the two children bore so little resemblance to each other and stranger still that Leah, so warm and gentle with her small daughter, grew still and pale when her son approached.

But he stopped thinking about the Goldfeders now, and began his lesson with the discussion of a composition problem, showing the students how a design might be spaced in a given area. The class was attentive, with some of the more diligent students taking laborious notes. During the afternoon hours most of his students were high school boys and girls who rushed to the settlement house as soon as the dismissal bell sounded in their classrooms. One very tiny girl chewed a bagel as she worked, her fingers and mouth moving with equal swiftness, and he smiled when she jumped with surprise as he took her hand and guided it across her sheet of paper, showing her how a simple wrist movement eased her task. He moved up and down the room, stopping to remark on one boy's colors and to gently correct another's perspective. On his third round he noticed that Leah Goldfeder had arrived and slipped quietly into her seat.

She looked tired and pale today, he thought, and was glad that he had good news to share with her. He watched as she worked and twice leaned over her to correct a linear pattern and suggest a different shade of green.

After class he touched her arm lightly.

"I have some news for you, Leah."

"Yes?" She was quiet and patient although he knew that, as always on Friday afternoons, she was in a desperate hurry to get home.

"I showed some of your designs to my old student, Goldstein, and he bought one and asked to see others. He thinks you have a real feeling for both fashion and fabric design, and he said to tell you he knows someone who is looking for a forelady and a designer. I told him I didn't think you would be interested, but still it's a great compliment." Charles Ferguson passed the crisp green check over and watched Leah's face soften with pleasure and the lines of fatigue slowly ease.

"That's wonderful," she gasped. "How pleased David will be. You have given us a wonderful Sabbath gift, Charles."

She took his hand and pressed it with surprising strength and swiftly left.

At the window, moments later, he watched her emerge from the building and hurry down the deserted street. The mauve shadows of evening streaked the gray cobblestoned street. One small boy, his workman's cap balanced jauntily on his head, ran by, clutching a brown paper sack. A single onion skidded out and rolled down the street, shedding its pale silken skin. The boy dashed after it and plucked it from the arms of a darkening shadow, and then Charles Ferguson could no longer see him because the darkness of night had overtaken the street before the lamps were lit. The art teacher thought of the wintry sunset that briefly bloodied the gray skies that stretched above his father's striped and somnolent fields. Next spring, he promised himself, next spring he would set out across the prairies. Next spring.

*

David Goldfeder, walking home through the deserted, night-washed streets, did not hurry. Under one arm he carried a sewing machine shrouded in newspaper which he had borrowed from his shop for the use of his brother-in-law Shimon Hartstein. His other arm was laden with books from the public library, including a picture book for Rebecca and a volume of fairy tales for Aaron. The boy had started first grade only a few months ago but already he was reading with easy fluency. They had been right, after all, to send him to the public school rather than a yeshiva. One cannot enclose oneself in a ghetto in a country which offered the opportunity to be free of ghettos. Anything was possible in the United States. Look what he, David Goldfeder, had accomplished in only a few short years. He had earned a high school diploma and was taking university courses. Such things would never have been possible in Russia where only a minute percentage of Jews were admitted to the universities. Even under the new Communist regime in which poor Yaakov had placed such faith, the words of the law had simply been twisted so that a new ideology was attached to ancient discriminatory practices. The killers of Jews had simply become proletariats instead of Cossacks. On the North Campus of the City College one evening, a fellow student, a youth with wild hair and burning eyes, had asked David Goldfeder to sign a petition on behalf of Eugene Victor Debs, the Socialist. David had refused, gently but firmly.

"I'm sure this Debs is a good man," he had said, "but if you want to know about socialism—sit down and I'll tell you about socialism."

The boy had moved uneasily on, looking nervously back at the thin man with the heavy accent who carried his notebooks in a brown paper bag and used the ten minutes between classes to sleep, sometimes snoring lightly through parted lips, to the controlled amusement of his classmates who also understood the bone-weary fatigue of the night school student.

And now even wider horizons had opened for David Goldfeder. He trembled at the memory of Professor Thompson's words and repeated them to himself again, as though they were a secret incantation whose repetition implied fulfillment.

"Your paper on Freud's theory of the subconscious was excellent, Goldfeder," the tall dark-bearded professor had said. "You approach the subject with considerable depth. Remarkable for an undergraduate. Psychoanalysis interest you?"

"Very much." David's heavily accented voice, as always, was soft, his words cautious. Psychoanalysis more than interested him. It absorbed him. Since his introduction to the work of Sigmund Freud he had thought of little else. It was as though he had searched in the darkness for much of his life and a great light had suddenly been thrust into his hand. Shadowy corners of doubt and fear were illuminated with reason and explanation. There was, after all, an answer to the question that had hammered at him since he looked down at the body of Chana Rivka, the gentle violet-eyed girl who barely reached his shoulder and whom he was to have married in a few weeks' time.

Chana Rivka's jaw had been broken. One arm had been jerked with such force that it had been dislodged from the socket and lay twisted against the tiny lifeless form like the ragged limb of a discarded doll. Chana Rivka had worn a ring, a tiny sapphire that had belonged to David's mother. The ring finger had been chopped from the hand and David tried not to think of how the jeweled circlet, with which his father had betrothed his mother and which he had given to his beloved on a starlit summer evening, had been wrested from the bloody stump. The severed finger had been found a few meters from the body by the small boys who trailed after the burial society in the aftermath of the pogrom, scraping up blood and scattered limbs, gathering crushed eyeglasses and handfuls of hair jerked from beards and earlocks.

Chana Rivka's death had filled David with a grief that clung to him like an engraved shadow and the thought of her killers suffused him with a horror that made him despair of life. How could men kill like that? What forces drove them to such excesses of hate? Did they actually hover so close to the world of the jungle that if they took one uneasy step backward they would fall upon each other in a frenzy of violence, fear, and greed? The questions tormented him and he had wrestled with them for five years, until he found hints of a possible answer in the observations of the Viennese doctor who had wandered solitary through the wilderness of man's anger and anguish. Psychoanalysis, the understanding of man in his most naked psychological being, gave David Goldfeder the courage to counter the desperation that had throttled him since the darkness of that terror-ridden Odessa night.

"You must do more work in the field. Your grasp of the material is unusual, extraordinary. You are a second-year student now, Mr. Goldfeder?" the professor had asked.

"Yes."

"You have had biological sciences?"

"Only one semester. I go to classes at night and laboratories are difficult to schedule."

"And in the daytime?"

"I am a pants presser."

"I see." Professor Thompson compressed his lips in irritation. It was ridiculous that a man of Goldfeder's unusual intellectual talents should spend his days pressing pants. Something would have to be done. Some sort of scholarship or loan arranged.

"You must think of medical school, Goldfeder. You must think of studying psychoanalysis in depth." Decisively the professor walked off to a faculty meeting as though a troubling situation had been settled.

Medical school. The thought teased David Goldfeder as he struggled home, clutching the sewing machine which seemed to grow heavier at every step. Psychoanalysis in depth. It was ridiculous, impossible. Even with scholarships. But still, perhaps he could juggle time. Perhaps it could be arranged. He would talk to Leah about it tonight, after the children were asleep and the boarders had dispersed to their rooms.

Slowly he mounted the steps to their apartment. The stairwell smelled of the ammonia and urine which drifted over the transom of the common bathroom and he pinched his nostrils against the acrid odor. The door to his own apartment was open and he heard the sound of excited talk and Rebecca's lilting laughter as she scurried after Joshua Ellenberg. The aroma of vegetables simmering in rich golden chicken broth, the yeasty scent of the newly baked Sabbath loaves, and the smell of burning candles banished the foul hallway odors and he closed the door firmly behind him.

"Good Shabbos," he said cheerfully, looking at the welcoming burning tapers. He realized with a kind of terror that he had almost forgotten tonight that the darkening sky meant the beginning of the Sabbath.

In the kitchen Leah was adding salt to the soup and he noticed that her wrist bore a light streak of blue paint.

"You had an art class today?" he asked.

"With Ferguson." She bent over the pot again, her face bright with the heat of the kitchen and the rush of preparing the large meal.

Once, standing on the deck of the boat that had carried them across the Atlantic, he had watched her standing in the wind and marked the way the color slowly rose in her pale cheeks, the blood warring against the resistant pallor of the skin and settling finally with ruddy radiance across her upturned face, turning the small dimple in the corner of her mouth into a tender pink bud. She had been pregnant than, heavy with the weight of Aaron and the memory of Yaakov's death. He had struggled against the unfamiliar stirring of longing and had gone below deck, leaving her to her solitary vigil above the endless waves. Now, in the cluttered kitchen, with her color so hauntingly bright, he was drawn to her and felt his weariness fade as he passed his fingers gently across her face.

"Tired?" he asked and bent his head, his lips searching for the blue scar of paint that trailed against her wrist.

Abruptly she withdrew her hand. A spoon clattered to the floor and she bent to retrieve it, calling too loudly for Sarah Ellenberg to come and help her. She did not turn as David walked from the room.

After dinner that night, she read aloud a letter from her brother Moshe, in Palestine. David listened to her soft voice rising and falling in rhythmic Yiddish and realized that he was beginning to think more and more in English. He had to strain to understand one or two of Moshe's references and he wondered whether this was because Moshe, too, had lost an easy grasp of the language of their childhood and was more at home now in Hebrew. David tried to concentrate on the letter now and not think about that brief scene in the kitchen. He and Leah had agreed upon a partnership when they married, a viable union against loneliness and despair. He had no right to demand more from her than he had offered that fall evening when they had talked without touching in the Odessa park, as the madwoman rushed off to meet a train that would never arrive.

His feelings for Leah had changed since that evening. From the small roots of affection, from the need to somehow fill the great emptiness left by Chana Rivka's death, a trembling love had grown. He knew, though, that Leah's feelings had not altered. And so he struggled to withhold his love from the woman who was his wife.

Rebecca scrambled onto David's lap and Aaron remained in a corner, his bright hair glowing in the soft circle of lamplight which was left glowing throughout the Sabbath, his eyes rooted to the pages of the *Blue Fairy Book.* Aaron loved the sound of his mother's voice but he did not listen to her words. Like David, Yiddish was becoming an unused language for him and Aaron allowed the words he understood but no longer spoke to flow over him as he read on in English.

Leah heard Moshe's deep voice behind the written words and in her mind's eye conjured up Henia's patient, loving face. She continued to read.

"This letter will reach you after we here, and you there, have celebrated the New Year and observed the Day of Atonement. We wish you and all of Israel peace. Our spirits are high this year because at last we have managed to drain the swamp on the northern border of our settlement and we are certain that in the spring we can at last begin planting.

"A thousand dunams will be given over to alfalfa which we can market and we will plant the rest with vegetables for our own use. Small Yaakov went with us to the market in Tel Aviv and returned full of excitement. Truly, we also were excited when we saw the new city built on the sands. There is so much to do here and so much to learn. Tonight I am on guard duty. We have tried mightily to befriend the neighboring Arabs but they return our overtures with attacks. I am sorry to tell you that Mottel Abramowitz who studied with us in Odessa lost an eye in such a raid. But we comfort ourselves with the knowledge that this is not Russia. Here, Jews are allowed to defend themselves. I wish we could persuade the rest of the family to leave the old country and join us here. Write to us soon. Our hearts are with you."

Leah refolded the sheets of paper and put them back in the envelope. She peeled the English stamp off the envelope and gave it to Joshua Ellenberg, who had announced that he was now collecting stamps for a hobby. Aaron knew that Joshua saved the stamps he begged from other people's letters and sold them to the old man who kept a coin and stamp stall on Canal Street. He wondered why his friend didn't tell the truth and turned back to the fairy tales which were less puzzling to him than the people around him.

"Your brother sounds like a marvelous man," Masha said.

She was wearing a new dress and as she talked to Leah her eyes laughed across the room to Shimon Hartstein. The dress was of a rustling brocade and when she reached over to pick up the weekend edition of the Yiddish *Morning Journal,* her skirt brushed against Shimon's knees. He blushed slightly and pressed the richly waxed curves of his handlebar moustache with nervous fingers. Twice last week Leah had heard soft voices behind Shimon's closed door and on the second occasion, late in the evening, she had recognized Masha's softly lisping voice. She had noticed too that whenever Masha emerged from her room to announce that she was going to the roof to collect her drying laundry, Shimon felt the urgent need for a breath of air.

"My sister is also a marvelous woman," Leah said. "I wonder if Moshe's Yaakov can be as cute as Yankele and little Chana?"

Shimon coughed nervously and looked away from Leah.

"Did you bring home the sewing machine?" he asked David, swiftly changing the subject.

"It's over there." David pointed to the machine which he had set down on a bench. "What do you want it for over a Sabbath?"

"My business secret," his brother-in-law replied, but leaned forward conspiratorially. "I bought a pattern for a new kind of shirt front. A dickey, they call it. They're like the shirtwaists the girls wear to go to business but without sleeves or a back. Just for show underneath the jacket and very cheap to make. I got a good buy on the fabric and I figure I can cut and sew myself and sell direct. I listen when the boss talks to the buyers and salesmen and all the names I got in my head."

"And I can deliver for you," Joshua Ellenberg volunteered. "I just put new wheels on my wagon. I can go all over the city."

"Wonderful," David murmured. "Everyone here in this apartment is a Henry Ford, at least."

"So what's wrong with a little ambition?" Masha asked, looking up from her paper. "It's better to have some ambition than to give up and put your head in the oven like that poor young woman on Monroe Street. Every week something like that in the paper, and then I think of poor Mrs. Moskowitz next door left with all those children. Ach, it makes me not want to read any more." But she licked her lips expectantly as she bent over yet another headline offering a reward for information about men who had deserted their wives.

"You had a good day, David?" Leah asked. She wanted to change the subject quickly, to steer the conversation into calmer waters, away from the shoals of suicide and desertion and the desperate race against poverty.

"A day like all days," he answered.

"You must have had something on your mind though," Morris Morgenstern said. "When I saw you at the bathhouse you looked right through me. Thinking about your books, maybe." He glanced with reverent eyes at the small mountain of David's texts in a corner of the room.

"No, I had something on my mind," David admitted and blushed slightly as everyone leaned toward him.

Even Aaron looked up from his book and small Rebecca left the basket of spools she had been patiently dressing in scraps of rags and climbed onto his lap. Her dark hair, thick and glossy like her mother's, smelled vaguely of the fresh lemons Leah squeezed into the home-blended shampoo. He pressed his cheek against her curls as he so often longed to do with Leah's long tresses when she brushed them each night, sitting on the side of the bed.

"What was on your mind, Papa?" she asked. "What's a mind, Papa?" David laughed.

"A mind is what helps you think, little one," he answered. "The most precious thing you have. Better than money or a thousand patterns."

"So what were you thinking in your mind?"

"About something a professor said to me. This professor—he's a smart man, a wise man—he thinks your papa should study to be a doctor."

His words were followed by a stunned silence. Sam and Sarah Ellenberg looked at each other and Sarah shrugged and raised an eyebrow quizzically while Sam nodded, their silent marital signals expressing amusement and incredulity. Morris Morgenstern and Label Katz stared at their hands and then at the ceiling as though to avoid embarrassing David Goldfeder by looking at him. The man had had a moment of madness. He was entitled. But until he recovered they would not intrude on him with their doubting eyes. The young women, Masha, Bryna, and Pearl, tried not to look at each other and when Bryna rose and announced that she would take a walk before bedtime, the other two quickly offered to accompany her. Their soft giggles trailed up the staircase and David heard Pearl say, "A doctor yet. I'm surprised he doesn't want to be president."

"To be president you have to be born here," Masha replied and the laughter began again.

When the door slammed behind them, Shimon Hartstein clapped David on the back and slammed his hands together derisively.

"Medical school now? All right, so you finished the high school and you're going to the college. But for medical school you can't work by day and go to school by night. And medical school is not free. What greenhorn goes to medical school?"

"There are scholarships," David answered feebly.

Secretly he agreed with Shimon and, more clearly than his brother-in-law, he saw the incredible obstacles that lay before him. Even if he did get a scholarship, how would they live? The extra income from the boarders could hardly support the family. And how could he pass the entrance examinations to medical school? He would be competing against men ten years younger than him, for whom English was a native language. The other applicants had studied in libraries and laboratories, not on rumbling subway trains and at the edge of an ironing board in an airless factory. The idea was insane, preposterous. He wondered how he had ever seen any hope at all in Professor Thompson's words.

"Of course there are scholarships," Leah said calmly.

"And on what do you live while he studies?" Shimon asked.

"I will get a job," Leah replied, as though she had thought the entire situation through and created a workable blueprint that would carry them through the next several years. "Only today Charles Ferguson told me that he showed one of my designs to a designer, a friend of his, who liked it so much that he bought it. In my bag I have the check. This man knows someone who is looking for a designer and forelady and he thought of me. From that I'll bring home what David brings home from the factory."

"And who'll run the house?" Shimon asked. "Who'll see to the boarders, the cooking, the laundry? That too you've thought of?"

"Certainly," Leah said. "Malcha. My sister. Your wife. With the money I have from that design and some other money I put aside from here and there, I have enough now to add to your savings and bring her and the children over. And while I work, Malcha can manage the house."

"Leahle," David protested weakly, thinking suddenly that he did not know his wife at all. How swiftly she had formulated this plan and he knew that she would set it into operation with equal swiftness. He remembered with what expeditiousness she had left her native village for the unknown experience of Odessa and how she had agreed, in a matter of minutes, really, to marry him and come to America. She was a woman who moved with sudden certainty, fording each new bridge with the courage of her intuition and the strength of the resulting resolve.

"Why is it so strange, David?" she asked. "Didn't my mother work so my father could study Talmud? So I will work and you will study medicine."

She was busy with the children, holding Aaron by the hand and carrying sleepy Rebecca. Walking from the room, she turned back at the doorway and said, "Tomorrow night, after Shabbos, I will write to Malcha and tell her to prepare for the journey."

Shimon Hartstein stared after his sister-in-law, his jaw slack with defeat and admiration. Something in the way Leah held her head, or perhaps it was the graceful slope of her shoulders, reminded him suddenly of his own wife.

"I wonder," he said musingly, "if my Malcha still wears her marriage wig."

4

"May I speak to you for a moment, Mrs. Goldfeder?"

Leah Goldfeder looked up from her drawing board and stole an impatient glance at her watch. Her heart sank. It was almost four o'clock and the sketches for the new shirtwaist dress were not nearly completed. In another hour she would have to switch from designing to her duties as a forelady and begin checking work, collecting materials, and finally, the task she disliked most, the personal inspection of the girls who worked under her to check that they were not leaving the factory with stolen fabric, patterns, or thread. She was rushed enough and now there was yet another interruption.

"Yes, of course. What is it?" she asked, adjusting her voice as always to conceal her mood.

Like all the employees at Rosenblatt and Sons, she knew the man who stood before her. He was Eli Feinstein, the chief cutter, and she knew too that it was only his speed and skill, both recognized as extraordinary, that kept him employed at the dress and blouse factory. Arnold Rosenblatt, the paunchy, balding man who ran the factory for his father and an older brother who was always mysteriously traveling in Europe, had often spoken derisively about Feinstein in Leah's hearing.

"That Communist," Rosenblatt had muttered when told that the cutter, one scorching summer day, had refused to continue his work unless everyone in the factory was given a fifteen-minute break and the factory was closed an hour early. The temperature in the airless workrooms had risen to ninety-five degrees that afternoon. One girl in Leah's section had slid from her stool although her foot was caught on the treadle, so that the machine continued its rhythmic progress while she lay in a faint so heavy that for a moment they thought her dead. After that there had been a series of small accidents. The needle of a sewing machine had pierced the thumb of a fifteen-year-old finisher and the blood had spurted upward, staining the low ceiling with the peristaltic scarlet gush. A girl's hair had been caught in the bobbins of a rapidly moving embroidery machine, and only Leah's swift move to disconnect the current had prevented the girl's head from being dragged into the machine's works. Finally the break had been granted and the factory closed a half-hour short of the usual closing time, to the great displeasure of Arnold Rosenblatt, who stood at the office door twirling his gold pocket watch and glaring at the backs of his departing workers.

"I should like to speak to you in private," Eli Feinstein said, bending closer over Leah's drawing board, looking critically at the half-finished design. Leah recognized that his tone was devoid of any request. He was, rather, demanding her time and his voice was calm with the assurance that he would not be refused.

She looked up at him, giving him for the first time her full attention and noticing, with surprise, how tall he was and how erect he stood. It occurred to her that she had never seen him before when he was not bent over the cutting table, his eyes rooted to the mountain of fabric piled before him, overlaid with tissue-paper patterns through which he would cleave with razor and knife, carving out sleeves and shirt fronts which he trimmed to size with enormous gleaming scissors. She had passed him perhaps a dozen times a day in as many months but only now did she notice that his hair was as dark as her own and grew with such thickness that it covered his head in wildly uneven layers. His eyebrows too were thick and grew together in a shaggy line, but beneath them his eyes were river-green and he looked at Leah as though he guessed a secret which he would not share.

"It's very late," she said. "I have something very important to finish here and then I must get back to the factory floor."

"I did not mean that we should talk now. Perhaps after work we might have a coffee together."

"That's impossible. I must get home. My children will be waiting."

She thought of the way Aaron stood at the front window each evening, his eyes raking the street, his bright hair blazing in the circle of lamplight. But always, as she approached the front door, he darted away, and when she came into the room he would be sitting at the table, clutching a pencil and earnestly absorbed in his homework, his eyes lowered against her greeting but following her movements stealthily as she bent to kiss Rebecca and to greet Malcha and his cousins.

"It will take only a few minutes," Eli Feinstein persisted. "And it is very important. Otherwise I would not bother you. It concerns your girls in the factory."

Leah considered, intrigued now by the man's urgency and calculated air of mystery. David, as always, would be working late at the library and Malcha would have the dinner ready. Joshua Ellenberg, who worked afternoons as a messenger boy for Rosenblatts, could tell them that she would be late.

"All right," she said finally. "I'll meet you downstairs then."

"No. Not downstairs," he replied swiftly. "Someone would see us there. At the Cafe Royale. I will be waiting for you."

He strode away before she could object that the Royale was blocks out of her way and there was, after all, a coffee shop right next door.

But then she shrugged, surprised to recognize that her annoyance had turned into anticipation and surprised, too, that the design over which she had labored most of the day was finished within minutes.

"A ruffle at the neck. Of course, that's it," she muttered to herself and tore the finished drawing off her pad without giving it another glance. Charles Ferguson would not approve of such swift work, she thought, but then Charles Ferguson was not working at a double job ten hours a day.

Leah woke each morning in the cold grayness of earliest dawn and thrust her shivering body into David's old winter coat and the fleece-lined boots Malcha had brought with her from Russia. It was

Leah's job to shovel the coal into the kitchen stove and coax the fire into life so that the kitchen would be moderately bearable when the children carried their clothing in to dress. By that time Malcha would be up, preparing breakfast, thrusting pots of water onto the stove so that there would be warm water for washing, and searching for the inevitably missing set of underwear.

In their bedroom, Leah and David dressed in the heavy silence that now shrouded their life together. In the exhausting pace of the last year, they had surrendered the need for words, as though talk would squander the energy so desperately needed elsewhere. David was attending classes both days and evenings now, carrying out a double program mapped out by Professor Thompson. He left early in the morning and often did not return until late at night, and then sat up for hours at the long table, reading and writing. Often, as the light of dawn streaked across the sky, Leah awoke alone in bed and walked through the silent flat to the table where David still sat, driven at last to sleep over his books. His head rested on pillows of papers and his pencil slid limply in his fingers. Her heart would turn over then, and she would lead him to their bed with the tenderness of a mother guiding a somnambulistic child, tucking him beneath their blankets still dressed, with a new day's beard sprouting harshly on his chin. Sometimes at such an hour he awoke and they made love too swiftly, observing still the silence that had become their secret language of determination and despair.

Leah, too, followed a relentless schedule. Rosenblatts, the factory to which Charles Ferguson's friend had recommended her for employment, was a mile away and she walked there each morning, joining the crowd of hurrying workers that poured out of the east side tenements only to regroup and reassemble in West Side factories and lofts. Leah was in charge of a group of twelve girls whose job it was to add the trimmings to the garments that were manufactured in other parts of the factory.

They sat in rows before her, smocks shielding their dresses from the debris of threads and cuttings which their machines spat out. Leah had insisted, since the accident with the bobbin, that they gather their hair up in snoods or kerchiefs, and sometimes, as she watched their bent heads enclosed in the colorful cloths, she was reminded of the kerchiefed heads of the women huddled in their separate section of the synagogue in the Russian village of her girlhood, staring at the pages of prayer books they could not read. But of course the girls who sat before her in the Lower Manhattan factory were young, some of them almost children. When they rushed into the factory in the morning their cheeks sparkled with color and their eyes burned with the brightness of dreams and hopes. Over the noise of the whirring machines, they chatted about young men, dances, the weddings of their friends. The high-buttoned shoes that pumped the treadles whirled, in the evenings, across the scarred floors of the dancing studios that had sprung up in the parlors of the larger apartments. But the most precious hours of their young years were spent in the narrow workroom of the factory under Leah's watchful eye. Too often, her heart thudded heavily as she reprimanded a girl whose chatter had caused her to damage a garment. Sometimes the young culprit would be only ten years older than small Rebecca, and Leah, thinking of her black-haired daughter, hardened her resolve that Rebecca would never sit behind a sewing machine while the days of her youth drifted by.

Leah was also charged with designing some of the less important items manufactured by Rosenblatt and Sons. Each week she brought her designs for bodices and chemises up to Arnold Rosenblatt's glass-enclosed office and handed them to the pale secretary who shivered slightly each time the harsh buzzer on her desk sounded. It was common knowledge in the factory that the idea of using waste fabric to manufacture cummerbunds had come from Leah Goldfeder's drawing board. Twice, during the year, Leah's pay envelope had contained an extra ten-dollar bill, which was Arnold Rosenblatt's grudging acknowledgment of the value of her work.

"Ten dollars!" Shimon Hartstein had snorted. "Do you know what kind of a profit that pig Rosenblatt got from those cummerbunds? He should be ashamed. The rich bastard!"

"Shimon," Malcha remonstrated weakly. "*Bitte.*"

"English! Speak English!" he shouted and Leah's sister swayed silently, fearfully in her rocking chair.

Malcha did not understand this angry, energetic businessman with his pomaded moustaches who had mysteriously replaced the shy, softly bearded young Talmud student she had married. The bridegroom of her marriage bed had delicate white flesh that lay loosely on his arms, but the man who had plucked her out of the crowds of immigrants at Ellis Island had held her in an embrace of hard muscle and spoke in a language she could not understand. Sometimes, watching the Hartsteins together, Leah wondered if Malcha were really glad that she had come to America—but she knew that her older sister, always quiet and quiescent, would never complain. She had, since her arrival, dutifully set aside her marriage wig and her dark hair had grown in again so that it hung once more about her shoulders as it had when she was a girl in Partseva. But the hair had lost its sheen just as Malcha, alone and lonely for too many years, had lost her vitality and initiative. She moved as a marionette might, set into motion by the manipulations of a benign puppeteer. Her parents had wanted her to marry Shimon and she had dutifully stood beneath the marriage canopy. Shimon had gone to America and for five years she had huddled in waiting. Now Shimon and her younger sister had propelled her to New York to run their household while they disappeared into the tumultuous world outside, and Malcha, mesmerized by the obedience that had become habit, did so with neither protest nor complaint. Malcha would not have so casually made plans to meet Eli Feinstein at a café.

"But what does it matter?" Leah thought, adjusting the broad-brimmed straw hat so that it cast a slight shadow across her face, concealing the fatigue. "So I'll meet Feinstein for coffee and be home an hour late." She was nagged by the worry that Aaron would spend that hour waiting at the window, an unread book balanced before him. What was wrong with the boy? she worried plaintively, washed anew by the curious currents of irritation and concern that thoughts of Aaron always set in motion.

"Good night, Mrs. Goldfeder."

Surprised, Leah looked up and saw pretty Bonnie Eckstein, who always had such difficulty threading her machine. What was the girl doing here? Leah knew she had left fifteen minutes earlier because she remembered sliding her hands across the girl's unresisting body. Once, years before, there had been an epidemic of petty pilfering and the factory girls had smuggled fabric and patterns beneath their clothing when they left. It was because of this that Arnold Rosenblatt insisted that each worker be searched by the forelady in charge of the section, a task which Leah performed with abhorrence, feeling herself as humiliated as the girls whose bodies she touched with swift impersonal fingers.

"Did you forget something, Bonnie?" Leah asked.

"Yes. My gloves." The girl picked up her hands to display the thin white cotton gloves she wore. She was fair-skinned and the color rushed to her cheeks with startling redness. Her gloved hands flew up to button her open jacket, but not before Leah saw the edges of a distinctive blue muslin which had been distributed for cutting only that day. It was obvious now that Bonnie had left the factory with the others, waited until she assumed the building was empty, and hurried back, using an excuse of a forgotten item to get past the watchman, and taken the fabric. The girl's frightened eyes followed Leah's stare and she threw her hands up to her face, blocking the tears that had begun to gush down across her mottled skin.

"I know it's wrong but I didn't know what else to do. I must get some more money. My father has trachoma and he can't even take the pushcart out anymore. My mother's still sick from the last birth and I have two little brothers. The small one has bronchitis. He coughs and coughs and there's no medicine. What can I do? I've got to have some more money. I thought maybe I could stitch the material by hand and sell the shirts. I didn't know what else to do. If

Yossi doesn't get the medicine he'll die. I know it." Certainty of the worst gave a strange strength to her words. She stopped crying and looked at the woman who stood before her, so tall and calm, her black hair a gentle crown beneath the straw hat. On the floor above them the cleaning woman moved with padded steps and they heard the light thud of her heavy water pail as she set it down.

"How old are you, Bonnie?" Leah asked.

"Sixteen," the girl replied. She was fifteen but added the extra year automatically.

"Bonnie, you must give me the fabric and I will put it back. Tomorrow I will teach you how to operate the embroidery machine. That work pays more, and Maria Calderazzo is leaving soon to be married. You can take her machine. But now, your brother must have the medicine. There is a nurse at the Irvington Settlement House who will help you. I will give you a note to Mr. Ferguson, whose studio is on the second floor of the Settlement House, and he will help you find the nurse."

She wrote a few words to Charles Ferguson, explaining the situation, and gave it to the girl, who seized her hand briefly, relief and shame flooding her face again with a harsh redness.

"You must never do anything like this again, Bonnie," Leah said firmly. "Never. There are other ways."

"Yes, Mrs. Goldfeder. And thank you."

The girl closed the door gently behind her and Leah, standing motionless for a moment in the dim light of the empty factory, heard the clatter of her feet as she rushed down the stairwell. She put the muslin in the storage cabinet and wondered sadly if they should lock all the cabinets each evening.

The incident with Bonnie had made her late for her meeting with Eli Feinstein and she walked quickly, still thinking of what had happened. She wondered what she would have answered if the girl had pressed her about those "other ways" to ward off poverty Leah had so easily mentioned. What were the "other ways" to find money for food and clothing for the armies of men and women who had brought trachoma with them as a part of their portable legacy after generations mired in the poverty and misery of the old country. The settlement houses and welfare agencies could do only so much and many of the immigrants were unaware of their existence. There had been, after all, no "other way" for her neighbor, Yetta Moskowitz, who had been deserted by her husband and left alone with four children. Heavy and clumsy with the weight of her pregnancy, Yetta had placed her head on a pillow within her open hissing gas oven. It was there that her children had found her dead hours later. The building rang with their anguished wails and the youngest complained over and over that she was hungry and her mother would not wake up. Always, Leah would remember that Yetta Moskowitz had used a carefully laundered, newly ironed pillow slip, embroidered in the thick blue satin thread of her dowry marks, for her final comfort. Her hair had been newly washed and the scent of lemon mingled with the acrid fumes of gas.

Thinking now of the Moskowitz children, dispersed among relatives, Leah reached the corner of Second Avenue and Twelfth Street and pushed open the door of the Cafe Royale.

The sounds of the mournful violinist floated above the bubbles of conversation that sparkled upward from every table. Scraps of Yiddish tumbled over arguments in French and collided with stern pronouncements in Russian. A tall blond man stood up and read from a tattered copy of *Eugene Onegin*. The two blonde women with him, both dressed in pale blue suits, clapped in unison and their gloved hands created a wondrously soft, sweet sound. A young man, wearing a suit and a vest from which a pocket watch dangled, waved across the room to a pretty girl in a high-waisted red dress. She joined him at the table he shared with three men dressed in work clothes, glasses of tea standing before them. They continued their argument without looking at the girl, who slid quietly into an empty chair and touched the young man's hand with her own.

At a small table a one-eyed artist sat, sketching the café's patrons. They drifted across his pad in gray pencil lines and Leah, glancing automatically at the artist's work, saw the figures of the bent newspaper readers, the arguing clusters of men, the groups of pale girls who sat together and watched the clock that would eventually drive them back to their barren bedrooms at the end of dimly lit boarding-house corridors. The waiters drifted from table to table, uneasily balancing glasses of tea and coffee and chunks of cake on the scarred aluminum disks that served as trays.

Cigarette smoke wreathed the warm room in a gray cloud that made Leah's eyes smart. Suddenly her name was called and she felt Eli Feinstein's hand on her shoulder, guiding her to an empty chair at a table where two glasses of tea had already been set down, next to two clumsy pieces of honey cake on which bright golden nuts nestled unevenly.

"I hope the tea isn't cold," he said. "You were so late I thought you weren't coming."

"I was delayed. Something at the factory."

"Oh?"

"Nothing very important," she said and was stung by the memory of Bonnie's cheeks reddening in shame and despair. Suddenly, without meaning to, she was telling Eli Feinstein the story.

"It's not so unusual," he said when she had finished. "The girl is very young and very poor. A sick father. A sick brother. What can she do?"

"Yes. Still, it is not right to steal."

"Nor to be stolen from. Her youth is stolen for poor wages. Her dignity is stolen. In a way this is why I wanted to see you, to talk to you. Think of how it would be if there were a fund at the factory for girls like Bonnie, a fund they could borrow from if there is such sickness in the family or they need help for other reasons. It's been done in other factories where the workers have been organized."

"You're talking about a union," Leah said. "Please. Do not play word games with me. You must say what you mean."

She sipped her tea. Eli Feinstein had sweetened it himself and she was surprised that he knew she took two sugars. Smiling, taking another drink, she looked at him.

"Once on the street I saw you buy a tea from a peddler. I saw that you take two sugars. I noticed."

"Then you have noticed that I am a forelady. Foreladies are not good people to talk to about organizing unions."

"I thought perhaps a forelady with eyes such as yours might be different," he said. "A forelady who hates the examination of workers, who thinks of ways to protect them, who worries about a little finisher with a sick brother. Such a forelady, I thought, might be induced to care even more. Maybe she would organize her caring so that it means something. Was I wrong, Mrs. Goldfeder, was I wrong to think that you cared about your comrades?" His voice was gentle but certain, playing against her feelings knowingly and expertly, a skilled fiddler wielding his bow against a recalcitrant instrument.

Leah looked up at him, fending off his words. The café violinist, who had wandered from table to table, cradling the café sitters in the cocoon of his mournful tunes, had gone to sit with the one-eyed artist and count the coins he had collected in the cup which dangled from his waist. It was the music that had unnerved her, she thought, the music and the use of the word "comrade." The music had swept her back to her wedding to Yaakov in Odessa and she remembered how they had sat in a circle then, the bridegroom and bride clasping the hands of their assembled friends while the violins played and they sang of bright tomorrows, of days of peace when comrades would stride forth together. There had been no tomorrows for Yaakov and the violins had been stilled; the comrades and the promises vanished, when the streets rang with agony and were littered with bloodied bodies.

"I care, Mr. Feinstein. I care about my husband and my children. I do not like words like comrade. You see, I was in Odessa in 1919," she said. Again, she was telling this man something she had not meant to reveal, thrusting out secrets of her past in defense against a future she did not want.

"I too am from Odessa. My wife was killed in that pogrom," Eli Feinstein replied. "I was away that day. In Karkov. Karkov." He offered the name of the town as though only that gave reality to all that had happened. Leah remembered now Moshe and Henia's neighbors, whose three children had been murdered when a mob raided the apartment while their mother was out shopping.

"I went down for flour and brown sugar. I needed a kilo of brown sugar," the woman had said over and over again, clinging to the memory of that sugar in its mesh sack as though it represented her sanity, her grasp on reality. Leah, remembering the terror of a distant summer day, often thought of the dress she had been wearing. It had been of yellow cotton, dotted with sprigs of tiny red roses. Karkov. Brown sugar. Yellow cotton with tiny red roses. Small weights of facts to anchor them lest they drown in the whirlpools of horror.

"I'm sorry," she said softly.

"No matter." Eli Feinstein stared at his tea. "I do not talk of communism and brave new worlds. I talk only of Rosenblatts and girls like young Bonnie. You know that Rosenblatts is one of the few larger factories that is still not unionized."

"Yes. I know that."

"It is because Rosenblatt frightens off those workers who try to organize and buys off others. You, I have the feeling, he can neither frighten nor buy. And there are others like you. Am I right to have such a feeling about you, Mrs. Goldfeder?"

Leah sipped again at the tea, cold now, and allowed her eyes to rise from the scarred linoleum-topped table and meet Feinstein's searching gaze.

"You must understand something, Mr. Feinstein," she said. "I am working to support my family. My husband is studying for entrance into medical school and we have two small children. Only my salary buys our food and clothing, pays the rent. I do not think I can risk my husband's future and my children's needs."

"But you wouldn't have to." He leaned forward eagerly and continued. "Look, there are a few important workers who make it possible for Rosenblatt to run that factory and keep his good-for-nothing brother traveling around Europe, his father in an old age home, his wife on Park Avenue, and his mistress on Fifth Avenue. Without them he'd have to close down."

"So he would close down for a week, two weeks even. Until he found new workers and then it would be the same thing all over again. Only you and I and the others who joined with us would not have jobs."

"But that's not true," Eli Feinstein protested. "The organizers for the United Hebrew Trade Unions have found out a few things. Like, for instance, Mr. Rosenblatt has a lot of creditors who watch what's going on with him very carefully. If he closed down, even for a day, they'd all be demanding their money and that would finish him."

Eli Feinstein fumbled in his pocket and found a folded sheet of paper which he spread out in front of Leah. It was a list of company names; some of them she recognized as the names of fabric companies whose cartons she frequently handled, and others as names of leading dealers in trimming and threads. Many of the names were unfamiliar to her but the figures next to them were staggering. Arnold Rosenblatt owed hundreds of thousands of dollars. The paunchy little man in expensive dark suits, whose chauffeured car waited for him each evening, who clipped his cigars with a small gold scissors, was in debt in every part of New York. His survival, she supposed, on a much grander scale, was not unlike that of her brother-in-law Shimon, who had established his own small business which existed largely on credit.

"How can you owe everyone so much money?" Malcha had asked worriedly, but her husband had winked and laughed.

"The man who sells me threads doesn't know that Label Katz from the trimming store also gives me credit. Blumberg, from the fabrics, I pay absolutely on time, and he tells Weinstein from the machines what a good customer I am, so Weinstein I can let ride for two, three months. Like in a circle, Malcha, I juggle," Shimon had replied with relish, and Leah had wondered if he would enjoy being in business so much if it were not such a game.

"In a circus, sometimes a ball gets dropped," David had observed dryly, looking up from a textbook.

"Just so long as it's only one ball, I'm okay," Shimon had replied.

But if Rosenblatt were unable to maintain the business for even a day, all the manufacturers with whom he dealt would become aware of his precarious situation and his delicate balancing act would be over, Leah realized, scanning Eli Feinstein's list again.

"These important workers you talk about—all of them are in agreement with you?" Leah asked.

"Some are less sure than others," he answered honestly. "But they are all willing to sit down and talk about it together, to see if it's possible. And you, are you willing?"

"I don't know. So much depends on this job. My husband's studies. My family. My parents are still in Europe and I want to make enough money to bring them over. The news from there is not good." She arrayed her objections like a merchant loading a scale and then, her voice still low, she balanced the other weight. "But I know it is wrong for people to work like that. It is dangerous for the girls in the building. I worry about the doors. If we ever had to leave the factory in a hurry, in a case of a pipe busting or a fire, we could never get out safely. And I know that the girls are underpaid. Six days a week—ten hours a day—no holidays. It's not right."

"But will you come to the meeting?" Eli Feinstein asked urgently, seizing a moment when her voice trembled against the uneasy balance of pros and cons.

The violinist had begun to play again, a mazurka she had often danced to with Yaakov's fine-boned hands resting lightly on her waist, the movements of his booted feet matching her light, slippered steps. Beneath the table, Eli Feinstein's feet twitched with remembered rhythms and his eyes grew clouded with the film of memories.

"Yes, I'll come to the meeting," she said. "Give me the address and the time."

Briskly he jerked himself free of the spell of the music and scribbled the information on a piece of paper.

She groped in her purse for change to pay for the tea and cake but impatiently he refused the outstretched coins.

"You are my guest. I invited you," he said and rising to his feet, he took her hand in his and his lips brushed her upturned palm.

"Well, thank you. And good night."

She hurried from the café, passing the table where the group of girls still sat, smoking cigarettes now, their pale faces veiled in smoke and their eyes roving to a corner booth where a group of young men argued over steaming glasses of coffee. Near the exit, a bearded poet read his Yiddish verses to listeners who marked his rhythms with bent teaspoons. Softly, as though fearful of snapping the delicate thread of their attention, Leah closed the café door behind her.

It was late when she reached home and from the street below she saw Aaron at his post in the window, anxiously watching the street. But, as always, he slid into the room when he saw her in the doorway. She waited a moment before entering the apartment, then lifted her hand and allowed her fingers to lightly touch the spot where Eli Feinstein's dry lips had met her skin.

*

Two weeks passed before the meeting which Eli Feinstein was organizing took place. The cool air of early spring melted into a sudden warmth and small shoots of young grass appeared beneath the cracks in the pavements. Through the factory window, where a lone ailanthus tree grew in a barren courtyard, Leah watched the lacy leaves sprout forth, their texture so delicate that the sun filtered through them and dappled shadows fell on the concrete pavement where, once again, small gray sparrows and starlings fluttered.

Several times, during those two weeks, Eli Feinstein stopped at Leah's worktable. Once he left a Yiddish newspaper folded to a particular page, and when she opened it, she found a story describing a fire in a factory similar to Rosenblatts. Four girls had been burned to death in that fire, and one survivor, a sixteen-year-old, would never walk again. A few days later he left a small pamphlet published by the United Hebrew Trades Association describing the need for organized labor and stressing the fact that organized factories, union shops, resulted in greater profits for the owners.

"What did you think of the pamphlet?" Feinstein asked Leah a few days later, when they met at the cart of a vendor who peddled cold drinks to the factory workers during the lunch break. They were in the courtyard and the bright sunlight danced across the cutter's face, sparking golden tones in his green eyes.

Leah leaned against the ailanthus tree and sipped her cold coffee.

"It makes it all sound so simple. Too simple," she said. "If everything were as described in the union pamphlet we could just go up to Rosenblatt and tell him that if we had a union he'd make more money."

Eli Feinstein laughed.

"You're a smart woman, Leah Goldfeder. Look, isn't that the girl you told me about??"

Leah followed his eyes to a corner of the courtyard where Bonnie Eckstein sat with a group of girls. Her face was flushed and she wore her pale blonde hair in the newly popular pageboy fashion. She was singing, a gentle song about a calf with mournful eyes, and the others were following the melody, singing with increased confidence so that soon their voices rose in a sweet chorus that vied with the harsh gong of the factory bell that summoned them back to their machines. Still singing, they gathered their things together and drifted back to work. Some of the tardier ones cast nervous glances at Leah. She and Eli Feinstein remained standing for a moment in the deserted courtyard, listening to the whir of the machines that had so swiftly replaced the sweetness of the singing.

"I can't get used to the idea that some of the girls are frightened of me," Leah said sadly.

"I know it's not a pleasant feeling," he replied. "We will see you then at the meeting tomorrow night?"

She nodded and he shook hands with her gravely before disappearing into the factory. Leah, following him a moment later, looked up and saw Arnold Rosenblatt staring down at her from his office window. The owner's eyes were narrow although his lips were creased in a thin smile, and when she entered the building, he tossed his cigar butt from the window with such force that it fell into a pool of sunlight well beyond the ailanthus tree.

The meeting was held in Eli Feinstein's small room on Catherine Street and every available space was occupied when Leah finally arrived. She had been delayed at home by Malcha's worried questions and a disturbing incident with Aaron.

"To a man's room you're going? A single man? Leah, what kind of thing is that to be doing?" Malcha's eyes were permanently wreathed with lines of puzzlement. Everything in this new world bewildered her—the streets which teemed with activity from early morning till late at night, the schools which were miraculously free for all children, the libraries which offered books for loan, the subways which swept her in minutes from one end of the enormous city to the other, her clean-shaven husband—but Leah, her own sister, was the most consistent source of puzzlement.

Leah's earnings sustained the household and it was Leah who examined the bills and arranged for their payment. Sarah Ellenberg had told Malcha that Leah earned more than her own husband. And Leah was increasingly content to leave the running of the house to Malcha, who had quickly mastered the mystery of the labyrinthine streets of the east side and scurried expertly from the Essex Street market to the open stalls of Hester Street. This division of duties did not trouble Malcha, but she believed that when Leah came home at night she should remain in the apartment and not go to classes or lectures at the settlement house or, as she was now preparing to do, rush off to a meeting. The children needed her. Aaron was growing more and more withdrawn, hiding from his mother as though she were a stranger yet obsessed with her arrivals and departures. Rebecca was a sweet child but headstrong and stubborn, always demanding her own way, unlike Malcha's own children, Yankele and Chana, who clung to their mother, following her obediently about the house, helping with the chores, and trailing behind her when she did her shopping.

"Little ghosts," Masha named the pale, quiet children, but then Masha had been very unpleasant since Shimon Hartstein's wife had arrived from Russia, and it was a relief to everyone in the flat that she was planning to move to California where a distant cousin had opened a drapery shop.

Aaron, too, had delayed Leah as she hurried to dress for the meeting.

"Mama, can I talk to you for a minute?" he asked, standing in the doorway and watching Leah brush her dark hair.

Impatiently she turned around, expertly spinning the mass of dark hair into a loose knot that rested against the pale-blue fabric of a new dress she had finished sewing only the night before. She did not mean to dress especially for the meeting, but it was pleasant to slip on a new dress and she remembered now how Yaakov had loved the color blue. It was a strange coincidence that Eli Feinstein so often wore shirts of a shade similar to the one Yaakov had favored.

"I haven't much time, Aaron," she replied. "Can you tell me tomorrow?"

"You won't have time tomorrow either. You never have any time," the boy said accusingly, scraping the floor with his scuffed shoes.

Leah looked hard at him, the anger rising hot within her. Her cheeks burned and her palms were moist. Aaron was almost ten now, tall for his age and stocky. He seldom smiled and when he spoke his voice was laced with a moody harshness.

"The boy is lonely," David maintained when Leah mentioned his sulkiness, but where her husband saw sadness, Leah sensed an anger and hostility which, like a magnetic force, attracted her own.

"Why don't I have time?" she shouted now. "I don't have time because I am working day and night. I'm working for you, Aaron, and for your sister and your father so that your lives will be better than mine. Do you think I like getting up when it's still dark and sitting all day in a factory? Do you? Answer me, Aaron! Do you?"

The boy stared at her wide-eyed with fear. His mother had always spoken to him in tones of quiet restraint, of indifferent reason. Sometimes, when he was smaller, he had courted her anger, almost hoping for a sudden burst of temper which would violate the removed calm, the cool control with which she spoke to him. Sarah Ellenberg shouted at Joshua with fierce fury and embraced him with equal fierceness, her anger somehow inexplicably linked to her love. But Leah's sudden burst of fury bewildered Aaron now and tears flooded his eyes, shaming him into new misery so that he fled his mother's bedroom, his shoulders shaking with small silent sobs he could not control.

Leah stared at herself in the mirror as though seeking to recognize, within her own reflection, that mysterious unpredictable stranger who shouted at a child without reason. Heavy-hearted, she continued to dress, and before she left the apartment she went to Aaron's room. The boy's narrow bed was empty. The words of regret remained frozen in her mind and a nagging sorrow added its weight to the fatigue that always cloaked her.

A half-hour later Leah stood uneasily in the doorway at Eli Feinstein's room and listened to the voices around her. The meeting was well under way and to her surprise almost every employee of any importance at Rosenblatt and Sons was present. Sam

Abramowitz, the general foreman, sat on the narrow cot with Moe Cohen who managed piece goods and Salvatore Visconti who headed the traffic department. The three men were all smoking small cigars and passing a single battered aluminum ashtray from hand to hand. Several machine operators and finishers sat cross-legged on the floor and Eleanor Greenstein, Rosenblatt's designer, elegant in a green organdy dress, occupied the only chair. Eli Feinstein himself was perched on a corner of a shaky bridge table, piled high with papers and pamphlets.

The room, small and dark, its single window looking across to a blank brick wall where a crippled dumbwaiter dangled, was similar to the rooms Leah rented to her boarders, but every inch of space was packed with books. Wooden crates overflowed with worn volumes and piles of journals, looped with twine, were ranged in every corner of the room. Someone pulled out a stool and handed it to Leah. She set it down where she could lean against the wall and, grateful for the support, she sat back and listened to the heated talk around her.

Some in the room had been involved in organizational activity, working quietly, for a considerable time. Salvatore Visconti, his English spiced with a heavy Italian accent, small particles of tobacco glinting in his thick brown moustache, told the group that every worker with whom he had spoken was prepared to sign up for a union shop.

"They know it's the only way we get any rights," he said. "The girls, they go to church to say Mass on Ash Wednesday. They come a half-hour late and Rosenblatt tells them they got to stay overtime to make it up. We say freedom of religion in this country. That's why we come over here. And the rich boss, he can't give maybe a half-hour a year for this freedom? Pah!" Visconti's tongue curled upward in a gesture of contempt and licked at a golden flake of tobacco which he spat into his hand.

"That's gravy, Visconti," Sam Abramowitz interposed. "A couple of hours off for church or *shul* is nothing. It's safety I'm worried about. You people don't see it but I know for a fact that there isn't a single safe fire exit in the whole damn place—begging your pardon, ladies, but this gets me excited." The little man bowed to Leah and Eleanor Greenstein and continued. "I had trouble getting through the front door yesterday. I had a delivery and the damn cartons were too big. So I get a brainstorm—I thought. We'll get them up through the windows. Only the windows on the second floor are locked tight. Some of them nailed down. Rosenblatt says the girls get enough air from the fans and he needs the security against break-ins. Well, he'd better get a watchman and get those windows open because if anything ever happens here they'll be calling him a murderer."

His harsh words left the room stunned into silence until Eleanor Greenstein leaned forward. Her cheeks were flushed and her eyes were dangerously bright.

"Sam Abramowitz is right. Protection is the most important thing. We must fight for it." Her voice trembled and Leah stared at her, surprised at the older woman's intensity.

"Well, it's not only fires I'm worried about," Moe Cohen said thoughtfully. "I'm worried about the wear and tear of every day, never mind emergencies. I don't know about you, Mrs. Goldfeder, but I lose half my people every year. They get sick or they get fed up with not having any benefits or holidays, and just when I get them trained they're off to one of Dubinsky's union shops. And I don't blame them. I tried talking to Rosenblatt about it but he squints up his eyes and starts yammering about laziness and pilfering."

Leah nodded. Her turnover rate was also disturbing. Her girls grew ill or found better jobs. Bonnie Eckstein was the fourth girl to work her embroidery machine in as many months.

"I too have talked to Rosenblatt," Eli Feinstein said. "The word union makes him crazy. He told me that once before, in his father's time, there was union talk in this factory. The old man had a lockout when he heard about it. He didn't open and the workers were out in the street. It was winter. They had no money for coal or food and after a week they came crawling back to him, begging him to open. He took out of their wages the losses from his own lockout. Some of them paid back for months. And Rosenblatt says he'll do the same thing."

"Only he can't do it." Eleanor Greenstein's voice was cool and controlled now and there was certainty in her tone.

She was a handsome woman who had designed Rosenblatt's line of inexpensive dresses for two decades and it was rumored that she had been mistress to both Arnold Rosenblatt and his father. Her ash-blonde hair was licked with silver and she wore it in a loose chignon which she patted occasionally with an impeccably manicured hand, her fingernails painted a pale pink. Leah, who often saw her in Arnold Rosenblatt's office when she delivered designs or time sheets, had been surprised to see the designer at the meeting in Eli Feinstein's small room. She listened attentively as the older woman spoke.

"There isn't a supplier Rosenblatt doesn't owe money to. And they're beginning to talk to each other and realize it. So far he's been able to calm them with talk of a successful fall line. And he does have good items for the fall. But if there's a strike and there's no fall line, there's no profit. No profit, no payments—and those suppliers will go after him. I think he'd rather have a union shop than a bankrupt shop. Believe me, I know. I have all the figures here. Arnold Rosenblatt needs us more than we need him." Eleanor Greenstein patted her notebook and smoothed her skirt. Her gray eyes met Leah's gaze and she smiled at her.

"All right. So it seems we're all agreed. What do we do now?" asked one of the younger machinists. He had been sitting crosslegged on the floor, but rose to stretch his legs and reach impatiently for a cigarette.

"Now we break down into committees and do separate jobs," Eli Feinstein replied. "We have to feel out all the workers and find out how committed they are. Most, I think, will go along with us, but we have to be careful. Very careful. When we're certain enough of our people, a committee will go to Rosenblatt. We'll tell him that we're through asking for our rights. Now we're demanding them. The right to a union. The right to safety. The right to decent benefits and decent pay. If we are all together, nothing and no one can stop us."

There was a brief outbreak of applause and Leah joined in, stirred by the restrained passion in Feinstein's voice. She remembered Yaakov, so young, so full of hope, making similar speeches in rooms even smaller than this one, rooms where a burnished samovar bubbled in a corner and a tiny crude press hurtled ink-blurred pamphlets onto the sawdust-covered floor. It was a long time since she had been to such a meeting, a long time since she had heard such calls for hope and solidarity.

Eli quickly proceeded to divide the group into smaller working teams. Eleanor was excepted because her position was too vulnerable. He himself would work with Leah and Salvatore Visconti. They would serve as liaison to Dubinsky's union, which might lend them support. The others in the room would canvass their fellow workers.

It was late when the meeting disbanded and Leah stood on the stoop for a moment, breathing the clear, fresh air. A group of girls jumped rope in front of the house, delaying the hour when they would crawl into a bed shared by other siblings in bedrooms crowded with cots and cribs.

> Rosie my darling, Rosie my own,
> Climb into my pushcart, I'll take you home.
> Tomorrow is the Sabbath, we'll eat *gefilte* fish
> Rosie, oh Rosie, you are my favorite dish.

They sang as the worn piece of clothesline turned rhythmically, and Leah smiled at a small girl whose braids bobbed up and down as she jumped. She turned to see Eleanor Greenstein standing beside her.

"Do you have children, Mrs. Goldfeder?" the designer asked.

"Yes. A boy and a girl."

"You're very fortunate. I had a daughter." The words were soft, almost a whisper. "Your work is very good, Mrs. Goldfeder. You should be doing much more designing. But of course you will. You know that." Lightly she touched Leah's arm and disappeared around the corner.

Leah hurried home, worried suddenly about what David would think about her involvement in the union and how Malcha would react to the frequent meetings. When she reached the house she glanced up at the window, but although a dim light burned within, no small face topped with fiery curls was framed within the casement. A sudden shaft of fear shot through her and she hurried up the stairs, but when she reached the children's room, Aaron lay curled up in bed, his body tense and rigid even in sleep. Rebecca lay in the bed next to him and a smile briefly lit her sleeping face. Leah drew the blanket around her daughter and hesitantly put her hand on her son's. At her touch, he reached out and his fingers curled about hers, pressing them lightly.

"Aaron," she said softly, and the boy's body relaxed as his hand dropped hers.

Slowly she went into the living room where David had fallen asleep over an anatomy text. Carefully she walked him to bed, his body as yielding as a child's beneath her supporting arms.

5

The weeks that followed were busy ones for Leah. She could not, of course, match the pace of Eli Feinstein and Salvatore Visconti, who worked tirelessly, inviting one worker after another to share their corner tables at the Cafe Royale or the Italian coffee shop on Mott Street. The two men spoke with a swift urgency and an earnest sense of concern that moved their listeners. Stirring sodden granules of sugar in their empty coffee cups, one Rosenblatt employee after another agreed to join the effort. Some were hesitant, even fearful, but others burned with enthusiasm. The young were the easiest to convince. They were not worried about families and responsibilities. Their lives lay in the future and they pledged themselves to improving that future with as much zeal as even Eli Feinstein could wish for.

Leah, too, spoke with the girls in her shop, inviting a few of them to her apartment where they talked under Malcha's disapproving eye and Shimon's open scorn. David, when she told him of the union effort, had approached it with his usual gentle concern.

"You are sure such work will not upset you?" he asked. "You have faith in this man, Feinstein?"

Leah nodded. She did not tell her husband how her eyes followed Eli Feinstein when they happened to be in the same area of the factory or how she would suddenly recall the words of a conversation she had had with him days before. She recreated in her mind his gestures and expressions, the way he tossed his head so that his black hair grew tousled or the habit he had of smoothing his thick dark eyebrows as he argued a point. Several times they had met by chance during the lunch break and sat together beneath the ailanthus tree, watching the shadowed pattern of the leaves and talking softly.

Near them, other workers, their eyes webbed with lines of worry, read the stark headlines of economic disasters. Two Wall

Street investment firms closed suddenly that month. A philanthropist from a renowned German Jewish family, who had given enormous sums toward the support of the Irvington Settlement House, jumped to his death when his family business collapsed. The settlement house closed on the day of the funeral and women and children stood grouped in bewilderment and grief on its steps, awaiting the cortege. In accordance with Jewish tradition, the hearse and its attendant caravan of black cars paused at the building which had given meaning to the man's life.

The widow remained in the car, but a small girl, who had plucked a cluster of morning glories from a vine which grew wild in the back of the bath house on Attorney Street, had thrust the flowers into the car's open window. A black gloved hand had reached out to take the purple flowers and to stroke the child's cheek.

An east side savings society had gone bankrupt and the director of another had absconded with the life savings of the families who had trusted him. Among those who lost their tediously accumulated savings was Leah's boarder Bryna. The girl had been planning a wedding in one of the new wedding halls on lower Broadway, putting off her marriage from month to month until there would be money enough to pay for the arrangements of pink roses which would in turn match the tablecloths and the bridesmaids' dresses. Enough luxury and opulence to last a lifetime would be crowded into that wedding day, to be captured in sepia photographs, bound into an album which would become a bulwark of memories, reviewed and relived. But in the end Bryna sold her wedding dress and she was married in the Goldfeder parlor with Malcha and Leah serving the guests tea and sandwiches. The bride, pale and subdued, stared at the corsage of carnations awkwardly pinned to her light-blue wedding suit and listened without interest as her furrier groom described the loft he had just rented.

"The Depression can't last forever," he said emphatically, but no one in that strangely quiet wedding party believed him.

Sam Ellenberg had been laid off and sat motionless in the kitchen all day, his jollity lost in worry, absently fingering the flap of flesh that lay where his ear might have been. The family's board was paid with the hoarded coins that Joshua, even in the worst of times, managed to bring home. Shimon Hartstein's newly established shirt business was struggling for survival. While the wedding guests munched their sponge cake and sipped small glasses of cognac, a family sat on the street below, surrounded by trunks, cartons, and battered furniture. Leah, drawing the drapes, wondered where they would go and was relieved, when she looked out the window after the wedding party, to see that they had in fact gone. Only a child's armless doll remained on the pavement.

The situation was similar all over the country, she knew. Charles Ferguson, returning at last from the long-anticipated visit to the plains of his birth, had visited the Goldfeders and shown them his sketchbook. In broad black crayon strokes he had created the world of those who lived in cardboard shacks sheltered by billboards, of thin, large-eyed children who wore wads of newspapers around their feet in place of shoes, and gaunt nursing mothers who milked their breasts to provide nourishment for their older children, sometimes even cooking with the thin mother's milk.

"Perhaps 1929 is not a very good time to start a union," Leah said dryly to Eli Feinstein the next day.

ood time to start a union," he replied. "And d they must get better. And I think that self is struggling to survive he will be more th us than in a year when things were good is head."

t David Dubinsky's International Ladies confirmed Eli's analysis. Leah joined Eli the meeting with the professional labor prosperous lawyer in his double-breasted

"Now is definitely the right time to go after him. He knows he doesn't have a chance. Even the whisper of a strike will finish him. And if it should come to a strike, we'll furnish you with picket signs and placards and whatever financial support we can manage. Our people have been pretty hard hit by the Depression and our welfare funds are getting low. But we'll do whatever we can. We're with you," the official said, and solemnly shook hands with each of them.

They left the office feeling nervous and exhilarated, knowing that the time of crisis was drawing near. Soon, certainly in the summer, they would have to confront Arnold Rosenblatt.

Visconti left them on the corner and Eli and Leah continued eastward, walking slowly and savoring the cool of the evening and the brief respite from talk and activity. A small boy stood on a corner selling rainbow-colored Italian ices and Eli stopped and bought two of the frosty sweets encased in thin paper cones. They walked on; they did not speak, and when they finished eating they dropped the wrappers in an open ashcan. Standing beneath the streetlight, Eli wiped his own hands with a large handkerchief and then reached for Leah's hand, deftly mopping a streak of strawberry ice that had leaked across her palm. Gently he touched each finger with the linen square and then lifted her hand to his lips and kissed it. They stood for a moment in the circle of light. Their eyes met and Leah felt suddenly suffused with a calm and tenderness she had not known for many years. She took his hand and, wordlessly, they continued to walk. Together they turned into the doorway of Eli's boardinghouse and walked up the stairway to the darkened room.

Inside at last, Leah leaned against the closed door, glad of the darkness that hid the tears which had begun to fall with an inexplicable suddenness. They streaked her face and Eli's lips dried them as they fell, his face pressed against hers, his hands gently stroking her hair, loosening the pins that held the thick dark coil in place so that it fell in velvety black folds about her shoulders.

"You are so beautiful," he said. "So beautiful."

"It's dark. You cannot see me."

The tears had stopped now and a shy smile played around her mouth. Her voice was soft, her words the flirtatious whisper of a young girl. She plummeted backward in time and felt her body ache with new awakenings, with the stirring of desire, both distant and familiar.

Eli pressed her to him, enclosing her in an embrace at once urgent but carefully tender. With a small sigh of release she allowed her body to melt against his and felt his strength press against her.

They made love on his narrow bachelor cot and when their bodies had exhausted each other and were spent at last, they lay pressed together, their fingers exploring each other's flesh as though their bodies, encased in twin pallor against the now familiar darkness, contained long-kept secrets which must soon be revealed. They did not talk and when she rose to go, he lay still and watched her as she dressed, rising only when she began to pin her hair in place. Naked, he stood behind her and stretched her hair across his open palms, kissing the exposed nape of her neck as she stood motionless, submissive. He turned her around, at last, and pressed her mouth against his own, then passed his hand gently across her face, dry now of all tears.

It was very late when she returned home and for once she did not go to the room where her children slept, but undressed quietly and lay down at once beside her husband who stirred but did not move to touch her.

She saw Eli Feinstein every day after that. He waited for her after work and they walked together through the crowded streets, sometimes stopping at the Cafe Royale for a cold glass of coffee, or at Goodman and Levine's on East Broadway, where they would munch a slice of dark bread spread with farmer cheese and sliced scallions and listen to earnest young poets, perched on high stools, read their works. The poets, long-haired and too thin, their clothes worn and patched, wrote of a world of freedom where there were neither rich nor poor. They sang of days of peace and plenty, of equity and solidarity when all men lived together. These beardless, bareheaded young men had abandoned the synagogue and they wrote with anger of the harsh yoke of religion, fighting private battles with their Orthodox fathers in a language those fathers would never comprehend. At eight o'clock, as though by signal, poets and listeners alike would disperse to claim good seats at the lecture halls and settlement house auditoriums. Then Eli would walk Leah halfway home, where she confronted Malcha's silent stare and the children's strange shyness, as though she were a stranger to whom they must be polite.

One evening, Leah and Eli listened as a young poet, still in his teens, his blue eyes harsh with anger and his pale hair falling wildly about his narrow face, read a verse he called "Yom Kippur—The Day of Atonement."

> Swayed by the winds of prayer,
> My father shivers in the synagogue,
> While I eat of the American dream,
> Bacon, lettuce and tomato on God's own fast day.
> They pray for mercy;
> I work for peace.

Eli listened thoughtfully to the small murmurs of shock and approval that followed the reading and watched the poet join a group of friends at a table across the room.

"He belongs to that world of his father;s more than he knows," he said. "All of them—our young Communists and Socialists—they think they have left the old Jewish world so far behind but they are wrong. They have taken it with them. What are their dreams of peace and social justice but the messianic vision? For all their eating of pork and bacon, they are religious still, working for the advent of the son of David, working for the day when the lion lies down with the lamb and there are neither rich nor poor."

"And you, Eli—are you too a religious messianist?" Leah asked teasingly. The books and pamphlets that crowded his room were political and economic treatises, but among them she had found a biblical commentary in Yiddish, thick volumes in Hebrew which she could not understand.

"Me? No. I am just a man who loves a black-haired woman," he answered, matching the mockery in her tone. He touched her hand and they rose to leave, going to his room where, slowly, relishing this precious respite against haste, they undressed each other. She gently unbuttoned his shirt, slipped it off, and folded it neatly while, as she bent, he unhooked her camisole and let his hand fall across the bare skin of her back. He caressed the expanse of naked flesh until her body trembled and she turned to him with her eyes and flesh moist with desire, aching with memory.

Now she began to arrive home later and later, but no matter what the hour, from the corner she saw the coppery flag of Aaron's hair at the window and knew that it would disappear when she turned into the entryway. When she bent over the children, seizing the excuse of a fallen blanket or a sudden cry from Rebecca who had begun to sleep fitfully, she sensed Aaron rigid and wakeful in the darkness, but his eyes remained closed and he did not move when she touched him.

"What am I doing?" she thought as she stood beside the children's beds, her body still warm from Eli's searching hands, his insistent thrust of love. It seemed to her then that she was not one person but several women—her children's mother, her husband's helpmate and companion, her lover's beloved. She remembered, suddenly, a wooden doll that had stood on her sister-in-law Henia's bureau in Odessa, the whimsical gift of a Russian friend. Its hollow body had contained a smaller doll, which in turn had opened to reveal yet another diminutive one, and that too contained a smaller doll—until five figurines in gradually decreasing sizes stood side by side, their identical painted smiles mutely jeering at each other. How similar she was to that Russian toy; one Leah after another broke forth, all of them contained within a single form. But perhaps one day she would be unable to replace them all in time and one small self would wander off and reveal her secret. She shivered and saw that her hands were trembling wildly.

"You're tired. Very tired," she told herself severely and went to bed, moving away from David on the narrow island of their feather mattress, as though to touch her husband would be to betray her lover.

She willed herself to sleep, mentally fashioning her life with her family and her life with Eli into two separate worlds. She inhabited them both with practiced ease, recognizing ill-defined borders and treacherous terrain which she traversed with calm and caution. Angrily, she stilled the small voice that told her that this could not last for long. Soon there would be a fork in her dangerous road and she would have to choose one path or another. But not yet. She lulled herself to sleep at last, rocked in a cradle of rationalizations and fragile reassurances.

Beside her in the darkness, David stirred to an uneasy wakefulness. She was home. He could not, would not, ask where she had been. There were hidden, silent clauses in the contract they had entered into on that park bench in Odessa. He would not violate them. But he trembled in the darkness with fear and clenched his fists with an anger he disowned. So much had been taken from him. He could not bear to lose her too—but then could a man really lose what he had never possessed? The anger left him then and he drew the eiderdown about her bare shoulder that gleamed whitely in a sudden shaft of moonlight.

"Please, Leah," he mutely begged and she stirred in her sleep, flung her arm across his body, and then quickly—too quickly—moved it away.

During the rare hours when they were home together Malcha watched Leah with worried eyes. They spoke of household matters, the need for new pots, light cloth to make summer clothing for the children. Their boarder, Morris Morgenstern, who had finally brought his entire family over from Poland, had decided to marry. He had proposed to Pearl, the shy factory worker, and to everyone's surprise she had accepted. Perhaps she had tired of reading Masha's reports of the golden sunshine of California and of visiting Bryna on

Saturday afternoons. She had long since given up her classes in elocution and etiquette at the settlement house. Small lines were forming at the corners of her eyes and a fan of gray had threaded its way through her stylishly lacquered bangs. In any case, they would be married and Leah and Malcha talked of whether or not they should take in new boarders now that only the Ellenbergs remained.

"I don't think we should," Malcha said. "Shimon's business is beginning to show a little profit. He wants me to begin coming in a few hours a day. I wouldn't have so much time for the house then and you know, it would be good to have more room. The children are getting too big now for boys and girls to share."

Leah nodded, noticing that Malcha spoke with new assurance. Her sister had grown slightly heavier and suddenly she had begun to dress in brighter colors and wear her newly grown, uncovered hair in the long pageboy style of the day. Today she wore a bright-green dress and her hair was caught up in a matching snood.

"And Leah, please, try to come home earlier. Does all this union organizing have to take up so much time? The children need you. You don't see it but Rebecca is nervous and Aaron—it's so hard for him."

Malcha's words were laced with warning and Leah stood uneasily and looked into the kitchen where Aaron was playing chess with his cousin Yankele—newly called Jake—while Rebecca and Chanele helped Joshua Ellenberg sort bright squares of silk according to size. Joshua was an acknowledged merchant now. He owned a large black valise balanced on the wheels of a discarded pair of roller skates. With the money he earned as a messenger boy at Rosenblatts he replenished his supplies and hawked his merchandise, pushing his valise before him and shouting mightily to proclaim the beauty and cheapness of his stock.

"What can I do, Malcha? What can I do?" Leah asked. Her eyes filled with sudden tears, but her sister swiftly snapped her sewing bag closed and hurried from the room, unwilling to hear any confidences that would change her fears to certainty.

Leah stood in the empty parlor, swaying from side to side as though in prayer, her hands pressed against her eyes. In the kitchen the small girls laughed at Joshua's jokes and Aaron explained a complicated chess move. Behind her the front door opened and she turned to see her husband, his arms loaded with books, staring at her in sorrow and concern.

*

Summer exploded on the east side without warning that year. They plunged from the soothing cool of a gentle spring into days of sizzling heat. In the hot, airless factory, the girls worked with their skirts pulled up to their laps and their sleeves rolled high on their arms. The men worked in their undershirts and the piles of fabric were damp with their sweat. Eli Feinstein stood at the high wooden cutting table operating the shears. He worked rapidly, stripped to the waist, and Leah, passing his post on her way to and from the office, watched the familiar curve of his bare back, the skin shimmering with sweat and the tight muscles tensing and releasing against the force of the shears.

Leah made Rebecca and Chanele light organdy dresses, and with the remaining pale blue fabric she fashioned a broad-brimmed summer hat for herself. She wore the hat as protection against the heat of the early morning sun and swung it by its satin ribbons after work as she and Eli Feinstein strolled the streets. Once, on such a walk, they met Charles Ferguson and he joined them at the Cafe Royale, sketching them as they chatted and sipped their glasses of cold coffee.

"How is your union effort coming?" the artist asked, his fingers deftly capturing Leah's shadowed forehead, veiled by the hat's floppy brim.

"Rosenblatt went off to Europe just as we were about to approach him. But he returns soon. We will talk to him then. The whole thing hinges on the fall line and there is still time," Eli answered. He lit one of the small dark cigars he sometimes smoked and watched Charles draw.

"Will you be on the committee that talks to him?" Charles asked Leah.

She smiled and licked the crystal grains of sugar that clung to her full lips. "I haven't come that far," she said.

"No, not that far," he replied and thought of the young woman he had invited to the concert at Carnegie Hall who had carried a borrowed purse and kept her money knotted in the corner of a handkerchief. Now that same young woman leaned forward and puffed playfully at Eli Feinstein's cigar. The small gesture answered many questions for Charles Ferguson. When he arrived home that evening he ripped the sketch from his pad, folded it carefully, and put it in a drawer where he kept a snapshot of his mother, the faded sketch of a girl he had met many years ago in the south of France, and a small book of El Greco drawings for which he had paid much more than he could afford.

The heat of the summer intensified as the days went on. Fire hydrants were wrenched open in desperation and barefoot children danced in the rushing waters. Even some of the yeshiva children joined them and their earlocks danced damply as they jumped about and were dry minutes later. Joshua Ellenberg sold ice water which he sweetened with cherry syrup, setting up his stand on packing cases near the larger factories. Women fainted in the streets and small children complained of muscle pains one day and the next lay motionless, their fever mounting and their limbs heavy and immobile. They were victims of the epidemic of infantile paralysis that accompanied the heat and engulfed the east side in a net of anguish and misery.

Malcha hung small cambric sacks of garlic around the children's necks and begged them to stay inside as though the dreaded disease were fazed by walls and doors, and could be repelled by odors. In mid-July Aaron and Yankele left for the settlement-house camp in the Catskills.

"I didn't know they had such a camp," Leah said to Aaron, relieved that in the mountains Aaron, at least, would be safe from the dangers of the disease, but unwilling to have her son leave her. She wondered, wearily, if any decision about Aaron would ever be simple for her.

"I tried to tell you about it that night—when you were dressing to go to that meeting," he replied moodily and they did not look at each other, fearful of the anger and shame their eyes revealed. She hugged him hard the morning he left, and although he did not return her embrace she heard his heart beat with fierce rapidity.

Sarah Ellenberg's sister, who had taken a bungalow near Peekskill, wrote to tell them of a similar cottage nearby which could be rented very cheaply. The families conferred and it was decided that if they all shared the rental it could be managed. A feeling of excitement and exhilaration gripped them. They had never had a holiday before. Shimon Hartstein would close his small factory for the week and Joshua Ellenberg had acquired a supply of thin cotton T-shirts which he would hawk to vacationing mothers.

"There they can't get things so cheap, they'll think I'm giving them a bargain," he said, thrusting the merchandise into his valise with its rollerskate wheels.

His father and mother nodded their agreement.

"Some head the boy has," Sam Ellenberg said.

He and his wife followed the directives of their small son without question now. When Joshua selected a particular corner as a good location to sell undershirts and furnished him with a supply, Sam Ellenberg, out of work for many months now, stood there and sold undershirts. It was Joshua who now brought the board money to Malcha each month, pulling a change purse out of his knickers and counting out the money. It had been a long time since Sarah Ellenberg had talked about getting her own flat.

The Hartsteins and the Ellenbergs, with Rebecca, left for the mountains on a Sunday evening. David had a research project and

Leah had to work that week but they would join the family on Friday.

Leah and David stood on the curb and watched the children pile into the hired car, loaded with valises and linens, jangling pots and pans, and Shimon Hartstein's sample case. One could never tell. Small shopkeepers in the country might be interested in his line.

Rebecca's tiny face, her cheeks pink with excitement, was framed in the window and Leah dashed forward just before the car pulled away. Seized by a strange premonition, she touched her daughter's upturned face as though it were a delicate blossom.

"Be careful," she said and Rebecca laughed and kissed her.

Then, with a choke of the exhaust, the car sped away and she and David stood alone in front of the house, neither of them ready to mount the steps and confront the empty apartment.

Silence stalked the simple dairy dinner they ate alone that night, broken only by polite requests for salt and sugar. Uneasily, they circled around each other in the dimly lit kitchen, desperately offering scraps of conversation to shield themselves against words they could not utter.

"It must be bitterly hot in the factory," David said.

"One of the things the union will insist on is adequate fans," she said. "Eli is definite about that."

She was glad of the excuse to use her lover's name, to roll it about in her mouth, remembering the way he had pounded the table at their last workers' meeting, insisting on those fans, on windows that would open to offer both air and adequate fire protection, on a stipulation for early closing when the summer heat invaded the factory, sending more than one girl reeling to the floor.

"He is a strong leader," David said, watching her closely. "Yes. Eli—" she pronounced the name and again a shiver caused her to tremble imperceptibly and her breasts grew full and firm. "He really knows how to involve people. I think we have almost everyone committed to the union cause now. But we have to wait for Rosenblatt to get home from Europe and he keeps putting off his return. Eleanor Greenstein says he's afraid of the polio. Did I tell you about Bonnie Eckstein—the young girl who comes here sometimes? Her baby brother caught it. They're not sure he'll live, poor thing."

"*Lieber Gott*," David murmured sadly. "I'm glad the children are out of the city."

"Yes."

Briefly, their thoughts wove together, joined by shared worry and shared love for the children. They sat together in the half-light of early evening and watched two cats wind their way up the fire escape outside the kitchen window.

"Leah."

He rose from the table and stood behind her, his hands gentle on her shoulders, his cheek, faintly redolent of soap, pressing against her own.

"Leah."

His hands roamed her body, found her breasts, grown soft again, clutched her upturned palms and pressed them against his mouth.

"Leah."

The sound of her name was a plea, a call to memory, and she wept against the softness of David's voice; he allowed her no defense because he did not attack. She remained motionless as his touch and breath probed her. His mouth was soft upon her neck, his voice sibilant in her ear, whispering words she did not want to hear. But when he pulled her up and pressed his body against hers, his lips searching out her mouth, she pushed him from her with a suddenness that shocked herself and left David standing in frozen disbelief.

"No, David, no! Please. You must leave me alone." She fled into the bedroom and flung herself across the bed they had shared for ten years, burying her face deep into the pillow and surrendering to a heavy dreamless sleep.

David went into the empty parlor and stood for a moment looking around the room. Malcha had covered the furnishings with white sheets against dust during the family's absence, and it seemed to him that he stood in a deserted chamber, abandoned to the ghosts of memories. It was a simple enough thing to walk away from a life—one covered the furniture, snapped a valise shut, and closed a door softly in passing. All that had been so laboriously built could be effortlessly destroyed; a single gesture, a few words wrought demolition. He imagined leaving Leah and then he imagined Leah leaving him. A febrile terror seized him and he sank into a shrouded armchair, clutching at it for support. He saw Leah and himself walking together and the shadow of Eli Feinstein slipping between them, prying their intertwined fingers apart. He felt a wild hatred for the unknown man who had captured his wife's love, and the fury of his hatred frightened him. Having consecrated his life to the struggle against such hate—was he now to fall victim to it? He sat on until the milky light of morning filtered across the sky and he knew at last what he must do.

When Leah woke the next morning the pillow slip was damp to her touch although she did not remember weeping. David had covered her with a light blanket because the night had grown strangely cool. David himself was gone. His breakfast dishes were neatly washed and spread across the empty drainboard. The apartment echoed with an unfamiliar silence and she wandered from room to room, smoothing the sheets on beds that had not been slept in. She stood for a long time in the doorway of the living room and went at last to straighten the cushion of a chair which sagged sadly beneath its loose counterpane cover.

A message was delivered to her at the factory that afternoon. David had been invited to join Professor Thompson on a field trip. He would be away all week and would join her in the mountains on Friday. She clutched the piece of paper and looked across the room to the worktable where Eli held a newly cut garment up to the harsh afternoon sunlight.

6

Both Eli Feinstein and Leah Goldfeder worked late that Monday evening and when they left the factory, the sky streaked with the gentle mauve shadows of the fading summer evening. They paused beneath a newly lit streetlamp and as they stood together in the pale circle of light, Leah showed Eli the note that David had sent her.

"And the rest of the household is also away?" he asked softly.

"Yes."

"I see."

They walked slowly on, their long shadows falling before them as the last vestige of light was sucked into darkness. Leah removed her broad-brimmed hat and swung it from its long satin ribbons, as they continued to walk westward, free of any sense of urgency about the hour. She felt strangely weightless, as though a decade of cares and worries had suddenly been lifted and she lived once again the life and dreams of the young girl who had danced across the coarse floorboards of an attic in rural Russia, her naked body capturing the dappled shadows of the swaying Lombardy tree. She took Eli's hand and executed a tiny waltz step. At once, his feet followed hers, so that two old women on the opposite side of the street stopped to watch them and smiled wistfully before walking on.

"They think we are innocent young lovers," Leah said teasingly as they rounded the corner.

"And so we are," he replied and kissed her lightly on the forehead.

They had dinner that night in a small Italian restaurant in Greenwich Village, and at the corner of Fifth Avenue and Twelfth Street they boarded a bright-red municipal bus and climbed to the upper deck. The summer stars glinted brightly above them and the great stores and mansions of Fifth Avenue sparkled on either side of the broad expanse. They held hands and she rested her head against him as the bus carried them northward where they could see the lights of the George Washington Bridge and feel the moist breezes of the Hudson River.

"Such a world," she murmured and lifted her hands as though to embrace the evening cool, to engulf and seize this strange freedom of riding aimlessly through the wondrously lit city in the arms of a man who sheltered her effortlessly and whose slightest touch moved her to tears and longing.

They went to Eli's boardinghouse that night, not going to his room at once but climbing to the roof, where drying sheets billowed out against the infrequent breezes like the sails of a mysterious boat and brightly colored children's garments hung from makeshift dryers in an array of small flags that danced and whispered in the quiet night. A group of women sat in a corner of the roof, still in their cotton housedresses, talking quietly in Yiddish, their hands clasped in their laps as though they had to be restrained into stillness. Against the balustrade, a young couple leaned and watched the street below. The girl's long fair hair was covered with a blue silk kerchief. When they turned to each other, the young man removed the small silk square, pressed it to his lips, and allowed handfuls of the shimmering hair to fall through his fingers before bending down to kiss the girl's upturned face. Slowly they turned and disappeared into the stairwell and Leah watched them with a sudden harsh envy.

How fortunate they were. They were young and free. They would marry in this new land. Their untouched lives stretched before them, uncomplicated by memories of bloodied streets and screaming children. They would not wake in the night clinging to the ghosts of dead lovers buried in distant lands or whispering the names of loved ones whose faces were slowly fading from memory. Twice now, Eli had wakened in her arms, his strong, tightly muscled body damp with the sweat of anguish, whispering the name of Mira, the young wife he had found dead when he returned from Karkov, a town he could never forget.

"What is it?" he asked her now, sensing the change of her mood. He cupped her chin and turned her face toward him, perhaps in imitation of the young man's gesture, but the words and feelings congealed within her, a bitter ganglion of silence that would not be pierced. She buried her face in his shoulder, relishing again the hardness of his body. The women turned to look at them but Eli and Leah ignored the accusing glances and left the roof.

In Eli's room, on that narrow cot, a small island of space in the room's bachelor clutter, they clung together, the passion of their bodies fighting off memory and guilt. Leah's dress was cast upon a nest of union pamphlets and her hat, that frivolous, pale-blue concoction of organdy and satin that matched her daughter's summer frock, crowned an open volume of Lectures by Eugene Debs.

Leah did not go home that night, but spent the night for the first time beside Eli, their bodies sandwiched together in the narrow space. They made love in the darkness and woke as the first streaks of morning light threaded the dimness, to come together yet again, like gluttonous children at a rare feast.

They did not go to work the next day, each phoning in their excuses separately. They walked together to the Goldfeder apartment where Leah changed her clothes and gathered a few things into a small wicker bag. The empty apartment was like a place suspended in time. In the kitchen the huge empty pots in which she had cooked so many meals sat on the stove, scoured and gaping. The coffee cup which David had placed on the drain-board after his solitary breakfast the previous day was still there, but there was a plate on the kitchen table and a cluster of dry crumbs formed the pattern of a flower across the checked oilcloth. David had returned, then, to pack some things and eat, and she thought of how he must have moved through these empty rooms trailed by the weary sadness that had haunted him throughout this year of silence.

She washed the plate and dried it carefully, as though the simple domestic action exonerated her. Eli sat in the parlor, impatiently reading a week-old newspaper, and she was grateful to him for not intruding on her now, for keeping his distance as she visited this life that had nothing to do with him.

Spurred by habit, she stopped at the door of the children's room. A small pink sock, belonging to Rebecca, dangled from the bedpost and she held it in her hand for a moment as though to capture the smell of her daughter's sweet flesh, thinking of the small girl's feet, so tenderly pink after a bath, the toes curled like fragrant blossoms. Aaron's slippers (he had forgotten them, then—would he be warm enough at the camp? she worried helplessly) lay unevenly beside the bed and she bent to line them up evenly, blue scuffed twins of felt. A longing for the children suffused her. They frolicked now in waters she did not know, against the shadows of mountains she had never seen, while her lover sat and read in their parlor, a live figure caught among shrouded furnishings. She was at once the deserter and the deserted, the bereft and the newly claimed.

"Leah, are you almost ready?" Eli called and she hurried to him, closing the door of the small room behind her.

They walked westward from the apartment to the docks and boarded an excursion boat that steamed its leisurely course around the urban island they called their home. The last time Leah had been at sea, during the crossing from England, she had been heavily pregnant with Aaron, newly married to David, and as burdened with loss as she was swollen with child. She re-remembered the long crossing and how she had sometimes stood on deck, staring down at the rolling gray-green waters of the wintry Atlantic. She had almost seen herself lowering gently upon the waves, drifting and swirling until all grief had washed away from her and she could sink effortlessly to the ocean floor.

But today, with Eli at her side and the sun bright upon their heads, the decks awash with the music of strolling musicians and the carefree voices of the holiday crowd of passengers, she fell in love with the ocean. She marveled at its blueness and was intrigued with the lacy caps of foam that topped each joyous wave. At lunchtime they munched frankfurters, thick with mustard and hairy with sauerkraut, and drank beer from heavy glass steins. She had never tasted beer before and it was the second time in as many days that she had eaten meat that was not kosher. But now, in this holiday interlude in her life, all things were permitted just as all things had been forbidden.

An accordionist played a swift polka and they danced, losing their balance as the small steamer dipped and bobbed. Eli's straw hat was carried off by a playful wind and they laughed as though this were the most amusing thing that had ever happened to them. The hat was retrieved by a group of young people, who invited Eli and Leah to join them and taught them the words of "My Darling Clementine."

When the boat docked in the late afternoon, their faces glowed with the sun and crowns of salty sea mist had settled into their dark hair.

They talked a great deal that night, offering each other stray strands of their own histories to be woven together at will. Weeks before, over a table at the Cafe Royale, Leah had told Eli about her first marriage, Yaakov's death, and the agreement she and David had made.

"I was never sorry I married David," she said. "He is such a rare man, so full of gentleness and compassion. But we never pretended to love. Never."

She had not told Eli about Petrovich and wondered later why she had not shared this fact with the man with whom she found it easy to share everything else.

Now, lying beside her, smoking a small dark cigar, Eli spoke to her about his wife, Mira, and the great void that had followed her death.

"Nothing seemed worthwhile then. I came to America only because I had to leave Russia where every face on the street had become a murderer's face. It didn't matter to me if I lived or died. I think I did not kill myself only because it did not seem to make any difference. Mira was pregnant when she died and I thought again and again of that child, my never-born baby. She was feeling life and I, too, with my hand upon her had felt the baby move within her, kick and move again. They tell me that an unborn child does not feel pain but I thought always of that small moving thing, lying there bewildered in Mira's dead body, waiting for the nourishment that did not come and curling up at last, in those drying waters, to die unborn. Do you know for years I turned my eyes away whenever I saw a pregnant woman? Then one night, just by chance, I went to a lecture at Cooper Union. Debs was the speaker. I listened to him and came to life again. There was work for me to do, there was a world that could be made better, there were other unborn children I could in some small way protect. I began to read and to write, to work for the union, for a world that will be perhaps a little bit better."

Leah listened quietly, thinking of the night David had explained why he wanted to study psychiatry.

"If we understand hatred, if we understand violence, we will be able to predict it and then to prevent it. There will be no more Odessas, no more dead Yaakovs and Chana Rivkas," he had said.

Dreamers both—her husband and her lover. They would root out evil, ferret out injustice, while she, who lay beside them, was blanketed in the bitter certainty that it could not be done, even while she struggled with them.

"They pray for mercy, I work for peace," the bearded young poet had sung and Leah, remembering his words, thought sadly that perhaps the prayers might be more potent than the work.

They went to work the next day, leaving Eli's room together and returning, with cheerful smiles, the accusing glance of one of the women who had watched them on the roof the night before.

"She thinks I am a woman of sin," Leah said, glancing back to the stoop where two women now stood, their light cotton dresses already damp in the morning heat.

"Do we care what she thinks? Do we care what anyone thinks?" Eli asked and he pressed her hand hard.

"No," she said and felt the taste of the lie turn her mouth bitter.

She did care. She cared desperately about what David would think, what he was perhaps thinking already. They had made an odd bargain that night in Odessa, but it was a bargain she had kept scrupulously until the heat of this summer. She dared not think of all that was now involved in that partnership they had entered into out of shared desperation. Their lives were so intricately interwoven now. David's studies, his bright persistent dreams, depended on her and her ability to support them. It was a debt she owed and acknowledged.

And she cared, too, about what her sister Malcha would think, Malcha who was always in awe and always slightly disapproving of Leah's choices. But there had been a new strength in Maicha's voice recently, a new spring to her step, and now, at last, perhaps her disapproval would outweigh her awe.

The children, Aaron and Rebecca, were too young to have any understanding of the situation, but she thought of Aaron's brooding green eyes, the tight curve of his lips, and of Becca's flower face, puckered into a bud of puzzlement. One day, of course, they would understand—understand and judge.

Caught between worlds, she stood balanced between her life with Eli—the factory and union meetings, the smells of his small room and the touch of his hand upon her body—and her life with her family in that apartment where they worked and played, struggling toward a future that would transport them from cluttered rooms and frenzied streets.

"I do care, in a way," she whispered softly and was relieved when Eli did not hear her.

After work that evening they took the subway up to 137th Street and sat on the hard stone steps of Lewisohn Stadium, listening to the strains of Mozart. Around them other young couples sat, clutching books and brown paper bags of sandwiches, leaning slightly forward as though fearful of missing a sound. Above them the summer stars hung in shimmering brilliance and the moon was a perfect crescent carved of burnished amber. These young people were David's fellow students, she knew, and wondered if her husband had ever granted himself the luxury of sitting beneath the stars and allowing the music he loved to drift over him. During the intermission, she saw a slight, dark-haired man with David's slow, deliberate gait ascend the steps, and her heart beat faster. But it was not David, of course, and she leaned back against Eli, her hands trembling and her dress damp.

As the evening grew cooler, Eli took off his jacket and wrapped it around her shoulders. The smell of his body clung to the garment and she pulled it tight around her, as though to envelop herself in his very essence. An odd memory occurred to her suddenly. During the early days of her marriage to Yaakov, she had sometimes wakened in the morning and slipped his discarded shirt around her bare limbs, fondling the material that had nestled next to her young husband's body and carried with it still the intimacy of his smell. In the bottom of her trunk, still neatly folded, was the blue cambric shirt he had worn the day of his death, the shirt she had mended again and again as an endless penance for the sin of staying alive, during those first mindless days of grief and despair after his death—those days before David had taken hold of her life and gently guided her until she had grown strong enough to guide herself.

"What are you thinking about?" Eli whispered.

"Nothing," she replied, and realized that it was the second time that day that she had lied to him.

The next day at work, Salvatore Visconti came to them with the news that Arnold Rosenblatt had returned from Europe. He would be in the office on Monday. This was Thursday. They would have only that evening to meet and finalize their approach before the weekend scattered them. Leah had to meet her family in the mountains and others, too, planned to flee the steaming city on the weekend.

"At my place then. We'll meet tonight."

"No. There's more room in my apartment," Leah insisted, and it was agreed that they would meet there that night.

Eli looked at her thoughtfully.

"Why did you want the meeting there, Leah?" he asked.

"There is more room," she replied, and saw the doubt in her voice reflected in his eyes.

The same group that had assembled for the first meeting in Eli's small room gathered again that night, with a few additions. Leah had asked young Bonnie Eckstein to come and represent the girls who worked in her section. Salvatore Visconti had persuaded two young Italian men who worked with him in the shipping section to participate. Eli was pleased to see them. He had explained to Leah that the unions often found newly arrived Italians the most difficult group to organize.

"They are used to a feudal system where they hand their lives over to a *don* and in return for their work he clothes them, provides food and housing. In America, bosses like Rosenblatt just became their *dons*," he had explained.

But Leah could understand that Salvatore's great warmth and his vituperative powers of persuasion would be difficult to resist, and she was not surprised when he reported that he had guarantees of support from every Italian worker at Rosenblatts.

Eleanor Greenstein arrived late and was at once given the most comfortable seat in the room. She wore a pair of green linen slacks with a matching jacket and Leah realized it was the first time she had ever seen a woman wear pants. She watched as Eleanor lit a small cigar, and offered her an ashtray. They all knew now why the successful designer had joined forces with them.

Eleanor Greenstein had a daughter who had left home in her early teens and taken a job in a factory in the South Bronx. There had been a fire and the girl had suffered burns on every part of her body. She had died after weeks of pain, screaming in agony through lips that were scorched into ribbons of blackened flesh. It was then that the designer had asked Arnold Rosenblatt to provide adequate fire protection in the factory. He had refused, ignoring her persistent argument, until she turned to Eli Feinstein and became part of the organizing effort.

Now she took out her notebook and, in her usual brisk voice, summarized the situation.

"We're into July now. The fall line is entirely cut, pieced, and basted. Monday we're scheduled to begin sewing and trimming. That's cutting it very close, and if we don't start work next week there'll be no shipments in August and no Rosenblatt line in the stores in September. If that happens his creditors will pounce on him and he'll be through. And not only on paper. All his personal money is in the business now. He needs that fall line. On Monday morning your steering committee will meet with him. We've got a ninety percent commitment from the workers to strike if he doesn't agree to terms. He can't face that down. Ten or twenty he could fire, but not the whole work force. He's a shrewd man. I think he'll see that our demands are reasonable. After all, what are we asking for? The right to collective bargaining. Paid vacations. Sick leave. And most important of all—adequate safety protection. A fire alarm system, windows that open, and accessible fire escapes." Her voice, always so cool and firm, faltered now and they looked away from her. Some said her daughter had been only fifteen years old when she died.

"Who's on the steering committee?" Moe Cohen asked.

"Eli Feinstein, Salvatore Visconti, and Leah Goldfeder."

There was a murmur of approval and Leah felt a small glow of pleasure. It was good to be part of a group and recognized.

"All right then," Eli said, taking control of the meeting. "When the steering committee gets back, if we have to strike we're ready. Everyone will be down in the street in fifteen minutes. We'll have the picket signs ready and Dubinsky's organizers will be waiting to help. But remember—this is going to be an orderly strike. If you're called names you keep on walking without answering. If Rosenblatt brings in scabs, close your lines and keep them from breaking through. If they manage it, let them pass without any violence from us. If the police arrest you, go along quietly. The union will make bail and get lawyers. Make sure everyone in your group knows what's happening. Any questions?"

Bonnie Eckstein raised her hand.

"If they arrest you, you get locked up in a jail. You can't get home?"

"That's what will happen," Eli said gently. "But not for long, Bonnie, maybe a few hours or just overnight."

Leah's heart sank. She remembered the strike at the Gay Paris Blouse Company only the year before. That picket line, too, had been an orderly one. The girls in their long dark skirts and neat white blouses had marched quietly around the building, some of them wearing their best hats as though they were on a festive outing, not fighting a weary battle for survival. Suddenly the police had arrived and made a mass arrest. The union lawyer had angrily demanded to know the grounds for the arrest and the police officers, clutching the arms of the young women and shoving them into wagons, had leered and answered, "Prostitution. Ain't they walking the street?" There had been a burst of laughter from the crowd. Leah knew that some of those girls had spent the night in filthy cells which they shared with criminals and prostitutes. She would talk to Bonnie before Monday, she decided. She would talk to all her girls. They must be prepared.

"Are there any other questions?" Eli asked.

There were none and the meeting slowly broke up into small groups. There was quiet talk and laughter as they lingered on, unwilling to relinquish the sense of togetherness that had grown between them during the long weeks of preparation and equally unwilling to confront their individual doubts and unease about the week to come. Leah passed around bowls of fruits and nuts and glasses of cold lemonade. The small gathering took on the ambience of a party. They talked louder and laughed with nervous exhilaration. Someone put on the radio and a few couples danced to the slow mood music until the tenant downstairs banged irately on a water pipe and the baronic tones of the news announcer replaced the lazy melodies. President Hoover was predicting a full economic recovery. Elections had been held in Germany and the new National Socialist Party had won 107 seats in the Reichstag. The Duke of Windsor continued his alliance with Mrs. Simpson despite the Queen's disapproval. The news bored them and they turned the dial and finally found more dance music, but the mood was broken. It was late and people began leaving, saying good-bye with unusual affection considering that they would all see each other at work the next morning.

"How is your brother, Bonnie?" Leah asked as she walked the girl to the door.

"He's better but he's still in the hospital. The doctors think that with a brace he'll be able to walk. That's what they think." Bonnie's eyes filled but she fought back the tears and hurried down the steps.

Eli and Leah remained alone in the apartment. Like a married couple skilled at coordinating small domestic tasks, they straightened the room and in the kitchen she washed the soiled glasses and he dried them. They did not talk but moved in easy rhythm as though they had done this many times before.

"All right. This is finished," he said and placing the towel on the sink, he took her in his arms.

"Not here," she cried wildly, stiffening suddenly.

"Why not here?" he asked in a harsh voice she did not recognize, and shrugged in defeat when she did not answer.

"Let us go to my place then, Leah. But you know, we cannot keep on like this. Soon we must talk about everything. Make decisions. This must be settled."

"Yes," she agreed helplessly and looked around the familiar room.

A small crayon drawing of Rebecca's hung on a kitchen cabinet. The child had done it as a first-grade exercise. "My Family" the printed block letters read and beneath there were stick figures of Leah and David, Aaron and Rebecca. The children's hands touched but the faces of the father and mother, drawn in magenta wax, were turned from each other, as though the child had guessed an uneasy secret.

"Let us go, Eli. Let us hurry," she said, with sudden urgency.

They did not go up to the roof that night, to look at the stars, but went at once to his room, where they clutched each other with a fierceness they could not control, scarring each other's flesh with hands and teeth, and waking from the light sleep that finally came upon them to cling to each other again. Once, in that thick darkness, she thought she saw a tear glisten in his eye but when she touched his cheek with her lips she felt only the rough dryness of his skin and the vague smell of the menthol lotion that was his one small vanity.

7

They awoke too early the next morning, but neither Eli nor Leah wanted to return to sleep. They dressed hurriedly in the half-light and Leah felt a curious relief at leaving the building before its women had assembled on the stoop. The excitement of the previous evening had left them at once exhausted and keyed up, and when they stopped for breakfast at the Garden Cafeteria on East Broadway, they ate in silence at a table near the huge windows that overlooked the busy street. Working men and women, their lunches wrapped in oil-stained brown paper or packets of newspaper wrapped in string, hurried past them. Peddlers with bolts of merchandise strapped to their backs lumbered down the street. Groups of rabbinical students, their black caftans sweeping after them, wafted down the street, their earlocks still damp from their morning prayers and ablutions.

"Where are they all running to?" Eli mused, dipping his hard roll into the glass of coffee which was almost white with milk and sugar.

"You should have an egg," she said.

"For lunch I'll have an egg," he answered, smiling as his thick dark eyebrows met.

She blushed, remembering that as they dressed that morning she had urged him to put on a lighter shirt and opened the window so that the room would be properly aired. She was becoming too proprietary, too wifely, worrying over this strong man whose ringing voice had the power to move so many to action and whose strong body excited her so. She was aroused by Eli's small secrets and weaknesses, the holes in his socks, the frayed cloth of his collars, the way he patted his cheeks with menthol lotion, slapping them sharply for color, and his habit of combing a streak of gray beneath a cluster of dark hair. His vanity amused her and made him even more desirable.

They reached Rosenblatts before opening time, but went at once to their work stations. Eli had emphasized the fact that all work must either be on schedule or ahead of schedule when the committee went in to negotiate on Monday.

"We must bargain from a position of strength and certainty," he had said. "Rosenblatt knows the kind of work we're capable of and he's not going to risk losing us. So everyone must be absolutely on schedule."

Leah planned to leave early because she knew there would be long lines waiting for the buses to the mountains and she was anxious to see the children. She worked quickly to make up for the time she would lose in the afternoon. Her girls drifted in and took their places at their machines. They rolled up their sleeves and told each other that the day seemed a bit cooler than the day before. Perhaps the heat spell was breaking after all and Monday would finally be cool. They glanced at each other nervously as they mentioned Monday because all of them knew what would happen then, although no one mentioned the possibility of the strike. There was a flurry of talk about a folk dance that night at the Cooper Union and an altercation when one of the Orthodox girls asked how they could think of folk dancing on the eve of the Sabbath.

"Come instead to our forum at the Young Israel," she urged. "We have a speaker just returned from Palestine."

Leah thought of her brother Moshe and Henia, his wife. It had been months since she had heard from them. A telegram had arrived just after the Arab riots assuring them of the family's safety, and then months of silence.

"Arab violence," David had said bitterly. "It was a pogrom called by a new name."

If they struck Rosenblatts and there was violence during the strike, would David label that too a pogrom? Leah wondered. A pogrom against the poor and defenseless. Jews would not be the only victims of the hate, ignorance, and avarice that would be unleashed against the workers. Reading Eli's pamphlets had taught her that.

The morning wore on and the girls talked less and concentrated on their work. The machines hummed rhythmically and from the pressing room they heard the repeated slamming of the hot irons. As each girl brought her finished pile of work up to Leah for inspection, Leah talked quietly to them about the implications of the strike.

"Carry very little money," she told them. "And bring a toothbrush in case there is an arrest. It may happen."

Bonnie Eckstein, in a new pink dress fashioned in a dressmaking class at the settlement house, smiled shyly when she came up with her work. She had thought of a stitch which would shorten the time required for embroidery finishing and she blushed when Leah complimented her.

"You're not worried about the strike?" Leah asked quietly.

"Not now," Bonnie replied. "I feel better knowing what might happen. But it's very hot in here. Can I open a window?"

"You can try," Leah said wryly and the girl smiled.

The first two windows Bonnie tried remained stubbornly closed, but she was able to force the third one open and the girls sighed with relief as a small breeze stirred the stagnant air. Leah got up then and tried the other windows, but they would not open and she turned back to her drawing board where she had begun a sketch for a shirtwaist that could be worn with slacks. If Eleanor Greenstein was appearing in public in pants, soon other women would and there would be a demand for tops that could be worn with slacks.

She worked steadily and looked up with annoyance at a sudden outburst of chatter. But that vague annoyance froze into a fear that sucked her breath away when she saw what was happening. Her pencil still poised in air, Leah watched a small stream of flame glide across the floor. The line of fire sliced the room into two halves and continued to roll on, consuming the small hills of scrap fabric that littered the floor and hungrily pressing forward. Blue sparks danced explosively upward as the fire reached a pool of machine oil and the stream of flame soared into a great fiery wave that threatened to engulf them. A girl screamed, shredding the air with her terror. Others joined her, one very young girl wailing softly like a small child who fears being heard.

The sudden crackling burst of fire jolted Leah. She jumped from her seat, dashed across the room, and flung the door open.

Smoke mushroomed in at them from the blocked hallway and they heard the pounding of feet and strangled shrieks of fear. Somewhere in the building a bell was ringing with harsh insistence; sounds of smashing glass and splintering wood could be heard. Men and women rushed down the stairwell but when they reached the next landing they began to scream.

"The door is locked. *Lieber Gott*, the door is locked!"

Above them a mountain of fire loomed and they rushed back, pouring into Leah's workroom where the flames were already breaking their bounds, raging strips of fire sucking at the hems of the girls' dresses, licking at the wood of the doors, subsiding mildly against the thrusts from the huge bolts of fabric with which the desperate girls were beating at them and rising again with renewed rage and fury.

"The windows," Leah shouted and headed to the one opened by Bonnie only minutes before. She stood on a chair and wrested it further up as the girls clustered about her, screaming and crying. It was three stories down to the courtyard where the ailanthus tree stood, its glossy leaves impervious to the blazing fires above it. Crowds were gathering in the courtyard and the bystanders gestured wildly to the trapped girls.

"Jump, goddamn it!" a man shouted and Leah saw that workers from the neighboring factories were dashing over with bolts of cloth, mattresses, layers of goods, anything that could be spread on the hard ground.

Lina Goldstein, the little orthodox girl, the smallest and lightest of them, was the first to leap from the window with Leah lifting her to the edge and urging her forward. Then others scrambled forward, fighting now for the chance of escape. From the floors above the screams of fear had turned into wails of agony.

"People are burning up," a girl screamed. "Human beings are on fire here."

The girl's own skirt was trimmed with a ruffle of flame and sparks glittered in her hair. Leah grabbed a bolt of cloth and wrapped it around her, beating out the scraps of fire with her hands. The girl had fainted and Bonnie Eckstein moved forward to help Leah. The two of them shoved the mummied form from the window and watched it land in the courtyard below.

The girls moved quickly now. One after the other they scrambled up to the ledge and hurtled to the ground, one girl landing on another as the ambulances wailed and the crowd below moaned in anguish and disbelief, shouting names up to the prisoners of the flames.

"Sadie Greenberg—is my Sadie there?" a man called.

"Papa! I'm all right, Papa." Tears streamed down the girl's cheeks and her elbow was streaked with blood. Bonnie helped support her and Leah bent to heave her up to the ledge and down to the courtyard. The girl's blood streaked the bodice of Bonnie's pink dress and her skirt was blackened. Crazily, Leah leaned forward and wiped the girl's cheek, wet with sweat and tears.

"Let me through, let me through!" Eli burst into the room, rocketing his way through the ranks of screaming girls. He picked up a chair and shattered a window, hacking at the strips of wood that blocked its access. Behind him, his face and hands black as coal, Salvatore Visconti worked with desperate speed. He picked up one girl and wrapped her, as Leah had done, in a bolt of cloth that shielded her from the flames. He passed the girl to Eli who tossed her swiftly down to the courtyard where firemen had at last spread a net so that the falling bodies were caught before they hit the ground.

"Eli, take Bonnie. Save her!" Leah shouted.

Bonnie, who had been working steadily beside her, had suddenly slumped to the floor and Leah felt her own lungs struggle for air as they were blocked by the invasion of smoke that had seeped in, rushing past the cloth she had pressed over her mouth.

Salvatore seized the barely conscious girl and passed her, unprotesting, to Eli. With relief, Leah saw her land in the net. New cries rose from the courtyard below. Crowds of children searching for their parents added their small shrill voices to the din.

"Mama. Mama. Please come out of the fire. Please don't burn up," a small boy in knickers shouted, but there was no answering call and the girl's voice added a plea. "Come home, Mama. Please come home. We'll be good."

Behind them the room swirled with flames that were leaping steadily toward the window. There was very little time left and the remaining girls screamed and clawed at each other in their efforts to escape. A seamstress dashed over to the remaining window which remained sealed closed, climbed up, and hurled herself through the glass. The jagged shards ripped her body and the outline of her form in the glass was etched with her blood. Another followed after her, muttering a "Hail Mary" as she hoisted herself up, leaving ribbons of skin dangling from the glass. A third girl tried to follow but her arm caught on the shattered fragments of pane. She broke loose, thrusting herself forward, and left a bloody hunk of flesh clinging to the window frame.

The girl behind her sank into a faint and fell backward into the flames. Leah ran to pull her out and felt the fire licking at her hands; Salvatore Visconti threw himself across the girl's burning body and beat out the flames, his body furiously rising and falling, his great shoulders heaving with sobs. Only when he lifted the slight black-haired girl in his arms did Leah realize it was his own daughter, tiny Philomena Visconti, who worked as a trimmer on the floor above. Eli took the girl from him and hurled her into the waiting net.

"She's all right, Salvatore," he shouted.

Salvatore nodded wordlessly, his face black with soot except for the neat lines etched by the tears of fear.

There was a sudden crash behind them and Leah wheeled around and saw the room's central beam collapse, charred to a length of cinders that crumbled and was consumed by the leaping flames.

"Leah! Now! You must get out now!" Eli shouted.

"But what about you and Salvatore?"

"Right after you. I promise. We'll come right after you."

The flames were rushing toward them now, lashing tongues of scarlet and gold, licking their way furiously forward. They were sandwiched into a narrow strip of floor. From the courtyard below the frenzied crowd shouted questions and directions up at them.

"How many are you?"

"Is my mother, Channa Schiff, there? Channa Schiff!"

"Jump, damn it! The building will go any second. Jump now!"

Eli leapt to the windowsill and Salvatore lifted Leah up beside him. Poised on the parapet, they clung to each other for the briefest of moments, veiled in a cloud of gray-black smoke. Eli's hair was dusted gray with clots of ash and his face was black with soot, matted over with sweat. But his green eyes were clear and bright and even against the acrid odor of the burning building and the scorching flesh, she smelled the fragrance of the menthol on his skin. He couched her face in his large hands and kissed her on the lips. Her fingers gripped his shoulders, but firmly he pried them loose and gently he thrust her forward.

A rush of air engulfed her, seemed to support her falling body. As she fell into the waiting net, all consciousness deserted her. Weightless and uncaring, she rested on the ground below, shaded by the lacy leaves of the ailanthus tree.

Within seconds the last supporting beam gave way, falling across the window and blocking it. The screaming voices of two women, trapped behind the curtain of dancing flames, were heard for a few minutes more and when the debris of the holocaust was cleared the bodies of Salvatore Visconti and Eli Feinstein were found, faces down, groping backward to the trapped women. Eli's fingers almost grasped the outstretched hand of a tiny blonde needleworker, who was buried two days later in a child's grave.

It was almost dark when Leah stumbled home that evening. The lights of the large synagogue on Eldridge Street were ablaze and congregants were already filing in for the Sabbath eve service. Hugging the velvet bags that held their prayer shawls, the worshipers looked after Leah as she walked slowly down the street, their sad eyes paying silent tribute to her grief.

Leah's long black hair, loose and knotted, tumbled about her shoulders and she wore a loose flowered housedress that a relief worker at the makeshift shelter had given her. Her own clothing had been scorched and shredded. She had lost a shoe in the fall from the window and she wore a man's slipper on one foot. Her hands, covered with soft yellow burn blisters and swathed in Vaseline-stained bandages, throbbed, though she was indifferent to the pain.

Her weary path seemed mysteriously familiar, and quite suddenly she realized why. Once before she had fled from fire and loss, running barefoot then through wooded hills and brambles.

Now she trudged slowly through urban streets, her mouth bitter with sorrow. Could one taste flames? She wondered and thought that she might laugh but did not. She was, it seemed, too exhausted for either laughter or tears. Painfully, she urged herself toward the house. When she arrived, she looked automatically up at the window where Aaron, his bright hair the color of those frightening flames, so often stood sentinel. But Aaron was away, she remembered. Everyone was away. It was Friday and the apartment was empty. They would be waiting for her in that mountain bungalow, miles above the river along which she and Eli had cruised and sung and laughed only days before.

Now Eli was dead. She reminded herself of the fact as though she might forget. Dead. Her love was dead.

Through the open windows of the synagogue she heard the voices of the men at prayers intoning the mourner's Kaddish, the prayer for the dead.

"Yiskadal v'yiskadash, shmei rabah..."

Silently, her lips moving, she mouthed the prayer after them and slowly climbed the stairs to her apartment. A sliver of light glowed beneath the door and when she opened it, David was sitting in the armchair, his face turned toward her, his fine thin features masked with a grief that matched her own.

"David!" She ran toward him and buried her head in his lap.

Gently he patted her shoulders and ran his fingers through her dark hair, allowing her sobs to spill forth until his clothing was drenched with her tears and his own, too, were falling freely.

"How did you know to come here?" she asked.

"The news of the fire was on the radio."

"Eli is dead," she said.

"I know. I went to the factory to look for you and they told me."

"Eli and I..." New tears came, choking off the desperate words. She could not finish the sentence, nor was there any need to.

"I know."

Gently he pulled her to her feet. Like a father caring for a small helpless daughter, he peeled her clothing off and filled the bathtub with hot water, carrying potful after potful from the stove. He led her to the steaming tub and immersed her in the soothing water; tenderly he bathed her, washing away the traces of soot and ash, the smells of fetid flesh and searing skin. He washed her long dark hair, freeing it of the smoky odors that had clung to it. Beneath his ministrations she wept, grew calm, and wept again. At last, he toweled her dry, dressed her in a clean white nightdress, and led her gently to the bed that had not been slept in for a week.

She fell asleep at once and slept heavily, waking now and then as young children do, to pound and scratch at the darkness, trembling and weeping wildly. He calmed her then, stroking her gently and pulling her down against the pillows. But at her side he lay wakeful and heavyhearted, as the velvety darkness faded into the gray, rose-streaked skies of morning.

*

"Death day," she thought on wakening and stirred restlessly within the sheets, damp with her sweat. Beyond her door she heard David talking softly and Malcha's indistinguishable reply. Malcha must have arrived during the night, then, Leah realized, and wondered if David had sent for her. No matter. She was grateful that her sister was there and grateful too that minutes later the front door to the apartment closed and David's step sounded on the outside stairwell.

Slowly she lifted herself from the bed, moved toward the mirror, and looked closely at herself as though her reflected image might reveal the terrible loss she had suffered. Her dark eyes, dulled with sleep, stared back at her; neither misery nor pain had carved new lines across her high smooth forehead. Her hair, newly washed, shimmered darkly and she thought of how Eli had loved the touch of its wetness, had played with it, draping it in sheaves of darkness across his face—or combed it with his fingers as she lay across his narrow bed after lovemaking. She reached up and touched a single soft curl, as though within its tendrils she might discover a ghostly caress, a lingering trace of tenderness. Then violently she pulled at the dark hairs, jerking them fiercely from her scalp, moaning with the pain and glad of it. She knew now what she must do.

She searched frantically in her bureau drawer and pulled out her heavy shears. Roughly she pulled her hair, layer by layer, as though it were a stubborn sheath of fabric, and hacked at it until it lay in severed, mutilated dark swathes across the bare wood floor. She had not shorn her hair when she married the youthful Yaakov nor had she covered it when she became David's wife. It was for Eli, who would be buried that day, that she had reserved that sacrifice. She plucked up one long dark curl and pressed it against her cheek, then carefully folded it into a scarf and put it in her drawer.

"Leah, what have you done?" Malcha, pushing open the door, stared at her sister. "Oh Leah, poor Leah," she said and cradled her in her arms, her fingers gently stroking the cropped head.

"I had to do it," Leah said, the first tears of that day of grief and loss twisting down her face.

"Yes. You did. Of course you did," Malcha replied and went to find a black kerchief for Leah to wear to the funeral that afternoon.

Long before the noon hour, the small funeral parlor on East Broadway was filled to capacity. Outside, crowds of mourners milled in the street and black-garbed men and women emerged in throngs from the subway and filled the tables of the Garden Cafeteria. Small children, their large eyes wide with startled wonder at a death so bright and terrible, lined the curbs. They held bouquets of wilted flowers, the meager offerings of tiny gardens cultivated in empty lots or sun-starved tenement courtyards. An old woman held a small boy by the hand and told him, in melodic zeugmas of English and Yiddish, that there had not been so large a funeral on the east side since that of the great writer, Sholom Aleichem, thirteen years before.

"Sholom who?" the child asked irritably.

"Sholom Aleichem. The great teller of tales," the grandmother replied.

"Oh."

The boy was unimpressed. He was not interested in writers, particularly writers who used a language he could not read and would soon forget. Eli Feinstein, on the other hand, had been a hero, a crusader for justice, a fighter. He had organized the workers. He had saved the lives of young girls fleeing in terror from the flames. The boy touched a hunk of charred wood he carried in his pocket. It was a fragment of the door that had once served as a portal to the

Rosenblatt factory. He had snatched it still hot from the flames, scurrying through the rubber-booted legs of cursing firemen to acquire it, Other children in the somber crowd that morning carried similar grim souvenirs—blackened fragments of glass from the windows that would not open, distorted hunks of metal burned to a ferrous brightness, singed scraps of fabric, a girl's barrette, a man's rimless spectacles.

A café artist had made a sketch from memory of Eli Feinstein, and an enterprising printer had run off hundreds of smudged copies which sold on East Broadway and Canal Street for twenty-five cents a copy. Joshua Ellenberg bought one and tucked it into his shirt.

Limousines carrying dignitaries drew up in front of the tiny building. Rabbi Stephen Wise, emerging from a long black car, almost stumbled over a little girl and bent to lift her to his shoulders, smiling into the wide startled eyes before handing the child back to her mother. Governor Franklin Roosevelt sent a representative and Mayor Jimmy Walker arrived with David Dubinsky. The crowds parted to admit them and the street filled with excited murmurs. Fingers pointed, heads nodded, and fathers lifted their children above the crowd to stare at faces that molded history.

But when Leah Goldfeder, her arm resting lightly on her husband's, her newly shorn hair covered by a black scarf, arrived, a hush fell over the crowd of mourners and spectators. Silently they stepped aside. In the small, stifling room where every wooden chair was occupied, seats were mysteriously found and offered to them.

She looked up only once, her dark eyes resting fearlessly on the plain pine coffin which was closed and draped with a prayer shawl. The corpse within it—the body of the man who had held her and loved her—was a mass of charred putrescent flesh and she had heard that even the most seasoned veterans of the burial society had wept as they prepared the body for interment.

She listened intently to the eulogy of the white-bearded rabbi who had come from Eli Feinstein's village in Russia and who had, so many years before in that distant land, intoned the service for Eli's young wife, her dead body heavy with its burden of undelivered life.

"A martyr," the rabbi called him. "A man who sacrificed his life for his people. A man who died for the sanctification of God's name—for a world of justice and right."

"Amen!"

The single word rose like a mighty prayer and trembled thunderously in the heat-heavy air. The aged rabbi wept unashamedly—the bewildered tears of an old man who accepts but does not understand.

David Dubinsky spoke in the thick, heavily accented English of those whom he organized to struggle for their rights. He reminded the mourners of the reasons for Eli Feinstein's death and for the deaths of all the men and women who had perished in what he called "the flames of greed" and "the fires of indifference."

"Renew your struggles. Take up their legacy. There must be no more fires—no more funeral pyres!"

"No more!" the crowd thundered back.

In the rear of the room Eleanor Greenstein slipped to the floor in a faint and was carried out of the room. But Leah Goldfeder remained seated quietly; her hands were clasped and David's hand shielded them, covering the bandages that blanketed her burns. She did not weep, although once, as the rabbi intoned the Kaddish—the memorial prayer for the dead—she swayed lightly from side to side and those standing nearby saw her lips move as she repeated the words soundlessly.

She and David did not join the parade of mourners who followed on foot after the horse-drawn hearse which carried Eli Feinstein's body through the streets of the lower east side. The wheels of the black carriage rattled across the cobblestones as it made the traditional pilgrimage to those places which had held meaning for the dead man. It halted at the tiny synagogue built by those who had emigrated from his village; it stopped at Rutgers Square, where he had gone to hear the impassioned words of Eugene Debs and returned to issue his own pleas for justice and right. At the Irvington Settlement, a chorus of children came out to sing in Yiddish a sweet song of hope for a better tomorrow; and at the Cafe Royale, where he had sought life and laughter during long dark nights, the artists and poets stood quietly and a guitarist played a mournful melody that had never been heard before and was never heard again. And then at last the hearse picked up its pace for the long journey to the open fields of Long Island, where a grave waited for Eli Feinstein in a newly opened cemetery, established, according to the ancient law, on the outskirts of a city.

Leah sat through the afternoon at the window of the parlor on Eldridge Street, and her son Aaron crouched in the doorway, a small witness to his mother's sorrow, his eyes fixed on her bent form. When at last the streets filled with returning mourners and Leah knew that the cortege had disbanded, she turned from the window, and leaning heavily on her son's arm, she allowed the child to lead her to her bed where she waited desperately for tears that would not come.

Brighton Beach
1933
8

Charles Ferguson looked up from his New York Times as the Brighton express careened wildly out of the darkness and soared magically above ground, triumphantly jolting to an abrupt halt at the Prospect Park station. He looked out the soot-encrusted window at the quiet Brooklyn station, almost deserted so early on a Saturday morning. A group of youngsters, one carrying an old army blanket and others cradling large brown paper bags stuffed with fruit and sandwiches, settled themselves on one of the wicker benches in his subway car. The tallest boy leaped up on the seat and proceeded to draw a moustache on the fading face of Franklin Delano Roosevelt which adorned the subway advertising poster, headed by the slogan "A New Deal for All America."

"Oh, Tony, cut that out," one of the girls protested.

"He don't need no more posters. He's pres'dent awready," the boy answered.

"Yeah. And my old man still don't have a job," another boy said, and they all laughed as though the thin, sad-eyed youth had uttered a great witticism.

It was easier, Charles thought, to accept deprivation with the equanimity of laughter, to use wit as an anodyne against desperation. He thought of all the hungry families who sat clustered around their enormous Stromberg Carlson radios, their faces expectant even through the introductory commercials. Clearly, the Depression would have been unbearable without Amos 'n' Andy and Fibber McGee and Molly.

There were, of course, those few who managed to struggle through pain and crisis supported only by their own strength and determination to survive and get on with the business of living. It occurred to him now, watching the same laughing, sad-eyed boy who had defiantly whipped out a bottle of beer and was drinking it without pleasure, that Leah and David Goldfeder, to whose home he was traveling, were among those few.

He looked out the window and watched the backyards of Brooklyn speed by and thought of the Goldfeder family, realizing with a start that it was almost ten years since Leah Goldfeder, then a shy young woman in her early twenties, had first entered his studio. He remembered how a hazy cloud of sunlight had hovered over her coronet of blue-black braids that afternoon, and he regretted again that Leah had finally cut her hair, shaping its thickness into a smooth heavy cap that hugged her finely formed head.

Ferguson had heard somewhere that on isolated Greek islands, young women whose lovers had been killed hacked off their own braids in paroxysms of grief and thrust them in the earthbound coffin. He had thought of those stories when he first saw Leah, her hair newly shorn, at Eli Feinstein's funeral. What would have happened if Eli Feinstein had lived? Charles Ferguson wondered. Would he be sitting on this BMT Brighton Beach express so early on a Saturday morning, en route to Aaron Goldfeder's bar mitzvah? Would Leah and David Goldfeder still be married?

Charles had watched his friends through the years that had passed since that long hot summer that had erupted at last in the flames of death and destruction. He had seen a new relationship slowly devolve between Leah and David. Slowly, like dancers in a tableau, they had moved toward each other, trading touch and glance, until they came together at last in a circle of stillness and light. He had not been surprised to receive news of the birth of their son Michael soon after their move to Brighton Beach.

After all, each life was a long road, inevitably marked with those blurred, uncertain *ifs*. What, then, *if* he had never left Illinois, *if* he had concentrated on his painting rather than his teaching, his life too would have curved its way down different, unknown pathways. Leah and David had been lucky, immeasurably and deservedly lucky.

In the grimy train window he saw his own face reflected and noticed that strands of gray had stolen into the wispy blond growth of his beard. His own luck was still concealed beyond an undiscovered detour. Each graying strand signified one of those mysterious *ifs*, and he stroked the silken silver threads as the youth in the next seat wrenched open the window and the salt smell of the approaching ocean filled the train.

*

Leah Goldfeder, too, had arisen early that morning and moved softly through the silent house. Always, upon waking, she followed a mysterious discipline and wandered from bed to bed, glancing briefly at each sleeping face, arranging a coverlet, smoothing a matted pillow. So too, on this spring morning, when the acrid scent of newly blossoming sorrel grass mingled with the odors of the ocean, she had looked down at David's sleeping face and lightly touched his cheek, shadowed by the morning growth of beard. How beautiful he looked in the half-light of dawn, she thought, and marveled at the mingled strength and gentleness of his sleeping face, feeling now a stirring within herself as her body called to his. Briefly she thought of crawling back into bed with him, of moving her hands across his sleeping form, of watching his body slowly stretch into wakefulness before he opened his eyes and took control of a new day. She knew how to caress his legs, moving her fingers gently and then, slowly increasing the pressure, up his thighs, slowly coaxing his sleeping sex into wakefulness until it sprang upward, firm and mobile, possessed of a vital life of its own. Then, at last fully awake, he would smile at her with his eyes and grasp her, holding her willing prisoner upon the bed, lashing her with kisses and embraces until she surrendered, admitting herself both victor and vanquished in this sweet battle which they fought again and again, relishing wound and victory.

But she did not waken him, recognizing that there would not be time this morning. She assuaged herself by planting a light kiss upon his sleeping face and allowing his hand to move and lightly touch her thigh before he turned and smiled and slept on.

Now she heard Michael, the baby, call to her from the small room which had once been a back porch and was now enclosed within huge panes of glass so that when she entered it each morning she shielded her eyes against the brilliance of the morning sunlight.

Michael stood in his crib, toddling from one end of it to another. His dark curls were clustered wildly about his head and she reproved herself for delaying the child's first haircut for so long. It was wrong, she supposed, but she wanted Michael to stay a baby, if only for a few months longer. It was the first time that she had enjoyed a child's infancy and she wished to prolong these precious days when she wheeled him about the streets of Brighton Beach in his stroller and watched him crawl across the grainy sands and rocks of the seashore. What luxury it was to feed the child in the cheerful warmth of a kitchen which belonged entirely to her and would not be invaded by stray boarders, or even her sister, who now called herself Mollie.

And, of course, there was the special sweetness of Michael himself, so relaxed and amiable, a child conceived in passion and carried with peace and certainty. David, citing a course in neonatology, had told her that there was a theory that the mental and emotional state of the mother during the period of gestation did much to influence the personality of the infant. Leah's own children substantiated that theory. She had carried Aaron during an agony of uncertainty, weighed down by her own sense of loss and suffering, feeling his growing weight within her as an unwelcome cancer that grew against her will. She had even resisted his birth and her breasts had refused to nourish the child. And when she had at last emerged from that forest of despair, when Yaakov's death and the assault she had suffered had finally been assimilated into a new life of her own choosing, it had been too late. The lonely child had grown into a bitter boy, as tense and rejecting as she herself had been through the years of his helplessness. Even today, she knew, as he made the requisite speech of gratitude to his parents, the speech demanded of all boys on their bar mitzvah, as though no child could assume the responsibilities of manhood without acknowledging a debt to childhood, her son's eyes would burn with anger, giving the lie to the words laboriously composed with the stoic assistance of the rabbi.

Suddenly tense, as she always became when thinking of Aaron, she lifted Michael from his crib and let him pull at her hair as she changed his diaper and listened to him sing a glad and wordless song.

Rebecca had been a cheerful child but she had lacked Michael's exuberance. She had been conceived on a night of shadowy memories after a day susurrant with repentance and memory. Her gestation had been a time of stoic calm, of resigned withdrawal. She was a child of sacrifice, borne by Leah as an offering to David who had supported and befriended her, who had become her husband through pain and compromise, rather than through promise and discovery. Michael had been born when Leah and David, husband and wife for a dozen years, had at last become lovers. Leah felt a special tenderness for her raven-haired daughter, but never had she felt the surging love that overcame her with small Michael, who wriggled now beneath her touch, tossing diapers to the floor, clutching at her face and bringing it close to his own for the great sloppy licks which he called kisses.

Sometimes Leah, pushing Michael in his carriage along the boardwalk, rocking him in tune to the beat of the ceaseless waves, thought back to that long year before Michael's birth. She remembered those months before their move from the crowded enclave of the lower east side to the Brooklyn streets, redolent with the smells of the ocean, the concrete pattern of the broad avenues broken by great fields of green in which Italian farmers, impervious to urban encroachment, grew tomatoes and broccoli, round rows of lettuce, and neat, sharply verdant patches of broccoli nodding under beads of crystal dew. Like all clearly defined expanses of time, she assigned borders to that period—emotional markers signifying a beginning and an ending. That time in her life had begun with Eli Feinstein's funeral and ended on the sunset evening when she turned to David and found her heart beating with sudden fervor and her body weak and fluid with desire.

She charted the days of that year with startling accuracy. Whole hours were returned to her in memory and she saw herself walking alone down streets she and Eli had wandered together during the brief season of their love. At the Cafe Royale, in those days of grief, she had sat at the same table she and Eli had shared with Charles Ferguson. A young poet had read a series of quatrains called "Sweatshop Inferno," dedicated to the workers of the Rosenblatt fire. She had listened dry-eyed to the impassioned lines, wondering why it was they seemed foreign to her, as though the horror of that holocaust had been endured by someone else, only dimly related to her. She had lost her lover and her friends, yet she sat here drinking coffee and allowing the words to scatter about her like careless pebbles. After the reading a plate was passed for the benefit of the survivors who were undergoing skin-grafting and the families of the victims. Like the other café sitters, she reached dutifully into her purse and placed a few coins on the battered aluminum dish. The collection was one of thousands being held all through the country. For weeks after the fire the money had poured in and a committee had swiftly been formed to administer the funds. Contributions had come from every part of the country and checks had arrived from England and the Continent. The sympathy and conscience of the world, deaf to the pleas of union organizers and workers, had been stirred by the sepia pictures of the flame-consumed bodies of young girls hurtling through smoke-drenched air.

"Too late. They realize everything too late," Eleanor Greenstein had said bitterly when she visited Leah. She had come to say good-bye. She was leaving New York for a small Vermont town. A manufacturer had offered her a job there and she had seized the opportunity for a new life.

"There is nothing left for me here," she said, looking out of Leah's window to the street below where the women sat on the tenement steps, watching the small boys shoot immies in the street and the girls jump rope double-Dutch, their feet beating a fierce rhythm against the hot pavement. "All I have here is a grave."

All our lives are dotted with graves, Leah thought, and wondered if anyone tended the graves in the small Russian cemetery where Yaakov and Chana Rivka, the attendant ghosts of her marriage, lay buried.

Part of the money raised in the collections would be used for headstones for the graves of those victims who had died without families. Leah realized, when she heard that, that she did not even know where Eli had been buried. She had not ridden out to the cemetery with the funeral cortege but returned home with David, to sit for hours at the window watching the purple shadows of the descending evening glide down and briefly veil the ugly streets in coolness and beauty.

"Why did you cut your hair, Mommy?" Rebecca asked, her small fingers regretfully touching the hacked ends of those pitch tresses that Eli had stroked for hours on end.

"To show that she was sad, silly," Aaron answered and led his sister away, as though, with mysterious wisdom, he understood his mother's grief.

In the kitchen, Malcha and Sarah Ellenberg whispered earnestly to each other and cautioned the children, stunned by Leah's silent mourning, to play in the street or on the roof. Firmly, like experienced nurses familiar with the spectrum of grief, they brought her plates of cold borscht, filled with nourishing vegetables, which she left uneaten on the table beside her. She remained at the window when they went to sleep but in the night they heard the door softly open and whisper closed. Through her own window, Malcha saw Leah walk slowly down the deserted street; minutes later David appeared behind her, a vigilant guardian trailing in the shadows of his wife's grief.

One afternoon, Leah went again to the pier and boarded the cruise ship on which she and Eli had spent their one golden afternoon which still rang in memory with song and laughter. The ocean was choppy that day and she stood on deck and watched the foam-capped waves roughly thrust themselves against the cruising vessel. The waves, as they rushed toward her, were bright green, the color of Eli's eyes, but they faded into a soft grayness as they broke. Did eyes retain their color in death? she wondered, and leaned so far over the rail, as though to search out the answer in the ocean itself, that a man standing nearby moved swiftly to her side and led her to an empty deck chair.

She sat in the sun for the rest of the brief voyage and when the boat docked, David was waiting at the pier. A patch of sunlight sat like a small crown on his dark hair and fine lines of worry rimmed his deep-set eyes.

"How did you know I would be here?" she asked.

"I followed you," he replied, and draped her shoulders with the sweater he had brought with him.

A strange calm suffused her and she put her hand in his, content to have him lead her home as though she herself had forgotten the route. Late that evening she placed the picture hat with its streaming ribbons in the bottom of her trunk, next to Yaakov's cambric shirt.

The next morning she went to Monroe Street, where a Hungarian woman maintained an improvised beauty salon in her apartment, and had the hair that she herself had viciously shorn with Shimon's cutting shears shaped into a sleek cap that curled smoothly about her head. She looked at herself in the mirror, registering the swift metamorphosis with relief and approval. She had emerged finally from a fierce struggle within a restraining cocoon of grief and achieved a quiet, heavyhearted acceptance of all that had come to pass.

Slowly, thoughts of the fire receded into a netherworld of shadowy pain, a world of gossamer memory through which Eli's strong and graceful form moved with purposeful certainty. Rosenblatt's factory never reopened and one evening in early fall,

Arnold Rosenblatt rented a room at the Astor Hotel, ordered two double scotches, drank them, and shot himself in the right temple. His suicide occurred two days before a municipal hearing into the causes of the fire, a hearing that resulted in legislation demanding fire safety precautions for all factories in the city.

That day the union paper carried a photograph of the courtyard cluttered with the bodies of the Rosenblatt workers and the solemn headline THEIR DEATHS WERE NOT IN VAIN. Leah stared for a long time at the front page of the paper which Bonnie Eckstein brought her, and then carefully cut the page loose and placed the clipping in a manila envelope where she kept letters from Europe and Palestine.

Gradually, the demands of day-to-day life encroached upon mood and memory. Shimon Hartstein's business, built on the bankruptcies that riddled the city, was thriving. Like an economic scavenger, Shimon darted from auction to bankruptcy sale, snatching up bolts of material, yards of thread, battered cartons of varied trimmings. He brought samples to Leah, who fingered the goods with practiced hands, draped a length of dark cloth into a fashionable calf-length skirt, and trimmed the waist with a strip of bright embroidered fabric, skillfully adding a pocket or a scarf to match. She easily translated the creation into tissue-paper patterns which were swiftly cut, sewn, and marketed under the label of "Fashions by S. Hart." It was Joshua Ellenberg who suggested the line drawing of a speeding hart as a trademark, and Leah sketched the graceful animal at the kitchen table one night while the children did their homework.

The simple line drawing was reproduced on labels and soon the small jobbers who sold to the larger stores were being asked for more styles bearing the hart insignia, and for the first time Shimon could suspend his juggling—he was receiving more checks than bills in the daily mail.

Now he no longer called himself Shimon Hartstein, but had become with painless ease Seymour Hart, and had renamed Malcha

Mollie. Chana and Yankele were now Anne and Jake, and the shy youngsters had suddenly become as Americanized as their names, as though a chimeric transformation had taken place. Chana and Yankele had clung to their mother's side like frightened children, still caught in the shadowy dangers of the *shtetl,* starting in fear at sudden noises, glancing nervously away from strangers, as though still entrapped in the loneliness and fear of their fatherless childhood in the Russian village where Jews lived their lives on the edge of terror. But Jake and Anne, he in store-bought knickers and jerseys, she in plaid pleated skirts and brightly colored blouses, were laughing youngsters who rocketed to popularity at school by treating their classmates to pretzels and egg creams. Sometimes Aaron, watching his cousins run gaily down Eldridge Street laden with brown paper bags of sweets, remembered the day they had arrived from Europe and stood shyly on the threshold of the apartment, each clutching a cloth sack from which the handles of worn pots protruded. He had liked his cousins better in those days, he thought, and always shrugged his shoulders and left the room when Jake, a good-natured boy, suggested that Aaron accompany them on their ritual Sunday afternoon excursions.

Rebecca occasionally joined the Hart family and returned with glowing tales of the golden dome of the Roxy theater where real stars twinkled. The seats in the theater were of red velvet, like the thrones of kings and queens, but she and Anne were particularly entranced with the ladies' room, which they visited several times during each film.

"Mama, the floors are marble and when you wash your hands you don't even need a towel. There's a special machine that breathes hot air and dries you," the child reported. David, studying at the dining room table, looked up and his eyes and Leah's locked in shared amusement.

Often during those months such moments passed between them. An understanding stretch of calm sheltered them as they shared quiet laughter or lengths of comfortable silence during which he studied and she worked at her drawing board while in the next room Aaron and Joshua Ellenberg played chess. When it happened that they were alone in the apartment and she made tea and brought the steaming glass to him, the small service made his heart rise in sweet contentment.

They were alone there one Sunday afternoon, a grim day when lamps had been lit in the early afternoon, creating small islands of light in the room suffused with wintry grayness. They had done their separate work while the radio played, Caruso's tender voice lulling them into a mood of melancholy nostalgia. Leah looked up from her drawing board and was startled to see that the colorless sky was suddenly soft with graceful domes of drifting pink clouds, laced with threads of fading gold. She switched off her lamp and went to the window, where she stood watching a slow darkness descend and, with shadowy ease, swallow the gentle clouds. As she watched, she heard David's soft step behind her and he stood beside her, his arm lightly touching hers.

Together, in the fading light that brushed their faces with soft-toned shadows, they watched the pink-gold sunset reluctantly surrender to darkness. They turned to each other then and David bent his head gently and kissed her on the lips. She raised her arms and placed them on his shoulders, pulling him closer to her, feeling his heart pump wildly against her breast. Again their lips met, this time with a fierce urgency, and his arms pressed tightly across her yielding body. The window was black with darkness and they turned from it, arms linked, as though having come together at last, they were now fearful of losing touch. Slowly, in the dark familiar bedroom where they had shared so many years of nights, together but alone, they undressed each other, their hands traversing each other's body with sensate wonder, newly discovering the mysteries of the flesh they had known so well.

He came into her with a force and strength for which she was unprepared but which her body welcomed with fierce acceptance, rising and falling in rhythm to the urgency of his love, until together they soared and wept in fulfillment and fell back in exhausted wonder.

They slept then, drowsing contentedly through the early evening hours as the apartment beyond their closed door filled with noise and light, with laughter and bustle. Their bodies entwined, they stirred luxuriously, murmured careless answers to the knock that came at last to their door, and when they emerged to join the family at the table, their cheeks burned and their eyes were soft. Across the room, Sarah Ellenberg and Mollie Hart smiled at each other with secret knowledge and the men became suddenly boisterous and teased the children, who giggled in wild freedom. All who sat around that communal table, laden with its weekend meal of cheeses and sour cream sparkling with vegetables, and bright-red borscht in which fragments of emerald-green scallions floated, were suffused with a sense of relief, as though an uncertain battle had at last been resolved.

Four months later Leah was pregnant with Michael, and the day she slipped on her first maternity dress, a blue-and-white checked shift which she designed and made herself (causing Seymour Hart to visualize a full line of maternity clothing), David came dashing up the stairs.

"I've been accepted. In the fall I begin the medical school at Downstate!"

Like a small boy overwhelmed with the enormity of his good fortune, he pulled Leah to her feet and whirled her around the room in a dance of unrestrained joy. They were still dancing, the stiff white letter of acceptance clenched in David's teeth, when the children arrived home from school. Rebecca, Anne, and Jake joined them in that frenzied dervish spinning, and even Joshua allowed a few minutes of business to be lost as he too grasped hands and tapped out rhythms of joy. Only Aaron stood shyly by, watching, although his coppery curls bobbed up and down in tune to the music and his eyes followed his mother's light steps with heavy wistfulness. But it was David who drew him into the circle finally, so that moving with awkward self-consciousness, he joined for a few minutes the spontaneous outbreak of joy. Then the widow in the apartment below banged with righteous fury on the water pipes and the dance was ended.

Exhausted, Leah sank into a chair and remembered with a sadness the summer evening when the Rosenblatt workers had danced to the music of the radio. The widow had banged on the pipes that evening too, but days after the fire she had waited for Leah on the steps, her eyes red with worry and regret.

"I'm sorry for stopping the party that night," she said. "How was I to know?"

She could not have known, of course, that for some of those dancers, the music they swayed to that night was the last music they would ever hear. She would not have denied them that respite of joy had she known that the next day their laughter would be frozen into screams of terror and the little young limbs would be scarred and mutilated. But now, months later, that regret had been forgotten and she knew only the irritation of the moment. Grimly, she protested the sounds of joy, pounding her broomstick against the metal pipes, drowning out the music that violated and emphasized the silence of her loneliness.

Seymour Hart read the letter of acceptance carefully and beamed at the assembled family as though David's achievement were his own. With his new prosperity had come a sense of omnipotence over the lives of his family and he smiled benignly at Jake's report cards, at the sound of Anne's off-key violin, at Aaron's intricately constructed model airplanes. It was as though his financial success had made everything possible, and insured the fulfillment of their talents.

S. Hart and Company had expanded and moved into new quarters and then had taken over a large factory as business continued to increase. Seymour acknowledged that the company's success was as much the result of Leah's talent as of his own shrewdness. Leah worked at home but she was listed on the payroll as a designer and each week her brother-in-law issued her a generous salary check. Occasionally she went down to the factory to supervise, but when she could not, pink-cheeked Bonnie Eckstein, who was Seymour's forelady, came up to the apartment and she and Leah together worked out problems in piecework on Leah's designs. They never spoke of the days at Rosenblatts or of the fire, although Leah knew that beneath the ring on Bonnie Eckstein's right hand lay a curling rim of scarred flesh where a spiraling flash of flame had eaten the skin through to the milk-white knuckle.

"Listen, we must celebrate. It's not every day that a greenhorn gets to study for a doctor, even in the United States of America. Let us go out this Sunday," Seymour suggested.

"No. You go with the children. David and I have work to do," Leah protested, smilingly avoiding her husband's eye.

Very little work got done during those weekend afternoons when the apartment was empty. More often than not, she and David, like guilty young lovers shyly searching out a secret place of privacy, would wait until the door shut behind the family and then fly into each other's arms. Like carefree honeymooners, they played house in the apartment which was their home. They teased each other away from work, each surrendering to the other's mood, whispering and laughing through the long afternoon of love and relishing the luxury of falling into easy sleep, their naked bodies pressed together, while in the street below children played and men and women shouted idle weekend pleasantries to each other.

Usually, as though by tacit understanding, no one even suggested that David and Leah join the Harts on their Sunday excursions, but this time Seymour was insistent.

"It's not to the Roxy that we're going or even Radio City. This is something special I want you to see with your own eyes."

Reluctantly, then, David and Leah joined the outing and dutifully followed Seymour and Mollie to the subway where they boarded the Brighton express and rode it almost to the end of the line. On the Brighton Beach station, they sniffed the sweet freshness of the salt air and craned their necks to see the ocean from the elevated platform.

It was late spring but Brighton Beach Avenue was already electric with a holiday atmosphere. Young couples, their towels and swimming costumes tucked into small wicker valises, trailed through the streets, eating potato knishes wrapped in greasy waxed paper and gashed with wounds of golden mustard. Seymour bought pink clouds of cotton candy for each of the children and carelessly dropped the change into the outstretched cannister of a young woman who walked slowly down the street holding a small boy, his feet wrapped in rags.

"Everyone makes promises but still there are children who go barefoot," David murmured and looked sadly after the woman.

"Soon. This Depression must finally be over soon," she replied.

"With the help of God," he said and abruptly turned and walked after the woman, quietly pressing a dollar bill into her outstretched hand.

The little group followed Seymour's decisive lead as he turned up Brighton Eighth Street and crossed two long avenue blocks. At Ocean View Avenue, where small multifamily red brick houses replaced the string of apartment buildings typical of the area, he stopped in front of a three-family red brick house girdled by a wide porch.

"A nice house, eh?" he said and his white teeth gleamed beneath his thick moustache.

His wife Mollie smiled proudly up at him. With chameleonic ease, Leah's sister assumed the protective coloring necessary for each changing segment of her life. In turn, she had been the dutiful daughter, the shy bride, and the stoically patient wife. Now she was the prosperous matron whose husband showed ambition and foresight, initiative and responsibility. As though to meet the demands of this role, her body had expanded. A wider girth was necessary if she were to exude the proper pride. Her white satin blouse stretched too tight across her full heavy breasts and her blue shantung skirt twitched importantly as she marched beside her husband.

"It's a very nice house," David agreed cautiously.

"By subway only two blocks to the medical college for you and fifty minutes to the factory for me. Two blocks away is a fine public school. A half a mile away is Coney Island Hospital. And all around nice synagogues, Hebrew schools, good shopping. Perfect for us." Again Seymour beamed.

The children were already scrambling about on the porch and Joshua Ellenberg had wandered out to the backyard, which he was measuring step by step. But Leah and David remained looking quietly at each other and then at the red brick house.

"What do you mean—perfect for us?" Leah asked finally, and Seymour, like a magician who has been waiting for his cue, reached into his pocket and flashed a key at them.

"It's ours. That is, so far, mine and Mollie's, and if you want to come in for a share—good—and if you want to rent from us the apartment—also good. I got it cheap. Six thousand dollars with only a thousand down. On auction."

"A foreclosure?" David asked grimly. The small lawn was bordered with bright tulips and he thought of the people who had planted the bulbs, planning for years to come. They had lost the house and the sweet promise of their planting.

"All right, so it was a foreclosure. Look, I don't want to make money on someone else's misfortunes, but someone else would buy if I didn't. Why shouldn't we have a little luck? We didn't work hard enough? We didn't wander long enough in the desert? Why shouldn't our children breathe the air from the sea? Tell me—it's a crime to do a little better for yourself?" Impatiently spitting out answers to questions they had not asked, he pulled out a fat cigar and turned from them to look up at the red brick house with the secret satisfaction of new ownership.

Leah turned to David and nodded. He too looked up at the small brick home again and its uncurtained windows stared down at him like strangely vacant eyes. As he watched, a seagull swooped lazily down, hovered above them for a moment, then rocketed skyward, shooting toward the ocean.

"For you the best apartment—the one with the porch. Mollie wants it to be easy for Leah to put the baby out," Seymour said cajolingly.

Leah felt the growing life within her stir and stretch against the walls of her womb. How wonderful it would be to pick up a small cosseted bundle of newborn child and settle it in the sunlight of an easily accessible porch. She remembered the small containers David had fashioned for Aaron and Rebecca during their infancies on Eldridge Street. Oversized wooden boxes were lined with pillows and comforters and cautiously balanced on the fire escape while Leah hovered over the window to shield the sleeping children from stray cats. Then they could not afford even a secondhand baby carriage and the fire escape was the babies' only source of sun and air.

Leah remembered how her neighbor, poor Yetta Moskowitz, had murmured one day, "For the poor even air is expensive." Yetta Moskowitz, a casualty of poverty, deserted by her husband and killed by her own despair. Her children, farmed out to relatives, still attended classes at the settlement house and Charles Ferguson had told Leah that the oldest Moskowitz boy was an evening student at the City College. In this solid brick house, with the breeze strong from the ocean blowing toward them, they would be insulated from the miseries of the Yetta Moskowitzes. Leah wondered what it would be like, after a dozen years of boarders and shared kitchens and bathrooms, to live alone in rooms that belonged only to their family, to know the privacy of a closed door which would not be thrust suddenly open, and the sweet aloneness of preparing a meal just for her own husband and children.

"What do you say, Leah?" Mollie asked, and there was a nervous shyness in her voice which Leah found reassuringly familiar. She did not want her sister Malcha, dutiful and shy, to be swallowed by this buxom Mollie who laughed too loudly and wore clothes of a rainbow brightness.

Impulsively she clutched her sister's hand.

"I say fine," she said. "And the third apartment will be for the Ellenbergs?"

"Who else?" Seymour glowed with his own munificence and flicked the long, delicate gray ash of his cigar onto the grass, grinding it slowly in. He enjoyed taking charge of other people's lives, of charting their destinies and reaping satisfaction from their achievements. What he had helped make possible he harvested as his own.

"The rent they'll be able to afford and Sarah will finally have her own place. Enough talk. Let's see the inside."

Three weeks later, on Aaron's eleventh birthday, they left the apartment on Eldridge Street for the last time. They watched as their possessions were loaded on to the moving van—the pots and pans packed in the same barrels that had accompanied them from Russia, still bearing the faded green and white tags of the Oceanic Steamship Line. The tenement-house stoop was lined with women and children who shouted out words of advice and encouragement and whose eyes followed the laden van with glances of wistful hope. Leah, her hand resting on Rebecca's dark hair, peered through the window of the hired car as it wove its way through the teeming east side streets, swerving to avoid a lumbering pushcart peddler, the driver shouting an angry curse at three yeshiva boys who dashed across the street, their earlocks flying. The car passed the Irvington Settlement House where posters announcing a summer lecture series were being hung, sped past the charred hulk of the building that had once housed Rosenblatt and Sons. The branches of the ailanthus tree were bare and the earth at its base was black with necrotic soot.

"We are doing the right thing," David had whispered to her, his eyes following her own to the gutted skeleton of the building where she and Eli Feinstein had stood suspended above flame and death.

And it had been the right thing, she thought now. She smiled down at wiggling, laughing Michael, her merry child born to this new beginning, soothed by the sea breezes and the distant crashing of weary waves against the shore. The two years in the red brick house had been rich and peaceful, banishing the past into penumbral memories. A new prosperity was slowly wafting its way through the land. The eagle of the National Relief Administration hung over every machine in their factory, and in Mollie and Seymour's living room a framed color photograph of the newly elected president, Franklin Delano Roosevelt, smiled down at them. Freshly painted banks had reopened their doors and men walked with new purpose.

"Will you be good in synagogue today? You don't want to ruin Aaron's bar mitzvah, do you?" Leah playfully asked squirming Michael.

The child chortled and sprang up, thrusting his fat little fingers through his mother's sleek dark hair and hugging her hips with his own fleshy small thighs.

*

Aaron Goldfeder glanced nervously around the crowded synagogue, the silk of the new prayer shawl his father had given him that morning cool against his neck. Nervously he fingered its fringes and felt in his pocket for the crisp folded pages of his speech. He mouthed the morning prayers dutifully while the incantations of the prophetic reading, which would be his responsibility during the service, trilled through his mind. Next to him his father intoned the prayers without looking at the prayer book, swaying to the intoned cadence with the habit of centuries.

"God, full of mercy," David Goldfeder's strong voice rang out and Aaron thought of how his father had stared moodily at the newspaper that very morning, somberly studying a picture of Hitler's brownshirted troops striding toward the Reichstag.

"Now they are marching. Soon they'll be killing. Leah, we must write again to your family. They must leave Europe."

"David, David, Hitler's in Germany. My family is in Russia." Leah had been disinterested, all her concentration focused on feeding Michael without letting him soil the light-blue outfit which Mollie had knit for the bar mitzvah.

"His river of blood will cross Europe," David replied bitterly.

But now, in synagogue, his voice rose to full strength. "God of compassion and healing," he sang, and Aaron wondered how his father who predicted rivers of blood could pray to a God of compassion.

In the pews behind Aaron the congregation murmured and swayed and he heard his sister Rebecca's giggle through the yellowing gauze curtain that separated the men from the women in this small seaside synagogue. He was grateful for the thin gossamer barrier because it shielded him from his mother's eyes, from the worried sweep of her deep stare that settled upon him, sometimes for minutes at a time. What was there about him, after all, that caused his own mother to focus on him with fear and bewilderment? When he was a small boy, absorbed in a game of chess or blocks, he would suddenly feel her eyes heavy on his bent back, as though her stare were possessed of visceral strength. He would continue to play, pretending that she was not there, studying his every motion and gesture. Sometimes in his sleep he felt her eyes upon him and wakened to find her staring down at him, a naked question puzzling her own dark eyes.

Once, months ago, he had asked his father about it, choosing a moment when David Goldfeder had laid his heavy medical texts aside for a moment and was carefully filling a pipe.

"Papa," the boy said hesitantly, carefully choosing the words he had mentally rehearsed, "sometimes Mama stares at me in such a funny way. Sometimes I think she doesn't even like me."

He could not look at his father but stared at the patterned rug, relieved that he had thrust the thought from his mind, allowed the words to be heard.

But David Goldfeder had not been shocked. He had looked thoughtfully at the boy who had always been just a bit too thin, whose coppery curls burned brightly on days of sunlight and gleamed with burnished splendor even in the grim light of winter. David reached out with a gentle finger and affectionately traced the line of freckles that ran from Aaron's nose to the crease of his green eyes which had always been too serious for a child.

"Your mama likes you—she loves you. It is just that she has had a hard life. Many bad things, terrible things happened to her, and sometimes people who have suffered have moods and feel sad when they remember too much. Perhaps when she looks at you like that, she is thinking of Yaakov, the man who gave you life, just as I have given you love. Such a memory may make her sad. You are a big boy, Aaron, with a big heart. Try to understand your mother."

David's dark eyes caressed the boy and he placed an arm in brief embrace about Aaron's shoulders. But his own answer did not satisfy him. He too had felt the brooding wondering of Leah's gaze as she looked at her son.

Aaron turned now and looked about the synagogue, smiling shyly at the familiar faces of those who had assembled to pay tribute to his passage into manhood. There were the old boarders who had shared his childhood—Label Katz the hatter, and little Mr. Morgenstern whose trimming store had kept Aaron provided with wooden spools to be fashioned into miniature soldiers or building blocks. Morgenstern's wife Pearl, another former boarder, sat with his mother in the women's section. Pearl had been a thin young woman, her pale skin almost colorless and her voice so soft that the other girls, especially Masha who had gone to California after his aunt Mollie had come from Europe, taunted her and asked her to repeat everything. But the woman who had kissed him that morning was portly, with packets of flesh dangling from her arms, and her small eyes were almost lost in the small mounds of pink flesh which were her cheeks. One child toddled at her side, she held an infant in her arms, and her body curved with the fullness of a new pregnancy. The Morgensterns had arrived in a large maroon

Chevrolet car and she had announced in a loud voice that Mr. Morgenstern was doing well, very well. The small shopkeeper seemed to have grown even smaller but his new suit was well cut and his feet were encased in shoes of burnished leather that captured the morning sunlight.

Just behind Mr. Morgenstern, Aaron saw Charles Ferguson, who taught art at the Irvington Settlement House and who had never come to visit the apartment on Eldridge Street without bringing Aaron a book, knowing with mysterious accuracy just when Aaron's interest had drifted from the Hardy boys to Robert Louis Stevenson and Daniel Defoe. Mr. Ferguson wore a beard now, a smooth blond growth threaded with silver, which he stroked now and again. Aaron touched his own chin and was comforted by the small, almost imperceptible hint of fuzz that met his exploring fingers.

David Goldfeder touched the boy's wrist lightly, fondly, motioning him to pay attention to the services. The cantor, a small, wizened man from whom a powerful tenor voice sprang forth with amazing strength, was summoning the bar mitzvah boy with the vibrant ancient melody to which all the men in the congregation had responded in their time.

"Let Aaron, the son of David ben Levi, of the tribe of Levi, approach the Torah. Behold how the son of the holy Commandments, the bar mitzvah, is summoned!" The cantillation rang with the strength of centuries and Aaron Goldfeder rose and slowly ascended the platform.

He stood for a moment before the open Torah scroll and watched its graceful bright-black letters dance before him, almost leaping upward from the yellowed sheet of parchment. The sun poured in from the window beyond the ark and settled on his bright hair. Crowned with warmth, he lifted the fringes of his prayer shawl, kissed them, and placed them on a corner of the open scroll. Softly at first he chanted the blessing over the Torah and then his voice rose in new strength as he sang the prophetic portion he had rehearsed week after week in the cantor's tiny office, with its pervasive odor of throat lozenges and camphored ceremonial garments.

His voice gathered strength and he sang the words of the prophet Amos: "Seek good and not evil that ye may live—thus spake the Lord of Hosts..."

The congregation sighed and the boy continued: "Hate the evil and love the good..." but before he could continue with the Prophet's exhortation, his throat rebelled. The voice which moments before had been the sweet tones of a boy had suddenly erupted into the depth of a man's tremulous tenor, and it was in the voice of a man that Aaron Goldfeder sang the concluding verse: "It may be that the Lord God of hosts will be gracious unto the remnant of Joseph."

The boy's face was red and there was a murmuring and chuckling throughout the congregation. The cantor patted him approvingly on his shoulder. It often happened, in the family of Israel, that a child's voice became that of a man on the Sabbath of his bar mitzvah, and it was considered good luck. David Goldfeder, his face glowing with pride, ascended the platform, embraced his son, and together they concluded the service.

In the women's section, Leah sat quietly, Michael at last asleep on her lap, and acknowledged the flow of "Mazel tovs" that rippled around her. She was swathed in a sweet serenity that had settled upon her as Aaron's voice trembled into manhood. The timbre of his new voice was a familiar echo that carried her back across the years to that distant day in Odessa when Yaakov had stood beside her beneath the wedding canopy and lifted his voice to sing the marriage vows.

"Behold thou art consecrated unto me according to the laws of Moses and of Israel," he had sung to her as they stood sheltered beneath the outstretched prayer shawl.

Now she was hearing that voice again, and she lifted a corner of the gauze curtain so that she might see her son's bright hair, burnished amber in light as his father's had been on their wedding morning. Familiar, too, was the curve of his back in the new navy-blue suit. Finally, in the moment of his new manhood, she had unraveled the mystery of his conception.

9

David Goldfeder had always loved the earliest hours of morning, when the first fresh segments of dawn, laced with the gentle quiet of a world still largely asleep, broke through the night. As a medical student it had been his favorite time to study and during his residency he had never objected being on call while others slept. Now, four years after Aaron's bar mitzvah, as a practicing physician, he still nurtured his fondness for the hours of the morning's sweet nascence. He cherished boyhood memories of morning walks when he wove his way through the tall and slender trees that lifted themselves defiantly against the wind and watched the darkness of their leaves slowly fade as the lights of morning revealed their fragile greenery. The little forest hut that had been his home must be deserted now. His brother, for whom his son Aaron was named, was dead; his sisters were scattered, and his parents lay buried in the small Jewish cemetery, not far from the grave of Chana Rivka with whom he had so often walked beneath those slender trees.

"I remember the trees more clearly than I do their faces. I can see the crippled stump of a giant pine that fell during a winter storm. Wet green moss had covered it, growing in the shape of a hand—a four-fingered hand. That I can see, but I cannot remember the color of my mother's eyes or the sound of Chana Rivka's voice," he had cried out during the psychoanalysis that was part of his training as a psychiatrist.

"But that is natural," his analyst had replied. "The forest is a symbol. The growing trees and the fallen one are also symbols. Think of them. See their shadows. Watch them sway and tremble, blossom and shed."

The gentle voice, belonging to the esteemed Dr. Simonsohn who had trained with Freud himself in Vienna, was quiet but insistent, and hour after hour, year after year, David had obeyed its gentle urging, sometimes with his fists clenched in anger, sometimes with tears coursing unnoticed down his cheeks.

With Dr. Simonsohn, David had discussed Leah's love for Eli Feinstein and his own feelings about it, buried for so long in an underbrush of shame and pain. He flushed them out slowly, painfully, and confronted them, in the emotional clearing his analysis had created.

"I hated him. Without even knowing him I hated him—and wished him vanished or dead. And I had no right to. We had made a bargain in Odessa, Leah and myself, and nowhere in that bargain had we talked of love. Comfort and sustenance, yes. Companionship, yes. But not love. I came to love her but I knew that her feelings remained unchanged. Perhaps I should have spoken. Perhaps if I had told her then of my love, courted her, and won her, she and Feinstein would never have become involved. Why didn't I tell her? Why couldn't I tell her?"

"You could not take the risk just then. You were afraid of losing her," Dr. Simonsohn said quietly. "Revelation must rest on some guarantee. You had none. So you remained silent."

"I hated him," David said in a low dead tone.

"Hate. What is hate? Another word for anger unreconciled. You are allowed your angers, David Goldfeder. You have a right to them. Face them. Allow them to percolate. Then they will not simmer and condense into that hatred you so despise."

Like warm water across an open wound, the words soothed him, and in the weeks and months that followed he talked more of that time, at last allowing his fear to flow freely and evaporate, while the smoke of Dr. Simonsohn's inevitable English cigarette drifted in gray clouds through the quiet room. From then on, slowly, the layers of bewilderment and terror peeled away until the day he left Dr. Simonsohn's office for the last time.

Now Dr. David Goldfeder strode briskly through silent streets barely silvered by the slowly rising sun, on his way to his first patient of the day, ready to take his own seat in the deep leather chair and watch and help as his analysand lay rigid in the couch and wandered through that wondrous forest of fear and feeling.

It was very early for an analytic hour: seven o'clock. In order to be at his office that early he had awakened in a heavy darkness. Leah, deeply asleep beside him, had not even stirred as he padded softly about the room, dressing. Of course, she had worked very late the previous evening and had still been bent over her drawing board when he closed his book and commented on the lateness of the hour.

"You go to sleep. I've only just got an idea. I've been playing about with it for days and now, suddenly, I see the whole thing clearly," she said and sent her pencil racing across the sheet in front of her.

"Why is it, Doctor, that I get my best ideas near midnight?" Leah asked playfully.

"Psychoanalysts have had little success in dealing with the secrets of the creative mind," he answered seriously. Like a priest committed to a demanding religion, he too worshiped his discipline and was unable to approach any aspect of it with humor. It was a dangerous tendency, and he had been warned against it by both Dr. Simonsohn and his friend and teacher Peter Cosgrove. He recognized it but still was unable to combat it.

"I would make a guess," he offered, "that at this hour, your mind is free of worry about the children and the house and you can focus more easily on your work."

"Yes, perhaps," she murmured, but he saw that she was totally involved in the drawing now and scarcely listening to him. Smiling, he passed his hand through the sleek dark cap of her hair, kissed her pale neck, and went to bed alone.

He could scarcely resent Leah's absorption in her work, he knew; it was that work which had made it possible for him to complete his medical studies. For years Leah had been the able breadwinner of the family, and thanks to her artistic ability and

Seymour's business acumen, the fortunes of S. Hart Inc. were soaring.

"Look, now I don't pay for advertising. My customers wear my ads," Seymour chortled jovially, referring to the hart trademark designed by Leah and soon the streaking hart was emblazoned on shirts and jackets, blouses and tennis costumes.

Banks had been swift to offer Seymour Hart the necessary loans for expansion, and he juggled large sums of money with the same dexterity he had displayed in the days on Eldridge Street when he used a borrowed bolt of cloth as collateral to pay a trimming manufacturer.

The Hart family had adjusted easily to the new prosperity. Mollie covered her entire apartment in deep-gold wall-to-wall-carpeting. Gilt-framed landscapes hung above her royal blue satin couch and she installed a false fireplace with an electric log that glowed rosily when a switch was pressed. She and Seymour slept on an enormous bed beneath a carved headboard facing a matching double bureau.

"It's beginning to look like Versailles there," David remarked wryly after a Friday evening visit to the Harts.

The Goldfeder home, too, reflected the new prosperity, but in their living room the polished wood floor gleamed beneath woven area rugs and the furniture was simple and neutral, punctuated only with brightly colored cushions. Their living room was dominated by David's large desk and Leah's drawing board.

After all the years of cramped living on Eldridge Street, the Brighton Beach house still felt luxurious to them, but Mollie Hart had already begun to speak disparagingly about the red brick house. It was too small. There was no need for them to live on top of each other. She talked longingly of places like Long Island and Westchester.

"After all, a doctor, a specialist, needs a good address," she told David when he completed his residency.

"Why? Where he lives adds to his qualifications?" he asked joshingly, always feeling a bit sorry for his wife's sister who had never claimed the right to plan her own life. With stoic acceptance she had rowed on in the random streams of her experience. As the wife of Shimon Hartstein, a poor man, she had diligently lived the life of a poor man's wife. As Mrs. Seymour Hart, married to a wealthy manufacturer, she moved into the role of a comfortable matron, obsessed with her home, her children's teeth (both Anne and Jake clamped their lips tightly shut against gleaming braces), and her own bright wardrobe.

"Why should my Seymour travel on the subway? From the suburbs he could drive, take a comfortable train," Mollie argued.

Neither David nor Leah chose to mention the fact that Seymour Hart spent very little time in the house on Ocean View Avenue. More and more frequently he found reasons for staying in the city, and he arrived home later and later when he arrived at all. Only that morning, David, leaving the house at dawn to meet his seven A.M. patient, had met his brother-in-law arriving home, his expensive suit rumpled, his eyes rimmed with an angry redness, his breath sour with whiskey.

"Very late conference. Out-of-town buyers," he muttered to David. "Listen, try to come home early tonight. I want to talk to you about something important."

David had nodded and now, walking toward his office, he wondered what it was that Seymour had on his mind, but when he reached the door of his consulting room, with professional precision he cleared his mind of all thoughts of his family, ran his fingers across the nameplate on his door as though still in need of reassurance that he was indeed David Goldfeder, M.D., and settled himself behind his desk to begin his long day's work.

During the early morning and late afternoon and evening hours, David saw his analytic patients. The rest of the day he spent at the large municipal hospital, not far from his office, passing from the frenetic, turbulent ambience of emergency admitting rooms to the insulated calm of the small consulting cubicles where he examined the miseries and emotional agonies of the city's poor. After two years of practice he still could not decide which aspect of his work he found more rewarding.

"I'm a professional schizophrenic," he complained to Peter Cosgrove.

"No," Peter replied, with academic certainty, "the work may be different but the struggle is the same."

Peter Cosgrove—tall and lean, whose family lived on the Connecticut side of Long Island Sound, who twice a year, in spring and fall, went into J. Press and bought his narrow rep ties and blazers and slacks, choosing only different colors, slightly darker than those he had chosen as an undergraduate at Princeton and during graduate school at Brown—it was Peter Cosgrove, confident enough of his own gifts, freed by his family's wealth and acceptance of the petty competitiveness typical of early academic life, who as a psychology professor at City College had spotted David Goldfeder's gifts. Now his student, the immigrant pants presser, surpassed his own knowledge, and Cosgrove proudly viewed David's achievements while continuing to offer encouragement and reassurance. Like his Phi Beta Kappa key, his doctoral dissertation, and his academic rank, Dr. David Goldfeder was included among his achievements. A rare friendship and appreciation existed between the two men, who spoke to each other with the complete freedom of those who have come from totally different worlds.

Peter was right, David had acknowledged. The struggle continued to be against those implacable enemies of the spirit—hatred and violence bred of ignorance and despair. Their dark shadow had clung to him from the bloodstained streets of Odessa to this calm, neutral consulting room where he sat patiently in his leather chair and listened to patients set their fears and feelings afloat in the room's dim light.

Jeffrey Coleman, David's seven-o'clock patient, arrived ten minutes late, but neither he nor David commented on the time lost.

Only a few months earlier, Jeffrey, a young black physics student at Columbia University, would have arrived even later, and often he had not arrived at all.

"Five minutes late—five minutes' hate," David thought, leaning back and waiting for Jeffrey to break the silence.

That silence was both their enemy and their weapon. Draped in its protective folds, Jeffrey had remained mute and constrained, sunk deep into the depression that was paralyzing his academic progress and frightening those professors who recognized his unusual gifts. A fund raised by those same professors was making the expensive analysis possible and while it was an unusual enterprise, Jeffrey Coleman was an unusual case.

He was a Southern black who had startled his Northern high school teachers with record-breaking scores on mathematical achievement tests. A Westinghouse winner, he was admitted to Columbia on a full scholarship and completed two academic years in one, and then suddenly became unable to study. In a waking sleep he attended lectures, but the equations and theories which he had handled with such ease had become meaningless to him. More dangerously, he slept very little and had almost no communication with those around him. He was indifferent to threats that his scholarship was in danger, and David found it difficult to understand how the boy had been persuaded to see him—a small subconscious streak of self-preservation, he guessed, although Jeffrey claimed he had come just to shut the professors up.

Still, they had struggled through the silence. Then, in the terrible quiet of the Manhattan consulting room, tales of Southern nights had unfolded—nights when men wearing hooded sheets careened through narrow streets, shattering windows and tossing fiery torches through doors of rooms where small black children crouched in fear and trembling. Scattered images, memories so masked with fantasy that they had to be sorted and scrutinized, dusted with fragments of dreams and pierced with sudden insights. Memories of blood and shouting and a mother's dark thighs suddenly exposed, kicking upward, twisting against the fierce thrust of the hooded man's purple throbbing penis, etched in the small boy's mind as a pale bloodied club. That remembered terror had festered within the child's secret thoughts.

David remembered the morning when that memory had at last been wrested forth. He remembered how Jeffrey's shoulders had quaked with relief and how he had rested afterward, suffused with a silent calm. The boy was almost well now, David thought. Perhaps he might even begin to arrive on time for his analytic hour, he mused wryly, as Jeffrey raised himself on an elbow and talked freely now, his brief battle against the silence won.

The newspapers that morning had carried the story of the newest Scottsboro trial and there had been a photograph of one of the young Negroes accused of the cardinal sin of the South—the sexual violation of a white woman. Even David, familiar with the case, his own contribution to the defense fund twice repeated, was shocked by the youth of the black boy in his overalls whose large bewildered eyes stared out of the front page of the Times. The accused was only a child in a striped T-shirt who, like Aaron, should be dashing out to a softball field after school, his arms raised high to catch a soaring ball, not manacled together in cruel handcuffs.

Jeffrey Coleman talked about that picture now, his hand clenching into a fist and unclenching so that the skin beneath his fingers turned pale ocher and became newly dark as the angry blood was pumped forward and then released.

"All of us, growing up down there, had the feeling that maybe it would be us who would end up in a white man's jail. You know, when I looked at this kid in the paper, I was sorry for him and glad it wasn't me. It's like we were born with a shadow, a kind of fear that followed us everywhere, warning us and scaring us. I remember when we first came up north I used to sit on the subway with my eyes down because down there if you looked at a white woman they could get you for the thoughts you weren't thinking. You wouldn't know about that kind of being afraid, Dr. Goldfeder."

"Yes I would," David replied softly.

The young man looked back in surprise. It was unusual for Dr. Goldfeder to offer an answer or an admission.

"I too have lived in that kind of fear," David said. He was breaking an important rule of Freudian analysis—revealing himself to his patient—but he sensed that it was important for Jeffrey Coleman to know that he was neither isolated nor unique. It was easy to understand Jeffrey's relief that it was not his picture of agonized pain in print. With stricken clarity David remembered looking down at his brother Aaron's body, hearing of Yaakov's death, and through the blindness of his grief, growing heavy with guilt at the knowledge of his relief that he, at least, was alive. What a fellowship of pain and guilt he shared with young Jeffrey. Was it that same fellowship that had sent a Jewish lawyer with a Russian name hurrying to the South to defend the black boys?

Aloud, his voice controlled and gentle but his accent more pronounced than usual, he said, "Jeffrey, all men live on the edge of a terror they do not understand. Some, the ignorant and impoverished, focus that terror on those who are different, who cause them uneasiness and fear. It is from such angry terror that lynchings come and also pogroms. For such men, for such frightened, ignorant men, the violence is a purge. If you cannot forgive them—and that I know is very difficult and perhaps too much to ask—try at least to understand."

The boy on the couch relaxed and the silence that hovered between them now was a quiet, comfortable one, broken only when David softly reminded his patient that the hour was over. They shook hands at the door, a habit of David's after each analytic hour, but this time the handclasp was not mere ritual.

David placed his other hand over the boy's outstretched palm so that for a moment Jeffrey's fingers were sandwiched between his two hands in a tender manual embrace.

"Thanks, Doc," Jeffrey said and left swiftly.

David stared after him. They had traveled such different routes—he and his young black patient. But the same tenacious shades had pursued them both. There was no great difference between the stricken streets of Odessa and the dusty roads of Jeffrey's Alabama hamlet. The doctor shivered with the memory of Chana Rivka's battered body and the patient writhed as he recalled his mother's rape. Doctor and patient would live with these memories the rest of their lives.

Lynchings, pogroms, and now the rantings of the little corporal in Germany. Adolf Hitler's picture had appeared in the column next to the story of the Scottsboro boys, and David, in a brief respite between patients, took up the newspaper again and looked at the black boy's luminous fear-filled eyes and the Austrian agitator's face, screwed into an angry mask of hatred. A familiar sadness settled on him and he folded the paper neatly and placed it with practiced control in his wastepaper basket.

The rest of the day passed swiftly for David. Patients came and went. He had lunch at the hospital and as he ate, he glanced through Lancet, a British medical journal, and noted that the Psychoanalytic Association of Great Britain had offered a formal welcome to the eminent Viennese physician Sigmund Freud. There was no mention of the fact that the father of psychoanalysis, ill with cancer of the jaw, was virtually being forced out of his native land by the Nazi Party.

"Look, how the blind send away the only sighted person in their midst," David said, showing the magazine to Peter Cosgrove, who had unexpectedly found himself downtown and sought David out.

"Well, perhaps they don't think they're all that blind or he's all that sighted," Peter replied. "Perhaps we're getting an exaggerated picture of what's happening over there. Maybe it's not all that bad."

"No, it's not all that bad," David said dryly. "It's worse. Look, Peter, Hitler came into power in thirty-three. Think of what he's accomplished in less than four years. He's done a marvelous job of stirring up the German people. Are we just to sit and wait for that to happen and say 'maybe it's not all that bad'?"

"Aren't you being a bit extreme—even a little paranoid on the subject?" Peter asked.

"I haven't been practicing psychiatry long but I have discovered one thing. Every paranoid I've encountered has a medically acceptable reason for his disease. I think, Peter, I have a historically acceptable reason for mine."

Peter did not answer, and as the two men sat silently drinking their coffee, each locked into thoughts separate from the other, a young woman moved toward them across the room. She stopped a white-jacketed intern, asked him a question, and followed his finger as he pointed to the table where Peter and David sat. Swiftly she made her way across the crowded cafeteria, and tapped David on the shoulder.

"Bonnie," he said in surprise. "What are you doing here?"

Bonnie Eckstein smiled and he thought that she had grown amazingly pretty, remembering her from the days at Rosenblatts when her eyes were haunted with worry and her small form stooped from the long hours at the machines. Now her eyes were bright with excitement. As Leah's assistant at S. Hart she had an exciting job for a young woman, and she moved with the easy confidence and grace of those who are secure in their own achievements and abilities. Her skin was still very pale but she had learned to dress in delicate colors that turned her pallor into a subtle asset. Today she wore a pale yellow dress and her fine light hair was scooped up into a French knot from which a few graceful tendrils teasingly escaped, licking her long white neck.

"Leah knew I was going to be in this area picking up some fabric samples and she asked me to drop by and remind you to try to get home early tonight. She tried calling the office but the service said you had already left."

"You see how it is, Peter," David said jokingly, "my wife no longer trusts my memory. Ach. Still, Bonnie, take a few minutes.

Have a cup of coffee or some lunch with us. Do you know my friend Peter Cosgrove? Peter, this is Bonnie Eckstein, my Leah's right hand and sometimes also her left."

Bonnie laughed and slid into an empty chair.

"I will have some coffee," she said. "The factory's been a madhouse today. Your brother-in-law Seymour must have a new idea in mind and he's been driving everyone mad checking hypothetical production schedules. You know, what if we had such and such a fabric and such and such a pattern and so many workers? He must have something in mind."

"And you can figure that sort of thing out?" Peter asked with interest. The girl's skin was so pale he could see a delicate network of veins on her neck and he found himself looking at her hands, surprised to see small roughened caps of flesh on the tips of her slender fingers.

"More or less," she answered.

"Well, you explain your secrets to Peter," David said. "I must get back. Tell Leah that I will certainly try but it has been a very busy day."

He rushed off, but as he stood at the elevator he looked back toward the table and saw Peter toss his head back in laughter and Bonnie smile shyly and then laugh too, her eyes fixed on Peter's face as though fascinated by the swift and spontaneous good humor for which Peter was famous among his colleagues.

The hospital clinic was very busy that afternoon and David worked steadily through the evening. Just as he was about to leave there was an emergency admission, an attempted suicide who had to be treated and sedated, then a conference with the family. The patient was an unemployed mason and his wife, a tiny colorless woman in a faded housedress, stared at David through pale frightened eyes as though he were a judge, not a doctor. She clutched the hand of her small son who had found his father bent over the bathroom sink, the blood from a severed wrist forming a sticky scarlet pool on the cracked tile of the floor.

"He needs a job. That's all. A job. To make him feel a man again," the woman said, tiny tears streaming down her papery cheeks.

David nodded. It was too late to disagree, to explain, and besides it would make no difference. He gave her a small bottle of tranquilizers and watched as the small boy, the son suddenly turned parent, led his mother from the room.

It was, after all, quite late when he arrived home in Brighton Beach. He had phoned Leah to say that he would eat dinner at the hospital but she had insisted that he come home.

"Mollie cooked a big brisket for everyone because I had to go to the factory this afternoon to talk to Seymour about something. And he wants to talk to you. It's important. For all of us."

"Yes. All right. I'll come home as early as I can."

But now, as he approached the house, he dreaded the family conference and felt the full impact of the day settle on him in a sudden rush of fatigue. All the lights in the house were on and through his own front window he saw Mollie and Seymour sitting at the table with the Ellenbergs. Perhaps Mollie was right after all, about a move to separate homes in the suburbs. It was really time that he and Leah lived their lives more privately.

Only the front porch was dark, but as he approached he saw Aaron move toward the stairway and the dim porch light briefly ignited his son's bright hair. The copper curls had been shorn into a crew cut, and Aaron at sixteen stood taller than David, his height emphasized by the lankiness he had inherited from Yaakov. The Abraham Lincoln High School sweatshirt hung loosely about Aaron's spare frame, and although David could not see his son's eyes he knew that they were shadowed by a watchful fear. The boy seemed to exist on the edge of doorways, hovering always at the corner of a window or peering down a darkened stairway as though lying in wait for a dread event. Even when he played chess with Joshua Ellenberg or worked out math problems with his cousin Jake, his eyes roved uncertainly about the room. He was on the high school track team, and David had gone to matches and watched Aaron streak by, noting always that while the other runners kept their eyes rooted to the track, Aaron as he rounded each bend lost time by glancing up at the bleachers as though to assure himself that his family was still there.

Aaron was a good student and his peers liked him and sought him out. Since his bar mitzvah, Leah had been more at ease with her older son, had reached out toward him. But Aaron's eyes remained wary and always his gaze moved toward doorways and windows, apprehensive and uneasy. The long days of his childhood, of his mother's strange, inexplicable vigilance, those years of closed doors and silent evenings when poverty and loneliness pervaded an apartment crowded with strangers, had become the adhesive penumbra of his young manhood, and even when he laughed, a strange sadness trailed his mirth.

How different Rebecca was, David thought, watching his dark-haired daughter glide into the light just behind Aaron. The elasticized sleeves of her peasant blouse were pulled down to reveal the gentle curve of her shoulders and her bright red skirt swayed against muscular tanned calves. At thirteen Rebecca was a small, more robust replica of her mother. Her black hair was brushed back into a luxurious ponytail caught up in a wood barrette. Her skin had Leah's delicate pallor, but even in winter a rosy sheen lit the girl's cheeks and her full lips curved gently upward in a small, teasing rosebud of laughter.

Gentle and carefree, pleasing and knowing that she pleased, Rebecca spent her days after school walking with her girlfriends down Brighton Beach Avenue, their arms linked about each other's waists as they whispered small secrets to each other and smiled at their reflections in plate-glass windows.

Mischievously, Rebecca dashed from apartment to apartment in the red brick house, snatching covers off Sarah Ellenberg's steaming pots, hiding knickknacks from her aunt Mollie's collection of china figurines, teasing her cousins with whispered innuendos or hints of high school cabals. And yet no one ever grew irritated with Rebecca. Her room was littered with skirts and sweaters, papers and magazines, which her busy mother patiently put away. Her school projects were never submitted on time and her household chores remained undone. In the midst of drying dishes she decided to make a phone call. The garbage she had meant to bring down remained on the porch while she gossiped with her current best friend. Joshua Ellenberg raked the yard when it was her turn and mixed the colored flour-and-water mixture to make the relief map of South America which she had forgotten to complete. He found her favorite cardigan on the boardwalk bench where she had left it and brought up the bag of groceries she left on the staircase. But she was their American princess, born in this New World which she claimed unequivocally as her own. Her laughter vindicated them all and secret promises trembling toward fulfillment rode on the waves of her constant energy.

"Hey, Dad," she called down to David from the porch. "They're all waiting for you."

"Dad," David marveled. He was Dad? He, a Russian immigrant, former pants presser, former night school student, fledgling psychiatrist? What a wonderful country this was, that could turn him, David Goldfeder, into a Dad.

"All right. So I'm here," he said. "Is Michael sleeping?"

But there was no answer. Both Aaron and Rebecca had disappeared into the house.

*

They sat around the table drinking tea as he ate the warmed-over brisket. The Ellenbergs clustered together in a corner, as though fearful of taking up too much room, always conscious of their role as appendages to the family, doggedly bobbing along in the swell of the rising fortunes of the Goldfeders and the Harts. Sarah Ellenberg had grown heavier and her husband smaller through the long years. Joshua towered over both his parents and directed their lives, a strange adolescent father to them in their childlike uncertainty. Joshua wore his hair in a crew cut like Aaron's, but he wore neatly pressed slacks and soft collared shirts to the high school where he was a perfunctory student who dashed away as soon as the last bell rang, speeding toward the Hart factory where he seemed to be everywhere at once. He jerked ringing phones from their hooks, sped through the packing room in search of a misdirected shipment, darted from the cutting table to the finishing room with newly cut fabric stretched before him. He knew everyone by name, workers and salesmen, customers and vendors.

"Hey, Max, how you making out with the ballerina skirts? Sadie—what did you do with that gross of pearl buttons? Get a move on—this order has to be at Kleins by Monday, the latest."

His parents were anchored in their bewildered failure but Joshua was speeding impatiently toward success, deftly turning pennies into dimes and the dimes into dollars that would pay his way into the world of commercial success toward which he had been steering since childhood.

Seymour Hart sat across the table from David, patiently stroking the small moustache which had evolved out of numerous pomaded experiments. The sleeves of his white-on-white shirt were rolled up but the blue-and-white polka-dot bow tie was still in place and as he sat he wound and rewound the heavy gold watch that sat on his thick hairy wrist. "More brisket, David?" Mollie asked.

"No." He pushed the plate away and wished that Leah would come in from the living room where she was critically looking at the sketches on her drawing board, her pencil poised with surgical readiness. She wore a loose light-blue middy blouse over a pleated skirt and her hair was cut close to the nape of her neck. She looked almost like a schoolgirl, he thought, and was wounded to notice the small knot of vein in her leg that gave lie to the thought.

"It's not good?" Mollie stood poised, fishing for compliment, anticipating insult. Rebecca giggled in the doorway and ignored her aunt's patient scowl.

"Come on, Aaron. Lux Radio Theater is just going on," she called, and Aaron and Joshua trailed after her into the bedroom, where Jake and Anne sat on the floor doing their math homework to the strains of drama beamed to Brighton Beach all the way from sunny California.

David spooned up the last of Mollie's compote, complimented her on the blend of stewed fruit, and pushed his dish away.

"So, Seymour—what's the big conference that I had to run home from the hospital for?"

"Seymour also had to run home. Maybe not from the hospital. From the factory. Sure, he's not a doctor, a specialist like you, but he's got plenty on his mind, plenty." Mollie slammed down two dishes for emphasis, at once pleased and irritated that she had caught her brother-in-law making too much of his position. After all, who was it who had made him a doctor if not her husband? True, Leah's designs had helped, but for years the bills for both families—and the Ellenbergs too—had been paid with income earned by S. Hart Inc. And S. Hart, after all, was her husband Seymour. She turned away and missed the amused glance Leah threw out to David, who had not bothered to reply to Mollie.

"Poor Mollie," he thought, remembering Seymour's eyes as he passed him on the stairway that morning, red-rimmed and drained of color. Seymour was getting too old to spend half the night in the beds of young girls. It was a long time since he and pretty Masha had flirted with each other in the Eldridge Street parlor. He was not up to that sort of thing anymore. David would have to talk to Seymour one of these days, not as a brother-in-law but as a doctor.

"Come on, Mollie. Let me talk," Seymour said impatiently.

He cleared his throat and, as though they had been waiting for a cue, the three Ellenbergs rose from the table.

"We go downstairs now. For us it's very late and soon it will be time for the President's radio talk," Sarah said. She was addicted to Franklin Delano Roosevelt, kept a scrapbook of news clippings about him, and pasted a color photo from the magazine section of the Sunday Mirror on her refrigerator. At Christmas she had knit him heavy socks and received an engraved "Thank you" from Eleanor Roosevelt which was wrapped in cellophane and enthroned on a separate page of the scrapbook.

"Good night," Seymour said without looking up and he waited until the door closed behind them before beginning again.

"You know, David, right now we—S. Hart Inc., that is—are a small outfit but for such a small outfit our name is getting pretty well known. But in order to reach further and become what we could become, we got to expand the line—do something different, exciting. There's a new day coming for ready-to-wear. The Depression is over. People are beginning to have money and they want to buy for that money. You notice they're building houses with a lot of closets these days. In those closets are going to hang a lot of clothes, most of them bought right off the rack. And, if we get into the market on time, a lot of those clothes are going to carry the S. Hart label. This is a new day for marketing on account of advertising. Believe me. And for advertising we got a built-in symbol with that little hart. What we need is to get ourselves a special line, classy, well made and inexpensive, borrow on orders to place advertising—radio, daily papers, Sunday supplements—and soon there won't be a shopper in America who doesn't look first to see if there's a little deer on the label."

Seymour lit a cigar and puffed a cloud of smoke upward, signaling that his presentation was over. Behind them Mollie breathed heavily.

David nodded.

"I believe you. I don't know much about business but anyone can see that there's more money around and of course mass production and advertising are the clues to the future. That even I can see. But Seymour, what's it to do with me? What are you telling me for? When you started the business you didn't ask my advice. When you expanded and when you expanded again you also didn't ask me. So why now?" There was honest puzzlement in David's voice.

It was Leah who answered him.

"Seymour is talking to you about it because this new line has to be something different. If we're going to take that kind of a chance, make that kind of investment, we have to offer something different from what most ready-to-wear manufacturers are shipping out. What we're looking for is an inexpensive line with high-fashion design. And for that we have to get a lot of different ideas, use different kinds of fabric. But most important are the designs and such designs I'm not going to dream up in Brighton Beach. For such designs I have to go to Europe, to the Paris shows. Maybe even to Italy to see what the designers there are doing. Then I can put out a line for the kind of market Seymour has in mind. The time is right, David. I can feel it. We've got to take the chance."

"To Europe?"

Immediately, the front page of the morning's Times flashed before his eyes. He saw the hate-twisted features of the moustachioed little German leader, his hand jerked upward in a Roman salute to his own avarice and evil. Europe now was a tinderbox, arranged by Hitler, ready to be ignited by a single incident. He had plucked Leah from too much danger and pain to allow her to travel back into that smoldering continent. What was the matter with Shimon? Didn't he read any newspaper besides the Women's Wear Daily? Even now, as they sat silently around the table, the deep tones of Edward R. Murrow's voice reporting from London boomed out of the children's room and they heard snatches of his report in the somber voice David had come to fear. "A rally in the Reichstag drew record crowds.... New provisions in the anti-Semitic Nuremberg legislation.... Books by Albert Einstein and Sigmund Freud are now banned in Germany...." The listeners in the Brooklyn dining room remained quiet, eerily sharing the incredulity of the seasoned announcer himself. Abruptly one of the young people turned the dial and soft music filled the air. Rebecca giggled, Anne laughed, and then the door closed and the four adults sat around the table, not meeting each other's eyes, as though unwilling to read therein the knowledge they shared with fear and certainty.

"You know what's happening in Europe now. And it will get worse. If that Austrian bastard has his way he'll make the Odessa of 1919 look like a playground. You want me to tell you it's all right to go back to that because of a few designs?" David asked bitterly.

Immediately, he regretted mentioning Odessa. Familiar lines of pain creased Leah's eyes and in the face of his wife, the assured, stylishly dressed woman with her black hair cut in the fashionable new cap and her figure rounded by childbearing and contentment, he saw the frightened young girl, still in her teens, her face pale beneath a coronet of braids, sitting silently beside him in a deserted park while gypsy violins played a mournful lament. But when Leah spoke her voice was quiet and controlled.

"Actually, it is because of what's happening in Europe that I want to go. I had a letter from Moshe. He has written again and again to Mama and Papa asking them to come to Palestine. They refuse and he cannot go to Europe. Neither can Henia and she is worried also about her family. The kibbutz is in danger from the Arabs and they're doing everything they can to settle what children they can get out of Germany into Palestine. I also have written over and over but letters are of no use. To my parents Germany is another world. My mother answered me that my father didn't even know who Hitler was."

"He's not mentioned a great deal in the Talmud," Seymour said dryly.

"So I thought, if I went to Europe, from Italy I could try to get to Russia and talk to them. Make them understand what's happening. If I didn't try, David, I would never forgive myself." She moved across the table and stood beside him, her hand resting on his shoulder.

Once again, David was astounded by the swiftness with which Leah made decisions. Having listened to Edward R. Murrow's somber voice, David quaked inwardly, worried and agonized, and made dire predictions. But it was Leah who molded the improbable into the possible. To work while he studied medicine, to fight for a union, to fall in love, to mourn and then to love again: all that was Leah's doing.

"I could go with you," he offered weakly, knowing that with the suggestion he acknowledged that she would, after all, make the journey.

"Could you leave your practice, the hospital?" Seymour asked. He could not, of course, and he shrugged in defeat. "What about the children?" he asked.

"Now it's May. I wouldn't leave until school was over in June. Aaron and Rebecca will go to camp and Michael will be with Mollie in the mountains."

"I see. It's all been thought out, arranged. What is there left to say?"

He wondered bitterly how many conferences they had held without him, making their practical decisions while he, the family *luftmensch*—the intellectual dreamer—pondered in his consulting room. But his resentment evaporated as he felt the touch of Leah's hand in his and the smoothness of her arm leaning against his cheek as she stood behind him, bending slightly so that his shoulder brushed against the softness of her breasts.

Mollie and Seymour rose to leave then, Seymour turning suddenly to touch his sister-in-law's hair and then to shake David's hand. As though embarrassed by the gestures, he hurried after Mollie and Leah and David remained alone in the empty dining room.

"In June," he said softly.

Her lips moved hard against his in silent answer and from the rear of the house they heard small Michael laugh suddenly in his sleep. But even as they stood in their urgent embrace, their bodies pressed together, their mouths sweet upon each other, the wail of an ambulance siren pierced the quiet night.

They moved toward the window and watched the flashing red lights of the emergency vehicle rip past their house and disappear, speeding toward Coney Island Hospital. The shrill warning of death and danger trembled briefly on the dark air, so fresh with the odors of newly blooming lilac and the salt sea. They remained there for a moment, arms entwined, sheltering each other from the fear and apprehension they would not name.

10

The slender blonde mannequin in the black suit walked slowly across the stage and pirouetted in easy, practiced movement within the circle of moving rose-colored light. The subtle spotlight followed her as she continued on across the raised platform, bending easily to show the flow of the skirt and lifting her arms in a graceful arc, embracing the perfumed air, to demonstrate the generous cut of the sleeves.

"*Charmant,*" murmured the small moustachioed man who sat next to Leah. "*Très extraordinaire.*"

"*Quelle simplicité,*" the woman seated behind her whispered to a companion.

"*Peut-ệtre de trop de simplicité,*" the other woman answered with a slightly derisive laugh.

The model, her perfect features frozen, twirled about once more, rounded the stage with laconic elegance, and disappeared behind the taffeta curtain.

The buyers and private patrons leaned forward on their small gilt chairs, some making almost imperceptible signs to the saleswomen who hovered discreetly about the room. A raised eyebrow summoned a middle-aged woman in a smart black dress, who bent her carefully coiffed blue-white head to answer a query. Silently, Madame's assistants glided about the room, offering pencils and order forms, whispering the answers to softly voiced questions. The suit was cut of heavy silk on a wide margin. There was, naturally, a brief waiting period. One had to be honest—it might even take several weeks. Madame would rather lose an order than disappoint a customer. No—there was no worry about individuality. Madame herself was limiting the production of the model.

Leah smiled thinly and dug the heels of her brown-and-white spectator pumps deeply into the thick mauve carpet. The small notebook on her lap, similar to the ones used by the buyers for the Fifth Avenue stores, contained an almost completed sketch of the suit. She worked quickly, keeping one hand cupped about the sheet of paper. The jacket of the suit was unusual, the stark simplicity curving into a fishtail at the back. Madame Chanel was truly a genius, using the simplest lines and the most obvious fabrics to create these stunning classic patterns. Of course, in mass production they could not work with heavy silk, but Seymour had found a southern manufacturer who was producing a polished cotton which would just suit this design. If they cut on a narrower bias and used fake pockets instead of the real ones (which the blonde model had so artfully demonstrated, turning them inside out in a deft movement), they would save both fabric and production time. And the rapidly expanding army of women office workers in America would love that suit. Leah wondered how it would look in the marvelous peacock-blue cotton Seymour had shown her—perhaps with a pale blue blouse. She smiled, feeling the surge of excitement that always filled her when she juggled fabrics and colors.

"Your order is complete, Madame?" A saleswoman stood beside Leah and smiled at her with patient insistence. Leah quickly covered her clandestine sketch and fumbled for an answer. She wondered if the woman had seen her drawing and remembered Seymour's earnest warning.

"Try to memorize the designs," he had said. "Because if they catch you at one show they'll pass the word to all the coutouriers and your invitations won't be worth the paper they're printed on."

Now she looked helplessly about and shifted uncomfortably in her seat.

"Can't you see that Madame is indecisive?" A man's voice, laced with irritability, shot the question out at the saleswoman who nodded apologetically and moved away.

Leah had noticed the man at other shows and had observed that he too carried a pad which he concealed beneath order forms and brochures. He was obviously employed as she was and although she was grateful for his swift intervention, she had stiffened when she recognized the guttural German accent that blanketed his fluent French. Still, she glanced at him and smiled. He acknowledged her with a nod, his lips curving upward in a slow smile which could also be construed as an invitation. He was a tall thin man with a black-and-silver moustache that precisely matched his hair, the two colors evenly vying for dominance. He was dressed in the requisite formal attire for a Paris fashion show: striped trousers, gray vest, and black afternoon coat. His cane and hat rested on the chair next to him and Leah thought that he was the sort of man who wore such clothing for a stroll in the park. He probably ran a small salon in Berlin on Unter der Linden or Kurfuerstendamm and his customers were plump *frauleins* from the provinces who increased their orders as his thick moustache tickled their pink-and-white palms in appropriate kisses of approval and welcome.

But the next model had moved onto the stage and she forgot about him as her fingers moved deftly and surreptitiously, making notes next to the tiny line drawings. "Green silk with gold *lamé* trim—afternoon dress—perhaps add extra stole for evening wear—skirt pattern similar to number five—both numbers can be cut in one operation..."

Behind her, Frederic Heinemann also filled his pad and wondered who the dark-haired American woman was. She was obviously new at this sort of thing to be so intimidated by one of Chanel's saleswomen. He knew she was American because he had caught a glimpse of her green passport when she opened her purse, and like most of her compatriots, she seemed to know no other language but English—although she seemed to have a slight accent. What arrogance Americans displayed when they refused to master another language. Their assumption seemed to be that the whole world had to understand them, and too bad if it didn't.

He thought of the little corporal, the Fuehrer, who insisted that it was a punishable crime to speak anything but German. Ridiculous little man, with his nonsensical talk about a master race. Frederic Heinemann frowned deeply. Master race, master language—such nonsense. People were people and languages were languages. What a relief it was to be away from Germany for this short trip to the Paris showings, to have left behind the streets filled with strutting youths in their dark shirts with that red-and-black swastika emblazoned everywhere. It was a fever—a temporary viral reaction to the diseases of defeat and unemployment and the contagion of inflation. It would pass, of course.

But meanwhile it was distressing and he did not blame his Jewish friends who were leaving Germany. Why should one stay in a country which denied them basic citizenship, the right to work? He had found it hard to believe when Heinz had told him that the ridiculous Nuremberg laws even denied Jews the right to listen to Bach and Beethoven, lest they corrupt the music. He had almost been relieved to find that Heinz was right. Such ridiculous legislation proved on what nonsense the entire regime was founded. Hitler and the maniacs he surrounded himself with—failures like Goering and Himmler—were Philistines. He had told Emanuel Schreiber that, but poor Schreiber was already insane with worry. His son had been sent to some sort of work camp because of an affair with an Aryan girl and then some of those Hitler Youth hoodlums had pasted crude anti-Semitic posters across the show windows of Schreiber's beautiful store on Tautzienstrasse. And then, of course, Hilde, who had worked for Frau Schreiber for years, had had to leave because of that mad law that made it a crime for women under forty-five to be employed in a Jewish household. Madness. He had advised Schreiber to be patient but his friend was determined to leave and Frederic Heinemann could not blame him. The Schreibers were in Paris now, waiting for a visa to the United States. He would see them this afternoon and try to persuade them to take some money from him. The Tautzienstrasse store had been sold for only a fraction of its worth and the house they had not been permitted to sell at all.

Damn—with his thoughts wandering this way he had missed sketching that last evening dress. But perhaps the dark-haired American woman had caught it.... With an effort he forced himself to concentrate on the show.

The last model, wearing a lemon-yellow evening dress with an accordion-pleated skirt, danced across the stage. The sleeves were like gossamer butterfly wings and the model moved lightly, balanced on her toes and coming to a graceful halt so that the patrons might see how gracefully the flowing fabric settled into rich folds. The girl's flaxen hair matched the gown and Leah thought that S. Hart might manufacture it in brown for brunettes, yellow for blondes. She visualized a series of dramatic color advertisements with each model photographed in a dress that matched her coloring. What was that song Aaron played on his guitar—"Black, black, black is the color of my true love's hair..." They could use that as the heading for an advertisement and the dress would be of a midnight-black crepe—they had a lot of such fabric left from a style cut last year which had not done very well.

The show was over and polite applause filled the room as the overhead lights flashed on. The audience, jarred back into the real world, blinked reluctantly and moved awkwardly, slowly returning to the demands of an atmosphere where lights were not muted and soft music did not soothe the air. Women adjusted their hats nervously and men felt for their wallets. The salesladies moved quickly about the room, answering questions and accepting checks and folded order forms. Someone opened the window and the sounds of early evening traffic on the Champs Elysées filled the room.

Leah slipped her papers into her large shoulder bag and pulled her bright-red cloche hat down over her sleek dark hair. After a week of attending showings in Paris fashion salons, she no longer felt any trepidation after a show. The patrons chatted in small groups at the exits, some making plans for dinner or the theater that evening. Several of the men viewers had disappeared and could probably be found at the models' exit, waiting for the lovely slender girls with porcelain features who seldom fulfilled the tantalizing promise of the rose-colored spotlight. Leah's exit would go unmarked just as her invitation (obtained by Seymour from a friend of a friend on a New York fashion journal, at considerable cost) went unchallenged at the door. In her smart red, belted dress and hat to match, she looked the role of a buyer for a small Manhattan shop and the only time she had ever felt any apprehension was that afternoon when the saleswoman approached her. She would take the Métro now, as she had every evening for the past week, and return to her small hotel on the Rue du Bac where, after a light dinner, she would spend the evening doctoring her sketches with as many details as she could recall. It was difficult to be accurate in the perfumed dimness of the showroom and occasionally she added small details of her own.

"Madame, excuse me if you will."

It was the moustachioed German buyer who stood before her now, his black leather portfolio tucked under his arm, his well-brushed gray felt hat in his hand. She felt herself stiffen but smiled politely and replied in the cool, controlled voice which she had cultivated through the years.

"You wish to speak to me, Monsieur?"

"Allow me to introduce myself." He held out a card which identified him as Frederic Heinemann, proprietor of a shop for women on Kurfuerstendamm in Berlin.

"I'm afraid I do not have a card with me," she said, "But I am Mrs. David Goldfeder and I am from New York City."

"So pleased, Madame." He bent to kiss her hand and as she had supposed the hairs of his thick zebra-striped moustache tickled her skin, causing her to smile and breaking her apprehension.

Together they walked out into the cool of the evening. The Paris sky had thickened into the purplish-blue tones of early twilight and the faint aroma of chestnut blossoms sweetened the air.

"Does Madame Goldfeder stay in this district?" Frederic Heinemann asked.

"No. I am a guest at a small hotel on the Rue du Bac," she replied. "And I am afraid that I must hurry there now, Mr. Heinemann. I have some work I must do this evening."

"Yes. I understand, of course," he said and glanced at his watch. It was not, after all, too late to visit his old friends, the Schreibers. "But if you will forgive me, Madame, may I make a great presumption in thinking that you might do me a great favor. I could not help but observe that you have great skill with the drawing pen."

Leah glanced warily at him. So there would be a price to pay, after all, for his protective intervention. She continued to walk toward the Métro station without breaking pace.

"I think we are involved in a similar undertaking here in Paris, Madame. And you are enjoying a singular success. You recall the voile evening dress shown by Madame Chanel this afternoon?"

"The one with the stole and small sheer cuffs?"

"Ah. Exactly. I neglected to copy it and I wondered if you might share your own effort with me. For a fee, of course. The ladies of my clientele are much involved with the cabaret life and this dress would sell well in my salon."

"A strange request, Monsieur. If indeed our projects are similar, then we are competitors. Why would I help a competitor?"

"Perhaps because your interests are in New York and mine in Berlin. And perhaps because I would guess that you are interested in ready-to-wear production and you see by my card that my clients are exclusively private. And most important, perhaps, because if you are of service to me, then perhaps I might be of service to you."

They stood at the station entry and a newsboy dashed by carrying the evening edition of the *L'Express* and shouting the headlines:

NEW ANTI-SEMITIC MEASURES INSTITUTED IN GERMANY! ARSONISTS ATTACK FRANKFURT SYNAGOGUES! DUKE OF WINDSOR GUEST OF HITLER!

"Has it not occurred to you, Monsieur, that I would not be particularly inclined to be of service to a colleague from your country, no matter how mutually beneficial such an arrangement might be?" Leah asked, staring after the newsboy.

Frederic Heinemann blushed deeply and his finely shaped hands trembled.

"You do my country a disservice to think that all Germans subscribe to the beliefs of Adolf Hitler. There are many of us who are horrified by him. But we are sustained by the knowledge that ultimately he cannot succeed. He is the craze of the moment, the unhappy political remnant of Weimar, the Great War, and the inflation. Soon, Madame, he will be as dusty and forgotten as the unsuccessful design of years gone past. I am as distraught and repelled by his words and actions as you are, Madame Goldfeder." He stood erect and Leah saw the small Medal of Honor in his lapel.

"With all due respect, Monsieur, I do not think you can be as upset as I am," she replied and took a copy of the *Paris Tribune* from another newsboy who stopped long enough to wait for the few centimes she dropped into his outstretched grimy hand.

"I assume that Madame is Jewish?" the man asked gently.

"You assume correctly."

"I wonder, Madame, if you would do me an even greater service than the one I originally sought. I have friends in Paris, newly from Berlin. They are a Jewish couple, the Schreibers. They have endured a great deal because of the Nazi madness and now await a visa to the United States. In your great country they have neither friends nor relations. I planned to visit them now, and if you could accompany me, it would mean a great deal to them."

The homeward-bound crowds were hurrying into the Metro now and they moved aside to allow them to pass. Leah looked thoughtfully at the elegantly dressed man who stood before her. The distress in his voice and the gentle urgency of his request had touched her and stirred a forgotten chord. How willingly good people believed that evil could not endure, that it had neither power nor tenacity but withered like weeds with weakened roots. Yaakov had dismissed with contempt Gregoriev's hordes and Eli had fought greed and injustice with only his own courage and conviction. David daily battled the invisible demons of ignorance and terror, and this successful German businessman, who reddened with shame for his country, did not give credence to the very newspaper whose angry headlines they shared together in the darkening street.

"If you will have dinner with me at the hotel, Monsieur, I will then visit your friends with you. It may be that my family can be of service to them. And, of course, we must compare our drawings and see how we can be of service to each other."

Her decision made, she smiled warmly at him and allowed him to help her into the cab he hailed to carry them to the Rue du Bac.

*

The Schreibers had found temporary refuge in one of the small apartments in that section of Paris known as the *Pletzel* which Jewish relief agencies such as the Hebrew Immigrant Aid Society and the Joint Distribution Committee had leased as German Jews began crossing the border into France. The streets of the *Pletzel,* those winding narrow alleyways clogged with men pushing handcarts and housewives engrossed in their marketing with the intensity of the poor, their string bags bulging with onions and potatoes and hunks of meat wrapped in Yiddish papers soaked with blood, trailed by small parades of sad and frightened children, reminded Leah of New York's lower east side. Here too, she supposed sadly, air was expensive for the poor. Twice their taxi swerved to avoid hitting groups of bearded, earlocked men, who looked to neither left nor right as they crossed the street, their heads bent together in earnest argument over a point of law. Like her father, their lives were lived within the Talmudic study hall where they erected elegant arguments on ritual purity for vanished priests whose Temple had been destroyed thousands of years ago or debated the disposition of a wandering goat as the traffic of urban Paris trundled by them. How safe they were, she thought, how unworried and insulated from the shouts of "Heil Hitler!" and the guns that were poised in readiness only a border away.

The long black gabardine of one rabbi was splashed by a speeding cyclist and he looked up with seeming mildness, followed the cyclist with his eyes, and shouted after him, *"Cochon!"* and then turned calmly back to his companions and continued his conversation in eloquent Yiddish.

Leah smiled and saw that Frederic Heinemann was smiling too. She had to remember to tell the story to David, she thought, and felt a pang of homesickness. It was almost three weeks now since the sun-drenched afternoon she had waved to her family from the deck of the *Queen Elizabeth*. They had, of course, all come to the pier to see her off: David, who had clutched her tightly in the night but wakened to mask his fear with calm; Aaron, withdrawn and silent, who suddenly, as the last warning call to dockside visitors hooted over the ship's bullhorn, grabbed his mother and bent his head to her breast so that her bosom was damp with her tall son's tears when he turned away, shielding his eyes with his hands; Rebecca, laughing and excited, dashing about the deck with Joshua Ellenberg in joyous pursuit; and a small Michael, who kept tugging at his mother's skirt and asking her what she would bring him from "Your *ope*."

"Perhaps your grandparents," she had said and the cheerful little boy in his carefully pressed sailor suit had nodded happily.

"All right. And a little car. And candy."

"Don't forget. Candy," he reminded her, as she hugged him tightly in good-bye. "And don't cry. You're not a baby. I'm the baby."

She laughed but the tears had continued to stream down her cheeks and David had taken her arm and walked to the railing with her.

"You don't have to go," he said gently.

"I know."

He took out a large clean white handkerchief, wiped her cheeks, and lightly kissed her hair.

He wore a small beard now, its fine dark growth threaded with streaks of early gray, and a gold watch was strung across the light-gray vest of his summer suit. How handsome he was, she thought, and how distinguished-looking, this man who had been in turn her friend and brother, her protector and companion, and finally her lover. She took his hand in hers and pressed it to her lips.

"Just three months, David," she said and he nodded, his arms enfolding her, his head pressed to hers.

Now, on this crowded Paris street, so foreign and yet so familiar, she thought of the weeks that still must pass and the borders she would have to cross before joining her family. A heavy sadness stole over her, and Frederic Heinemann, as though sensing her change of mood, leaned forward.

"Madame suffers from *la tristesse*?" he asked softly.

"Yes, I am missing my family," she replied.

"I too think of a friend now," he said. "My young friend and companion, Heinz. It is the hour and this magic Paris light. But you will return to your family and I to my friend. I have the true *tristesse* when I think of those who cannot return."

The cab stopped on the Rue des Rosiers, before the entry of a narrow gray stone apartment building. Concrete pots of dusty red geraniums stood on the windowsills and the steps were cluttered with small children who jumped up and down, weaving their way teasingly in front of the heavyset concierge, a tired woman in a faded housedress who was listlessly trying to clean the steps with a basin of water and a stringy gray mop.

The narrow stairwell smelled of urine and cheap talcum powder, and the odors of stewing vegetables and frying garlic seethed from each open apartment doorway. Twice, as they made their way up the steps, apartment doors opened slightly and Leah saw pale frightened faces peer from the narrow slice of light before the heavy doors slammed shut.

The Schreibers lived on the top floor; Frederic Heinemann knocked sharply twice, waited a moment, and knocked again. The door opened slightly, and quickly he took Leah's hand and they slipped inside.

"Ah, Frederic, I knew you would come. You see, Ilse, he has come, our good friend. I told you he would not disappoint us. I told you."

"You told me many things," the woman said dryly, but her husband, a small dapper man impeccably dressed in tie and waistcoat even in the unbearable heat of the small flat, did not answer but embraced his friend and held out a hand of welcome to Leah. Frederic Heinemann introduced them.

"This is Madame Goldfeder, a coreligionist of yours from New York City. I had the good fortune to meet her at a showing this afternoon."

"Ah yes. The Chanel showing. Was it interesting?" Herr Schreiber asked, leaning forward. His wife coughed in annoyance.

"This surely must be the peak of absurdity, Madame Goldfeder. Our only son is interned somewhere in a camp. We do not even know where. We have lost our possessions—everything we worked for. We live among cockroaches in this flat for refugees and we do not even know where we shall take refuge, but my husband must know about Coco Chanel's latest fashions."

Frau Schreiber, taller than her husband, her blue-gray hair swept elaborately upward, flicked a piece of dust from her black linen dress and clapped her hands together as though the movement might magically spirit her out of the tiny hot apartment and back to her beautiful home on a tree-lined Berlin boulevard where her faithful maid, Hilde, would shortly serve iced tea in the tall frosted glasses bought on a shopping trip to Venice.

The sounds of an argument in Yiddish rose from the street below and Ilse Schreiber moved to the window, her eyes filled with sudden tears. She had loved those glasses and had punished her son severely once for dropping one on the tiled kitchen floor.

"Ilse. Leave the window open. It is hot." The small man's voice was firm. "Perhaps our guests are thirsty."

"Yes. Of course." Immediately she was the considerate hostess and the cold coffee she offered them came on a battered aluminum tray which she had covered with an elegant linen cloth.

They talked over coffee and Leah listened with horror to their stories of life in Germany.

"If you have eyes to see what is happening and you are Jewish, you have only two choices—suicide or emigration," Herr Schreiber said in a stoic, matter-of-fact tone that made Leah shiver.

"It will pass," Frederic Heinemann insisted, but his voice lacked conviction. His friend shook his head.

"No, Frederic. We are a people who have survived many things. Our entire history is founded on the supposition that things will pass. In Hebrew we have said again and again '*Gam zeh yaavor*'—This also will pass.' We have repeated this after pogroms, persecutions, even forced conversions. We will wait. We will endure. It will pass. But even we, history's most patient, most optimistic victims, now know that this sickness that has consumed Germany, this Nazi fever, will not pass so quickly. Do you know, Madame Goldfeder, that in the weeks before we left Berlin, Ilse and I went to a funeral almost every day—and each funeral was that of a suicide. We are a people who glory in life. We raise our glasses and call out '*L'Chaim!*' 'To life!' Yet each day another Jew chooses to surrender that precious life. Why, Madame?"

But it was Ilse Schreiber who answered, her voice dry and bitter.

"We went to the funeral of Professor Ehrenkrantz who was forced to leave the university. Of Dr. Eisenstadt who could no longer perform surgery at the clinic he himself had established. Of Frau Riegenbaum whose son was arrested because, like our own Leon, he committed the crime of falling in love with a German girl and might contaminate her with his Jewish blood. Ach—when people lose their livelihoods and their families and, in some cases, even their homes, to what purpose do they go on with their lives? Your questions require no answers, my husband."

Leah stirred her coffee and felt her heart thunder with a fear she had almost forgotten. She remembered, suddenly, the vegetal odors of a summer woodland and the sour breath of fear.

"But surely the German people will soon realize the insanity of the situation," she protested, not wanting to acknowledge a reality she could not escape.

"The German people. Forgive me, my dear Frederic, but there are very few with your courage and humanity in our country and you yourself know that your safety and that of your friend Heinz is not assured if you continue to befriend Jews like us. Picture, Madame, a citizenry which passes the office of a veterinarian who has, in all seriousness and adherence to the law, posted a sign saying 'Jewish Dogs Not Treated.' The passersby nod, as though such a legend were reasonable, understandable, and walk on. Think of people who have been friends and neighbors for many years, who go to the cabarets which are now all the social life of Berlin, elegantly dressed, some of them in gowns purchased in my husband's own establishment on Tautzienstrasse and still unpaid for, where they listen to anti-Semitic songs and jokes, so pleased at being able to forget the debts they now do not have to pay to Jews who lent them money in good faith or allowed them to charge in their shops. Surely a Jewish pharmacy is not an international banking enterprise, yet our friend Teutsch, the pharmacist, had to close his shop because his Aryan customers declined to pay 'filthy Jewish debts.'

"Quite suddenly, a woman who has belonged to my reading group for many years crosses the street to avoid talking to me. The greengrocer, with whom I have had an account for many years, faithfully paid on the first of each month, ignores me as I stand at the counter. But all this is nothing. Believe me, they do not want only our money and our possessions. They want our lives as well, our friends the Nazis. And the people will not object. The people will cheer them on as the Romans cheered their gladiators."

Frau Schreiber sat back quietly and her husband put his hand over hers, wordlessly acknowledging the truth of her words. Finally, he spoke and his gentle voice was laced with exhaustion.

"Yes. They have a dream now, Hitler and his gangsters. They have a cure for all of the Fatherland's ills—for inflation, unemployment, and war debts. All evil is caused by the Jews and to save Germany it must be made 'Judenrein'—free of Jews."

"And it will not stop with Germany," his wife added. "The world is to be turned into an Aryan wonderland, ruled by blond, blue-eyed giants and served by *untermenschen*—therefore the world itself must be made Judenrein."

"You think then that Hitler will truly plan another great war?" Leah asked.

"With all due respect to Frederic who disagrees with me, I think it a certainty," Herr Schreiber replied. "Hitler talks now of the Sudetenland and claims he wants that poor piece of Czechoslovakia because of the German population there. But what of the German population in Alsace-Lorraine, in Rumania, in Hungary, and in the Netherlands. Surely he will want to 'protect' all those nationals. With such a pretext and with the rest of the world idly watching and posing no opposition, he simply refuses to recognize borders and treaties."

"My husband—he is a psychiatrist in New York—agrees with you," Leah said slowly. "That is one reason why I came to Europe now. I mean to try to go to Russia—to persuade my parents there to leave. David, my husband, is convinced that no place in Europe will be safe for Jews in a few years."

"It is not safe for Jews now," Frau Schreiber agreed. "Think of it, Madame Goldfeder, I sit here and drink coffee with you and I do not know where my son is—whether he is alive or dead. Is that possible? You too are a mother. Tell me, is it possible to add sugar to coffee and try to decide between a green scarf and a blue one when one does not know whether one's child is alive or dead, healthy or in pain?"

She did not cry but stared at the flimsy white curtains that hung at the narrow window, encrusted with grime that weighed them down, as though the grim fears of all those who had sought refuge in the furnished flat on the Rue des Rosiers clung to the gauzy fabric.

"Life must be lived, Madame," Leah replied, but did not meet the other woman's eyes, fearing the encounter with familiar grief.

"But please, my dear friends, let us talk now of the future,"

Frederic Heinemann urged. "I have the presumption to think that perhaps Madame Goldfeder can be of service to you."

"Only if it is in your power to offer us affidavits, Madame," Mr. Schreiber said. "There are those who ask why more Jews do not leave Germany if the danger is so great. The truth is, many have nowhere to go. Other European countries hold similar dangers or are opposed to Jewish immigration. The British have closed off Palestine to all but very limited numbers of Jews. The South American countries are asking exorbitant fees for entry permits and the United States has exacting quotas and requires affidavits of support. My wife and I are eligible under the quota but we have no family or friends to provide the affidavit. If you could help us in that way we would be most grateful."

"I shall cable my husband tonight and tomorrow morning we shall go together to the American Embassy. I shall do anything I can to help you," Leah said.

She and Frederic Heinemann rose to leave and when the two men shook hands Leah saw Frederic Heinemann slip a folded bill into Herr Schreiber's hand. Impulsively she pressed her lips to Frau Schreiber's cheek. The German woman's skin was paper-thin.

"Have courage," Leah said in Yiddish. "We will do what mothers have always done. We will hope."

Tears blazed brilliantly in the German woman's pale eyes. She made no move to hide them but stood erect and said firmly, in a clear voice, "Of course, we will hope, Madame. Hope—*Hatikva*—you see how well we have chosen the title of our people's anthem."

That night Leah wrote long letters to her brother Moshe in Palestine and to her family in New York. Her meeting with the Schreibers had convinced her that the situation in Europe was even worse than they suspected. She told both her brother and her husband of her increased determination to make the arduous journey to Russia as soon as her business at the Italian showings was completed.

*

The Bessarabian Express moved at a rapid pace during the daylight hours, but as night swept across southern Russia, with a stern, dark swiftness that banished daylight without the gentle benediction of sunset, the wheels turned more slowly and occasionally ground to a full stop as though the motorman himself had been narcotized by the thick folds of night. Leah Goldfeder had drawn the thick green-velvet curtains of her compartment even while the silvery-pale summer daylight still lit the forests where slender pines swayed gracefully and stretched skyward, interspersed by narrow birch groves that shimmered with ghostly luster.

The Russian farmers had had a good summer and when they passed cultivated countryside, the feathery wheat was thick across seemingly endless acres. Field workers, stripped to their waists, vaulted upward on their tractor seats and waved to the passing train. At short station stops, crowds of children boarded the train and sold the passengers the first fruits of the summer harvest—thick green pears and strangely shaped cylindrical apples with a fruit of tender, sweet whiteness beneath the gleaming red peel. The children were barefoot but sunburned and cheerful, and the most enterprising group—on whom the lessons of the Communist collective had clearly been lost—carried with them garlands of braided wild flowers which they sold to the women passengers. Leah had bought such a necklace, remembering then how she and Malcha had braided similar strands on lazy afternoons, lying near the small creek and hiding from their mother who searched them out to help in the kneading of dough, the chopping of fish, or to assist in the small dusky stall she called her shop. Malcha had used the long-stemmed wild lilacs while Leah searched out the bright-red blossom they called "Blood of Russia," which she threaded with delicate golden buttercups. She had made just such a braided floral crown for Yaakov during the brief lost days of that marriage which seemed to her a dream now except when she looked at Aaron's flaming hair.

As the train sped on through the fields Aaron's father had known and loved, she recalled the lean toughness of Yaakov's body and remembered how that garland of red and gold flowers had sat atop his coppery curls and fallen at last to the clean, newly cut wooden planks beside their marriage bed. In the morning it was wilted and the proud "Blood of Russia" was tattered, drying petals.

As the train sped through fields aglow with the soft-petaled sunlight of the fragile buttercups, her eyes unexpectedly brimmed with tears. She wept then, for the first time in many years, for the brief months of her first marriage and for the terrible years of uncertainty that had marked the childhood of Yaakov's son who had been denied his father's name. She had advised Frau Schreiber to hope, but how often, in those lost years, she herself had turned from hope. It was then that she had drawn the drapes of her compartment and turned in sad resignation to the papers in her portfolio.

The sketches she had made at the French and Italian shows had been mailed to Seymour. She and Frederic Heinemann had agreed to work together, comparing their drawings and pooling their ideas. They had arranged to correspond with each other and Frederic Heinemann had been pained when Leah suggested that her letters to him should be signed by Charles Ferguson and posted from Charles's address.

"If Aryan veterinarians are forbidden to treat Jewish dogs, I do not think the authorities will look kindly on your relationship with a Jewish firm in New York," she said gently, trying to inject some weak semblance of humor into the situation that those who gathered in the Schreibers' tiny rooms on the Rue des Rosiers regarded as ludicrous.

But Frederic Heinemann had not laughed.

"All this will pass. It must. If I did not believe that it would pass I would be fearful for myself and Heinz. Such a regime tolerates no irregularities, no friendships that are too involved and beyond the norm." He sighed and clasped and unclasped his fine long fingers.

But as her stay in Europe was prolonged, Leah was convinced that there was little cause for optimism. In Italy she watched Mussolini's blackshirted young Fascisti march up and down dusty boulevards. They were much admired by citizens and tourists, who spoke admiringly of the wonder of trains that now ran on time and the new highways and bridges that were solving unemployment problems in Italy the way Hen Hitler, in his wisdom, had solved them in Germany. On the small steamer that carried her across the Adriatic Sea to meet her rail connections for Russia, she saw groups of Jewish passengers huddled together. Unable to obtain visas elsewhere, they were en route to the Asian countries, carrying their battered suitcases, their sacks of cooking utensils, and their carefully shrouded Torah scrolls to the mountains of Japan, the teeming streets of Hong Kong. She was relieved then that Seymour had been able to obtain visas for the Schreibers and had written offering Herr Schreiber employment with S. Hart.

Now, as the train thundered on through Bessarabia, along the coast of the Black Sea where tiny fishing hamlets were still lit by wicks fitfully nourished with kerosene so that they danced nervously in the velvet darkness, she put the final touches on the sketches she had made in Rome. She would post them in Odessa, she thought, and go on to her parents' village in the morning. Her hands trembled as she worked and once she lifted a corner of the drape and stole a fearful look at the lights of the city where her journey had begun.

"Almost there, almost there," the whirling wheels of the train sang, and she shivered slightly and gathered her things together, barricading herself behind her suitcases and watching small groups of passengers assemble in the narrow train corridor. A young mother, her pale, almost colorless hair neatly tucked beneath a dark-blue kerchief, knelt to lift a sleeping child and Leah wondered if Michael, her small laughing boy, was sleeping too, in the cool of the distant mountain country in New York State.

Odessa had changed very little in the seventeen years since she had left, and as she wandered the cobblestone streets in search of a driver who would take her to her parents' village, she chided herself for thinking that the city would be any different. The changes had occurred within herself and her own life. The streets she had known as a student and later as a young bride were immutable. Their names had changed—the Boulevard of the Czars was now People's Square—but the streets themselves were the same. New lives filled the flats and cafés where she and her friends had sat and talked, planned and dreamed. There were, of course, small monuments to those plans. Here, on a familiar corner where Yaakov had once mounted a cobbler's bench to argue for shared distribution of food, there was now a cooperative restaurant for workers. A small industrial district had grown up and over each small factory building the red flag of the Revolution fluttered. On her way to the post office, Leah passed groups of young women, each holding the hand of a small child and carrying a tin lunch box. They were, she supposed, on their way to one of the many government nurseries where the children stayed while the mothers worked in the factories.

The post office, where she mailed her letters home to the family and dispatched the last of the Italian sketches to Seymour, was not far from the square where she and David had sat on that autumn evening so many years ago. She walked over to it and saw that the café across the way, where mournful violins had played songs of hopeless love, had been torn down and replaced with a Komsomol meeting hall decorated with an enormous picture of Josef Stalin. The small park itself was deserted at midmorning on this summer day, but in a shaded corner, near a ragged hedge, two boys kicked a scarred black-and-white soccer ball at each other. No, they replied in answer to her strange question, posed in the scraps of Russian she had all but forgotten so that she had to rip the words into her consciousness, they knew of no old woman who frequented this park, though they often played here, even in the evening. They had never seen such a woman. But was it true that Leah came from the United States, and if so did she know Clark Gable? They had stood for hours in the line to see *Mutiny on the Bounty* and they hoped to see it again. Leah disappointed them when she admitted that she had never seen Clark Gable, even from a distance, and they were incredulous when she explained that the distance from New York to California was like the distance from Odessa to Paris. However, they were pleased when she found some American coins in her purse and argued over the one stamp she gave them until she found another.

The driver whom Leah finally located, however, knew of the woman she inquired about.

"Bryna Markevich—a name like that. I remember her. Sometimes when I was a small boy and played here she tried to give me coins or candies. She was always running to the train station. There was some story about her husband that my grandmother told me. I think it was that he deserted her and she could never believe it, and so she kept waiting for his train. Yes—I'm sure that was it." He nodded with satisfaction.

The driver, who sported a glossy Stalin moustache, was very young, barely twenty. He must have been a toddler, wheeled in a stroller, when Leah left Russia. He was Jewish but spoke no Yiddish and he wore the bright-red scarf of the Komsomol. A child of the Revolution, born to the glories of the brave new world, he was unable and unwilling to believe in the terrors of the years gone by.

He did not conceal his incredulity as Leah told him the true story of Bryna Markevich.

"She was not deserted. Her husband was killed in the terrible pogroms of 1903. He was on a train journey and she could never believe that he had been so brutally murdered and was not coming home."

"Come now." The young driver was scornful. "That is all reactionary propaganda. Russians did not murder wantonly like that. The Jews suffer from historic fantasy—we call it, at my dialectic seminar, a delusion of history. Do you know what xenophobia is, Madame? It is the Jewish disease which they have no desire to cure. Believe me, I know. I live in a family of such sufferers. My father—and he fought with Gregoriev, mind you—sees an anti-Semite behind every Gentile face. Surely an intelligent woman from the United States of America knows better.

"Three years ago, maybe four, we had a terrible winter here in Odessa. Blizzard followed blizzard and there was difficulty obtaining fuel. The public places, the parks and squares became mountains of snow and when at last the spring came and they were able to clear through the melting snow, they found the old woman, Bryna Markevich, frozen to death on a bench in the park. Like a statue she sat there, a Bible open on her lap, they say, and the snow-diggers were frightened and would not touch her. It was the police who carried her away, her hair bright with ice and her breath frozen about her open mouth. Some say they buried her sitting up because they could not force the body to recline."

He laughed harshly but she heard the fear in his voice and asked no more questions. They drove the rest of the way in silence and when they reached the village of Partseva, he opened the car door for her, a small courtesy she had not expected.

The village square, with its cracked cobblestones and leaking pump, was exactly as it had been. The town hall, recalled through the years as an edifice of importance whose polished floors had the official odor of carbolic and where windows of real glass framed the gold-edged sunset of the vast Russian skies, was a modest two-story building. Through the doorway she saw a harassed clerk sip cold tea and nervously tap rimless spectacles against a splintering wooden counter.

Leah, in her navy-blue suit with a cape to match, of her own design and Seymour's manufacture, stood nervously near her hired car. Her arrival had already spiked curiosity and small groups gathered to stare at her in front of the planked tables that served as open-air counters for the village vendors. There were very few men in the square, and the small, wide-eyed children stared at her, hiding behind their mothers' skirts.

In this village they had not forgotten Yiddish and she heard the shrill whispers of the children.

"Look Mama, she does not wear a *shetel.*" The strange woman who had arrived in a motorcar wore no marriage wig, and Leah nervously passed her fingers through her cropped black hair and noticed that the women, who moved closer to her now, automatically adjusted the squares of cloth that covered their shorn heads. Their marriage wigs stood in brocaded cases in a corner of the closet, reserved for the Sabbath. That, too, she had forgotten and she felt a strange melancholy for all that had been lost to her—her father's voice, her mother's light laughter, the voices of her own children tumbling from infancy to childhood. Life happened too quickly—passages were too swift. Names deceived and places were lost.

"Leah—Leahle—is it you, after all these years?" The woman who rushed toward her was their neighbor, Shaindel Lichter, and Leah's heart leapt up, remembering that it was Shaindel who had traveled to Odessa for Leah's marriage to Yaakov, carrying with her an embroidered matzoh cloth which adorned the table in Brighton Beach on Passover. She fell into Shaindel's outstretched, welcoming arms and breathed in the remembered smell of camphor and garlic, mingled with a fragrance of lilac talc—a powder which Shaindel ground herself from the purple blossoms that grew so profusely in her tiny courtyard. Amid all that she had forgotten, all the spidery memories that had drifted into nothingness, Leah remembered herself, a small girl with long black braids, importantly pounding away with mortar and pestle in Shaindel's garden, her small being suffused with the scent of lilac which she could never forget.

"Ach, Leah. Such a journey. You must be hot. Come, have some water."

The crowd of women and children parted respectfully as Shaindel led Leah to the communal water pump which stood in a corner of the square.

Leah drank thirstily from the tin cup which dangled from a rusty chain, tasting in the cold sweet water the remembered subtle metallic flavor of the waters of the town stream. She looked wonderingly about her, marveling at the scene that had changed so little since her childhood. Russia had endured a revolution but the village of Partseva remained as it had been. Leah watched as a young woman plodded toward the pump, a small child clutching her skirt and two buckets balanced across her shoulders on long poles. She filled the buckets at the pump, bending her body low with a dancer's easy balance as though the arduousness of her life had trained her body to perform with skill. A few drops of water fell on the fair-haired child, who laughed suddenly and coaxed smiles from the tired faces of those around them.

"So tell me, Leah—how does it feel to be back in Russia? And how is your David? The children we know about it. Your parents, God bless them and keep them to a hundred and twenty, read us your letters and show us the pictures. Ach, I should have gone to America then too. Look at you. A noblewoman you look to be. And David is a doctor?"

"Well, I am not a noblewoman but David is a doctor," Leah said, wiping a trickle of water from her chin. "But I must see my parents. Will you come with me, Shaindel?"

Suddenly she was afraid. Perhaps she would be a stranger to the man and woman who had given her life, perhaps they would be alien to her. Seventeen years had passed since she had seen her parents and although they had written and exchanged photographs, she could not summon up a mental image of her mother and father. It was a curious inability. She had not seen her brother Moshe and his wife Henia in as many years, yet she could close her eyes and see them—tall Moshe and his delicate wife whose fragility had not prevented her, when she surprised a group of Arab marauders near the kibbutz children's house, from banishing them into the darkness with blasts from her rifle. But Leah's parents remained shadowy figures to her—they drifted through her thoughts only as a silent bearded man and a sad-faced woman who had always been bewildered by their second daughter. She had crossed an ocean, and then a continent, to see them, but now she felt restrained by this strange hesitancy.

"Such a question. Of course I'll come with you," Shaindel said. She was thoroughly enjoying her importance as Leah's guide and she straightened her blouse, rolled down her sleeves, and brushed her full dark skirt. "Come, I will find someone to mind my stall."

Shaindel's stall was a long planked table, tented by two frayed blue cotton blankets, on which small jars of medicinal herbs and sweet-smelling powders were arrayed. Now Leah recalled Shaindel's reputation as a curer. There was no doctor in the village and the nearest Jewish physician, who also served as a dentist, lived in Odessa. There were few automobiles in the village and saddle horses and carts drawn by donkeys stood in front of the inn. With transport so limited, Shaindel's business thrived. She distributed her homemade potions and drugs, applied massages, extracted teeth with a huge pair of pliers, and, on occasion, served as midwife and cupper.

"So you still are mistress here in town of the healing arts?" Leah asked.

"Yes, but much is changing. The state controls all medicine now and the law is that doctors must treat any citizen who comes to them. Of course, the fees then belong to the government and many are against this. But I say that as long as sick people get good care we should be happy and thank God. This is not the same Russia you left, Leah."

"The same and not the same," Leah said. "I'm not the same Leah."

"That I can see," Shaindel said and her ample body shook with laughter. "You were such a small, skinny girl. Now you're a woman. But your hair, Leah. You had such beautiful hair. Why did you cut it?"

"It's the style in America," Leah said and remembered the afternoon she had cut her hair, hacking away at it with kitchen scissors as Eli Feinstein's body was prepared for burial.

Walking slowly now, she followed Shaindel down the village streets, so much narrower than she had remembered them, across wooden walkways to the narrow path where she had grown up and where her parents still lived. Women, sweeping their wooden steps with straw brooms, paused to stare after her, and small children, playing games of jackstones in the dust, looked up curiously. To all of them Shaindel called proudly, "It's Leah, daughter of Basha and Avremel, come from America." The women nodded and their tired eyes took careful note of her tailored blue suit, the quality of her handbag, and her sheer silk stockings encased in the neat brown-and-white spectator pumps. Two small girls, barefoot, in homemade dresses fashioned from the same bolt of dull plaid cloth, trailed shyly after her, jumping into the shadow of a house when she turned to smile at them. She opened her bag, thinking to give each a coin, but at that movement they dashed away and disappeared into a doorway, like frightened little animals.

Word of her arrival had reached her parents and they stood leaning against the wooden porch rail of their frame house, staring down the narrow path. Grayer and smaller than she remembered them, not touching but gripping the railing, they stood together and watched the tall dark-haired young woman, in foreign dress, who was their daughter, walk slowly toward them. So they had stood when as a young girl she had left the narrow street and the tiny house for the world of Odessa, and in this same posture of anxious despair they had welcomed her home as a young widow of nineteen who would have to fashion a new life in a new world. So they stood, passive and submissive, schooled in the rhythms and patterns of their history. Things had always happened to Jews as they waited in the shadow of their porches for the sound of approaching footsteps or stood behind bolted doors in anticipation of a harsh compelling knock; it was the role of the Jew to allow them to happen, while they clutched the rituals and routines of their faith, clinging for support to fragile wooden railings.

"Papa, Mama," she shouted and dashed toward them. It was only after she had grasped them both and felt her father's hands in gentle strength against her temples, his red lips like a soft bright flower blooming within the gray foliage of his beard, that she saw the tears that glittered in their eyes. Her own cheeks were wet and the tears of her parents mingled with her own as they embraced and wept and embraced again, oblivious to the stares of the small crowd that had gathered in front of the house.

Her father wore the black caftan and the high skullcap of the Talmudic scholar. His robe was belted around bulky ill-fitting trousers of the kind which Seymour sent in regular parcels each year. Leah's mother had aged greatly and her head was too small for the marriage wig which tottered on it. She moved with the fearful slowness of the old and the fragile. She wore a flowered cotton dress which Leah remembered Mollie buying for her, and where its folds were too large, she had fashioned a cord to pull the fabric closer to her diminished form.

"Nu? Why are we standing here? Come in, Leahle. And you too, Shaindel." The frail old woman herded them into the house and they sat around the table almost shyly as she hurried to prepare tea. The small room was fragrant with the odors of newly baked honey cake and golden spongey loaves. These delicacies had been Leah's favorites as a small girl and her heart turned because her mother had remembered that over the acres of vanished years. How must it be for her parents to live on in this house that their three children had deserted for distant lands, east and west. Did this dimly lit, quiet room echo with the laughter of vanished children on quiet winter evenings? Did her mother steal up to the small loft room where they had slept and touch the empty beds as Leah sometimes did when Aaron and Rebecca were not sleeping at home? Did her father sometimes look up from the mountain of black-bound Talmudic texts that rested always on this table, and see their shadows whirl in the empty room—hers and Mollie's and tall Moshe's? Their pictures, portraits dutifully sent each year at Chanukah, were ranged in gilt frames on a small oak chest. Leah stared at a photograph of Moshe and Henia and their three children, posed among newly planted trees upon a stark mountainside. Their oldest boy, young Yaakov, held an unplanted sapling, its bulky roots shrouded in cloth, in his hand.

"Moshe's children look so beautiful. I would love to see them," Leah said wistfully.

"Yes. God bless them," her mother said. "Moshe keeps writing us that we must come to Palestine. Some of the parents of the other pioneers have done that and there is a special house for them on the kibbutz. But we are old and this is the village where we have lived our lives. How can we leave?"

"I'll show you how you can leave," Shaindel said. "You take a suitcase and put in it your Shabbat cloth and Avremel will put in it his *tallis* and *tefillin* and you close the door and say '*Shalom.*' That's how you leave." And the fat woman leapt jovially up to demonstrate in pantomime the simplicity of the venture.

Leah's mother served the steaming tea in tall glasses, and as they drank and ate the cake still warm from the oven, Leah told them about her family and Mollie's, about the prosperity of S. Hart and the way they lived their lives.

"But Seymour and David still pray three times a day in a *minyan* at the synagogue?" her father asked anxiously.

Leah did not answer. It had been years since either her husband or her brother-in-law had attended a daily prayer quorum and recently they had seldom attended services even on the Sabbath. But her father's eyes searched her face and golden crumbs of sponge cake trembled on his beard as he waited for her answer.

"Yes, Papa," she said at last. "They are still good Jews."

She offered the untruthful answer, acknowledging that there was no danger of her lie being discovered. Her parents would emigrate neither to the United States nor to Palestine, but would remain on their porch, gripping the wooden handrail, awaiting the destiny that God meted out to the Jewish people.

Still, all that evening and the next day, she tried. She walked with her parents through the village, stopping to greet old friends, to answer questions about children and brothers and sisters who had left for America years before. With her mother and father at her side, she walked across the fields to the small cemetery, established according to biblical injunction at a distance from the town. Within the small graveyard, where wild flowers gutted the sloping graves in a frenzy of color, wild red roses entangled with sunny masses of goldenrod and threaded with hardy clumps of deep purple clover, they found Yaakov's grave. Leah stood quietly while her father intoned the Kaddish, tears flowing down his cheeks. Then she bent and searched the ground until she found a small smooth stone which she placed gently on his headstone.

She knelt to pluck up a few weeds and touched the stone, roughened and weathered through the long seasons. Her tears, too, fell freely and the Hebrew inscription danced before her clouded eyes, the sunlight bouncing off the twisted letters that grew larger and smaller through the saline curtain of her grief until at last the tears stopped and the letters etched in stone fell still beneath her gaze—"Yaakov, son of Eli, gathered unto his fathers at the age of twenty."

"*Shalom,* Yaakov," she whispered and broke loose a wild rose which she placed next to the smooth stone. Its thorn pricked her and she welcomed the pain and the hot blood that seared her fingers.

Slowly they walked back to the village, following the long purple shadows of sunset that stretched across the vast sky.

"Mama, Papa, you must make plans to leave Europe—to come to Mollie and me in America," she said. "We will make you a good, comfortable life."

"My life here is good and comfortable," her father replied. "I have my books and the study house. Your mother has her home, her small business. You and your sister have built lives in America and Moshe has his own life in Palestine. We have our lives here. We are too old to move to a land where we do not know the language. We want to die where we have lived."

Her mother nodded in agreement. They had reached their small home and in the yard a cruelly stunted apple tree shaded a patch of barren earth, its small burden of fruit slowly blushing into redness.

"We planted that tree when we were married, when I came to this house as a bride. Each spring I have watched it bloom and each fall we have picked the fruit of its branches. That is what I want for my old age—to smell the sweet flowers and eat of the fruit of our tree," her mother said.

"But your grandchildren—Mollie's children and mine—don't you want to see them?" Leah asked.

"If I could. If I could," her mother answered sadly. "But they are of your life, Leahle. You will see that when your children are grown, their lives belong to them and your life belongs to you. I wish I had known that when you left for Odessa. You claimed your life very early and if your father and I had granted you that right there would have been less pain for all of us. For your own children, learn from our mistake."

They sat together on the porch, smiling at the neighbors who made their way down the street, the children carrying pails to be filled at the communal pump, the women hurrying home with their straw baskets laden with produce, with small red potatoes, flowering stalks of beets, bright green bouquets of sorrel grass, pearly-headed scallions. All of them slowed their steps as they passed the house of Leah's parents, straining for a look at the daughter from America who wore a bright red dress and whose stockings were of a sheer, shimmering silk.

"You know, Papa, in Paris I met a Jewish family who recently arrived from Germany," Leah said.

"It is a terrible thing that happens there," her father replied sadly. He spoke as though Germany existed on a distant planet and his weary voice was heavy with resignation and acceptance. Terrible things happened to Jews everywhere from time to time. The only thing to do was to wait and pray and a remnant would survive and create new generations. *Shaarit Yisrael*—the remnant of Israel.

"But Hitler will not be content only in Germany. He wants to conquer all of Europe and wherever he goes there will be terrible danger for the Jews," Leah continued, her voice tense and urgent.

"Hitler? Who is this Hitler?" her mother asked. She sat in the shadow paring an eggplant she had removed with surgical skill from the plant that grew at the side of the house.

"I told you," her father replied impatiently. "That new Haman who has become the dictator of Germany."

"Ah yes. The little man with the moustache. He looks like Perel Lieber's younger son—the one who went to America and never sent for his wife and children—he was never heard from again. Do you remember Perel Lieber, Leah?"

"Mama," Leah said impatiently, her voice rising in familiar irritation, "I am not interested in Perel Lieber although it is interesting that you think this Hitler resembles a Jew. He considers Jews to be obscenities, subhuman creatures, and he intends to make Europe free of *Jews—Judenrein* is the word he uses. Have you heard that word, Papa?"

"Many have threatened to make Europe—no, not only Europe, but the world—*Judenrein,* Leah. But do not worry. It will not happen. It has not happened. We must have faith and study and pray and live where God has sent us." Her father lifted his head and charted the progress of the lowering sun. Slowly he rose from the wicker seat and went into the house, emerging with the blue velvet bag that contained his prayer shawl and phylacteries.

"I must go to the evening service now," he said, and joined the small parade of bearded, slow-moving men who walked down that narrow path, their long shadows streaking the splintered planks that served as sidewalks, each cradling a worn velvet sack.

Leah sat on in the quiet dimness and then joined her mother in the kitchen where she took up a paring knife and sliced the potatoes in neat ivory squares as she softly told her mother about her children—Aaron of the blazing curls, laughing Rebecca, and small Michael, born to joy and gaiety. Mollie's children were such good students and Mollie and Seymour had a beautiful home. Anne played the violin and Jakie's hair curled the way Moshe's had as a boy. Softly she talked on, answering her mother's questions about the grandchildren they both silently acknowledged she would never see.

She left early the next morning. The car she had ordered arrived just after sunup to give her enough time to take the Bessarabian Express in Odessa and begin her journey westward to Le Havre where the *Queen Elizabeth* was accepting passengers for the return voyage to the United States. She stood again between her parents and embraced them, feeling her father's hands, gentle against her temples as he blessed her in words she did not understand. Her tears mingled with her mother's as they kissed and then kissed again, unable to release each other until the driver harshly pressed his horn. The automobile negotiated a laborious turn down the narrow street, and she looked back; through streaming tears she saw her parents standing together in the half-light of dawn, their hands clutching the wooden porch railing.

There were letters waiting for her in Paris and as she sat in her room on the Rue du Bac, looking down at the sparse traffic on the street below, she read that Seymour had received her sketches and that production on the new line of S. Hart originals had begun. The children were all enjoying the summer and they had all attended Bonnie Eckstein's sudden marriage to Peter Cosgrove. The ceremony had been performed by a judge and Bonnie's father had refused to attend. He had, instead, rent his garments and observed seven days of mourning for the daughter whom he now considered dead to himself and his people.

"It is an oddly appropriate match," David wrote and Leah, knowing Peter and Bonnie, understood his feelings, but thought too of her father's sweet innocence when he asked if Seymour and David still attended daily prayer quorums. Her father would see nothing appropriate in this marriage between a New England Protestant and a Jewish immigrant girl. In a Left Bank stall, lithographs by an artist named Marc Chagall were being sold and Leah bought several because they reminded her of life in the village of her birth. But one such lithograph, portraying a bride and groom in dizzy dance beneath a glorious, starlit heaven, she saved as a wedding gift for Bonnie and Peter.

On that last day in Paris she went again to the narrow streets of the *Pletzel* and climbed the dank stairwell of the building on the Rue des Rosiers where the Schreibers had lived. But it was another frightened German Jewish woman who opened the door cautiously, her children clinging fearfully to her skirt and her own eyes wide with fear. That terrified stare told Leah more than she wished to know and she turned her eyes away and asked about the Schreibers. They had left for America, the woman said, and the Joint Distribution Committee had assigned the apartment to them. The tiny flat, with its frayed rug and ragged grimy curtains, served now as a way station in misery. Leah reached into her purse and pulled out a handful of francs which she held out to the woman. Proudly, the woman shook her head and the door was softly closed and bolted. But from behind the closed door Leah heard a threnody of sobs and a child's voice pleading "*Bitte, Mama, bitte.*"

Two days later she boarded the Queen Elizabeth carrying a copy of the *Paris Tribune.* The headlines screamed the news of Fascist ascendancy in Spain, the Abyssinian riots against Italian occupation, and new anti-Semitic measures in Germany. Leah stood at the rail of the ship that slowly made its way out of the harbor, her eyes drifting from the headlines to the slowly disappearing coast of France. A sad-eyed priest, standing at her elbow, glanced at her paper and then at the gentle curve of the shoreline.

"Let us say good-bye to Europe, Madame," he said softly. "I fear that it will never again be the great good Continent we have known."

They stood together on deck, allowing the salt spray to seep into their clothing, and watched the peaceful lights of the port city disappear into the purple twilight.

Scarsdale
1939
11

David Goldfeder arose early that Friday morning, the first day of a September still searing with summer heat. It was the sheer habit of years that awakened him because he was due neither at his consulting room nor at the hospital. He had decided to turn the Labor Day weekend into a four-day holiday and he glanced approvingly out the window at the sun-speckled leaves of the large maple, relishing the luxury of four days of leisure. Briefly, he glanced across the bed where Leah was still deep in sleep and was tempted to awaken her. Her dark hair, grown long again, was strewn across the pillow and her flesh was soft and rosy within the folds of her sheer white nightgown. He leaned over to kiss her and she smiled, murmured something unintelligible, and curled up into renewed sleep. He sighed in disappointment but told himself firmly that it would be unfair to deprive her of rest when they would be entertaining guests throughout the weekend. The Goldfeders' sprawling Scarsdale home became the gathering place on holidays and the Harts, the Ellenbergs, the Cosgroves, and poor Mr. and Mrs. Schreiber were expected that afternoon. No, it was best for Leah to sleep as long as she could.

Feeling virtuous, he padded down the hallway, past the large sunny bedroom where his daughter Rebecca slept, her arms still draped around a large panda Joshua Ellenberg had bought for her at the World's Fair. Rebecca was seventeen now, a senior at high school, but to them she remained the gay laughing girl whose childhood they had jealously guarded. David smiled when he noticed how the panda's bright black nose gently nudged the soft full curve of Rebecca's breast. Their little girl was quickly becoming a woman, he thought, remembering that Leah had been married to

Yaakov when she was a year older than the girl who slept with the large stuffed animal in her arms. Very softly, he closed her door.

Michael, too, was asleep, his bed barricaded by intricate Erector Set creations and his wall papered with posters from the General Electric exhibit at the World's Fair. Michael worked for hours, sometimes days, on a single bridge or building, kept it intact for weeks, and then suddenly dismantled it and cheerfully created something new. He shook his dark curls vigorously as he worked and laughed excitedly when a new idea struck him. A happy child was a small miracle, David thought, and as he passed Aaron's empty room, the neatly made bed caused him a brief pang of misery.

But then, perhaps Aaron would come home after all, this holiday weekend. It was a good sign that he had completed his summer school courses at New York University. His roommate, Gregory Liebowitz, who had shared Aaron's intense political involvement over the past two years, had been virtually paralyzed by the turn international events had taken this summer of 1939 and had dropped his courses and disappeared on what he called a "thinking hike." But then Gregory had been more introverted than Aaron, more isolated, coming as he did from a home still completely rooted in the traditions of the world David and Leah had left twenty years before. Aaron, at least, had had David to confront with his disillusionment and impotent fury when it became at last perfectly clear that Germany and Russia would form an alliance.

David remembered, as he walked through his quiet house, how Aaron had waited for him in his office the day the headlines proclaimed the news. His oldest son was over six feet tall, with the lean, taut body of the trained runner. His bright hair was closely cropped but even so curled defiantly, and his chiseled features were tense, the young face always sharply wary of nameless dangers. Dressed in the faded dungarees and plaid cotton shirt which constituted his uniform, Aaron pointed wordlessly to the *Tribune* headline which David had read, with sinking heart, hours earlier:

GERMANY AND RUSSIA SIGN TEN YEAR NON-AGGRESSION PACT; BIND EACH OTHER NOT TO AID OPPONENTS IN WAR ACTS; HITLER REBUFFS LONDON; BRITAIN AND FRANCE MOBILIZE.

"Dad, how could they do it? The People's Republics signing a treaty with that Nazi scum?" Aaron's voice was incredulous, betrayed. The headline violated everything he had believed in and worked for during the two years that had passed since he left their Scarsdale home to live near the University—a move which Leah and David had encouraged, each quietly hiding a painful sense of loss.

"It is time for him to establish his own identity, to find himself as Aaron Goldfeder, his own person, not as the son of Leah and David," David had said, using clinical terminology to shield himself from the intense private pain he felt as he watched Aaron pack. Increasingly, as his practice expanded, he found he was treating young men and women who had no sense of themselves as individuals and were divorced from their emotional lives. Alienation, his colleagues called it and offered learned theories on its origin—the sudden advent of mass production, the speed of their times, automobiles, movies—the explanations were manifold but the young people continued to writhe in emotional misery and David was determined that his own children should discover themselves.

"Yes, of course," Leah had agreed but her voice was frayed with worry. She enjoyed no ease in her relationship with Aaron. It was as though she and her bright-haired firstborn were trapped in an emotional maze, always chasing after each other, their outstretched hands just missing, their voices echoing down newly deserted corridors. She would watch Aaron sometimes, his face tight with concentration as he struggled with a chess problem, his lean body always keyed and taut. She felt suffused with a pride and love she could not display because there was no peace between them. Left alone in a room, they faced each other uneasily, fought for words and avoided each other's eyes. It would, of course, be better for all of them if Aaron lived at school. He had never liked the large Tudor home on the gentle Westchester hill which they had bought shortly after her return from Europe when it became clear that the new line of S. Hart International Originals was going to make them all rich.

The arrangement she had made with Frederic Heinemann had been a reciprocal one. She sent him sketches of American designs and fabric swatches and he in turn went to the European shows and shared his drawings and insights with her. The letters were still mailed to and from Charles Ferguson's because even hopeful Frederic Heinemann no longer dismissed fears of the Nazi influence as irrational. His letters were increasingly worried and he was determined to arrange for himself and his friend Heinz to leave as soon as the establishment on Kurfuerstandamm could be sold.

"He admits finally that the countrymen of Schiller and Goethe are experiencing an interlude of insanity," little Mr. Schreiber observed wryly. Schreiber now managed the import and export division of S. Hart, and when Leah visited their bright apartment on Washington Heights it was difficult to recall the grim misery in which they had lived on the Rue des Rosiers. Only the picture of their son, a serious-eyed, thin young man in university cap and gown, stood silent witness to the grief they had known and would never forget.

Aaron himself had no interest in the business and stayed away from both factory and office—unlike Joshua Ellenberg, who had enmeshed himself in the firm as soon as he graduated from high school.

Aaron shared none of Joshua's purposeful direction. He had been a good student at Scarsdale High School, but a pervasive dreaminess clung to him. Often, during his last years at home, Leah felt that he moved through the house as though he were an uncomfortable guest in their midst, observing and judging the ambience of their lives. The small boy who had stood sentinel at a tenement window had grown into a tall young man who moodily listened to other people's laughter and sat silently through meals at which the conversation of his parents and his brother and sister percolated with ideas and opinions. The New Deal had served its purpose. The federal government should take a more active stand against segregation in the South. Scarsdale High School should encourage an exchange program with foreign countries.

"What do you think, Aaron?" David would ask. "What does it matter what I think?" the boy invariably replied and waited for the twin shafts of pleasure and shame which followed his rudeness—shame at the pain he had caused his father and pleasure at the distress he knew Leah felt. But she did not reprove him in anger or indignation as she often cautioned Rebecca and Michael for lesser offenses. Instead she sought him out in his room and sat tentatively at the edge of his bed or stood uneasily in the doorway.

"Aaron, is something the matter?"

"What could be the matter?"

Like awkward strangers, they fenced verbally with each other, sparring with questions and answers but never allowing the sheer metal edge of their lonely anguish to pierce the mesh of delicate defenses it had taken them so many years to weave.

"What do you want to study?" she had asked when he graduated from high school.

"I don't know. I need time. Leave me alone."

He hurled the words at her as though her question had been an accusation and she did not think to defend herself, knowing that she had earned his anger in other places during other years. Aaron talked vaguely now of studying political theory, and the friends he brought home from the university were thin, almost gaunt, young men, who remained for hours in his room, talking softly while the portable phonograph played *The Songs of the Lincoln Brigade*. Above the music they heard Aaron's voice, impassioned and fluent, and the murmurs of agreement that followed when he expounded a theory. Within this group of intense young people he was totally accepted and they left him no time to experience loneliness and apprehension. There were important things to be done, books to be read, the problems of the world itself to be sorted out, solved. They were the generation to confront and conquer poverty, hunger, unemployment. There had to be a more equitable way to distribute wealth. How could Aaron reconcile his Scarsdale home with the Harlem slums he passed on the train that carried him from one life to the other? In the Scarsdale living room his mother and his uncle studied production figures. In his Greenwich Village apartment a poster hung over his sagging daybed proclaiming that "Communism is Twentieth Century Americanism."

When he came home alone he sat silently in the living room looking contemptuously about at the comfortable furnishings, the soft draperies and deep rugs, as though comfort itself were a personal affront, a conspiracy against him and his tortuous ideals. He smiled only when small Michael laughingly hurled himself at him and enticed him out to the grassy lawn to shag fly balls. A great joy and love soared between the two brothers, nine-year-old Michael and Aaron the nineteen-year-old political theorist. It was always Michael who could make Aaron laugh and Aaron who, during Michael's childhood illnesses, read endlessly to him and squatted on the floor, following his small brother's instructions on the Erector Set and Tinker Toy creations. Michael had always been a pet to him, never a challenge, and he cherished the small boy for the peace that had come to the household with his birth.

Leah, straightening Aaron's room when he returned to the city, found mimeographed sheets issued by the Young Communist League, the Young People's Socialist League, crumpled receipts from the Friends of the Spanish Fight for Freedom, clippings from the *Daily Worker*.

"He is in the family tradition," David remarked dryly. "Let him find his own way. Besides, I notice that he is not too involved in politics to neglect taking Lisa Frawley out to miniature golf."

Lisa was a young friend of Rebecca's who always managed to visit when Aaron was expected home, despite the fact that his visits to Scarsdale grew more and more infrequent. When Leah phoned and insisted that they meet in the city, he took his parents to small downtown theaters where they sat in hard-backed seats and watched plays by Aaron's hero, Clifford Odets.

"You see," Aaron would cry exultantly, "he understands poverty. He understands art."

"Your mother and I also understand poverty," David said, looking at the scar on his wrist where the flesh puckered into a grinning welt—the scar earned when he had studied while pressing pants before traveling uptown to his studies at the City College. "I think you too must have some memories of poverty, Aaron. Perhaps you recall the apartment we all lived in on Eldridge Street. Do you remember that there was a fire escape just outside the kitchen window? When you were an infant—we had been in America only a few months and I did not yet have steady work—your mother made a crib for you from a wooden crate and so that you should get fresh air, she put the crib on the fire escape and watched it while you slept because cats ran up and down that fire escape. For hours she sat there and watched. We had a neighbor there—poor Yetta Moskowitz—who used to say that the poor couldn't even afford air and she was right. For us, air was a luxury. So we too understand poverty."

"Those were the years that your father worked as a pants presser—twelve, sometimes fourteen hours a day," Leah added. "We haven't forgotten."

"But now you have your life's ambition," Aaron retorted bitterly. "A big business for Mama and Uncle Seymour, a fancy east side office for you, and a house in Scarsdale."

It was not long after that conversation that Aaron moved from the dormitory on Washington Square to a small cluttered apartment on MacDougal Street which he shared with Gregory Liebowitz, who was intensely involved in what they called the Movement. Their small rooms were piled high with mimeographed sheets deploring the lot of itinerant farm workers, of the down-trodden Okies, the tragedy of Spain, and the moral supremacy of the Soviet Union. A large poster of Mother Bloor smiled benevolently down on them. Leah, on an infrequent visit, maneuvered her way through the cluttered room and thought of a similar room where stacked pamphlets had served as furniture and a narrow cot had sufficed a dark-haired young woman and her green-eyed love. She saw that younger Leah, now, as a distant friend.

Aaron's involvement in the Movement intensified and he talked about leaving college and working full-time for the Party. No wonder, then, that he had felt so bitterly betrayed when the Hitler-Stalin pact was signed that sweltering August afternoon. A colleague at the hospital had told David that one of his patients, a committed Communist, had attempted suicide when he learned of the Von Ribbentrop mission. A group of Socialists at the City College had draped their red flag in black bunting and initiated a brief hunger strike. In the cafeterias on the upper west side, men and women carrying book bags and brief cases stopped each other and asked in earnest distress, "Do you believe it?" "Is it possible?" "Can you believe it?"

Aaron had read the headline he flashed at David but he too remained incredulous. Together he and David had gone into the doctors' lounge at the hospital, where they listened to H. V. Kaltenborn's cracked and strained voice give the details of the pact. A young black surgeon, active in a group called Doctors for Peace and Universal Justice, switched the station and they listened to Edward R. Murrow, speaking hoarsely from London, confirm the report. The surgeon had ripped a pin, a red enameled caduceus, from his white jacket and tossed it into the wastepaper basket before slamming out of the room. David looked at Aaron and saw that there were tears in his son's eyes.

"Your mother predicted this three years ago when she came back from Europe," he said.

"My mother always predicts everything," Aaron replied bitterly. "Ballerina skirts, the stock market, and even the Hitler-Stalin pact. Wonder Woman."

David did not answer. Aaron needed time, he told himself. It was Aaron who had suffered the agonies and hardships of those early years; it was he who bore the scars of their struggle, of Leah's losses, and, finally, even the acid imprint of her success.

Aaron had returned to class although Gregory had left the city and another friend paraded with a group of Zionist Socialists in front of the doors of the Russian Consulate, carrying signs which linked the hammer and sickle with the swastika.

Well, now Aaron had had a week to assimilate his distress, David thought, and surely he would come to spend this Labor Day weekend with them. Things would surely get better.

David opened the front door and sniffed in the freshness of the morning air. The last of the roses were in bloom and it seemed to him that their scent grew stronger as their season waned. What pleasure the garden had given him, these past three years. Mollie had been right, after all, to urge this move to Westchester on them—right for the wrong reasons. His sister-in-law, ensconced in a much larger house a few miles away, berated him for tending to the garden himself, urged Leah to hire more help, and drove an enormous Buick which she discussed with as much enthusiasm as she discussed the academic and social achievements of her children. Mollie, after all, was Mollie. He smiled and bent to lift the *Times*, which lay neatly folded on the brick steps, and his eyes still followed the yellow roses as he automatically flipped to the headlines. Always, in the years afterward, when he thought of the war in Europe, he remembered that strong late summer scent of blooming roses, their sweet doomed fragrance filling the early morning air, and the shock of the headline, so long anticipated and still so frightening: HITLER'S ARMIES INVADE POLAND!

"It's begun," he thought dully and like his tall son, tears filled his eyes and he wept with bitter credulity and pain for a world so newly at war.

*

Joshua Ellenberg heard the news of the Polish invasion on an early broadcast as he waited for the stock market report. Angrily, his fingers curled around the small copper model of the Empire State Building which he had purchased just months before at the opening of the World's Fair. The World of Tomorrow, he thought bitterly, and remembered how he and Rebecca had stood for hours to witness the opening ceremonies of "The Court of Peace." The Germans had already destroyed all hopes of peace and if they had their way, those Nazi bastards, they'd destroy all his tomorrows as well. And Joshua's tomorrows were so carefully planned—programed and saved for since his childhood. He knew, had always known, where he was going. He wasn't going to spend his life living in the shadows of the Harts and Goldfeders the way his parents had lived in the back rooms and basements of their homes. And he had already managed to end that period, to achieve for his mother the dream of her own home. When the Harts and Goldfeders had moved to Scarsdale, he had borrowed money from Seymour and used it to buy the Brighton Beach house for his parents. Now, at least they had an income from the tenants in the house and he himself was free to rent a room in Manhattan and continue to mold his secret plans into sweet reality.

He had even risked discussing his blueprint for the future with Rebecca, on the night the World's Fair opened. Hand in hand, they had walked through the gardens where fountains sprang up from nowhere, among buildings ribboned with sparkling waterfalls, edging their way through excited crowds calling to each other in many languages. Rebecca had worn a navy-blue skirt and a white blouse with the small red hart dancing on its pocket. She had danced herself, twitching excitedly to the tune of "The Sidewalks of New York" which followed them wherever they wandered in that lovely wonderland. They giggled as Elsie the Borden cow spun around with 150 friends on a revolving milking platform and they craned their necks as the brightly colored parachutes plunged earthward past giant-sized Life-Savers. In the amusement park he won a panda for her and she clutched it as they watched Oscar the

Obscene Octopus wrestle a very small blonde girl who wore very few clothes.

Rebecca's long dark hair was loose, held in place by a bright-red headband, and when she moved, twisting easily to the improvised dance step, her body was soft and graceful and her smile, so gay and free, made his heart beat with an arhythmic trembling.

"Oh Joshua, I'm so happy. Thank you for taking me. It's all so beautiful," she cried.

"That's all I want to do, ever, Becca," he said, the words breaking recklessly out of the carapace of secrecy in which they had been shielded since their shared childhood. "All I ever want to do is make you happy, take you places and give you things. And I will. I'm going to be as rich as your Uncle Seymour, Becca. Only I'm not going to sink all my dough into Seventh Avenue. I've been studying the stock market—Wall Street. I'm trading already. Do you know that I already made enough money to pay your uncle back the money he lent me for the Brighton Beach house, and now I've paid the whole house off! All from one killing in the market. You can make a lot of money now and I know just how to do it."

"Of course you do, Joshua. You've always known how to make money. Remember that first vacation we had in the mountains with your cousins—the time Mama was in that awful factory fire at Rosenblatts? I'll never forget how you went to all those bungalow colonies selling the cotton shirts you shlepped up there." She laughed and remembered how she had trailed after him and called out, mimicking his own voice, the call of the child peddler: "Get your bargains, get your shirts, cheaper than on Hester Street, cheaper than on Orchard Street!"

"I remember," Joshua answered shortly.

She had not, after all, understood a word he said. She was a baby still, too young to understand that he was talking about a real future, a long future, that they would share together. He wasn't talking about a couple of pennies' profit on a shirt from a peddler's cart but real money, the kind of money that bought houses with swimming pools and tennis courts, limousines with liveried chauffeurs. The kind of money her friend Lisa Frawley's family had. But there was time. He would wait for her to grow up. His baby, his Becca.

But now, with this news broadcast, there suddenly did not seem to be as much time. If Germany had invaded Poland, then England would have to support its commitment and declare war on Germany. And if France and England went to war, how long would it take before the United States plunged in? Hadn't President Roosevelt and his wife entertained the King and Queen of England at Hyde Park just that summer? Still, perhaps England would not jump in. They had preached patience, nonintervention, before. Anything could happen. He must not panic. His country was still far from war and his dream was still intact. It would take more than a war to interfere with Joshua Ellenberg's plans. After all, how many other nineteen-year-olds could buy their parents a house—and for cash? He looked approvingly at himself in the mirror, smoothed Vitalis on his thick fair hair, and liberally applied a shaving lotion Rebecca had admired. In a half-hour he would meet his parents at Grand Central and they would ride up to Scarsdale together. But they weren't going to make the *shlep* by train forever—no sir. Joshua Ellenberg's next purchase would be a car—a four-door Ford in baby blue, Becca's favorite color.

"When the moon comes over the mountain..." he sang as he slammed the door behind him, and he dropped a nickel in the blind newsdealer's plate before going down into the subway but did not take a newspaper. These damn journalists and news announcers exaggerated everything. He had time, plenty of time.

Rebecca Goldfeder and her friend, Lisa Frawley, walked down White Plains Road, carefully weaving their way in and out of the gently swaying shadows of the leaves that dappled the broad thoroughfare. They carried their tennis rackets under their arms and Rebecca allowed the can of balls she carried to swing loosely at her side. Lisa's long blonde hair hung in silken smooth folds about her shoulders, but Rebecca's thick dark curls were caught up in two ponytail bunches that bounced at either side of her finely shaped head and were tied with strands of bright pink wool that offset the crisp white cotton tennis dress her mother had designed for her.

Rebecca had begun playing tennis only a few months before and attacked the game with her usual enthusiasm. She always focused all her energy on the particular project in which she was involved, approaching it like a storm with a whirling vortex aimed in a set direction. Rebecca concentrated fiercely on her goal and then, like a dispersed wind, she abandoned it without regret. The previous year she had been addicted to horseback riding and haunted the local stables, having cajoled her parents into giving her lessons. Both Leah and David had been reluctant. Horseback riding, for them, was vaguely associated with midnight marauders, hoofbeats in the darkness, booted Cossacks galloping past houses where frightened children crouched. Still, they overcame what they acknowledged to be their "ghetto neurosis" and allowed Rebecca to ride. The day after her first show, in which she jumped the highest hurdle set up in the Scarsdale Riding Academy corral, she sent her jodhpurs to the cleaners and tossed her boots into the back of the closet.

That winter she had bought an expensive pair of figure skates, and bright felt skirts which she wore with heavy, cable-stitched white sweaters. She went daily to the frozen expanse of Twin Lakes until she could carve her name in elegant letters on the blue white ice, then hung the skates on a basement hook and gave two of the felt skirts to Lisa. Now tennis was her passion and she haunted the red clay courts of Scarsdale High School, fretting about her game and whether her favorite court would be available.

"She should stick to something," Leah worried.

"She will. She's only seventeen," David replied. He himself admired Rebecca's single-mindedness. Well, she had come by it honestly. Hadn't her mother known how to concentrate her energies and become mistress of her craft? And without a single-minded approach would he be a psychiatrist today?

The two girls ran lightly as they approached the courts.

"Of course they're not crowded today," Lisa said contentedly when they saw two empty expanses. "Everyone is probably home listening to the radio. My father hasn't moved from it all day. I don't understand him. The war's across the ocean, for heaven's sake—in Europe!"

Lisa's voice implied that Europe was a distant planet and Rebecca remembered how months before when everyone in Scarsdale had been upset by a devastating fire which had torn through Greenwich, Lisa had shrugged indifferently and asked, "What's all the excitement?—Greenwich is in Connecticut."

"My grandparents are in Europe," Rebecca said. "In Russia."

"Oh, that's all right then," Lisa said. "Russia's on Hitler's side."

"Lisa, you're so—so shallow," Rebecca said impatiently and laughed in spite of herself.

Lisa too laughed. "Shallow" was not a derogatory adjective, when used about a pretty girl at Scarsdale High School in the autumn of 1939.

"Well, I hope your brother Aaron thinks so too. Your friend Joshua may like 'deep' women but I'll bet Aaron, for all his Modern Library giants, doesn't mind my being 'shallow.'"

She smiled, thinking of the many hours she had spent with Rebecca's brother the past spring and fall, the quiet and the laughter, the long talks over lukewarm cups of coffee, the early-morning bike rides, that made up her time with the tall red-haired boy who quivered at her touch, but spoke about things she did not understand.

It had begun one afternoon when Lisa had come to call for Rebecca. Her friend was out playing tennis and Aaron had looked up from a political theory text he was reading on the terrace to tell her so.

"Oh darn. I wanted her to bike along the Bronx River Parkway with me. It's such a perfect day. When your sister gets hooked on one thing she can't think of anything else."

"I'll bike the Parkway with you," Aaron offered, tossing his book aside. He did not smile but there was pleasure in his eyes and his tense, thin features relaxed as they rode into the wind and followed the curving road up to the crenellated fortress of the Kensico Dam. The pleasure deepened as they rested side by side in the tall grass and then his long muscular arms reached about her, cradling her body while his lips tenderly touched her cheeks and eyes and finally came to rest, first gently, then with fierce certain strength, against her yielding lips. When they stood, locked in a sweet silence, to mount their bikes again, Lisa's body was deliciously moist. At home she stared at herself in the mirror, ashamed of her ignorance. Since that day, she had haunted the Goldfeder house each weekend, her heart soaring when Aaron's hand touched her shoulder and he said, in that oddly quiet voice of his, "Do you want to walk or bike this afternoon?"

"You can ask Aaron yourself," Rebecca said now, twirling her racket. "He called to say that he'd be up this afternoon and my mother asked if you'd stay for dinner. There'll be quite a crowd—the Harts, the Ellenbergs, the Cosgroves, and Mr. and Mrs. Schreiber—they're from Germany and their English isn't too great, so talk slowly."

"Sure, I'd love to come. At my house they'll still be wrapped around the radio," Lisa said and felt her breasts harden at the thought of sitting across the table from Aaron, remembering the hand that had moved so gently across her arm, strewn with dancing bands of the palest orange freckles.

"About Joshua," Rebecca said carefully. "Joshua is just like a brother to me. You know, we practically grew up in the same house."

"Well, he may be like a brother to you but I don't think you're like a sister to him," Lisa replied. "Oh, look, the far court is empty. Let's run for it."

The two girls in their gleaming white tennis dresses dashed across the grassy slopes of the lawn, passing a middle-aged couple in street dress who sat with their heads bent close to a large portable radio, listening to a news commentator analyze the situation.

"One remembers now," the announcer ruminated sonorously, over the faint static, "the day Mr. Chamberlain abandoned Czechoslovakia to Hitler. 'It is peace in our time,' he said, but Winston Churchill replied, 'Britain and France had to choose between war and dishonor. They chose dishonor. They will have war.' And today, Churchill's prophecy has come unhappily true.

It is only a matter of hours until England must make its move. We stand on the threshold of a world at war." The radio was clicked shut and the couple, without looking at each other, moved on.

On the shaded tennis court Rebecca Goldfeder tossed a new white tennis ball into the air and slammed it over the net, laughing when it fell neatly into a corner on the opposite side and rolled off into the purple-flowered shrubbery. Overhead a plane flew low, hovered briefly, and then soared upward with startling speed. Rebecca stared after it, then took a new ball and offered Lisa another serve.

*

By late afternoon, almost all the guests due at the Goldfeder home had arrived. Leah, in a long dark skirt that swung gently around her calves and a cowl-necked white blouse, passed plates of miniature stuffed cabbages. Charles Ferguson accepted a drink from David and watched his elegant hostess, her dark hair threaded with glinting strands of silver and pulled back into a graceful chignon, circle the terrace. He thought back to that distant wintry day when a timid young immigrant woman whose blue-black braids were woven into a coronet stood shyly at the door of his studio. He remembered too the librarian on East Broadway who had told him of a red-headed boy who had insisted that his mother looked like the princess in "The Sleeping Beauty." He had recognized that child to be Aaron Goldfeder and although he had not thought of Leah as a princess then, there was certainly something queenly about her this afternoon. Among designers, he knew, she was considered creative royalty. Her fashions took prize after prize and if Seymour Hart was fast becoming a millionaire, he owed his swift rise to Leah's talents and ingenuities. Certainly, much of her work was derivative of the major European designers, but it was a talent to know from whom to improvise. Charles himself still wished that Leah would return to serious painting, but the design fever had seized her early and her career had been spurred by her need to make a living for the family while David studied medicine.

David himself, Charles thought, had aged scarcely at all. True, a small tuft of gray sat spongily in the center of his beard, but thin men with their spare frames and narrow features clearly had the advantage in the years of advancing age. Charles touched his own corpulent middle and looked with satisfaction across the porch to where Seymour Hart sat, pleased to notice that Leah's brother-in-law was loosening the belt on his plaid slacks. The heavyset manufacturer laughed too loudly, breathed too hard, and ate too much. His pudgy daughter, a year or two older than Rebecca, dangled too many charms on a heavy gold bracelet and circled her eyes too thickly with violet moons. Mollie Hart wore too much rouge and her hair was dyed a too brassy red. Even their son Jakie's white buck shoes and V-necked tennis sweater were, after all, too white. The Harts were a family given to excess just as the Goldfeders were given to understatement. Charles Ferguson enjoyed wrapping people up into neat judgmental packages and he smiled, pleased with himself and with his friendship with the assembled group that had weathered so many years. Other things in his life had inexplicably vanished or faded into a whirling mist of forgotten days and dark, disappointed nights.

"You seem content today, Charles," Leah remarked, sitting down in the lounge chair next to him. "Doesn't the war in Europe worry you?" Her voice was calm but he saw the tiny lines of strain about her fine eyes.

"I'm too old to fight and too young to despair," he replied and then banished all lightness from his tone. "But I know it must worry you."

"Yes, I'm worried. My family is still over there. I warned them. Three years ago, when I went to Europe."

She spoke quietly but Mrs. Schreiber, who sat near her, leaned forward, seizing on her last words.

"We all warned each other," the German woman said. "My husband and I warned our friends and neighbors. Our poor lost son warned us and we in turn warned him. England and France warned Germany and Germany warned the world. But the warnings were never enough. We would not believe and if we believed we would not act."

"I think your pessimism is premature, Frau Schreiber," Charles Ferguson said gently.

"No. I have lost a son. My pessimism was too late," she replied and went to join her husband at the far end of the terrace where the men gathered around the radio which was issuing periodic news bulletins interspersed with baseball scores.

"Where are the children, Leah?" Charles said. He had noticed how Leah leaned sharply forward as a car sounded on the street or the phone rang within.

"Aaron isn't here yet. I wonder where he can be. I'm a bit worried."

She walked to the terrace railing and leaned forward, looking into the dimming light, watching for her tall bright-haired son who had spent so many hours of his boyhood watching for her.

"Oh, he'll be here any minute, Aunt Leah," Joshua Ellenberg said. He was carrying a tray with glasses of iced tea for his parents, still the dutiful son he had been since childhood. "See, there he is now."

He looked down the hill which Aaron was swiftly climbing, glad that his friend had arrived, annoyed at him for causing worry. Well, that was Aaron. Joshua deposited the glasses at the small table at which his parents sat and went off to join Rebecca, who was holding Bonnie Cosgrove's small daughter on her lap while Michael fashioned a paper plane out of the front section of the Times, creating a graceful wing from which the face of Hitler addressing a cheering crowd leered.

"Your prodigal brother returns," he said to Rebecca, and Lisa Frawley, who had been standing nearby, moved to the brick steps which Aaron was climbing two at a time. When Lisa was sure he had seen her she moved off and began an animated conversation with Annie Hart, automatically laughing with an elegant toss of her long blonde hair at something Jake Hart said, although she had scarcely heard his comment.

"You don't really like Aaron, do you?" Rebecca asked.

Bonnie's child giggled and a spot of pearly saliva gleamed on the shoulder of Rebecca's white tennis dress. Joshua leaned forward to wipe it off and felt his body throb as it drew closer to her dark skin with its smell of perspiration and Ivory soap.

"I like Aaron. But I can't stand this Bolshevik crap he's been spouting. Particularly since he really doesn't know anything about the working class and the famous intolerable 'conditions' he's always discussing. You don't find out much about factory workers in the library at Washington Square College. I could tell him a few things about the old days at Rosenblatts and even about the new days at S. Hart. I guess I'm just tired of being the listening post for his theories and hearing everyone worry about 'poor Aaron.'"

"He does get these horrible moods," Rebecca admitted. "But I think his politics have changed since last week. The Hitler-Stalin pact really got to him. Daddy said he was so shocked he could hardly believe it. And poor Gregory Liebowitz just took off—dropped his courses and everything."

"Yeah—it got to all of them. The sudden light of reality. How could their marvelous idealistic Soviets do that? The world of tomorrow takes giant steps back into the Dark Ages. Hitler and Stalin exchange the kiss of survival. I hear them in the coffeehouses downtown." He raised his voice to a cruel pitch and imitated the conversations that were repeated daily through the city. "I can't believe it. I won't believe it. It's not worthy of the Communist system. System—phooey!" He spat the word out as though it were an obscene epithet. "Systems don't make any difference, Becca. The only thing that makes any difference is what you do yourself in the world. Everyone has to go after his own. Did a system build S. Hart? It wasn't a system that made your mother a designer and your father a doctor. It was their own guts and work. They did it all themselves—just the way I'm going to."

"But what are you going to do?" Rebecca asked teasingly.

Bonnie's child had fallen asleep on her lap and she arranged the little girl's head on her shoulder and looked at Joshua. He did not answer, but small beads of sweat rimmed his lips and his large hand shook slightly. A small thrill of pleasure ran through Rebecca and she wondered, with sweet guilt, why it was that her body delighted in making Joshua Ellenberg nervous.

Bonnie Cosgrove, swaying gracefully on her heels in the manner of the newly pregnant woman, took the sleeping child from Rebecca. Michael walked down the garden path between Mr. and Mrs. Schreiber, listening with delight as they told him the German name of each of the flowers his father had planted with such gentle delight. The Schreibers adored Michael, sent him small gifts from time to time, and often took him out to concerts and theater. He had become their surrogate son, replacing the serious-eyed young man in the photograph whose voice would never again lift with laughter. Charles Ferguson took up the large sketch pad which he carried everywhere, and filled it with rapid charcoal drawings. Peter Cosgrove and David bent over a medical text while the Ellenbergs, their heads close together, dark-gray hair touching silver, listened to the radio which had been playing all afternoon. Bonnie Cosgrove, her child asleep in the stroller, read the newspaper, her hand resting on her stomach where new life grew as she read of distant death.

Aaron and Lisa disappeared into the house and emerged moments later through the garage, mounted on bicycles which they pedaled with urgent speed.

"We'll be back before dinner, Mom," Aaron called and Leah waved and watched them streak by, the full afternoon sun turning Aaron's cropped hair the color of new-lit flame.

"Don't worry, Leah. They'll be back in time for dinner."

Leah turned and saw her sister standing beside her. There had been times during these past years when she scarcely recognized Mollie. The sister she had known—the pale, dutiful bride, the frightened wife and mother—had disappeared and were absorbed by the overweight woman whose hair changed color too often, whose rings and necklaces matched the bright two-piece dresses bought during endless journeys to department stores for display to a husband who seldom noticed his wife. But now she saw the honest worry in Mollie's eyes and Mollie's plump hands clenched painfully together just as they had been so many years ago when she trembled beneath the marriage canopy.

"No, Malcha, not to worry."

The sisters stood together on the porch and watched a boy and girl walk by hand in hand and then went into the kitchen to begin setting out the meal, their thoughts gliding sadly back to the distant troubled land of their birth.

*

The Bronx River Parkway snakes its way gently northward and its sloping shoulders are thick with long grass and shaded by young maples and graceful willows. In some places the trees intertwine to form a bower and wild hedges create a natural wall. At the break of dawn on the Sunday morning of that Labor Day weekend, Lisa Frawley and Aaron Goldfeder parked their bicycles against such a hedge and locked themselves into the sweet dark room created by the walls of leaf and bark. Thus concealed from the road, they stretched full length on the grass and allowed the sweat accumulated on the ride to dry into delicious coolness on their arms before turning to each other and generating a new, electric warmth fired by skin and touch. Aaron's arms looped about her body and his mouth pressed hard against her soft lips, biting them suddenly and forcing his tongue into her mouth which yielded open in pain and pleasure. She took his hand from her back and pressed it against her breast, needing his touch against the painful hardness that filled her.

"Aaron." Her voice, usually so gay and light, was shy now, almost nervous. "Do you like me? Really like me?"

He smiled and rolled away from her, pulling up a long thread of grass and biting at it. When he was with Lisa his eyes lost their brooding melancholy and lit with an amused gladness. She seemed to him a delightful child, a small innocent girl, and he wondered why it was that this childish, wondrously naive quality of hers called forth his own urgent bursts of manhood. The girls he knew in the city, the girls who worked with him in the Movement writing and mimeographing literature, the girls who sat next to him in seminars devoted to an examination of the Hegelian dialectic—What, he wondered now, would Hegel have thought of the Hitler-Stalin pact? Probably he would have dismissed it as the product of a period of synthesis—left him wary and distant. Once, after a party when he had drunk too much Chianti after singing too many songs about the liberation of Madrid, Aaron went to bed with an earnest coed who wore her thick brown hair severely cut in a butcher-boy bob. She delivered a cogent argument on the biological tragedy of the woman and moaned and writhed when he silenced her with his body. But he never saw her again nor had he wanted to, fearing her seriousness, her complexity.

It was Lisa, his sister's friend, a child like Rebecca herself—a golden Scarsdale princess who wore a matching cashmere sweater set with little twinkling buttons, who skied in the winter and played tennis every day in the summer—whom he sought out, feeling soothed and safe when he was with her. Lisa, who had once said that she thought Hitler was "sort of cute" and whose father, a prominent land developer, was convinced that Hitler had done great things for the German people and pointed out the Autobahn and the wonderful garden apartments for workers. Her father quoted Colonel Charles Lindbergh extensively, and Lisa's mother kept a stack of wrapped copies of Mrs. Lindbergh's books which she gave as gifts for a strange variety of occasions.

"Of course we're against what he says about the Jews being warmongers but Daddy is sure the stories we hear are exaggerations," she had told Aaron.

"They're not," was his answer, but that was all he had said, not wanting to argue with Lisa, to surrender the pure simplicity of his relationship with her. There were so few times in his life that he felt this simple, clear ease and joy and he protected its brightness, refusing to cloud it with arguments and polemics and knowing that this sweet golden child was no match for any arguments he would offer.

"Come on, Aaron," she asked again now, the shyness gone from her voice and replaced with the bullying insistence of the spoiled girl. "Tell me. Do you? Do you really like me?"

In reply, he leaned over her, his face full upon hers, and lifted her from the ground to kiss her once, and then again.

"Now what do you think?" he asked softly. "Isn't that a dumb question? Do you think I get up at five in the morning to cycle with a girl I don't like?"

"Oh, Aaron."

She sighed and slid back into the tall sweet grass, but later that night, after the hectic events of the late afternoon and evening, as she lay in bed in her pretty pink bedroom where the starched white organdy curtains rustled at the windows, she remembered that he had not, after all, answered her. His final reply had been the strong mysterious pulsing of his body, lost within her. She remembered too, then, looking back as they left that wooded bower and seeing, with shock, the soft grass matted with a dark red clot of her girlhood blood.

Lisa and Aaron returned to the house at midmorning and found the family again assembled on the terrace, grouped around the radio.

"Good morning, this third of September, 1939," a breezy announcer said and Lisa thought that she would always remember the third of September as she did the date of her birthday. The day I became a woman—my woman day, she thought, and went to sit near Aaron's father.

David Goldfeder was stretched out on a lounge chair, an atlas of Europe open next to him, and as he clasped and unclasped his hands, Lisa noticed his graceful narrow fingers and the strange pink scar that rose to an angry welt on his wrist. She wondered if Aaron would resemble his father when he was older and then reminded herself that David Goldfeder was not Aaron's natural father.

Leah was writing a letter and her eyes were red, as though she had been crying; Lisa was startled. She had never seen her own mother cry, not even when her grandmother had died. The sun rested harshly on Leah's face, revealing the worry lines that circled her eyes and trembled in the corner of her mouth.

"I am writing to your grandparents," she told Aaron, without looking up. "Now, there is no question about it. They must leave. At once."

"Leah." David's voice was tired but his tone remained weighted with patience. "Your letter will be useless. They cannot leave now. The only possible way would be to travel east—to Palestine or the Asian countries—China, Japan. No Jew can go through those parts of Europe which Hitler controls."

"But they can't go to Palestine. You know what Moshe has written about the difficulties in getting even children in. The British refuse to relax the quota. As for China, Japan—can you see Papa and Mama going to China and Japan?" She laughed harshly and then began to weep, so softly that Lisa was gripped with fear.

"All right. Write. I'll be in touch with HIAS, the Joint Distribution Committee. Maybe there are channels, ways..." But

David stared straight ahead as he spoke, his gaze acknowledging that there were no channels, no ways.

"Look, something may happen," Aaron said. "Hitler may back down. England may be able to work out a compromise of some sort. You know the French cabinet still thinks it can get Mussolini to mediate. Hitler marched into Poland on Friday and this is Sunday and nothing has happened yet. Perhaps there is some hope that France and England will stay out, will negotiate a peaceful settlement." Aaron advanced his arguments with a sudden burst of desperate optimism. Lying on the grassy incline that morning, with Lisa Frawley nestled beside him, the sun high in the sky and cyclists cruising down the parkway, it had suddenly occurred to him that it was a sweet miracle that he was so young, the sun so strong, and that his life stretched before him as the sun-dappled highways stretched before the holiday cyclists.

"Ah, you haven't heard the news, Aaron." Joshua Ellenberg stood in the doorway, Rebecca just behind him. "Britain declared war on Germany this morning. France will come in anytime now."

"My God." Aaron held Lisa's hand tightly and looked about the terrace as though he were seeing it for the first time, noting the strange crook in the branch of the elm tree and the way the purple morning glories wound their way around the bright green trellis.

"Aaron—you're back! Aaron, play catch with me!" Michael, in short blue pants and a snowy white shirt, hurtled across the terrace clutching his pink Spaulding ball which he tossed so wildly that it fell onto David's lap and rolled across the atlas.

They all laughed, glad to leave the war for the moment. Michael scurried after his ball and pulled Aaron after him onto the lawn. Rebecca and Lisa followed Leah into the kitchen and helped prepare the brunch. David, rising abruptly, asked Joshua if he would help him paint a picket fence in the backyard and surprisingly, Joshua agreed. The fragrance of a baking pie floated over from the neighboring house. It was as though a sudden addiction to domestic normality might dispel the terror that now engulfed the world they knew.

Aaron received a phone call that afternoon from Gregory Liebowitz, his apartment mate. He had to return to New York at once. Something had come up. It was only later that Leah realized that Aaron had come without a suitcase, but when David drove him to the station he had a large valise with him.

Aaron stood beside her when he said good-bye, grown to such a height that she, tall as she was, came barely to his shoulder. The sun set his hair ablaze and when he kissed her he held her tight and she felt his body taut and supple within her arms. A gratitude stirred within her then because Aaron seldom kissed her and had not embraced her since the day she sailed for Europe, three years earlier.

He kissed his sister too, then walked briefly in the garden with Lisa Frawley, who did not return to the house but rode her bicycle slowly home, her eyes so bright with tears that she had to swerve wildly to avoid being hit by a passing motorist.

Aaron tossed a gleeful Michael high into the air and shook hands with Joshua.

"You were right, you know, about the whole Communist business. It was a lot of crap," he said.

"We all make mistakes. Take care, Aaron." Joshua's eyes held Aaron and he covered Aaron's hand with his own. Later, Rebecca, remembering that handclasp, that exchange of glances, realized that Joshua had known what Aaron meant to do. Shrewd Joshua who always anticipated everything.

Two days later, as Leah sat at her drawing board and listened to the radio playing a recording of King George's address to his people—"For the second time in the lives of most of us, we are at war"—the phone rang. The thin ready voice of a long-distance operator asked her if she would accept a collect call from Aaron Goldfeder in Montreal. Then Aaron's voice was on the line, bristling with strength, excitement.

"Ma—listen, don't get upset. Gregory Liebowitz and I took the bus up here and enlisted in the RAF. You understand, don't you, Ma? We had to."

Her heart sank and the room dimmed. She struggled to a chair, grasped the phone, and said in a strong voice, "Yes, Aaron, I understand. I'm proud of you." Tears streamed down her face but her voice remained calm. They talked for a few more minutes. The boys were leaving for England for special training. He would send his address as soon as he knew it. There were a lot of interesting guys in their unit—a whole American Zionist group from Chicago had enlisted.

"This isn't an ordinary war," Aaron said. "This is a war against evil."

"Yes," she agreed. Her palms were moist and a headache pounded distantly, obscurely, behind her temples. "You'll write."

"Of course."

"Aaron—take care. Please."

"You too, Ma. You too. Is Dad there?"

"No."

"Tell him... no, don't tell him anything. He'll understand."

Her voice was calm when she said good-bye and she remembered back over the years how she had watched for her small son's fiery curls at the window as she rounded the corner of the narrow streets of his childhood. She and her son had spent their lives stealthily concealing their desperate concern for each other. But now, at last, perhaps too late, the distances were narrowing, the blind alleys of their emotional maze were sealed off. She held the silent phone in her hand and touched her lips to the mouthpiece.

So much remained unsaid between them. Her son was going off to forge his future but the secrets of his past remained unrevealed, mired in the emotional thicket that separated them. Perhaps he was leaving for Canada only to leave her. How would David say it in that concise psychological vocabulary of his—that Aaron had found an intellectual solution to emotional problems—a rational escape from an irrational fear. If she had only spoken to him, told him, explained, he might not be in a distant city waiting for a plane to carry him across the ocean, into a battle that was not yet his. But no. Aaron had done what he had to do just as his natural father, so many long years ago, had done what he had to do. They had come full cycle then, she thought wearily, and overcome by a fatigue strangely fierce and febrile, she rested her head in her arms, her hand still clutching the silent receiver.

Later that night Gregory Liebowitz's mother called. She was a widow and Gregory was her only son. Tears clouded her voice and her accent grew thicker and thicker as her grief obscured the English learned so late in life that it could never be the language of her heart. At last, she spoke only in Yiddish and David listened as Leah too switched to the language of her childhood, calming the other woman with assurances and rationales that she herself could not be comforted by. The boys would be fine. The war would be over soon. A month. Perhaps two. The boys would be safe. God would watch over them.

"But why did they have to go?" the woman asked yet again.

"Because it was only right that they should," Leah said firmly.

But when the other woman hung up, she sat quietly at the small phone table, clutching the receiver, her shoulders shaking with sobs she could not control, and David guided her upstairs to bed and sat beside her, his hands buried in her dark hair, and listened to the sound of her helpless weeping until she fell at last into a heavy sleep.

12

When Moshe Abramowitz was a young pioneer in Palestine—years before he hebraized his name to Abrahami—he traveled to Cairo on kibbutz business. It was then that he wrote to his sister Leah Goldfeder, in New York City, that the Egyptian city was more provincial than the Odessa they had known in their youth. But the war in Europe had infused the sleepy Middle Eastern metropolis with new life. Traffic was heavy and constant through the narrow streets of the ancient quarters and along the great boulevards constructed in the nineteenth century by French and English architects who yearned for the broad expanses of the Champs Elysées and the stately ambience of Trafalgar Square. Trucks were loaded and unloaded at the Bab al Hadeed railroad station and maneuvered their way past the indifferent, massive statue of Rameses II, en route to the British army encampments, scattered throughout the city and its suburbs. Along the Avenue Fuad the First, everyone hurried. British army vehicles thundered heavily by, creating great clouds of fine white dust, reminders that the broadest boulevards could not long vanquish the encroaching desert. Their horns sounded stridently, and barefoot, large-eyed children dashed away from their careening desert wheels and jeered after the jeeps which inevitably were forced to stop by an immobile oxcart, halted in the center of the broad busy street. The peasant driver, in a dusty robe and grimy *kaffiyeh* headdress, imperturbably smoked a cigarette while the ancient beasts, with stoic exertions, dropped steaming turds in neat towers of stinking detritus on the sunwashed pavement. The British drivers, their faces pink with impotent rage, shouted expletives and shook clenched fists, but the dark-skinned peasant ignored them, except for a smile which revealed astonishingly pink, toothless gums.

Bureaucrats in minor government offices worked more quickly, importantly wielding their rubber stamps with the speed and precision of a soldier handling a Bren gun.

Shopkeepers extended their hours because the British soldiers who flocked to Cairo on leave from posts in the Middle East and North Africa brought with them their leave pay. The precious sterling piled up in the cash registers of the self-effacing businessmen, who issued gold-toothed grins beneath their red-tasseled caps, and sold the boys from the Cotswolds and Shropshire linens embroidered on the banks of the Nile, brass rubbed to a soft shining glow in the metalworkers' bazaar, and daggers which were offered with handwritten certificates of authenticity—each rusted weapon was pre-Christian, early Christian, a relic of the bloody days of Luristan.

The merchants pressed their sales with urgent confidences, oily whispers of sacrifice and esteem.

"I promise you, my good sir, this I give you as a bargain for only ten pounds. Also you must do me the great honor of drinking a small coffee with me. I say ten pounds and I am losing money, but even so, I know you go soon to fight for freedom so I will make you a special price of nine pounds. But please, you must take more sugar in the coffee and drink while my servant wraps your excellent purchase."

Patrons thronged to the sidewalk cafés with their round tin tables shielded by striped umbrellas whose brave reds and bright greens had long since been faded by the relentless desert sun. The waiters scurried about, always hurrying, always delayed. They wore black pants that glistened with grease and sweat, bright red cumberbunds, and shirts that had been pounded to a startling whiteness on the riverbank. The thin, busy waiters, who balanced several tall glasses of cold coffee on their arms with mysterious dexterity, knew everything about the life of Cairo. They knew who was in the city and who had left. Points of origin and final destinations were their secrets, transmitted from ear to ear for a modest *baksheesh*, or tip.

Salim, the headwaiter of the Cafe El Ibrahim, opposite the British Embassy, offered his information with the ice water he served after each cup of Turkish coffee. Sir Archibald Wavell was in earnest conference with a man named David Arthur Sandford. This Sandford, Salim confided, was a peculair man who drank only hot water and honey. In the café, the merchants absorbed this knowledge as though it had an obscure value, and the journalist at a nearby table noted the name of Sir Archibald's visitor in his orange Penguin paperback. Within hours he knew that Sandford had been consul at Addis Ababa and lived in Ethiopia as a gentleman farmer and confidant of poor Emperor Haile Selassie, who had been exiled by the Italian Fascists.

It was Salim whom the merchants asked about the identity of a bearded stranger in British uniform who sat picking at an order of eggplant fried in sesame oil and reading a Hebrew newspaper. He was a Palestinian Jew, Salim told them, named Avram Akavia. It was truly miraculous but this infidel Jew spoke an impeccable, classical Arabic. The merchants nodded admiringly and switched to usage of a Delta dialect.

The journalist had no need to research the background of Avram Akavia. He was known throughout the Middle East as the Jewish secretary to Major Orde Wingate, who, in turn, was known as the T. E. Lawrence of the Jewish community of Palestine. Just as Lawrence had dreamed of an Arab army, so Wingate imagined regiments of Jewish soldiers. The journalist shrugged at the thought. Jewish soldiers, indeed. He was a Londoner and knew the East End well. What sort of army could be raised from among those earlocked, bearded merchants of Whitechapel or the pale students of law and medicine who haunted the inns and academies? Of course, he had been to Palestine and he had to admit that the pioneers on the new agricultural settlements there were a different breed. Still, what could they do with that swamp-ridden Galilee that the Arabs themselves had deserted? The Zionists were mad, and Wingate, for all his brilliance, had been affected by their madness.

But still, what the hell was Wingate's secretary doing in Cairo, eating eggplant in the fall of 1940? Idly the journalist juggled his pieces of information, handling them in his mind like the isolated, ill-fitting sections of a jigsaw puzzle, moving them about until at last, by some obscure, chimeric connection they came together and he understood that Orde Wingate would be involved in a campaign in Ethiopia. Of course, that was it—and that accounted for the moderately inflated numbers of RAF troops in Cairo. He looked up as two young RAF men whom he had not seen before sat down at a neighboring table. Poor chaps, he thought. They think they're still on parade, ridiculously got up like that in khaki, sporting their wool berets in the desert heat. They somehow did not look British. Red hair, like the taller boy's coppery crown, was common in Wales. They were Welsh, he decided. Satisfied, he slipped a half-crown, covering both payment and insurance, into Salim's outstretched hand, and left.

The two young airmen put their red berets on the table, loosened their ascots, and asked Salim to bring them large Coca Colas.

"Americans," the waiter reported to the leather merchant who sat in the doorway puffing on a nargileh. He did not bring them Cokes but set before them large glasses of orange *gazoz,* in which small pieces of shaved ice floated like deadly slivers of glass. The shorter airman lifted the glass and twirled it around.

"When this war is over," Gregory Liebowitz said, eyeing the ice shavings distastefully, "I am going to make me a fortune."

"Spoken like a true communist turned socialist turned capitalist," Aaron Goldfeder replied. "And may an old comrade ask how you are going to make this fortune?"

"I'm going to import ice-cube trays. First I'm going to bring them into England and then into Egypt. Then I will work my way across Africa. I will consider it an altruistic endeavor—my contribution to the downtrodden of this earth."

Aaron laughed, remembering Gregory's good-humored arguments in the pubs of Bournemouth where they had been sent from Canada to get their initial training. The only places that had been on limits to the RAF troops had been The Prince of Wales and

The Golden Swan, and neither proprietor had shown any sympathy for the American predilection for ice cubes in their drinks.

"Say, look at that guy over there," Gregory said and pointed to the table where Avram Akavia sat reading a newspaper. "That's Hebrew the bloke's reading."

Aaron smiled at the anglicism. Gregory Liebowitz, Aaron guessed, would go through life using the English expressions he had acquired so readily.

"You're right. It's a Hebrew newspaper. I didn't even know there was such a thing. I wonder if I could read it." He stared hard at the man. "I guess he's a Palestinian Jew. I've got family in Palestine. Moshe, my mother's brother, is on a kibbutz in the Galilee. You know, the rumor is that a lot of Palestinian Jews will be coming out here. This Wingate has a mania about training a Jewish army. He worked with a couple of units in Palestine and thought they were such great soldiers that he's asked for a contingent to serve with him in North Africa."

"Maybe he'll pass the word about Jews being such great soldiers to the guys in our unit," Gregory said wryly, touching the small out-puffing of flesh just below his eye.

Gregory was a short, plump young man with a gaminlike face, gifted with a sharp, swift sense of humor and a fierce instinct for justice. The two qualities neatly balanced each other, giving Gregory the talent for self-mockery. At home it had been Gregory who worked intensely on Movement literature, traveling to migrant encampments in Pennsylvania in vain attempts to organize the itinerant workers, but it had also been a puckish, half-drunk Gregory who drew a moustache on their poster of Mother Bloor. Gregory had joined the RAF in passionate reaction to the Hitler-Stalin pact and had persuaded Aaron to enlist with him. Although he longed to do battle with the avowed foes of humanity, the only wound he had sustained since joining His Majesty's forces had been earned in a private boxing match with a young giant from the Canadian Rockies named Pierre. Pierre had culminated a series of observations on the cowardice of *"les Juifs"* and Gregory's role in the Crucifixion with speculation as to whether a circumcised penis could actually sprout seed to germinate a new generation of Christ-killers.

"Ah, *le pauvre petit*. They cut it all away. No juice come from there, *bébé*—no more little Jewish Christ-killers," Pierre had said, sneaking up on Gregory as he unbuttoned at the urinal.

Gregory's years of fighting in the schoolyards of P.S. 107 and DeWitt Clinton High School had prepared him for such an encounter. Leisurely he turned, pivoted slightly, lifted his penis high, and sprayed Pierre in the face with a forceful stream of urine, aiming the last golden spurt, which stank of ammoniated beer, at Pierre's eyes.

"Jewish piss blinds," Gregory said, calmly buttoning his fly as the astonished Canadian wiped his face with wads of toilet paper. "It's our secret weapon."

He walked slowly out, knowing that Pierre would follow him, his clenched fists ready, when the huge airman, with a curdling yell, hurtled out of the latrine and plummeted with him to the ground. The fight had been a fierce one and Gregory had emerged with two black eyes, one of which never healed properly, a bruised cheekbone, a chipped tooth, the admiration of his entire squadron, and, ultimately, Pierre's friendship.

That brawl behind the latrine had brought Gregory and Aaron to the attention of the training sergeant. A few days later they had been separated from their unit and, with another group of selected men, sent to the Middle East for special training. David Goldfeder had often told his son that it was the small insignificant incident that often altered the course of one's life. His father would be amused to think that Aaron was sitting in a Cairo café because Gregory Liebowitz had been in a fight with a French Canadian backwoodsman.

"Well, I think our fellow soldiers are getting the message," Aaron said. "We did all right during that desert bivouac."

"Not bad for two kikes from the sidewalks of New York," Gregory admitted.

He and Aaron had been the only ones in their group not to panic when a sudden sandstorm swept down upon them. Together, they had controlled the group, ordering the men to freeze in place and to cover their eyes against the angry air-tossed pellets of sand that could permanently injure sight. It was after that storm that they stopped hearing the words "kike" and "sheeny" as they walked by.

The bearded Palestinian neatly folded his newspaper, summoned Salim, spoke to him in Arabic, and paid his bill.

"So what do you say, Aaron? You still think your bar mitzvah class prepared you to read this guy's newspaper? Let's see." Gregory stood up and held his hand out to Avram Akavia.

"*Shalom aleichem*," he said, automatically using the traditional greeting extended from one Jew to another. "I have a bet with my friend here that even after five years of Hebrew School he can't read a word of your newspaper. Can he try?"

"*Aleichem shalom*." The stranger returned the greeting in the prescribed manner and smiled. His skin was tanned to the color of the soft bronze they had seen in the metalworkers' *suq*, and when he held his hand out his skin was hard, covered with calluses the texture of worn leather. "My name is Avram Akavia and I am from Palestine. You are British Jews?"

"I'm Aaron Goldfeder. This is Gregory Liebowitz. We're American but we signed up with the RAF in Canada."

"Ah yes. I have just been reading in this newspaper that you are so interested in that a surprising number of American Jews are crossing the border into Canada to do just that."

"Why not?" Gregory asked gruffly. "It is our war, after all. Hitler has said it himself—it is a war against the Jews."

"Yes. I agree. It is a war against civilization and democracy. I cannot remember who it was who said, 'You can judge a civilization by the way it treats its Jews.' It was your president John Adams, I think."

"You've got me," Aaron said, returning the smile.

He took the newspaper Avram Akavia handed him, glanced at it for a moment, then shook his head ruefully. "I can read the letters but without the vowels I'm lost."

"Ah—but a prayer book you can read, can you not?" the Palestinian asked.

"Sure."

"Good. We are lacking men for a minyan for the Kol Nidre service tonight. We thought we should have to leave the camp and go to the Old Synagogue here in the city. But if you can join us we shall be assured of a quorum."

"You know," Aaron said wonderingly, "I'd forgotten about Yom Kippur."

"Please then—you will come?" Akavia's English was clipped, his accent British, but his sentences had the strange convolutions that David's speech occasionally revealed. Tonight, Aaron thought, across the world, David and Leah, Rebecca and small Michael, would all be going to temple. And he, in this strange city rooted in a desert, would share the same prayers, the same sweet mournful chants.

"We'll come. But where will the service be?"

"The large tent in B Garrison. You'll see a Jewish flag on the post and a small shield that says 'Gideon Force.' Come at seven. Shalom aleichem."

"*Aleichem shalom,*" Aaron replied, wondering at the greeting that came so effortlessly to his lips.

"Gideon Force," he repeated aloud as he watched Akavia stride briskly down the street in the direction of the British High Command.

The headquarters of B Garrison were south of Cairo, where the city abruptly ended and the desert began. Across the endless stretches of pearl-white sand, wooden walks had been stretched to border a military city in transit. Huge mess tents with the odor of bacon clinging to the olive-drab canvas, dormitory tents, their poles sagging beneath the weight of drying laundry, and staff headquarters squatted clumsily on the sandy expanse. Small Arab dogs ran in packs between the canvas shelters, their skin loose across their fragile skeletons. They howled in concert and then sat in mournful silence.

Gregory and Aaron, in their dress uniforms, walked down the streets of the tarpaulin enclave. Aaron shivered slightly. The chill of the desert evening was always a shock after the heavy heat of the day. They passed groups of soldiers who gathered around a harmonica player and sang the songs of the last war with nostalgic gusto. "It's a long, long way to Tipperary... Pack up your troubles in your old kit bag... Show me the way to go home..." This war, their own, was still too young to have created a new repertoire so they borrowed from their fathers' music, because this tentside singing was as important to them as the long desert marches and the daily rifle practice.

Other groups of men dashed about the sand in improvised games of soccer, and an ambitious group of commissioned officers had painstakingly managed to set up a court for bowls, which they practiced with great seriousness, as though they were playing on a Yorkshire green, not on an arid, endless desert.

But there was no activity near the large tent over which flew a banner imprinted with a Jewish star, flailing bravely in the mild desert breeze. Here, there was a sweet quiet which Aaron recognized—the strange silence of solitude which encompassed every congregation immediately before the Kol Nidre prayer was offered. The blue-and-white flag, lifted in a sudden gust of wind, billowed out against the sky which had darkened to a pale gray, streaked with the bloody tentacles of the dying sun struggling against the desert night. The sight of the flag moved Aaron to a strange emotion of pride and wonder. It was a paradox of history that a Jewish army of sorts—admittedly wearing British uniforms but still made up of Jews who lived in their ancient homeland—was assembled on the soil of the land they had fled as slaves. In Jewish history, Egypt was the symbol of every land where Jews had lived as strangers and died as victims. The Russia which David and Leah had fled, where Aaron's natural father had had his skull bludgeoned, had been a modern Egypt. David reminded them of that each year as they sat at the Passover table and read the injunction reminding them that each Jew must celebrate the Passover as though he himself had been released from Egypt.

Aaron hesitated for a moment before entering the tent, allowing himself to summon up the picture of his family's seder table, of his father's calm and comforting voice, his sister's bright laughter, his small brother's high sweet voice and always, always, his mother's large, searching eyes. His letters from home were irregular but comforting. That fall Rebecca had left for Bennington College and his mother had started going into the factory on a daily basis. The only thing that puzzled him was Lisa Frawley's persistent silence. She had not answered any of his letters from England, and Rebecca wrote to tell him that she had gone away to school for the last year of high school. He had thought that there was something special between himself and his sister's friend, but perhaps her silence was her way of telling him that what had been was over. She had been so young then. They had both been so young, and the pine needles beneath their yielding bodies had been so soft and sweet. A confining melancholy sealed him off from the other soldiers in the tent and he was startled when Avram Akavia pressed his hand in quiet welcome and drew him forward to meet the other worshipers.

In the end there had been no need to worry about a prayer quorum of ten. Twice that number of soldiers stood on the raw-wood tent platform smiling uneasily at each other.

"Let me introduce you," Avram Akavia said, and Aaron and Gregory circled the room with him, shaking hands with soldiers named Shimon and Elitzur, Asaph and Chaim, Nehemiah and Ezra. The names rocketed Aaron back to his days at the Hebrew school on Brighton Beach Avenue, to lengthy incomprehensible Torah readings in hot synagogues, but the Nehemiah who stood before him was not a biblical figure but a good-natured, freckled boy who wore a BEF sharpshooter medal on his tunic. Asaph, however, like his biblical namesake, was a medical officer who had earned his degree at the Hebrew University medical school. The last soldier Avram introduced them to was a tall boy named Yaakov, and as they clasped hands Aaron looked up at the Palestinian soldier's face and experienced a sudden flash of recognition. In those gold-flecked dark eyes he saw his mother's familiar stare, and when Yaakov smiled his lips fleshed out too fully, as Leah's did. Avram Akavia had used only first names in the introduction, but Aaron could feel Yaakov looking hard at him.

"May I ask your family name?" the Palestinian soldier said hesitantly.

"Goldfeder. I am Aaron Goldfeder, the son of Leah and David Goldfeder. And you—"

"I am Yaakov Abrahami, the son of your mother's brother, Moshe."

The two young men remained still for a moment and then moved swiftly toward each other and reached out, arm upon arm, the fingers of each biting into the strong arm muscles of the other. They clasped each other's strength in welcome while their eyes burned in recognition, igniting an affection startling in its spontaneity.

"Neither of you knew that the other was in Egypt?" Avram Akavia asked in surprise.

"My father mentioned in a letter that my cousin had joined the RAF but I thought he was in Canada."

"And I knew that Yaakov was serving with the British but I thought he would be defending Jewish settlements in Palestine," Aaron said. "In fact, I thought that if we got any leave at all I would take the train to Jerusalem and visit my uncle's kibbutz."

"Perhaps we will do it together. It would make my father so happy! But come, let us join the others. The service is about to begin." Yaakov tossed an arm over his cousin's shoulder and together they advanced to the rough bench set up in front of the platform.

A tall young soldier, sun-bronzed, his bright golden hair covered with the red beret of the British Expeditionary Forces, stood on the small rough platform holding a Torah. Like the assembled soldiers who had draped silken prayer shawls over their rough khaki uniforms, the Torah too was girded for battle, garbed in a strong gray canvas cover. Akavia glanced toward the tent entry and saw the evening shadows obscure the last shreds of light. He nodded and the group opened their prayer books and listened to the startling deep tenor of the soldier-cantor ring through the quiet desert night.

"Kol Nidre," the strong resonant voice sounded—"All vows, bonds, promises, obligations, and oaths with which we have vowed, sworn, and bound ourselves from this Day of Atonement unto the next Day of Atonement, of all these we repent. Let them be absolved, released, nullified, made void and of no effect; they shall not be binding nor shall they have any power. Our vows shall not be vows, our bonds shall not be bonds, and our oaths shall not be oaths."

"Amen!" chorused the khaki-clad congregation, who fingered the fringes of their prayer shawls and repeated the chant in unison, banishing with fervent chorus the worry over the battles that would be fought and the blood that would be shed before the next Day of Atonement. Grimly they thought of the prayer they would recite the next day—"Who shall live and who shall die—who by fire and who by water—" and trembled with the certain knowledge that some of them would surely die, some by fire and some by water.

Toward the end of the service a British major quietly slipped into the tent. He was a lean man, somewhat shorter than most of the tall soldiers around him. He wore a dark beard and moustache that reminded Aaron of David's. His deep-set eyes strayed from the open prayer book, which he read without difficulty, to the soldiers, who bent and swayed at prayer. His head, oddly large on that compact muscular body, was covered with a pith helmet and his field uniform was almost threadbare.

"That's Orde Wingate," Gregory whispered, and Aaron turned to look at the British officer who was said to hold the key to the North African campaign.

The service continued. The soldier-cantor's voice rose and fell, caressed the ancient melody and issued rhythmic warnings, chanted promises. The light in the tent flickered, then burned bright with new strength. Aaron looked at his cousin. They stood shoulder to shoulder, these tall young grandsons of Avremele, the stooped Talmudic scholar, whose sad eyes stared out of the twin framed photographs—one hanging in Yaakov's small kibbutz room and the other perched on the marble mantelpiece of Aaron's Scarsdale home.

The two cousins talked late into the night. They each had some snapshots with them and Aaron showed his cousin photos of Rebecca in her tennis dress, smiling mischievously into the camera, of Michael building a model airplane, of Leah and David staring seriously out over the brick walls of the terrace. He looked at Yaakov's pictures of Moshe and Henia and his brothers, Daniel and Ethan.

"You look so much like my mother," Aaron said. "You have her coloring, her eyes."

"But I am named for your father—your natural father—Yaakov Adler. And it is you who have his coloring. When my father speaks of him he calls him the *Gingi*—that is the Arabic word for redhead," Yaakov said.

"What has your father told you about him? My parents, of course, have seldom spoken about him and sometimes, you know, I've thought about what he must have been like. I've even wondered if he and my mother were really happy together. I know they were very young but still..." Aaron's voice trailed off and Yaakov Abrahami thrust backward in memory, focused on childhood tales of the old country—the land of Czars and commissars, of suffering and pogroms—to retrieve the half-forgotten tales of his unknown aunt's first marriage.

"They were happy, my parents always said. It was a love affair, not an arranged marriage. They had not been married even a year when he was killed. I remember that my parents did not go up to Palestine with the rest of their group. They waited until your mother was able to cope, to organize her life. Perhaps until she married David Goldfeder. I don't know. They didn't know, even when they sailed for Palestine, that she was pregnant with you, Aaron. For some reason she kept that a secret. But yes, I think they were happy together. Why do you ask such a question, Aaron?"

Aaron did not answer. He could not tell this cousin, so newly discovered, of his childhood fear that his mother had perhaps not loved him because she had not loved the dead father who had given him life. The mystery remained his own emotional conundrum, and when he closed his eyes that night he summoned up his mother's face and saw again the doubt and agony in her eyes as she hovered over him while he feigned the heavy sleep of exhausted boyhood.

*

Immediately after Yom Kippur, intensive training began for a campaign, the ultimate aim of which was still kept secret from the contingents of soldiers who readied themselves for it. Rumors were rampant and Salim distributed whispered information with the cups of steaming Turkish coffee he slid across the tin-topped tables of the El Ibrahim café. He sprinkled a name here, garnishing it with a rumored date there, served it up with a vague speculation. Squadrons were disbanded, reshuffled, and formed anew. Yaakov, Aaron, and Gregory were assigned to the same unit, with Yaakov serving as a squadron leader.

"If Wingate were smart," Gregory said one afternoon, "he'd put Salim on his payroll."

"Oh, Wingate is smart and Salim is probably on his payroll," Yaakov answered. "But Salim must be on a dozen other payrolls, which I am sure Wingate also knows. To you Salim whispers about Italian Somaliland. To someone else he says Abyssinia. We hear that transport has been requisitioned for the spring and that there is no transport. Salim says that by Christmas Haile Selassie will be back on his throne and that the Duke of Aosta is dying of cancer. But he told Nechemiah that the Duke is mustering an enormous army to take on a French force and he told the Reuters man that ten thousand men are attached to Gideon Force. The confusion that Salim spreads with his Turkish coffee is Wingate's special creation."

"Psychological warfare," Aaron said, looking up from a letter he had just received from home. "But one thing's for sure. Wherever we're going we'll be doing a lot of compass marching. That's the thing Wingate's been concentrating on. And he's got Yaakov in as advance man because Yaakov's used to marching without roads or highways."

"Well, it's true that the Negev and the Galilee don't have too many modern highways, but I don't think the kind of hiking I did for my botany classes could be classified as military marching." Yaakov had been in his third year of botanical studies at the Hebrew University in Jerusalem when war broke out. He had had Haganah training and he joined the British army the same day Aaron had crossed the border into Montreal to become a British airman. The shadows of the Odessa pogrom, the specter of defenselessness, had reached across the years and spurred these cousins, the children of survivors, to do battle for their own survival.

"You have had a letter from home?" Yaakov asked.

"Yes. Finally. It takes mail so damn long to get here from New York. This letter's dated the beginning of November and here it is almost Christmas. Not too much news." Aaron scanned the thin sheets of tissue paper, reading scraps aloud. "My mother's pretty involved in the lend-lease contracts and the factory's so busy they've even got Aunt Mollie going in. My father's practice is flooded with more and more refugees. They're 'totally and irrevocably traumatized,' he says. He's got a sort of textbook or clinical approach to letter writing. He talks that way too. To borrow from his own jargon, I'd say it was a defense mechanism. He's such a damn sensitive man that he's got to protect himself. Rebecca's settling in pretty well at Bennington after her violent protests about the futility of going off to school at a time like this. Pretty dramatic, our Becca, but a lot of fun. She's pretty much in the dark about what happened to Lisa Frawley—a girl I used to like. Went off to school in the West somewhere and was never heard from again. And there's a postscript from Michael—he wants me to send him stamps. It doesn't matter from what country—just send them to him. My old pal Joshua Ellenberg is probably teaching him how to sell them. The little devil—he thinks I joined the army just to set him up as a stamp collector. Everyone sends their love to you, Yaakov, and Gregory, my mother underlined three times a sentence telling you to write to your lonely mother—so write to your lonely mother, write to your lonely mother, write to your lonely mother."

"Oh shut up," Gregory said. "I'm trying to listen to the bloody loudspeaker. An announcement's coming through. Probably about a special Christmas dinner catered by Salim. Roast ass or sautéd ox buttocks. No—there are movement orders posted at HQ. Any volunteers to go over and see?"

"We'll find out soon enough," Yaakov predicted and nodded sagely as Nechemiah, the freckle-faced sharpshooter, burst into the tent.

"We're moving," he said breathlessly. "All of Gideon Force. Our new posting is a place called Soba, near Khartoum, in the Sudan."

"The Sudan," Yaakov said thoughtfully. "My friends, a veritable miracle. One of Salim's rumors turns out to be the truth. We are off to Ethiopia to put Haile Selassie back on his throne."

*

The camp at Soba more closely resembled a ransacked native village than a British operational center. But it was from this camp that the British hoped to launch their objective of achieving a revolt in Ethiopia from within the embattled country. Ethiopian volunteers had flocked to Soba when the news of the British initiative spread through the area with the help of Salim and men like him who peddled their gossip with skill and discretion. Some of the native volunteers had arrived with their families and Amharic-speaking women, in their long colorful skirts, baskets of laundry balanced on their heads, roamed the camp, issuing soft reprimands to the hordes of half-naked children who trailed after the arriving British soldiers.

On their first evening in Soba, Aaron and Gregory, tossing a ball, had become aware of a small boy, his flesh limp on fragile bones, his eyes burning like dark coals in his thin black face. It occurred to Aaron that the child was Michael's age and he reached into his pocket and offered the boy a half-melted Hershey bar.

The boy's name was Ato, he told them, and he had been hiding in the scrub bushes of Mount Belaiya since the Duke of Aosta's Italian forces had crashed through the village, meeting the mild resistance of the unarmed population with savage assault. An Italian militiaman's sword had slashed savagely through the air and severed Ato's father's head from his body in a single thrust, so swift and efficient that as the head toppled to the ground and rolled off into the bloodied dust, the decapitated body staggered for a few steps, the headless form motored by sheer nervous impulse, and then collapsed into a lifeless heap from which blood streamed relentlessly. Ato had gathered up his father's head and carried it up the mountain where he talked tenderly to the frozen features, opened and closed the dark staring eyes until the eyelids froze in place, and combed the sticky dark hair with fragrant pinecones until at last a gentle older tribesman heard the boy's frantic weeping and helped him to bury his father's head beneath a thistle bush on which heavy purple blossoms grew.

Ato had stayed on Mount Belaiya with a group of other refugees and traveled with them to Soba when he heard of the arrival of the Gideon Force. He followed Aaron everywhere now, attracted by the American soldier's red hair. He had never seen hair of such a color before, and he insisted that its radiance meant that Aaron was descended from the sun itself.

It was Yaakov who recognized Ato's value. The boy knew the paths to Mount Belaiya and spoke both Amharic and English, which he had learned from a missionary to his village. He understood animals and nursed a passionate hatred for the Italians who had destroyed his village and murdered his father. When Yaakov told Avram Akavia about Ato, Wingate's secretary insisted that the boy be part of the entourage that would escort Haile Selassie to the headquarters camp at the foot of Mount Belaiya. Because Ato would not leave Soba without Aaron, Aaron and Gregory were also assigned to the advance contingent. Again Aaron thought of how small incidents altered one's life. Because he had offered a piece of chocolate to a small boy who reminded him of his brother Michael, he was now part of a historic mission that would escort the Ethiopian emperor back into his kingdom.

When Aaron was a small boy Seymour Hart, on one of his Sunday "outings," had taken him to a science fiction film where the expanses of the moon had been portrayed as desolate naked fields, scarred by yawning fissures and steaming lava pits. The children had been frightened by the film and for weeks afterward, as a child awakened screaming in the night, Mollie had berated Seymour for his lack of judgment. The chasmed area west of Belaiya, through which the small British unit passed with tortuous slowness, reminded Aaron of that film and he sometimes thought, as the men moved slowly forward, that it was the brutal enervating heat that had dredged up the remembered nightmare of his childhood and that even now he was caught up in a fading fantasy. But the hot wind that seared his face and sent the perspiration streaming down his thighs rooted him to reality. The stench of the dead animals that littered the road mingled with the odors of men's vomit and feces and he knew that it was not a science fiction creation he was recalling but the terror of war that he was actually experiencing. Beside him Gregory marched, his face set in grim lines of despair.

His body bent and straightened as he slowly pushed himself forward, riddled by the cramps of dysentery.

As they pressed forward they hacked out a road of sorts with machete and ax. Small Ato darted in and out among them, weaving his way through gorges and small hillocks entangled with vines and scabrous brush. They passed the corpses of camels, their pale flesh already being consumed by the low-flying vultures which trailed knowingly after them, their widespread wings briefly shadowing the sun-drenched plateau. The birds hooted at each other and blood dribbled from their huge sharp golden beaks.

"Damn fools to bring camels here. This isn't their kind of country," Yaakov said bitterly that night as they sat beside a low burning campfire.

"Not much of a choice. The lousy Italians managed to grab every damn mule in East Africa," Gregory said.

He leaned back in exhaustion. The cramps had disappeared but he felt himself light with weariness, weighed down by a peculiar pressure about his head, and his body trembled with febrile intensity. A new cramp caught him unawares and he writhed in pain, pulling his legs up so that he lay curled in fetal position.

Aaron looked at him anxiously.

"You'll feel better in the morning," he said.

Together, he and Yaakov piled every bit of clothing and covering they could find on their friend. Feebly, they tried to coax him to laughter when he could not sleep, to mine his resources of dry cynical humor, but Gregory lay back convulsed with fever and shivered even beneath the heavy covering, and when he spoke it was in the wild voice of delirium.

"No medical officer. No quinine. Nothing but the stink of those lousy camels," Yaakov grumbled.

"Is it worth it?" Aaron asked wearily, wiping Gregory's forehead with a damp cloth. Bitterly he remembered David's warning that Hitler meant to destroy all civilization. Looking about him, at the desolate lunar landscape shrouded in shifting gray shadows, he wondered if all the world would look like this if Fascism succeeded.

"Of course it's worth it." Yaakov's voice was impatient. He confined his anger to the lack of water and quinine but never did he doubt the importance of the long-range goal that had set them down in this ravaged African wasteland. "You know what Wingate told us just before we came here? It was at a meeting of Jewish volunteers in Khartoum and he said: 'Whoever is a friend of Abyssinia is a friend of the Jews. You are here for the sake of Zion.' We must believe that, Aaron. It makes some sense of what is happening here. In the morning Gregory will be better."

But in the morning Gregory was dead, his body curled into a rigid arc, his hands reaching toward the vanished fire as though to seize the warmth of the lingering embers. They fashioned a litter for the body and Aaron covered his friend's face with his own tunic.

"For the sake of Zion," he said softly, bitterly. "You are dead for the sake of Zion."

During the rest of the march he thought of the letter he would have to write to the widow Liebowitz, telling her that her only son had died of dysentery in Italian-held East Africa. But in his dream that night it was his own mother, Leah Goldfeder, who wept with wild abandon and hacked off her long dark hair with kitchen scissors, wildly calling his name: "Aaron—Aaron!" Her grief pierced his sleep and he rose to comfort her and saw the enormous stars frozen into the galactic sky and heard the gentle steady breathing of his cousin who lay beside him.

The day after Gregory's death, they finally reached the foot of Mount Belaiya. A cheer rose up from the exhausted soldiers as Haile Selassie, the proud Lion of Judah, his uniform impeccable and his jet beard trimmed despite the rigors of the march, drove into temporary headquarters in the truck that they had maneuvered through the agonizing terrain. Aaron remained grimly silent. In the late afternoon there was a brief burial service for Gregory and two other casualties of the devastating march.

Aaron stood over the gaping hole that would serve as a temporary grave site for the puckish-faced boy who had shared his MacDougal Street apartment. He remembered Gregory his fellow student arguing an obscure point of Hegelian dialectics; he thought of Gregory his co-worker in that network of impossible dreams they had naively called the Movement; he pictured Gregory his friend laughingly flirting with Becca, squeezing laughter out of the ordinary, planning an ice cube consortium in Cairo; he wept for Gregory who hated cruelty and injustice. Aaron remained there as soldiers in fatigues, caked with the dry red floor of the Ethiopian forest, covered the grave, and he stood there still as the scarlet sun disappeared around the other side of the mountain. It was small Ato who finally plucked at his tunic and led him to the campfire where they sat together in the gathering darkness.

Gregory's death had somehow steeled Aaron, girded him with the emotional armor he needed for the days that followed. Gideon Force was in full operation. The Italians were mystified as to the size of the British army and scattered before the approaching troops. They did not believe that only a few hundred British soldiers had been able to mobilize the enormous Ethiopian guerrilla force. Salim and his confederates had done their work well.

The Ethiopians and British marched on, taking over Fort Burye and Musaad, heading toward the goal of Addis Ababa. The British contingent was imbued with new confidence and although the heat was relentless and they still marched through wild country, cutting their own path and taking their bearings from compass readings, there was a vital new excitement. The heavy heat-soaked air rang with song. The Palestinian Jewish soldiers taught Aaron their songs and sometimes, even as he lagged behind, he found himself singing the ancient Hebrew choruses by himself. "Who will build the Galilee... We will build the Galilee... Let us sing before Him a new song, a song of victory, a song of triumph..." The Hebrew words came with surprising ease and now, when he heard Yaakov speaking Hebrew with Asaph and Nechemiah, he found himself following the conversation.

"Perhaps when all this is over you will come with us to Palestine," Yaakov said the night after the successful assault on the fort at Jigga. They stood on a low hill, their blankets wrapped around them, watching a herd of gazelles leap with electric speed across the plain below. Behind them Ato brewed coffee over the glowing embers of a mess fire.

"When this is over, I never want to see killing again," Aaron said. "Not anywhere in the world."

Yaakov remembered always the heavy sadness that permeated those words and he was glad, afterward, that he had suddenly taken his cousin's hand in his own and felt Aaron's fingers unclench and respond to his touch.

It was the next day that they marched on the fort at Dambacha, their confidence still high. But outside the fort they were met with a fierce Italian assault. The Ethiopians and British had no sentinels, no defense positions, and their first warning of danger came from small Ato, who had ridden ahead astride a mule. Desperately the boy's shrill voice rose in a shout that pleaded caution; again and again the child shouted and then his voice gurgled as an Italian bullet pierced his throat and sent the blood soaring into his strained larynx. But Ato's shouts, mangled and anguished, continued until he slid from the mule, frothy pink blood streaming from his mouth. Aaron cursed, cocked his Bren, and thrust himself forward.

"Stay back, you damn fool," Yaakov shouted. "Stay back!"

He watched as Aaron's helmet tumbled inexplicably from his head—later they learned that the Italians, short of ammunition, had catapulted stones toward the approaching British and Ethiopian troops, and Yaakov supposed that it was such a stone that hit the helmet. He saw Aaron's bright hair aflame in the searing sunlight and saw his cousin pivot forward, into the heart of the battle where the small boy had fallen from his mule. That was his last glimpse of his American cousin, so newly found.

He did not see him again during that battle, nor was Aaron in the group of survivors that regrouped along the bloodied escarpment in Burye. Neither was he among the corpses who carpeted the forest floor, the stench of their swiftly decaying bodies mingling with the foul vegetal odor of damp dead overgrowth.

When Akavia took the roll call that night, he wrote beside the name of Aaron Goldfeder: "Missing in action. Presumed dead."

And that night too, Yaakov Abrahami began the letter that took him two days to complete:

> Dear Aunt Leah and Uncle David,
>
> It is with a heart full of sorrow that I write to tell you that my cousin Aaron, your beloved son, was lost in a battle near Dambacha. There is some hope that he was taken prisoner by the Italians. It was a miracle that Aaron and I met in Cairo and a gift from God that I came to know and love my gentle cousin. Please believe…

The letter went on to describe Yaakov's last conversation with Aaron and it was David who noticed how the ink had run because Yaakov's tears had fallen across the paper as he wrote. But it was Leah who kept the letter in her night table drawer to be read and reread in the darkest hours of the night. Her son was lost to her. She had forfeited the chance of explaining to him the mystery that had haunted his childhood and forged so wide a gulf between them that neither tears nor laughter could bridge it. This, at last, was her punishment for the years of silence, for the love withheld and the dark shadows of doubt she had cast across her son's bright youth.

"Aaron," she said quietly, "please, Aaron, come back to us."

But the night remained dark and silent. A weak, aimless wind tossed the dry leaves of the maple tree and they scraped thinly across the flagstone garden path.

13

Rebecca Goldfeder's desk in her Bennington dormitory room was a reflection of Rebecca herself. It was littered with projects begun in a storm of enthusiasm and abandoned abruptly in a lull of indifference. A pile of index cards chronicling the history of French Renaissance poetry toppled over notes on the life of Chaim Soutine, which in turn were littered with a collection of transparencies for a research paper on pre-Columbian art, a ripped nylon stocking, a half-knit argyle sock, and a pile of letters, most of them from Joshua Ellenberg and the last one still unopened because all Joshua's letters managed to read alike. He was working like a devil because the factory was now open on a twenty-four-hour basis. They had undertaken uniform contracts in addition to the lend-lease orders. He hoped she was eating properly, not working too hard, and not worrying too much about Aaron. Joshua himself was certain that Aaron was safe, a Prisoner of War. Rebecca glanced at the picture of her family which somehow managed to dominate the clutter on her desk. It had been taken on that long ago Labor Day weekend—it was odd how two years could seem an aeon when events that had occurred during her childhood in Brooklyn seemed vivid and recent. In the photo she and Michael were grimacing at each other, her mother and father were staring with great seriousness into the camera, and Aaron stood behind her mother, also grave, with his hand poised just above Leah's shoulder. Studying his face now, she thought of how rarely he had laughed, of how he had always seemed to live on the periphery of the family.

Joshua had been more central to their lives than Aaron, who had moved farther and farther away from them, loosening up only with Michael. Yet, despite this distance, Rebecca had always felt a near twinship with her older brother. They had shared the loneliness and poverty of the years on Eldridge Street and the emotional tundra that had seemed to separate her parents during those early years—an iciness that had melted miraculously with Michael's birth, or perhaps before that. She and Aaron had never talked about their parents' relationship, but it had united them, and for all the differences in their personalities they had been much closer than she had realized. How close she had realized only when the news that Aaron was missing in action had arrived in Scarsdale, delivered by a somber British consul who drove up to the house in a black Ford Anglia, wearing a morning suit and a homburg hat as armor against their grief. It had happened in the Ethiopian campaign, the man had said in that impeccable accent that appeared to defy hysteria, and when David had brought the atlas, he had carefully marked the area where Aaron had disappeared and told them hesitantly that there was a chance, just a mere chance, that Aaron had been taken prisoner.

It was to that chance that they all clung.

"In Jewish law," David had said, "two witnesses must see a body before a person can be assumed dead. In Jewish law, our son lives."

As though to affirm his faith in that law he had suddenly began attending synagogue again on Saturday mornings, often with Michael and Leah at his side.

"Poor Daddy," Rebecca thought now and completed the letter she had begun earlier.

October 4, 1941

Dear Mom and Dad,

Well, it's taken me a while but now I realize that you were right to insist that I return to Bennington. I have begun to get involved in my courses again although it does seem absurd to be studying twentieth-century literature when no one knows whether there will be a twenty-first century. These pessimistic thoughts are not encouraged up here where most people think that the tide of the war will change. Hitler's luck cannot last forever.

The best thing about my courses this year is that I am taking sculpture with a really terrific new young professor, Joseph Stevenson. Actually, I call him Joe because you know that one of the great things about Bennington is the terrific informality between faculty and students. Joe and I have had some terrific talks and he is very optimistic about the outcome of the war.

It took me two years but I finally did look up your old friend Eleanor Greenstein. She has a really neat little factory near Bennington and a couple of design majors in the work-study program are apprenticed to her. We had a good visit and she told me how you worked together at Rosenblatts when you were just starting out. It's funny, Mom—I can never think of you as just starting out—I always see you as a prize-winning designer who knew just what to say and when to say it. Anyway, Mrs. Greenstein invited Joe and myself to a sort of party this afternoon so I had better hurry and get dressed. Did I tell you that one of Joe's sculptures won a prize at the Museum of Modern Art? He's really terrific.

Please try not to worry too much about Aaron. Somehow, I have the feeling that he is all right and that I would *know* if he wasn't. You probably have a fancy clinical term for that, Dad, but I know he's all right.

Tell Michael to stay out of my room and I love him—and all of you.

Your
Becca

Rebecca reread the letter, frowned at her notoriously illegible handwriting, and added several quick drawings to the corners. One showed a ponytailed girl in an oversized man's shirt studying at a desk; another depicted the same ponytailed girl in a loose sweater and plaid skirt, working at a potter's wheel; the third drawing was of a serious-faced young man wearing enormous horn-rimmed glasses. Rebecca pointed an arrow at him across which she wrote "Professor Joseph Stevenson." She smiled, quickly folded the letter, and put it in an envelope, dislodging a pile of letters from Joshua. Poor Joshua. She would definitely write to him tomorrow.

Rebecca dressed quickly now, selecting a soft blue wool of her mother's classically simple design, admittedly patterned on Madame Chanel. Still, it had been her mother's idea to add the stole which Rebecca draped dramatically around her shoulders. Leah had been right, after all, to insist that Rebecca take at least a few "good" dresses, prevailing over Rebecca's objections that all the girls at Bennington wore were skirts and sweaters or rolled-up dungarees with their fathers' cast-off shirts. And of course most of the girls did dress like that except for a few who wore artsy-craftsy Bohemian clothes, tramping across campus in loose homespun dresses that created a curious tentlike impression, and another small group of girls who seemed to have arrived at Bennington through error and dressed in the style of the Midwestern campuses—loose mohair sweaters with plaid skirts and spotless white dickies, high white bobby sox and polished loafers with shiny pennies sparkling against the leather.

Rebecca, who had grown up in a home where styles and fashion had been a natural part of the atmosphere, was amused by the variety of uniforms on display at Bennington. If Lisa Frawley had come to Bennington with her as they had planned, how they would have laughed together at the pretensions of the tall blonde girl whose face was powdered to a snowy whiteness and who dressed always in a black leotard with various overlong faded cotton skirts, although she was not even a dance major. But Rebecca had not even heard from Lisa since her friend had abruptly left Scarsdale High School in the middle of their senior year, just about the time Aaron had been sent from England to Egypt. Rebecca had heard that Lisa was going to boarding school somewhere in the Midwest, but when she phoned the Frawley home to ask for her address, Lisa's mother was cool and evasive—almost hostile, Rebecca thought, but then Rebecca knew herself to be oversensitive. Lisa was terribly busy, her mother said. She knew Rebecca's address and if she were interested she would write. At school there were the usual foolish rumors and speculations and Rebecca slammed indignantly out of the locker room when one of the girls announced that Lisa had left school because she was pregnant. That was sheer nonsense, Rebecca protested angrily to Joshua Ellenberg. After all, she and Joshua knew that the only boy Lisa was at all interested in was Aaron. Joshua nodded and suggested that Rebecca would be wise not to write Aaron about those foolish rumors. Rebecca agreed and after a while Aaron's letters no longer mentioned Lisa. Rebecca had called the Frawley house again when they learned that Aaron was missing in action.

"I thought Lisa would want to know," she told Mrs. Frawley.

"I'm very sorry, of course, but I doubt that Lisa is very concerned about your brother anymore," Mrs. Frawley said and she hung up without saying good-bye.

Rebecca seldom thought about Lisa now but she did miss her at times like this when she was dressing for Eleanor Greenstein's party. And she would have liked to talk to Lisa about Joe Stevenson, something she could not do with her Bennington friends because Joe, after all, was a member of the faculty.

It was through a curious accident that Rebecca had, from the first, ignored Joe's formal academic title. She had registered for the introductory course in sculpture at the suggestion of Charles Ferguson, who admired some of the small figures she had done in a summer workshop. She arrived early for the first class and found herself alone in the sunlit studio. A hunk of moist clay was on the worktable and idly she picked it up and tried to mold it. It was too hard and she sliced it on the wire and flung it on the hard wood table.

"Uh, uh. Not so hard."

A sandy-haired young man in an open-necked blue cambric work shirt and faded jeans had come quietly in and stood beside her. He took the clay from her, worked it into an oval shape, and flung it down with a swift practiced motion. He picked it up, touched it, sliced it, and threw the two separate parts and then blended them. Again he tested its texture and she noticed that his dexterous fingers were scarred with traces of pale red clay and a small plaster scar ran along the rim of one lens of his enormous horn-rimmed glasses.

"There, now you can work it," he said. "The trick is not to throw the clay too much—just enough to make it malleable."

"Thanks," she said gratefully. "I've just had this one sculpture workshop and I don't know anything about it. I would have been pretty embarrassed at not even knowing how to work the clay. By the way, my name is Rebecca Goldfeder."

"Oh, don't worry," he assured her, "most of the girls in the class are beginners. My name's Joe."

She assumed then that he was one of the male graduate students at Bennington and they talked easily, working together at the table, playing with the clay. She told him about her other classes and explained that she had chosen Bennington because of its unstructured atmosphere and its creative arts department.

"You want to be an artist, then?" he asked seriously.

Rebecca was startled. At home she was still treated as a small child whose whims had to be indulged. Her enrollment at Bennington was simply another offering in a constant buffet of pleasure and amusement. But no one had ever seemed to have serious expectations of laughing, enthusiastic Rebecca Goldfeder. She was cuddled and indulged, her whims satisfied, her brief passions assuaged. More than ever, since Aaron had been reported missing, her parents had relied on her for a flippant gaiety that would relax the tensions in the house. Now this serious-eyed young man was looking at her, asking her if she wanted to be an artist, assuming that she had a serious goal in life, and she found herself oddly pleased and flattered.

"I don't know," she said honestly. "I think I have some talent and I've done some work. My mother is a designer and although I'm not interested in that field I've always liked to draw and paint. I'd like to sort of experiment this year and see how good I am and what I'd really like to do. You see, at home no one seems to expect me to do any serious work—everyone's pleased if I'm just happy. Sometimes I felt that that was my job. But being away from the family, I think I'll be able to concentrate on real work and maybe get an idea of what I want to do. Because I know I want to do something—to make my life count."

Joe Stevenson nodded.

"It's easy enough to imagine why parents feel that way—why they want their kids to have everything fun and easy. It happens most with people who have been through some hard times themselves. Then they think that joy and ease is a kind of heritage they can give their children. They don't realize that their kids want—and need—something more."

"That's true. That's the way it is with my parents," Rebecca said and in a rush of words she told him about Leah and David's early days in America, the east side apartment, the Brighton Beach house, and finally the Scarsdale home and then the war. She talked so swiftly and with such ease that she was startled when the bell rang and students trailed into the studio and took their places at the worktables. She was even more startled when one of the girls nodded to her and then turned to Joe and asked, "Did you have a nice summer, Professor Stevenson?"

He *was* not a graduate student but the teacher of this class—and she blushed deeply when he grinned at her and took his place in the front of the room where, perched on a high stool, he explained the aims of the introductory course.

She rushed out after the lecture and halfway to her dormitory she heard running steps behind her and knew that young Professor Stevenson was hurrying to catch up with her.

"Hey," he called, "you're not angry with me, are you?"

She had anticipated amusement in his voice—she was Becca who amused everyone, who made them laugh and smile and bring her small presents in exchange for a teasing comment, a cute reaction. But there was no amusement in Joe Stevenson's voice, only worried concern. And so she stopped and waited until he was at her side and together, with measured pace, they continued their walk, not heading toward the dormitory but in the direction of the gentle Vermont hills where the leaves of the maples were already slashed with streaks of scarlet and the heads of the oak trees glowed orange and gold against the steel blue sky.

She missed the dormitory meal that night but in a small village restaurant she ate a spicy slice of Portuguese sausage on a thick home-baked roll, drank sweet black coffee, and learned that Joe Stevenson came from the Alameda Valley in California where his family had lived since the days of the Gold Rush, when they had come to root treasure from the ground and turned instead to growing golden citrus crops in orchards that ran for sun-blazened acre after acre. Each year they felled the trees whose harvest had been weak, digging up the roots so that the strong trees would have more room to expand. It was that soft fragrant citrus bark that Joe first used to carve the small animals and forms that sprang magically to life under the blade of his blunt penknife. At the rich banks of the shallow stream that bordered the orchard, the small boy dug up heaps of malleable mud of such a peculiar consistency that when he formed a small head, it grew obediently beneath his fingers and hardened in the strong sun. Often by summer's end he had whole families formed of river mud, living quietly at the edge of the stream, only to be washed away in the torrential California rains. At school his gift was quickly discovered and an excited art teacher offered him tools and clay, wood and the use of paints and kiln, and finally, when she could no longer teach the boy, he went on to San Francisco and the art academy whose great windows were flooded with light. Earnest teachers taught him how to work with his materials and how to look at the work of other sculptors. He was twenty when he completed the academy and went on to the Chicago School of Fine Arts. Then there had been the Fulbright year in Italy and that terrible sense of wonder and fear when he gazed at the marble forms in the Piazza della Signoria—wonder at the work a man's hands and eyes could accomplish and fear because his mind and fingers ached to fashion their own message but might-not-might, could-not-could. He did not know and was afraid to find out. Now, his doctorate earned, he confronted that terror, teaching and working. He thought now that he was happiest teaching others, freed of the doubt about his work.

Joe reminded Rebecca of Charles Ferguson and she told him about her mother's teacher and then about her mother and father, about small Michael and Aaron, whose hair sometimes matched the burnished golden crowns of the oak trees they walked slowly past. When she spoke about Aaron, she began to cry, surprising herself but not Joe Stevenson, who held her hands gently and offered her a handkerchief streaked with ocher clay, and touched her hair lightly when her tears stopped as inexplicably as they had begun.

It was night when he took her back to the dormitory and they stood on the stone steps, not touching but standing in sweet silence for a long minute before she quickly turned and hurried inside. Since that first day, they saw each other almost daily, sometimes by arrangement but sometimes by chance, as though a mysterious tropism brought them to the same corner of the campus. On weekends they went together into the Vermont hills, their sketch pads underneath their arms. They walked for hours, stopping to picnic on the cheese and beef that Joe carried in his knapsack and to draw the stark trees, bereft of their foliage, that stood in haughty desolation, scraping the near-winter skies. Wrapped in their cocoons of heavy sweaters, they stretched out on a bed of soft fragrant pine needles and watched the sun sink low into the sky and become a huge golden ball balanced on a net of slate-gray clouds that slowly borrowed color and became threaded with fine gold streaks. Against this sky their friends, the barren trees, trembled fearfully, and they, on their bed of pine, felt the wonder and loneliness of mountains melting and disappearing into night. They came together then, in wonder and loneliness, and the loneliness melted, leaving only the wonder and the sweet lovely scent of dry, new-fallen pine needles.

She stood before the mirror now in her blue wool dress, her long black hair brushed about her shoulders, and wished that it was a weekend morning and she and Joe Stevenson were not going to a party, but up unknown mountain trails where the last wild flowers of autumn trembled in the frost-kissed air.

"Rebecca Goldfeder—Rebecca Goldfeder. Your escort is here."

The bored voice of the proctor summoned her on the intercom and she looked at herself once more in the mirror and hurried downstairs to the common room. Joe, in a heavy tweed jacket and khaki trousers, stood in front of the fire watching the flames, oblivious to the cluster of girls on the couch who were seemingly absorbed in Edward R. Murrow's broadcast from London, diligently knitting heavy argyle socks to be tucked into Bundles for Britain boxes, and wondering how Rebecca Goldfeder, that dark-haired New Yorker whose lips were really too thick, had managed to snare Professor Joseph Stevenson.

*

Eleanor Greenstein lived in a large modern house, perched on a ledge of rock that overlooked a young pine forest. Each room in the house had its own stone fireplace and the dark wood floors were polished to a soft glow and covered with bright rugs. The furniture was low and angular, making the large rooms seem even larger.

"This was what I wanted when I came up here," Eleanor had told Leah and David years ago when they first visited her Vermont home. "I wanted space. Light. Room. I've spent so damn much of my life in crowded apartments, crowded factories, crowded streets, that sometimes I think I'll never have enough room."

Leah remembered then the tiny cubicle that had served as Eleanor's office at Rosenblatts, the cubicle that she, as a young factory forewoman, had entered with such trepidation, her own designs clutched nervously between damp fingers. And it must have been from a tiny apartment that Eleanor's young daughter had fled, striking out to find her own life and falling instead into her fiery death. It was not surprising that Eleanor had fled to these vast green mountains to establish her own small factory. It was also not surprising that she had built this spacious home where she lived alone, relishing the open area of the rooms, the huge windows that overlooked endless trees and skies, their view unhampered by confining draperies. On winter mornings a great white world stretched out before the designer, who lived with the terrifying memory of wild, encompassing flames, fiercely burning, spinning closer and closer, burning away all space, wiping out all paths of escape.

Leah had not told Rebecca anything of Eleanor's history when she suggested that she contact her old friend who, like Seymour Hart, had exploited mass production and ready-to-wear clothing and created a successful business enterprise.

"She has a lovely home and knows a lot of interesting people," Leah told Rebecca.

And she had written to Eleanor of Rebecca's arrival at Bennington, knowing that her old friend and mentor, who had herself lost a daughter, would do her best to help Leah's daughter.

Eleanor Greenstein did know most of the interesting people in the Bennington area, and Rebecca and Joe accepted a drink from their hostess and followed her about the room as she introduced them to her other guests.

"This is Rebecca Goldfeder, the daughter of an old friend from New York—the designer, Leah Goldfeder, she does all the S. Hart originals, you know—and her friend Joe Stevenson. Judge Lewis, Professor and Mrs. Henriques, Natalie and Alex Gormley, Dr. Harrington..."

"Goldfeder. I know a Dr. David Goldfeder. Are you by any chance a relation?" Dr. Harrington asked.

"I'm his daughter."

"Ah. You must tell him that I congratulate him on his article in *The Psychoanalytic Quarterly.*" Dr. Harrington was a black psychiatrist and Rebecca remembered now seeing a book by him on David's desk.

"I'll tell him. He'll be pleased," she said.

The other names were familiar to Rebecca and Joe and they sat down on the white wool rug in front of the fire and listened to a conversation between Judge Lewis, a widely respected jurist, and Dan Henriques, a visiting professor of political science at Bennington.

Rebecca, whose thoughts were never far from Aaron and the war that had so profoundly affected their lives, listened closely to Dan Henriques, who had just returned from a fact-finding tour of Europe. The tall man's angular face was weary and as he spoke his voice fell lower and lower, as though he had repeated the same thing too many times and was now convinced that no one really listened.

"It's obviously just a question of time," he said. "The United States will have to go in—it must go in. Lend-lease, the Atlantic Charter, refugee aid—they're all sops. We're not just witnessing a war between opposing nationalist forces—this war in Europe and North Africa is a struggle for civilization itself."

"Come now, Dan. Don't you think you're overreacting a bit? The war is in Europe—it's between the nations of Europe. We're on the other side of the Atlantic. We've got to think of America first."

"What a good name for an organization," petite Mrs. Henriques murmured sarcastically. "Perhaps we can get Charles Lindbergh, the marvelous Lone Eagle himself, to head it."

"Or perhaps that great friend of justice and tolerance, Father Coughlin," her husband added sarcastically.

Judge Lewis's face flushed to an angry pink.

"Dan, you've known me long enough to know what I think of men like Coughlin. It's too bad that the noninterventionists are attracting reactionary rabble like him, but that doesn't mean they're wrong. A man like Lindbergh's a patriot. He's right when he says that the President's first duty is to protect his country from war, and it seems to me that Mr. Roosevelt is doing just the opposite—he's warmongering."

"It wasn't Franklin Roosevelt who sank the *Reuben James*" Dan Henriques said shortly.

The group in the room was quiet. Among the sailors who had been lost on the American destroyer, wantonly sunk by a German submarine on that angry autumnal sea, had been two Vermont boys whose pictures, draped in black ribbon, were displayed in every shop in town. One of the boys had a chubby, friendly face, covered with freckles, and the other had graduated at the top of his class from Bennington High School. Joe Stevenson had been commissioned by the Vermont Arts Council to sculpt busts of the two boys and Rebecca had sat with him as he studied their portraits. In Vermont, the sinking of the *Reuben James* had not been a distant, unpleasant news event but a grim reality that had pierced the comfortable insulation of their lives. The freckle-faced sailor's fiancée was the cashier at Food Fair. She wore his small anchor pinned to her smock as, red-eyed and trembling, she bagged their groceries, offered them change. The mother of the second sailor was a finisher at Eleanor Greenstein's factory, and since her son's death she had eaten lunch alone, at a corner table, looking out toward the mountains.

"I don't want war," Dan Henriques said harshly. "No sane, civilized man wants war. But we're not dealing with sanity or with civilization. Germany is a nation crazed with power and hungry for even more power. They've marched on countries that were committed to peace. They've declared war on civilian populations. They've established concentration camps."

"Dan, concentration camps are as old as martial history. Cicero talks about them. Herodotus. They're part of any war. Warring nations routinely isolate saboteurs, enemy agents." The judge took another glass from Eleanor and settled back in his comfortable chair.

"Not camps like these," Dan insisted. "Have you heard of them? Terezin, Auschwitz, Dachau, Matthausen, Treblinka. Surely there are not millions of saboteurs and enemy agents—yet millions of Jews, gypsies, dissenters, and God knows who else, fill these camps. I saw them myself, Judge. Our study mission could not get into them but I saw their gates and their wire barriers—electrified wire—and I spoke to people who have been inside."

"Again this hysteria. The Red Cross have been inside. They've reported nothing unusual." The judge's voice was calm, soothing. He was an old man and he had seen a great deal. He gathered all his accrued wisdom and dispensed it; he was a trained pharmacist of history, distributing pellets of reassurance, placebos of precedents.

"All right. We ourselves were not inside the camps. But one thing I guarantee you. Very few of those who are inside will ever come out. Those camps are designed for death. They are part of Hitler's program—the one he proclaims himself—the rendering of Europe *Judenrein*—free of Jews."

Rebecca experienced a shock of recognition, remembrance. She had heard those words before, in the trembling voice of Frau Schreiber, in her father's heated discussions with Peter Cosgrove, in her mother's hushed conversations with Mollie. "Free of Jews." She thought of her grandparents in Russia, the old man and woman whom she knew only through the faded photograph that stood on their fireplace. Her grandmother's large dark eyes matched Rebecca's own. In the photo, her grandfather held a book, a large volume of the Talmud which he balanced uneasily before him, as though to shield himself from the camera's eye. But such a book would not shield him from guns and bayonets, from angry blows and savage kicks. She did not know the gentle old man who was her mother's father, but she melted with fear for him and was grateful when Joe Stevenson took her hand and slowly traced the pattern of her veins.

It was only then that she found the courage to ask Dan Henriques a question—the question that had plagued her since the war began for her family on that Labor Day weekend when Hitler marched into Poland and Aaron had left them to disappear in the wilds of North Africa.

"But you do think that in the end the Allies will win, don't you?" she asked, her voice so low they had to strain to hear her.

Dan Henriques hesitated for a moment and then he replied in a voice so flat that it carried the sound of death.

"No, I don't. Unless the United States comes in and comes in very quickly, I don't see a chance for the Allies."

"Here now, Dan, you're being inconsistent," the judge said reprovingly. "On the one hand you're condemning the isolationists like Lindbergh and then you say the same things they say—that the Allies have all but lost."

"No, that's not true," Henriques replied. "Lindbergh and his people advocate coming to terms with Hitler and Mussolini. But I am saying that it is impossible to come to terms with barbarians. I'm not advocating an accommodation with Fascism but a battle against it. If we don't combat it then all of us, all of us here in this room, are condemned."

The assembled group sat mute, looking about the large room with its polished floors and woven rugs, its cheerful prints and its fenestral vista of trees and mountains. A fire blazed, the table was laden with plates of meat and salad, the smoked-glass pitchers sparkled with wine, music played—and all this was threatened. All of them, gathered together on this peaceful Vermont hillside, sat under sentence of death and desolation.

"Come—enough talk! Let's dance."

Eleanor Greenstein jumped into that sea of silence to rescue her party. Quickly she put a new record on the phonograph and couples rose to dance.

> Give me one dozen roses,
> Put my heart in between them,
> And send them to the one I lo—ove...

Rebecca and Joe were caught up in the swirl of dancers and moved rhythmically across Eleanor's polished floor, stilling the fearful uncertainty in their hearts with the wild beat of the music, their feet tapping out the rapid dance steps, her body swaying and dipping, supported by his strong hand, his easy grace.

"You're as good a dancer as your mother," Eleanor said admiringly when Rebecca, panting for breath, sank down next to her.

"As my mother?" Rebecca was surprised. She had never seen Leah dance or even listen to dance music.

"Oh yes. I remember a big meeting at your parents' apartment on Eldridge Street. After the meeting someone turned on the radio—your Uncle Seymour's old Stromberg-Carlson—and we danced and danced until the woman downstairs began banging on the pipes with a broom."

"My mother danced?" Rebecca asked. "And my father?" It was more difficult still to think of her father, that quiet bearded man who spoke in the gentle voice of his profession, ever moving his feet fast enough for anyone to protest.

"No—not with your father. He was away then. I remember now. It was the night before the fire at Rosenblatts. She danced with a friend—a good friend. Eli Feinstein. He died in that fire." Eleanor's voice grew vague, almost dreamy. Abruptly, she got up to prepare the coffee.

"Eli Feinstein," Rebecca thought. The name sounded familiar, but she could not remember when she had heard it. She would ask Aaron who he was. The thought was quick, automatic. Aaron would know. He was the guardian of their vanished childhood, the archivist of places and names. But of course, she could not ask Aaron. He was gone, taking with him their shared heritage of childhood treasures, of feelings unarticulated but cherished. A rush of anger at her absent lost brother overcame her. He should not have gone off and left her alone. He should not have allowed himself to disappear, to be lost in a military action in a country she had never even heard of, that she had difficulty finding on the map. Abyssinia—Ethiopia—it did not even have a proper name. What was the point of it all—of the anguish he had caused their parents, of Michael's swift and terrible nightmares that made the young boy awaken in the middle of the night trembling in his bed, drenched with sweat, calling for a brother who would not come. It was not even their war. She wanted to believe the reasonable arguments of the white-haired judge, but she remembered then the photo of her grandparents, the dark-eyed woman and the gentle-faced man, he clutching his worn tome of Jewish wisdom. Of course it was their war and of course Aaron had been right to go. Her anger was overweighed by guilt, regret, and then a bitter sadness washed over her and she leaned back, exhausted, and studied the flames that danced teasingly in Eleanor Greenstein's stone fireplace.

*

The first snows fell early that winter. By mid-November the mountains of Vermont were covered with layers of glistening whiteness that would not melt until late spring. The white-capped peaks of the highest mountains strained toward the low-floating blue-gray clouds, heavy with nascent storms. Rebecca and Joe drove to Scarsdale for Thanksgiving and although Leah prepared a beautiful dinner and the large house was filled with guests, Aaron's absence pervaded the festive dinner table. It was the first time Joe had met Rebecca's family and throughout the meal she sensed her father's eyes studying the tall sculptor and her mother's apprehensive, too polite reactions to their guest.

Joshua Ellenberg poured the wine, helped Leah with the carving of the turkey, made sure his mother had a stool to elevate her foot, now painfully crippled by arthritis. When conversation at the table lagged, he filled the vacuum with raucous humor.

David sat back and stroked his beard, prepared to be amused. God knew there were few enough opportunities for laughter these days. His patient load had tripled. He was one of the few psychiatrists in New York with a knowledge of Yiddish, and welfare agencies were constantly referring newly arrived refugees to him. Of course, his knowledge of Yiddish did not ease the therapeutic task of helping a Polish woman who had become separated from her children during their flight assimilate the loss; nor could it soothe the agony of a man whose wife had been detained and then disappeared somewhere in the Satanic maze they called Nazi-occupied Europe. He thought of the woman who had sat in his office earlier in the week. Years younger than Leah, according to the chart he held in his hand, she looked years older. She kept her gloves on but he knew that one finger of her right hand was missing, surgically removed when it became insensate after a frostbite sustained while crossing the mountains of her Czech homeland. She had set out on that journey with her small daughter, a ten-year-old, tiny for her age. Her husband and son had been arrested in an "action" and sent to Terezin. But Gentile friends had hidden her and the child and helped them to arrange this journey to freedom across the mountains. The small girl wore bright red mittens and the mother held the small mittened hand in her own, clutching the frightened fingers that were flesh of her flesh, offering her child the only thing she could—the touch of her hand. Almost narcotized by a sudden snowfall, they had tramped on through the mountain, and the woman felt that she was walking in her sleep, wending her way through the endless columns of tumescent icy whiteness. Time passed but she could not account for its passage, aware of it only because of shifting shadows, gliding light. They trod lightly, fearful of the sound of cracking twig, startled when an overburdened branch snapped. The mother glanced down from time to time at her hand, frozen now beyond feeling, and was comforted by that brave red mitten still clasped within her grasp.

The falling snow alternately blinded and hypnotized her but she spoke comfortingly to the child, sang her small songs through frozen lips, assured her that the border was not far away, spoke of joys past, promised joys to come. And then they reached the border, scrambled across the dilapidated barrier, and she looked down at last, turning to the child who would be at her side, wearing the red mitten she had clutched so tenaciously for so many frozen miles. There was no child. Somewhere along that mountain path as the mother stumbled more asleep than awake, the small girl must have fallen into a snowbank, the mitten slipping from her hand to become her mother's only memento of a child who had always been too small for her age.

The woman carried the mitten with her everywhere and she showed it to David. Gently he stroked the red wool, talked to her with as much calm as he could muster, his own eyes awash with tears he could not shed. He longed to tell her that he too had a child who was missing, lost in this terrible, senseless war, just as the small girl ("tiny, so tiny for her age," the mother repeated again and again as though it were a clue to that loss so overwhelming that it could not, would not, be comprehended) had been lost among those mountains, so soft with new-fallen snow-flakes.

Instead he offered the woman advice he knew would be ineffectual—advice he had followed since the day he held the communication from the British consul in his hand and learned that his bright-haired young son was "missing in action and presumed dead." As colleagues had well-meaningly, futilely, advised him, the bewildered father, as he had advised Leah, so he advised the Czech woman who sat before him clutching the scrap of red wool, faded by snow and tears.

"Try to think of other things. Concentrate on the future, not the past. You must live for this world now, not for one lost. You must get a job, make friends, go out, build a new life. Yes. Even laugh. You must try to laugh. You have not forgotten how."

Now at his Thanksgiving dinner table, he followed his own prescription of laughter and turned back to Joshua, giving his full attention to the joke that was forthcoming.

"Yes indeed," Joshua continued, "the Jews have three worlds: this *velt*, the next *velt*, and Roosevelt!"

The group around the table laughed. Rebecca leaned over to Joe and explained, "The Yiddish word for world is velt."

"You don't speak Yiddish, Joe?" Leah asked.

"No. I'm not Jewish, Mrs. Goldfeder," the sculptor replied.

"Oh. Of course. So stupid of me," Leah murmured.

She should have known from his name that he was not Jewish but she paid so little attention to casual conversation these days. Her thoughts were always riddled with worry about Aaron and about her parents, from whom there had been no word for months. She worried too about Moshe, feeling a great closeness to this brother she had not seen for twenty years, whose son had so befriended her son. Through the secret Yiddish code buried in Moshe's letters, which were of course subject to British censorship, she had divined that he was involved in illegal immigration—the smuggling of Jewish refugees onto the shores of Palestine.

"We go nightly to the seashore," Moshe had written her, "and walk with Uncle Mavet and Aunt Sacanah."

Mavet meant death and *sacanah* meant danger. Both death and danger were possibilities for those Jews being smuggled into Palestine in defiance of the British White Paper which restricted Jewish immigration. It was an irony of history, Leah thought, that Yaakov, Moshe's son, wore a British uniform and fought bravely with the British army, while his father broke the law of Britain. What was it David Ben Gurion had said—oh yes—"We will fight Hitler as though there were no White Paper and the White Paper as though there were no Hitler."

"Come on, Joshua. Another joke," Rebecca commanded. She had slipped automatically back into her role in the household, that of a princess, ready to be pampered and entertained by Joshua Ellenberg, her court jester and sometime knight, depending on her need.

"Sorry, I'm fresh out of laughs," Joshua said. "Maybe Joe has one."

The group turned expectantly to the sculptor, who held his hands up in good-natured despair. Leah studied Joe Stevenson more carefully. He had a fine face and a firm sense of himself. Before dinner he and Charles Ferguson had discussed current trends in painting and she had been impressed with his knowledge. He possessed a quiet gentleness and the artist's patient, considering forbearance. But surely Rebecca had no real serious intentions. He was a professor and so many years her senior. She was a child—just nineteen. Nineteen. Leah herself had been only eighteen when she married Yaakov and Rebecca's age when Aaron was born. She looked at her daughter, who was helping Mollie clear the table, somehow relieved to see that a small flower of cranberry sauce clung to Rebecca's chin. How like Rebecca, their little girl, their baby, she thought. She had always been a careless eater. She risked her daughter's annoyance by wiping her chin with a linen napkin. Of course, Becca was not serious about this sculptor—it was simply a student-teacher relationship, like her own friendship with Charles Ferguson.

Later that afternoon, Charles drove Joe to an exhibit at the Hudson River Museum and Joshua and Rebecca sat in the living room, talking quietly. Joshua told her about the feverish pace of work at S. Hart. They were overcommitted and Seymour was spending this Thanksgiving weekend in Washington on company business.

"I didn't know people did business on Thanksgiving," Rebecca said and Joshua grinned. Seymour's Washington weekend would consist of a half-hour meeting with lend-lease officials and many hours with a tall blonde model who spoke in a breathy voice that did not mask her mountain-country accent.

"Your mother's been coming down to the factory regularly," he said. "She anticipates a whole change in fashion because of the fabric shortage and she's got a line with shorter skirts and brief bolero jackets ready to put into the works for spring. It's good for her, too. Takes her mind off Aaron."

"Aaron. You do think he's all right—a prisoner somewhere but still all right?" As always since childhood, she had turned to Joshua for protection and reassurance, but this time his eyes avoided hers.

"How can I tell you that, Rebecca? The only thing anyone can be sure of is what they control themselves."

Michael came into the room then and Joshua grinned at the dark-haired boy.

"Come on outside, Mike. We'll have a catch," he said.

"Uh, uh." The boy shook his head and opened a Flash Gordon comic. "I don't feel like playing ball now. I'll play in the spring when Aaron comes home."

"Michael." David Goldfeder stood in the doorway, his voice gentle but firm. "Go out and play ball with Joshua now. We don't know if Aaron will be home in the spring. I have explained that to you. We don't know, Michael, if we will ever see Aaron again. We hope we will but we cannot know. Meanwhile we continue our lives. So please put on your jacket and have a catch with Joshua."

Michael looked up at his father, then followed Joshua out of the room.

"Oh Daddy," Rebecca said and her eyes filled with tears. She reached out for her father's hands but they covered his face, concealing the grief that twisted those gentle features into a mask of misery. His body trembled briefly as he struggled for control, and when he looked again at his daughter his face was calm. He sat down beside her, a brief smile of apology teasing his mouth upward.

"Rebecca, you are very fond of this Professor Joseph Stevenson?" he asked. His arm rested on her shoulder.

"Yes. Very," she answered. "Don't you like him?"

"Very much." Slowly he lit a pipe and gently blew out a wreath of blue smoke. "We have not talked about this a great deal but you know your mother and I have always expected our children would continue our heritage. We are very upset that he is not Jewish."

"Oh, Daddy!"

She was surprised and almost impatient. It had been years now since her mother had kept a kosher kitchen, and her parents had only resumed going to synagogue services since Aaron's disappearance. Of course they were generous to Jewish causes and Aaron had been bar mitzvahed, but she herself had attended Hebrew school only briefly and even then sporadically. She could barely read the prayer book. Naturally, she knew she was Jewish and was proud of it, but what possible difference could it make to her that Joe was not Jewish? Her parents had never seen anything strange in the marriage of Bonnie and Peter Cosgrove, so why should they object to her relationship with Joe?

"Look, Daddy," she said, as though he were a student having difficulty grasping a basic simple concept. "Joe and I aren't getting married, but even if we were, would it really make any difference to you that he wasn't Jewish if he was good and kind and I loved him?"

"Yes," David replied without hesitation. "Perhaps I cannot explain it or justify it in the intellectual terms you seek, but it would make a great difference to me and to your mother—to your Aunt Mollie and your Uncle Seymour."

"Uncle Seymour—so busy in Washington. You see how ridiculous that is," Rebecca retorted. The color rose high in her cheeks and she stormed out of the room, slamming the door behind her.

David sat on in the darkening room, thinking of the Czech woman and the small girl whose frozen body lay buried under hillocks of snow. How swiftly children slid from one's grasp, how easily their hands slipped away leaving parents abandoned, clutching at scarlet scraps of mittens and bittersweet memories of laughter and tears.

The rest of the Thanksgiving weekend passed pleasantly enough, but David did not find another opportunity to speak to Rebecca alone. He kissed her good-bye as she drove off with Joe Stevenson that Sunday morning, promising to call, as was his and Leah's custom, the following Sunday evening. But when he made that promised call it took hours to establish a connection because long-distance lines all over the United States were jammed. On that Sunday, ten days after Thanksgiving, eighteen days before Christmas, Japanese planes bombed Pearl Harbor and the phone wires of America, from coast to coast, throbbed with anxious voices that repeated Rebecca's tearful question.

"Oh, Daddy," she asked, "now we're at war—really at war, aren't we?"

14

During the weeks and months that followed that black wintry Sunday, it was impossible to forget for a moment that they were indeed at war. The desperate battles in Europe and the Pacific permeated every aspect of their lives. Colorful posters appeared on the commuter train and subway which David now traveled daily in an effort to conserve gasoline. He read his Times under the accusing finger of a grim-faced Uncle Sam who declared in bold block letters, "I WANT YOU!" He answered the invitation of a soaring eagle whose great wings enfolded the message "America Is Calling!" and became an air-raid warden. With dozens of other older men, their thinning hair streaked with gray, their eyes worn with worry, he reported each Tuesday night to the Civilian Defense Training Center in White Plains and was issued a metal helmet, an enormous flashlight, and a mimeographed training manual which he memorized like the conscientious student he had always been. David's young secretary heeded the call of the poster he had hung above her desk and resigned to become a "soldier without a gun"—a worker in a defense plant. He hired an older woman and took the girl out to lunch where she wept into her untasted shrimp salad and thanked him for the month's salary he gave her. Her fiancé was in the South Pacific and her brother had been a midshipman on the USS *New Orleans* at Pearl Harbor.

Former patients came to see him, wearing uniforms which never seemed to fit properly. Some spoke shyly, hesitantly, of fear. Others worried him because of their fierce enthusiasm, their impatience for action. All of them shook hands solemnly and promised to write, but few did. Jeffrey Coleman, the young black science student who had been one of his first analysands, arrived one afternoon. He did not wear a uniform but an extremely well-cut J. Press gray flannel suit. He had recently completed his doctorate at Princeton, was married to a pediatrician and the father of a chubby baby whom he had named David. He and his family were en route to a place in

New Mexico called Los Alamos where he was involved in research important enough to earn him a draft deferment. It was not a deferment he had sought.

"Those bastards in Germany are doing in boots and uniforms just what the sons of bitches down South did in hooded sheets when I was a kid. I wouldn't mind getting a crack at them."

But he was a disciplined man and went off to do his mysterious work in that melodically named settlement at the edge of the New Mexican desert.

David's patient load increased and he became a medical consultant for the local draft board and joined the staff of a veterans' hospital.

With difficulty, he found a huge world map which he hung in his Scarsdale study. He and Michael transferred colored pins about as the military action progressed and intensified. Guam. Wake. Hong Kong. Borneo. Singapore. The Netherlands Indies. The Philippines. They exhausted their supply of bright pins and resorted to thumbtacks.

White satin banners appeared in their neighbors' windows on which blue and red stars were carefully stitched. In a house whose blinds were always drawn now, not far from the Scarsdale station, such a banner appeared with a gold star stitched across it. David had known the boy who lived in that house, had watched him over the years run up and down the steps, toss a basketball, walk a large Irish setter. It was astonishing, unbelievable, that the boys he had watched dash across the track at Scarsdale High School and bike down the Bronx River Parkway were dying in jungles in countries some of them had never heard of before they donned their uniforms.

"What color star do we hang for a boy who is missing in action?" Leah asked one evening in the deadened, fatigued tone that so often overtook her now. Only with Michael could she summon up the gentle, light voice of hope and confidence.

The question she asked did not anticipate a reply and it was a blue star that she hung at last, sewing above it a fringe of gold.

Waves of gray crested Leah's dark hair now and she earned her fatigue on the night train she traveled at least once a week to Washington. She had been named to a war planning board commission as an adviser on fabric and design. S. Hart was open twenty-four hours a day now, turning out Leah's coveralls designed for the women who formed the vast army of defense workers. The small hart ran across the pocket of the coveralls, but now its horns were curved into a graceful V for victory.

The nation became obsessed with that V as the war went on and it became clear that victory was distant, ephemeral, and perhaps—although they dared not articulate such a thought—impossible. In David's consulting room, grown men stretched across the tweed couch and wept, women scratched at their bodies and pummeled their faces in despair.

Michael tore up the badminton court in their backyard, turned the earth, and began a victory garden. Feathery carrot greens, acrid tomato plants, tender beet and onion greens flourished where once they had sat on cushioned chaise lounges and watched Rebecca and Aaron volley for serve. Leah sniffed at the fragrant greens and remembered her parents' kitchen garden in Russia. Her eyes filled with tears and she hurried back to her drawing board, banishing her worry over her parents and Aaron with fierce addiction to her work.

It was Michael, too, tall for his age and heir to David's sharp lean features and his mother's velvety black hair, who organized a brigade of youngsters. They trailed through the neighborhood with wagons collecting wastepaper and tin cans. In the Goldfeder garage, they stamped and hammered the cans down to packets of flattened tin, roped the newspapers into great piles, and set aside a bushel basket to be filled with emptied toothpaste tubes.

Michael worked with a fierce determination which frightened David. The boy's nightmares were less frequent now but he spoke of Aaron incessantly, making plans for the camping trip his brother had promised him. He clipped from the newspaper Bill Mauldin's best *Willie and Joe* cartoons and the streamers of *Sad Sack* which appeared daily in their local paper. He was saving them for Aaron, he explained. There was a drawer in his room in which he kept such things for his brother. Its most prized content was a glossy photograph of Betty Grable in a bathing suit inscribed: "For Aaron Goldfeder, When He Comes Marching Home." Michael had written to the actress and explained that his brother was missing in action but Michael was sure he would be home any day now. And he was sure. One day he would be sitting in front of the house—a sunny day—and Aaron's shadow would streak before the pavement in front of him and then he would be caught up in his brother's strong arms.

That November, as the family sat in the living room and listened to the report of the Allies' invasion of North Africa, Michael went to the map and drew a circle around Ethiopia. It would not be long now. The Allies were closing in on the area where his brother had disappeared. He clipped pictures of Omar Bradley and George Patton from the newspaper. These were the men who would rescue Aaron. David listened to him quietly and searched out Leah's eyes across the room. Her gaze was heavy with despair and the familiar unbidden sudden tears stood in her eyes and rolled down her cheeks in crystal splinters of grief. She was tired, so very tired.

The fatigue had become a part of her. It weighed her down when she went one afternoon, as required by the Office of Price Administration, to Scarsdale High School, to collect their ration books. There, in the huge gymnasium, on whose polished floors Aaron had leaped for baskets and run the mile, she waited patiently on the line that said "F through H." The letters were cut out of red, white, and blue construction paper, lest anyone forget why it was necessary to stand on this line and wait for their families' needs to be reviewed and the booklets of stamps needed to purchase sugar, eggs and meat, shoes and gasoline, to be meted out. It was a long line and Leah shifted impatiently. Although she had traveled back from Washington on a night train and spent the morning at the factory setting up production schedules for an urgent uniform consignment, she knew she was not alone in this bone-racking weariness. These were not times where one asked for preference on slow moving lines.

It had rained that morning and the gymnasium smelled of the damp rubber galoshes the women wore. The woman ahead of Leah wore the overalls of a defense worker. Her hair was caught up in a bright bandanna and on her metal lunch box she had pasted a decal that read "Silence Is a Weapon." Just behind her a pale young mother in the uniform of a postal worker stood, holding a blond toddler by the hand and reading a V-letter. Leah turned and further up the line she saw Lisa Frawley's mother standing with regal indifference. Priscilla Frawley wore her long gold hair, the same color as her daughter's, piled high; her slender form was encased in a simple black suit which Leah's professional eye recognized at once as an original Chanel. Her long legs (Lisa had inherited those legs) shimmered in nylon stockings and she stood on her black ankle-strapped platform shoes as though upon a reviewing stand. Leah caught her eyes and smiled and the tall blonde woman turned swiftly away but not before a hot red dotted her cheeks and her eyes filled with a betraying febrile anger. The fury of that glance impelled Leah to wait at the gymnasium door and reach out to touch Priscilla Frawley as she hurried by.

"Please, Mrs. Frawley," she said, "there is something I must ask you."

"Yes?" The blonde woman launched the question on wings of ice and it hung frigidly above them. "You know that my son Aaron is missing in action?"

"I'm sure I'm very sorry."

"Then perhaps you'll understand why I ask—why I must know. Was there a child?"

She asked the question, knowing that she had known for months what the answer would be—wondering why it had taken her so long to confront that realization.

Priscilla Frawley stared hard at her and the fury drained from her eyes. It was over. It was done and it had not after all been Leah Goldfeder's fault. It had not been anyone's fault. Other women rushed past them as they stood there together, both mothers, both caught in a war, riven by anxiety and uncertainty, forced to endure long lines in overheated gymnasiums.

"There was a child," she said. "A boy. Born dead. Strangled in the cord. I hope your son is found but Lisa is out West now, building a new life. It was terrible for her and it is over. You understand?"

"I understand."

The two women shook hands then and walked their separate ways. As she drove home, Leah wondered if the child, her dead grandson, had been born with a shock of red hair. She remembered Aaron as a baby and the way the sun had turned his clusters of red ringlets the color of burnished copper. Would she ever hold such a copper-curled baby again, she wondered, and mourned quietly, in that brief drive along tree-lined streets, for the strangled baby and his father whose infancy and childhood she had squandered in doubt and misery and whose young manhood was denied her.

The pace of work at S. Hart Inc. had intensified. They had undertaken a special government contract for WAC uniforms and it was difficult finding factory workers. Mrs. Schreiber worked in the office now but Mr. Schreiber, along with other German immigrants, had been called to Washington as a consultant to military intelligence. He sat at a Pentagon desk, bent over maps and documents, grimly, methodically avenging the death of his son, murdered for the crime of loving an "Aryan" girl. It had been months now since there had been a communication from Frederic Heinemann and by tacit agreement neither the Schreibers nor Leah mentioned their valiant German friend.

Jake Hart, Mollie and Seymour's son, enlisted in an officers' training program and their daughter Annie became engaged to an Air Force lieutenant who received his overseas orders immediately after presenting Annie with a ring. They were married in a swiftly arranged garden wedding in Mollie's backyard, and Leah sat beside Rebecca and Joe Stevenson who had traveled down from Vermont. How swiftly the years had gone. It seemed such a short time ago that Annie had been a small girl newly arrived from Europe, too fearful to walk down Eldridge Street without holding Rebecca's hand. Now the cousins were young women, Annie a bride whose husband was off to war and Rebecca—she glanced at her daughter who sat beside Joe Stevenson, her eyes too bright, her color too high. Rebecca, Leah thought half wistfully, half gratefully, was still their Becca, their baby.

Joshua Ellenberg did not enlist. As Leah and Seymour Hart spent more and more time in Washington and traveling around the country in an effort to obtain fabric and other materials and contracting out jobs to other factories, he assumed more and more responsibility at S. Hart. Often he slept on a cot in the office, waking to check a production schedule, trace a missing shipment, or operate a cutting machine himself for a rush job. He instituted a payroll savings plan and took out an ad in *Women's Wear Daily,* announcing that the workers and management of S. Hart had bought over $100,000 in war bonds. Twice he dutifully reported to his draft board as summoned and received a medical deferment because of a mastoid operation during his early childhood. It occurred to him as strangely ironic that a self-inflicted ear injury had kept his father out of a war he had chosen to avoid while he would be deprived of serving in a war he would have chosen to fight. But he was too busy to brood about this—so busy in fact that he missed Annie Hart's wedding and no one told him that Joe Stevenson had traveled down with Rebecca.

He installed a loudspeaker system in the factory and the sewing machines whirred to the tunes of "This Is the Army, Mr. Jones," "They're Either Too Young or Too Old," and "Don't Sit Under the

Apple Tree with Anyone Else but Me." In the packing room, the huge shipments were wrapped as the speakers wistfully resounded to "When the Lights Go on Again" and "You'd Be So Nice to Come Home To." Sam and Sarah Ellenberg, who worked together in the packing room, achieved modest success for their duet rendition of "Praise the Lord and Pass the Ammunition," delivered with the Yiddish inflection that seemed to grow more pronounced with each year. But every hour on the hour, work stopped as everyone listened to the news and always there was a dull, defeated silence afterward, followed by a record, frenetically whirling at too fast a speed.

It was Joshua, too, who organized a blood drive—once a month the long cutting tables were cleared and covered with mattresses as Red Cross units moved in with their donor equipment. The first donor at S. Hart was Leah, who watched as though hypnotized while the scarlet blood slowly filled the bottle that hung suspended above her. Into whose body would her blood feed, she wondered. Had another mother's blood fed into her son's veins? She clenched her fist as she had been advised to but did not weep. Such thoughts no longer brought tears.

The third time Joshua Ellenberg was summoned to his draft board, his physical examination was more exhaustive. Twice a young doctor, his own uniform still newly creased and his army-issue stethoscope brightly reflecting Joshua's flushed pink face, bent over the mastoid scar.

"Ever give you any trouble?" he asked Joshua.

"None," Joshua replied firmly.

Three weeks later a letter arrived; and after reading it, Joshua called the bus station for the Bennington schedule. He had just time to visit a jeweler and tell his parents and his assistant at S. Hart that he would be out of town for a few days.

As the bus, crowded with soldiers and sailors who blocked the aisle with their bulky duffel bags and passed around pint bottles of bourbon wrapped in paper bags, wound its way up the stark New

England mountains, he twice took out the small leather box and looked at the diamond ring inside, cushioned on its tiny royal-blue velvet pillow. Twice, too, he reread the letter, as though searching for a mistake. But he knew that there was no mistake. If family men, fathers of small children, were now being drafted, it would take more than a mastoid operation to keep Joshua Ellenberg out of the army. And he did not, after all, want to miss this war. It would, of course, slow down his plans, throw a crimp in his operation, but just briefly, just until they managed to beat those bastards. He hoped he'd be sent to Europe. The Japs didn't interest him as much as those damn Nazis. The bastards. He read the letter again, beginning to like its sound.

> Having submitted yourself to a local board composed of your neighbors for the purpose of determining your availability for training and service in the land or naval forces of the United States, you are hereby notified that you have been selected for training and service therein…

"Selected." He liked the sound of the word, smiled, and once more opened the little leather box. In the dark bus, the small diamond glinted like a distant star.

It was late when the bus reached Bennington and although he had planned on seeing Rebecca at once, he went instead to the Bennington Inn and phoned her dormitory. She was not there but he was given a phone number where she could be reached.

He dialed, feeling a sudden uneasiness which evaporated when he heard Rebecca's familiar voice on the phone. As always her tone was high and sweet, her greeting enthusiastic, expectant, as though everyone who called Rebecca Goldfeder had something pleasant and exciting to impart to her.

"Becca. It's Josh. I'm here in Bennington."

"Josh! That's marvelous. Are you here to see Eleanor?"

He remembered then that Eleanor Greenstein had undertaken production of a Hart contract. Of course, he would call Eleanor and maybe even go over to see her operation. It might be interesting to start up on his own in a small town after the war, especially since Becca seemed to have gotten used to that sort of life. On her visits to New York she was impatient to get back to Vermont, often cutting her vacation short by several days. It was highly possible, with S. Hart expanding so rapidly, that after the war Seymour might be interested in establishing a rural plant. Maybe a subsidiary company. Hart and Ellenberg. He doodled the name, then crossed out the Hart and wrote instead "J. Ellenberg Inc."

"Well, I'll get over to see Eleanor. But I came to see you. I've got some news for you," he said. He reached into his pocket and touched the small jeweler's box. The ring within it was bigger than the diamond Annie Hart's flyboy had given her.

"News? About Aaron?" Her voice trembled with fear and he was briefly irrationally, jealous of her brother, his friend whose loss hung over their days in a lingering miasmic mist.

"No. Sorry. This news is about me."

"Oh? Give me a hint. Is it good news?"

"That depends. Listen, it's sort of late but since you're out anyhow, suppose I take a cab to wherever you are and walk you back to your dorm and we can talk," he suggested.

"No. That is—I'm studying for a big prelim—with a friend. I'm staying the night here. But I'll meet you first thing in the morning. For breakfast. Okay?"

"Here at the Inn," he said. "Nine. Is that too early?"

She laughed. "Nine-thirty. And Josh?"

"Yes, Becca?"

"Sleep well."

"Good night, baby."

But he did not sleep well. The curious uneasiness returned and he awakened twice in the night. Instinctively he reached for the small jeweler's box and looked to that starlike diamond for reassurance.

Rebecca surprised him by being on time, and when he saw her in her plaid skirt and duffel coat, her long black hair glossy beneath a red knit beret, he wished he had thought to change to sport clothes. He felt out of place in his wide-lapeled suit, white-on-white shirt, and narrow silk tie in the sunny dining room where the other men wore tweed jackets and V-necked sweaters with slacks that were too baggy yet looked somehow just right.

"Josh! Oh, Josh! How marvelous to see you here."

She hugged him and his arms closed about the soft curves of her body, that sweet body he had watched shed its small-girl fat and flesh out into the graceful form that moved so sweetly within his outstretched arms. His Becca. His baby.

They had breakfast and he watched with amusement as Rebecca smothered her pancakes with golden maple syrup, and primed him for news of the family. During their childhood together, in the apartment on Eldridge Street, it had been his job to cut her food to her liking and he remembered how she had coated her toast with sugar, her cereal with blankets of butter. She had not changed. All of life's sweetness and richness were due her and she claimed them without embarrassment or hesitation. Patiently he gave her news of the family.

Her mother was in Washington just now. There was talk of rationing clothing and the Office of Price Administration wanted Leah's opinion. David and Michael might join her there on the weekend, taking the train with Mrs. Schreiber, who spent every weekend in the capital with her husband. Peter Cosgrove had volunteered for a special military psychological unit and Bonnie was once again working at S. Hart. Carefully, they avoided talking about the news that had brought him to Bennington. She told him about her work as a Red Cross volunteer. She was, she said laughing, the slowest bandage-roller on campus. During a silence as they sipped their coffee, he remembered to tell her that he had heard that her old friend Lisa Frawley had been married in California. An older man, they said.

"Yes. Lisa sent me a marriage announcement and I wrote her a note. But she didn't answer. I wonder why."

He shrugged and when he did not answer she slipped on her coat.

"Let's walk," she said. "I'll show you my favorite places."

Arm in arm, they strolled the hill-bound campus. They passed groups of laughing, chatting girls, their heads bent close, their long hair swirling about windswept faces, eyes very bright, wool scarves trailing after them in woven streaks of color. The red and white of Harvard. The orange and black of Princeton. It was January, 1944. In Casablanca, Winston Churchill and Franklin Roosevelt talked of the future of Europe, and across North Africa boys from Spokane and Duluth cleaned their rifles and mended uniforms shredded by jungle thorns. But in Bennington, Vermont, sharp wintry winds kissed the air and young women in plaid skirts and loose mohair sweaters allowed themselves to forget the war and speak instead of Matisse and Mahler, of Kant and Weber.

A light snow had fallen during the night and was now stretched across the earth in a crusty lacelike frost that crackled beneath their feet.

"Do you remember how you used to pull me along the street in a wooden box when it snowed?" Rebecca asked.

"Sure. We had the runners that Aaron pried off a rotting sled someone had thrown in the garbage. Up and down Hester Street we went on snowy days. I was selling scarves that winter. That little guy who boarded with us, Morris Morgenstern—he married Pearlie—got me a gross somewhere. You held them in the carton while I pulled you and hollered about what a bargain they were. You know what the other peddlers called you? The *shmatte* angel." He smiled and looked at Rebecca, his "angel of rags" grown to this beautiful, laughing young woman.

She laughed now, a rich throaty sound that made his blood tingle.

"I'll have to remember to tell that to Joe. I'll bet I'm the only girl at Bennington who ever helped sell *shmattes*."

"Oh yeah. Joe. Joe Stevenson." Joshua pulled up the collar of his coat. He had forgotten Rebecca's sculptor friend, or perhaps, he acknowledged reluctantly, he had not wanted to remember him. The uneasiness he had felt the previous evening washed over him and he took Rebecca's gloved hand, pressed it tightly within his own, and put both hands in his pocket.

They had left the campus now and were walking across a field where a copse of slender birch trees formed a natural windbreak. As they passed beneath the trees, a cushion of snow trembled on a low-hanging branch and fell, grazing Rebecca's cheek. He took out his handkerchief and gently wiped the powdery crystals from her skin, then passed his finger across her face. Her skin was soft as velvet beneath his touch and she waited patiently, submissively, for him to minister to her, as he always had.

"Joshua," she asked softly now, as they stood beneath the snow-laden trees, listening to the wind whistle in mournful threnody through the branches, "what was the news that made you come here?"

For answer, he reached into his pocket and took out the letter from the draft board. She held the crisp official paper and read it carefully.

"You too, then. First Aaron and now you. You have to report in a week. That's not much time, Joshua." Her voice was heavy and all laughter had fled from her eyes.

"Time enough. Time for us to get things squared away. Becca, baby, I wanted to wait until you finished college—I wanted you to have your fun, but like you said, now there's not much time. So I want you to wear this now."

His hand trembled slightly as he reached into his pocket for the blue velvet box. He passed it to her and she held it hesitantly, then fumbled with the catch, her fingers made clumsy by her thick red wool gloves. She opened it at last and stared down at the ring, holding it a distance from her body, like a child handling a bewildering and unpredictable toy.

"Do you like it?" he asked shyly.

She had never heard Joshua's voice so soft and uncertain before. She took her glove off and lifted the ring from its blue velvet bed, holding it so that the sunlight sparkled on the glinting ice of the perfectly cut stone.

"It's beautiful," she said. "But Joshua—it's an engagement ring."

"Of course it's an engagement ring. Becca, baby, you must have known that's what I always wanted, always worked for. I love you Becca. I've always taken care of you. I always want to take care of you."

As she struggled for an answer, three fighter planes from a nearby air force training field flew in formation overhead, winging in low and then soaring upward in swift and graceful corps, their noise drowning out her words.

"What did you say?" He shouted to make himself heard above the noise of the planes, but they had disappeared so suddenly that now his loud voice ripped through the strange heavy silence they left in their wake.

"I said 'I love you, Joshua,'" she replied slowly, shyly.

A large smile spread across his face. Doubt, uncertainty, vanished. Of course she loved him. Of course. She was his Becca, his baby.

"Sure you do. So put the ring on already."

There was so much to do. Maybe Rebecca would come back to New York with him today. They had to tell her parents, his parents. Maybe they could even get married when his basic training was over. A small wedding, like Annie Hart's but indoors. And then perhaps a brief honeymoon. He knew an inn in Connecticut. His body pulsed and strengthened, shivered with anticipatory delight.

"I can't put the ring on. I love you, but not that way. I love you the way I love Aaron. Like a friend, like a brother. Oh Joshua,

Joshua, why did you have to spoil it?" Her voice broke and she was crying now, the tears spilling down her cheeks, one of them splashing across the blue box and staining the bright velvet.

He stared at her in pained disbelief. His heart sank and his limbs grew light with sudden weakness. Her hand was outstretched and he took the ring box from her, snapped it shut, and put it back in his pocket. On the tree nearest them, a fragile, snow-laden branch snapped and soft mounds of snow slid silently to the frozen earth. She continued to cry, her face contorted into that familiar knot of misery which tears had brought her to since babyhood. Her full lower lip jutted out and her nose grew red. With the habit of years, he took out his handkerchief, still damp with snow, and wiped her tears. He took off her red beret and smoothed her long dark hair. When she still sobbed, he pulled her to him and holding her gently, he rocked her into a slow calm. He soothed her with weary patience, warding away her sorrow at the terrible hurt she had inflicted upon him. A harsh wind rose and whistled wildly through the copse, breathing coldly upon their upturned faces, but still they stood there swaying, clinging to each other for comfort, her red beret tightly grasped between his fingers, ungloved and raw with cold.

*

Six months later Joe Stevenson brought the mail up to the apartment he and Rebecca had shared for almost a year. Among the circulars was a tissue-thin V-letter covered with Joshua's broad uneven handwriting. He was "somewhere in Europe." Things were pretty hectic. His unit was a terrific bunch of guys. His best buddy was a Choctaw Indian who had taught Joshua some great curse words. They were really giving those Fascist bastards a run for their money. He hoped things were going all right at home. "Good night Becca baby. Take care." That was all.

It was the first letter she had had from him since they had stood on the crusty hillside sheltered by a fragile wall of birch trees. She read it over and her face crumbled. Quickly she went into the small bathroom and locked the door so that Joe Stevenson, who was embarrassed by tears, would not see her cry.

15

The night before he left Vermont to report to the New Jersey army base for basic training, Joe Stevenson awoke in the unquiet dark, felt the familiar, comforting pressure of Rebecca's head upon his arm, and saw the silver moonlight splash briefly and wondrously across her face. That was the way he would remember her always—lying there across love-rumpled bedclothes, her face lost in sleep as a slender shaft of argentous light drifted across her cheek and rested briefly on the thick dark hair that fanned out across the pillow.

He carried a picture of Rebecca in his wallet, one taken in the Vermont hills they loved so well. In the snapshot she stood against a tree wearing a light-colored turtleneck sweater and dark slacks. Her head was tossed back and a stray maple leaf clung to her dark hair. She had been laughing; a half-smile was frozen on her full lips and laugh lines creased the corners of her large eyes. The picture wore thin as the war progressed. He stared at it lying across a three-decker bunk in a Texas training camp and held it in his hand as he leaned across the rail of the troopship which carried him into the European Theater of Operations. The Europe he had known as an exchange scholar had vanished and now, like other soldiers, he talked of the ETO, the Second Front, the French line.

On leave in London, he huddled in a shelter as bombs sounded dully on the concrete shield of pavement above him. He took the picture out then too, and showed it to a young mother who clutched a fair-haired baby. The white-haired child laughed wildly, improbably, at the sound of the muffled rocket blast.

"Are you married then, Yank?" the woman asked, passing the picture back to him. "She's a pretty gel."

"No. I'm not married," he said and wondered again why it was that he and Rebecca had not married.

They had, of course, talked about it often, and it was acknowledged between them that sometime, in a vague, mysteriously deferred future, there would be a formal ceremony that would put the stamp of legal commitment on their lives and their love. Before he left for the army—his draft notice, too, arriving after years of deferments he had not sought—Rebecca had insisted that they marry. But then such a marriage had seemed to him unfair, selfish, and he had refused, gently and firmly. One did not take a wife and go to war. It had been one of the few times he found himself able to say no to his gay dark-haired girl, who had received so few denials.

But had he been right, after all? he wondered, as the London shelter tumbled into a sudden darkness. He took the child from the trembling young mother and held it gently, his fingers smoothing its fine white hair. Women screamed and children cried in the subterranean darkness—then with that swift British assertion of determined control, there was sudden order, sensed though not seen, and a girl's sweet clear voice began to sing, "There'll be blue birds over, The white cliffs of Dover..." Around him other voices, old and young, strong and faltering, took up the song and when they had sung the last chorus, their voices surging upward with hope at "Tomorrow, just you wait and see," the lights flickered weakly on again.

He too sang and, because he could not look at Rebecca's picture in the darkness, he thought of the shaft of moonlight gliding across her black hair. No. It would not have been right to have married then, a feeling shared, he knew, by Leah and David Goldfeder. He thought then of David's troubled gaze and Leah's large sad eyes.

Rebecca's parents had never openly objected to him nor to the unorthodox pattern of the life he and Rebecca shared in Vermont. Even at Bennington, it was unusual for an unmarried couple to live openly together. But he had been welcome at the Goldfeders' Westchester home although he and Rebecca made it a point never to stay overnight there together. Only once, in his hearing, had David spoken of their relationship, and even then, the reference to their different faiths had been oblique.

A letter had arrived from Palestine, from Rebecca's uncle Moshe, her mother's brother whom she had never met. Because it was written in Yiddish, David translated it for them as they sat over coffee. It had arrived during the bad days of the war, when the harsh voices of weary newscasters brought them bloody accounts of the invasion of Sicily and Michael moved the tacks on the war maps in David's study, in uneasy circles, until at last it became clear that Allied troops would win the Italian peninsula in the end.

Moshe's son Yaakov was fighting with the Jewish Brigade of the British army in Italy, and Moshe himself was involved in the illegal operation of smuggling refugee Jewish children from Europe into a Palestine sealed to those children by a quota system. He wrote cautiously about this clandestine operation in familial code.

"I am sure you remember Uncle Beryl," he wrote his sister. "I find myself using some of the business tricks I learned from him."

Their Uncle Beryl had been a genius at sneaking Jews past border guards. Once, David told them, he had put three young Jews in enormous kegs of beer and when the Russian guards had stopped them, he had offered them drinks, his ladle scraping the heads of the emigrants. "The guards complained that there was hair in their beer but they drank it anyway and asked for more," David recalled, laughing.

Moshe's letter concluded on a pessimistic note. He told Leah that he had all but given up hope for the safety of their parents in Europe. The soldiers of the Jewish Brigade had intelligence reports on the European camps for Jews. Their reports made him pray for his parents' deaths rather than hope for their lives. In Palestine the Jewish community looked to the future and prayed that the skills of men like Uncle Beryl would benefit them all.

"It's ironic," David had said then. "My brother-in-law and his family risk their lives for Jewish survival and we here in America treat it so lightly."

"What do you mean, Daddy?" Rebecca asked.

"I mean you, Rebecca," David said heavily and left the room too quickly, allowing the heavy oak dining room door to slam.

"You mustn't think he really minds that you're not Jewish," Rebecca reassured Joe later. "I mean, I suppose he does mind in a way but he would never make an issue of it."

Joe had not answered her then but he knew that while David and Leah would not have objected to their marriage, they were relieved when they did not, after all, marry.

But why hadn't they married? The question that had teased him in the London shelter recurred weeks later, as he shivered in the hills north of Saint-Vith, waiting with his unit to launch the assault which the freezing infantrymen, in their khaki wool face masks and double thickness of leather mittens, did not even know was called the Battle of the Bulge.

He thought about it as his platoon trekked doggedly through the winding roads of frozen mud, coated with snow and ice, and followed a mysterious network of paths. They ascended evergreen crested hills that overlooked narrow rivers bordered by steep banks that meandered through the dense hill country. Men sang softly or cursed bitterly as the snow and ice invaded their combat boots and icy rain crept into their helmets. They were approaching Christmas of 1944, a Christmas they hoped to celebrate by controlling the foam-locked waters of the Roer River.

"I'm hoping for a white Christmas," the lanky soldier marching behind him sang. "Hey, Stevenson, who you dreaming about? Your girl?"

"I've got my mind on Betty Grable. You think I'm un-American?"

Joe shifted his backpack and held his rifle high as they forded one of the small brooks that riddled the Schnee Eifel hills they were now passing through. Here they heard the sounds of long guns, the thunder of an onslaught of artillery. They checked their rifles and forgot about the water freezing into ice within their boots. A strong wind, heavy with the breath of unfallen snow, battered their faces raw, and their lips bled where they had bitten through the frozen skin.

Rampant rumor flew through the columns, as swiftly as the snow that broke into brief fitful flurries around them. The Germans, it was said, were launching twenty-two divisions against them. The entire Sixth SS Panzer Division had been deployed for a confrontation. Now it was confirmed that there were Germans dressed in American uniforms, speaking English and manning captured American tanks and trucks. Intelligence officers moved through snowdrifts, issuing instructions.

"Don't trust anyone. Ask questions they'd have to be from stateside to answer. Who won this year's World Series? What does 'hold the mayo' mean? Where is Yankee Stadium? What does 'mairzy doats' mean? Who was Nick Carter?"

Joe Stevenson, sculptor-in-residence at Bennington College, began to sweat within the heavy folds of his uniform.

"Who the hell won the World Series?" he asked. He did not even know which teams had played.

It occurred to him then that it was highly probable that he would be killed, and at a rest stop he wrote a long letter to Rebecca and immediately tore it into pieces, thrusting the pale-blue scraps of tissue-paper V-mail into the trunk of a tree strung with ribbons of ice. He might die and he had never confronted his life. He had feared his gift, doubted his talent, and so he was not a sculptor but a teacher of sculpture. Just as he had feared to commit himself artistically, so he had feared to commit himself personally. Many things had prevented him from marrying Rebecca, he realized now, the teasing conundrum routed at last. He could not have married her before he knew himself as an artist, as a man. Nor, he recognized, with startling clarity, could he have expected Rebecca to marry him until she too had faced herself. It had been too easy for her to slip from her parents' home into their cocoon of easy, uncommitted love.

Rebecca, too, had played with her talent, struggled very briefly with it, and then allowed the war to excuse her from meeting its demand. She worked now in Eleanor Greenstein's factory. Like her mother, Rebecca had a sharp eye for detail, a natural talent for piercing design and production problems. Eleanor, struggling with a harried schedule of government contracts, needed her help. The job became Rebecca's war effort. It was a natural niche and Rebecca had slid into it as easily and enthusiastically as she had slid into all the other situations in her life.

These thoughts came to Joe on Christmas Eve, on the day he killed his first German soldier, a very young man, almost a boy, whose pale-gray eyes Joe picked out with the sights of his rifle. The young soldier's steel helmet fell from his head when he toppled over, and Joe saw that his hair was milk-white in color, the same shade as the curls of the child he had held in the London shelter. After that he did not seek out the eyes and faces of the men he aimed to kill. In that same battle he somehow lost Rebecca's picture and then had only the memory of the moonlight sliding across her sleeping face. Months after that same battle, he woke in a sweat. The eyes of the soldier he had killed rolled about loosely in his dream and somehow collided with the brooding stare of David Goldfeder. It was a dream of drifting orbs and wooded paths, but he had no time to puzzle out its meaning.

It was winter's end now and the rumors that rushed through the columns of those who had survived the march from Saint-Vith were fleshed with tales of the concentration camps deep within German-occupied territory. It was to these camps that Jews and gypsies, communists and dissidents had been taken. It was said that such camps—they were as large as small villages and towns, in fact—were surrounded by electrified wire and from within their confines was heard the barking of dogs and the soft desperate weeping of children.

Joe remembered, then, that long-ago day in Scarsdale (was it only a year and a half ago?) when David Goldfeder had read the letter from Palestine in which a son had wished his parents dead rather than exposed to the mysteries of those camps.

"But nothing could be that bad," he thought uneasily and wrapped himself in his sleeping bag, knowing that he had seen things that were beyond imagination, rational assimilation. He had seen the throat of the good-natured lanky Texan who marched behind him pierced by a bullet and the man choked by his own blood foaming up through the perforated flesh. He had marched past a burned-out Panzer tank to which the body of a corpse clung, the skin clinging blackly to the exposed bones of the skeleton from which flesh and uniform had been scorched. The man lay with his feet pointed upward, still encased in their tightly laced combat boots, tied with an impeccable military knot.

He had bitten earth and felt the mud grit against his teeth and cake his eyes when he heard the unearthly cry of "Moaning Minnies" and watched them leap across the fiery orange skies. He had listened then, waiting for the reptilian hiss of the projectiles, and watched the missiles hurl earthward and rip the air with red fires of hate and destruction.

Often on the march now they passed burned-out houses where women and children rooted in the rubble like foraging rodents. Once he saw a small girl, thin cheeks smeared with ashes, one blonde braid oddly longer than the other, scream with excitement as she discovered a spoon and waved the silver utensil in the air. The sun glinted across it and the child suddenly cried—perhaps because she had seen her own small face mirrored in her treasure.

During a brief skirmish among the scrub pines that dotted that mountain network, he was surprised by a German corporal moving swiftly toward him, pistol raised and cocked.

"Stevenson, look out!" the GI next to him screamed in warning and Joe seized his bayonet and plunged it through the flesh of his attacker, feeling the blade's force as it ripped through the layers of uniform, speared soft mounds of skin and body meat, severed muscle and artery. He was a sculptor, as familiar with human anatomy as the most expert surgeon, and he used his weapon now with fierce, blind skill, knowing instinctively when he had severed the carotid artery. He withdrew the bayonet as the blood spurted blackly forward, drenching his dead assailant's gray uniform. Carefully, the skirmish over, the German dead across the fragrant pine needles, he wiped the blade to which shards of pale-pink flesh hung, tossing away a small piece of human meat, the epidermal skin bluely ribboned with vein. His fellow soldiers looked at him with rare admiration, but he wept that night and for nights afterward. He who had spent his life creating in wood and clay was now skilled at destruction with rifle and bayonet. Bitterly then he would place one hand on another and feel the weatherbitten crust of his skin, the broken edges of his nails, and wonder if his fingers would ever be free enough of death to work for life.

Finally, he went to speak to his commanding officer. He explained, with some diffidence, that he was an artist. He wanted to be reassigned to some unit that might use his skill—perhaps public relations, information. The officer looked hard at Joe, noticed how his hands trembled and how a tic jerked his lip up and down. Two weeks later he received orders directing him to report to a British public information unit near Breslau which was preparing for the occupation of surrendered territory.

The British adjutant who briefed him for his new assignment wore the gray mask of exhaustion and his instructions were terse, his voice stretched to a weary thread.

"This isn't simply an 'occupation of surrendered territory.' We're going into a concentration camp which was principally used for the internment of Jews. I don't know what stories you've heard but whatever you see is going to be worse than anything you can imagine or anticipate. We're sending a sizable information and propaganda team in because here, more than anywhere else, we've got a chance to show the world the kind of bastards we've been fighting, what Nazism is, what it's been responsible for. In this war there's no need to fake 'Hun atrocities.' No propaganda expert with science fiction inclinations could dream up the things these bastards have perpetrated. You're an artist, Stevenson. Go in there and draw what you see. And I hope you have a strong stomach."

Joe did not salute. The adjutant had turned away, as though too tired to bother with routine military etiquette. It was said that this would be the third such camp he had entered. He came from Bournemouth and his name was Geoffrey Silverstein.

Joe was issued several drawing pads and the familiar thick black drawing pencils of the kind he and Rebecca had used during their sketching walks in Vermont. He caressed the familiar smooth casing of the pencil and ran his fingers across the clean white paper, feeling a sensual surge of excitement at the touch of these new materials. Idly, he drew a small leaf. It was April, the threshold of spring, and small shoots of grass were already thrusting their way through the burned-out war-weary earth. The wild dogwood trees were tumid with buds and the leaves of the silver birch trees were threaded with fragile veins. As they drove, they passed through meadows of newly leafing trees and felt a hint of warmth in the early spring wind. The season's promise lulled them into a dreamy calm which was startlingly shattered when they approached the place called Bergen Belsen, a forbidding gated enclave over which pale-blue smoke floated in a perpetual somber cloud.

Joe, a BBC broadcaster, two photographers, and a writer were in one of the last jeeps which rolled down a road fringed with barren elms whose leafless arms stretched agonizingly skyward. Tacked to each tree was a white notice reading *"Danger! Typhus!"* The near-dead trees heralded the truth of the warning, as though they themselves had been stricken, but the lead British tanks ignored the warning and plunged on. They rumbled down a stretch of road carved out of the fir wood whose fragrance filled the air but mingled with an odd putrescent odor. The cavalcade of tanks was followed by scout cars and Bren carriers. When Joe's jeep finally advanced, the air was thick with petrol fumes and clouds of dust enveloped the single pole across the roadway, lined on either side with wooden huts. This was the entrance to the camp which was being surrendered that day to the conquering British.

Joe took up his sketch pad and rapidly drew the group of smartly dressed German officers who awaited the British forces. They stood at rigid attention on the porch of one of the small huts, their faces frozen, their eyes hard. With deft strokes Joe etched in the forked-lightning badge of the SS, the three rows of medals proudly worn for this historic occasion by a Hungarian colonel, and the elegant epaulettes of the Wehrmacht officers, who alone talked easily with each other, as though today consisted of a boring formality which would be stoically endured before they returned to their clubs and tailors, their homes and families.

Papers were presented and signed and now the British drove another 200 yards to a high wooden gate with crisscross wiring. Irrationally, irrelevantly, the gate reminded Joe of the last afternoon he and Rebecca had spent together in New York; they had visited the Bronx Zoo, wanting to be among children, to briefly lose themselves in innocence and laughter. He realized almost at once why the entrance to Belsen reminded him of that day. The entry was like the entrance to the zoo and from the rows of green wooden huts, fit only for the containment of animals, poured the odors of zoo—the sickening stench of ordure, the dead waste of rotting vomit and excrement, of sour stagnant water.

He stared at the barbed-wire fences that surrounded the compound and fought the nausea that welled bitterly in his throat, but could not conquer it. Bile-bitter vomit filled his mouth. There were people behind those fences. A simian throng of men with shaven skulls, their skeletal bodies enveloped in ragged striped pajamas, gazed at them with huge-eyed stares, their bony fingers clinging to the wire fence. A strange sound arose from them—a half-credulous cheer threaded with a sudden wild weeping.

Joe felt his own cheeks grow wet and the tears stood hot in his eyes and streaked down his cheeks. The BBC broadcaster, weathered by the long war to a hardness of mouth and eyes, stood on the seat of the jeep, stared across the sea of pajama-clad figures, the wave after wave of grotesque moving skeletons that surged toward them, arms outstretched, and wept. He sat down as though his legs would not support him and unashamedly opened a large khaki handkerchief to sponge his tears. A woman dressed in rags came up to him and gave him a budding branch of dogwood. He took it and pressed her fingers to his lips, as though to assure her, to assure himself, that somewhere in the world humanity and tenderness survived. Joe, with trembling pencil, drew the weeping officer and the ragged woman.

There was a sudden silence as the sound of the loudspeaker crackled and the voice of Colonel Taylor, the administrative officer, resounded through the compound.

"The forces of the Allied armies have liberated the Bergen Belsen Concentration Camp. Because of the danger of typhus we ask you to remain here until the disease can be controlled. Food and medical supplies are on their way. You are a free people but please do not leave Belsen while the disease is rampant. For your sake and for your own welfare. We wish you well. We wish you—life."

There was a great murmuring in the crowd as the announcement was translated into a dozen languages. Women clung to each other and wept. A group of French women linked arms and softly sang the *Marseillaise*. Then, as though the realization of their freedom had only just penetrated their consciousness, they ran to the gate that separated the women's camp from the men's compound and thrust it open by the sheer force of their fragile bodies. There was new weeping and sudden shouting as husbands and wives, brothers and sisters, even parents and children, found each other.

An old man, wearing the obscene striped pajamas that fell across his skeletal frame like a ragged tent, peered into the face of each passing woman calling, "Are you my Esther, my darling Esther?" Twice Joe passed him and hours later still heard his plaintive call. The woman's name, the lost Esther, was part of a threnody, a lament of loss and longing, and the searching man's voice joined other seeking voices as darkness fell. "Moshe—Avremel—Henia—" Their calls were threaded with soft weeping, with a gentle, despairing keening. There was no strength left for savage grief, and the survivors in an agony of exhaustion braced themselves to endure a life they had long since surrendered.

Throughout that long day and longer night, Joe wandered the camp, his nostrils slowly becoming accustomed to the stench of death and decay, his eyes growing used to scenes that belied credence. His pencil moved across the pad automatically, as though independent of his weary body and benumbed sensitivities. Later, looking at those drawings, he could not remember the moment of their execution. That day was splintered for him into fragments of horror, some preserved on paper, some consigned to shocked memory.

There was a potato patch near the kitchen in the men's compound—a small patch of land covered for the winter with sodden straw. Across it lay a cadaver, its bones shining through the sheerest skin, the fingers frozen around two potatoes that had rotted within the frozen hand. The corpse was that of a woman, they saw, because a limp breast lay exposed, a neat bullet piercing the delicate blue-white flesh that might once have nursed a child. Perhaps it was the corpse of Esther, sought on this day of liberation by a man who might be her weeping lover, her frantic husband, her distraught father. Joe did not know, would never know, but he drew that poor corpse and wrote across the stark line drawing, "Esther?"

There were other lifeless bodies on that bed of straw, and the British soldiers, some weeping still, lifted them and set them gently on the ground, organizing mounds of corpses for burial. Some were still alive, if just barely, and these light bodies they carried, like quiescent children, to the building which had quartered German officers but which was now a hospital for the victims of those officers.

Twice that afternoon, Joe Stevenson put aside his pad and pencil and took up a shovel. In the waning light of that spring afternoon, he helped to dig a mass grave which was quickly filled with the bodies of men and women plucked from barracks which the dead had shared with the living. The earth was spongy, soft with the release of spring, and the bodies, clumps of bone and staring skulls, slid easily into the soft, accepting soil. The British soldiers' faces were tight with anger and some wept as they worked but they were orderly and organized. The corpses had to be buried at once because of the threat of epidemic. They affixed small placards to each mass grave. One hundred corpses. Seventy-five. One hundred and thirty. There were 13,000 unburied corpses in liberated Bergen Belsen, and the survivors, bony wraiths with haunted eyes, wandered the burial grounds, peering into each yawning abyss. "Esther," the voice of the searching man called, and other voices joined him, calling yet other names, but there were no answering cries. The spring air smelled of grief and rang with mourning.

Evening shadows moved across the sky and all about the camp small fires blazed, their tongues of golden flame licking the silvery green sky.

"What are they burning?" Joe asked a tall British sergeant, who wiped his hand again and again on a handkerchief black with earth.

"Their huts. Tonight the whole camp will be on fire and a good thing too. Who could have believed this. Is it possible? Did it happen? Is it happening?" He gestured wildly about, his arms taking in the horrors of the camp, the small incidents of a day that would never be forgotten.

As they stood there a woman clad only in a loose envelope of potato sacking and carrying a tiny bundle in her arms approached. When she saw them standing there she started and they realized uneasily, but too late, that it was the uniforms they wore that had awakened the electric fear in her great dark eyes. She scurried past them and they saw that the burden she sheltered within her arms was a child, stiffened in death, its ivory exposed bones gleaming brightly with eyes still open and the small mouth gaping wide in a scream which would never be articulated. The British sergeant knelt and vomited and Joe walked quickly on, falling into a procession that wound its way to the last grave to be dug that day.

The weary group was led by an old man whose gray beard trailed down his trembling chin. He had been a famous rabbi in his native Hungary, someone had told Joe, and he had been allowed to keep his beard and the tattered prayer shawl he wore about his shoulders because the Germans often used him as a figure to ridicule. They would stand him on a platform with a sign reading "*Jude*" hung about his thin neck.

"This is a Jew," they would tell visitors and they allowed small children to pull his beard and throw the prayer shawl over his head, as though the old rabbi were an animal on exhibit at a zoo for their amusement. All this the man, to whose synagogue in Budapest thousands had swarmed to share his wisdom, had endured with stoical dignity. It was a dignity that the Germans could not shatter and which was visible on this day of liberation. The rabbi walked very slowly, and holding his arm in gentle support was a British soldier on whose uniform the six-pointed star of the Jewish Brigade glistened. He was, Joe realized, a member of the famous Palestinian unit which had fought with such heroism throughout the European theater. The two men, the soldier and the rabbi, were followed by other shadowy figures, soldiers and prisoners, and together they ringed the chasm hollowed out of the earth which would be the burial place for nameless, faceless dead.

They stood briefly in silence, and then the old man's voice, strangely melodic, rose in the ancient chant of mourning, the Kaddish.

"Magnified and sanctified be His great name in the world which He has created according to His will.... May there be abundant peace from heaven and life for us and for all Israel..."

His frail voice gathered strength and was joined by the deep basso tones of the Palestinian soldier and then by other voices. Feeble men, in the ragged pajama uniform of the inmate, their lives ravaged by war, prayed for that elusive "abundant peace." British soldiers, their eyes bright with the pain of all they had seen that day, swayed in that prayerful attitude of centuries, and prayed in the hesitant Hebrew learned long ago in the back rooms of English synagogues. The women who rimmed the semicircle of worshipers moved their lips silently but remained dry-eyed until finally a small boy with a high sweet voice sang the final plea: "May He who maketh peace in the heavens, spread His peace over us and over all Israel and say ye all Amen."

"Amen," they intoned and tears fell then, and they clutched each other and watched as the British soldiers tossed shovelful after shovelful of earth across the corpses. It was a children's grave they filled and the bodies were very small.

Joe's voice too rose in that final "Amen" that resonated through the area and seemed to shatter the sad blue mist of smoke that hovered so persistently over them.

He woke the next day to the foul stench of death and realized, with horror, that it no longer nauseated him. No sudden seizure of vomiting or revulsion overtook him and he was able that day, and during the days and weeks that followed, to wander the camp with his pad and pencil, stopping now and again to do what was necessary—to assist in carrying a sick woman from the vermin-infested prisoners' barracks to the hospital created from the officers' quarters, to help with the digging of a grave, to make a small drawing of a cowboy for a small boy who sobbed and sobbed but was wondrously silent when Joe gave him the picture.

One day he saw a small girl holding her smaller brother on her lap. Both children were covered with layers of filth and large blood-encrusted scabs scaled their bodies. But their faces were clean because the small girl had wet a scrap of cloth from her ragged dress with her own saliva and had scraped her own face, and then her brother's, free of dirt. She had fashioned a comb from a fallen twig and was determinedly pulling it through the boy's tangled mass of dark curls. Joe took out his own pocket comb and offered it to her. She looked at the black plastic comb as though it had magic powers and ran her fingers across its teeth. For a moment Joe feared she might cry but instead she smiled and the sudden brightness of her small face was the first sign of gladness he had seen in this expanse of death and grief, bounded by barbed wire, cut now but still threatening with its message of evil and hate. The girl turned back to her task, passing the clean new comb through her brother's hair but singing now—a sweet song in Yiddish, remembered perhaps from some distant day when loving hands had combed her own tousled curls.

He saw other children at the camp and while some had the typical deathlike beaten gaze of morasmus and all walked too slowly, their childish gaits burdened with sadness, their natural quickness slowed by grief and fear, they did not have the skeletal, malnourished look of the adult survivors. Later, he learned that this was because the adults in the camp had organized themselves to care for the children. When there was food the most nourishing portions were saved for the little ones, and commodities and drugs were stolen for the small prisoners, some of whom had never known freedom.

"They are our hope, you see," a young black-haired woman who had somehow organized a small school within this compound of devastation, told him. "If the children do not survive, if they do not become the next generation of our people, then all those who died here lived for nothing and died for nothing."

He looked across the yard where a group of boys had organized a game of ball. They ran awkwardly, their legs matchstick thin, their small hands flailing the air, jumping for the ball which the Palestinian Jewish soldier had fashioned out of a neutralized hand grenade, artfully wrapped round with khaki socks. One small dark-haired boy, who leapt with surprising agility, reminded Joe of Rebecca's brother Michael. When Joe looked more closely he saw that the child was the brother of the little girl to whom he had given his pocket comb. She watched the game and he saw that she, like his own Rebecca, had dark hair and a warm wide-lipped smile. With a sudden shock, he realized that only years and geography separated Rebecca and her brother Michael from the orphans of Belsen, the frail large-eyed children who were the last hope of those who had died and those who had survived.

Palestinian Jews taught the children circle dances. They sang as they danced and a Palestinian soldier sang lustily, the rich Hebrew resounding against the soft wind that cooled the hot spring afternoon.

"What does the song mean?" Joe asked.

The soldier finished the refrain, then replied, "It means that we dance because our heart is one heart from one generation to the next and because the chain of those hearts remains unbroken." He sang softly in the Hebrew, *"Ki libenu lev echad, Minay oz v'oz edad, Ki od nimshechet hashalshelet."*

"Because the chain remains unbroken," Joe thought. That chain which linked Jews one to the other: newborn infants born to the thousands of murdered men and women buried in mass graves below their birthing place, a fragile old rabbi to a strong young Palestinian soldier; which linked Rebecca and Michael Goldfeder to the small girl who combed her younger brother's hair with a fallen twig. It was a chain which he knew now, on this day when the air rang with song and was sweet with the breath of a new season, that he must not break. He could not stand beneath a wedding canopy with Rebecca nor could he dance with her in such a circle of joy and continuity. Again he thought of his lovely love as the silver moonlight slid across the gentle curve of her cheek and his eyes filled with tears.

He wrote Rebecca a long letter, filling page after page with all he had seen during the eternity of weeks he had spent at Belsen. He enclosed some drawings he had done, feeling somehow that they explained much that he could not articulate. In a few months, he told Rebecca, he would be separated from the army but he would not return to America. He would go to France and work in a studio in Paris. It was time that he faced himself and that was something he had to do alone. Alone. He stared at the word and went to the window.

Small campfires were lit every night at Belsen now and young people sat and sang beside them. He watched and listened as they sang, their arms intertwined, their bodies swaying. "*Ki od nimshechet hashalshelet*... Because the chain remains unbroken." He sealed his letter and mailed it that night. There was a full moon and as he walked back to his tent from the post box, he followed the trail of its silvery light across a field of new young grass.

*

Joe Stevenson's letter arrived in Bennington on a very hot summer morning and Rebecca Goldfeder held it loosely in her hand when she went to answer her phone. It was just noon, she remembered, and the letter had arrived early that morning. She had read it over several times, and studied the drawings Joe had enclosed. She understood and yet did not understand but knew with certainty that her heart was twisted with grief and she moaned softly with the pain of it. The phone rang several times before she answered it, and when she heard her mother's voice she knew that she would cry.

"Becca!" Leah was shouting. "They've found Aaron. He's alive. He's just been released from a Prisoner of War camp. Aaron's alive and well!"

Rebecca did cry then and she did not know, then or later, whether the tears that streamed down her cheeks that morning were for her newly found brother or her newly lost love.

16

The city of Bari, a sleepy port on the Adriatic coast of Italy, had emerged from the anguish of the war with its curious timelessness intact. Polished black landau carriages, pulled by limpid-eyed horses festooned with fragrant garlands, continued to circle the cobblestoned piazza overlooking the gentle rolling sea. University students hurried to classes in ancient red brick buildings, grabbing hot sausage rolls to eat en route from the vendors who followed each other up the narrow curving streets. There were, of course, fewer young men in town than there had been a decade earlier. The war had made the young men of Bari impatient and many had departed for Venice and Rome, some embarking for the United States and South America. But their departures did not disturb their sedentary elders. They were young men—they would see the world and return. Meanwhile, those who sat in the cafés which rimmed the harbor dipped oversized spoons into bowls of rainbow-colored *gelato* and looked out to the harbor, marking the arrival and departure of familiar boats and strange ones.

The women wore the eternal mourning costume of Italy. Their shapeless black dresses showed rust in spots and their black cotton stockings wrinkled about legs that occasionally were surprisingly well shaped. They stopped to chat with each other, balancing their battered aluminum trays of newly baked dough on their heads with indifferent ease. They went twice a day to the communal baker's oven for the rising of their pasta dough and then worked together in the gardens near the square. There they sliced the mounds of spongy yellow dough into thin spaghetti strips or helped each other operate the small iron machines that fashioned it into macaroni elbows, petaled shells, or tiny snow-flakes of *tubettini*. They talked as they worked, looking up to shout reprimands at the small boys in short pants who hurtled through the streets, teasing groups of girls in flowered skirts who walked together, arms intertwined, singing the newest songs from Radio Roma. They looked up, too, when the

American *signorina* who had lodged for the past week in the small pension near the university passed. She was, they agreed, *molto bella,* very beautiful, and they had been surprised to learn that she did not speak Italian. They had thought, at first, because of her long black hair and dark eyes, that she would know their language but it was of no importance. She would leave Bari soon. They had lived all their lives in a port city and the vagaries of travelers were no mystery to them.

Rebecca Goldfeder moved quickly down the narrow streets although she had neither an appointment nor a destination. In the large red leather purse which had been her first purchase in the straw and leather market of Florence, she carried a packet of neatly addressed envelopes for posting. These were dutiful letters to her parents and brothers, to Eleanor Greenstein and her other friends in Vermont. They were worried about her, she knew, and so each letter was designed to reassure them and she laced her sentences with cheerful asides and drew small pictures along the margins. From Milan she wrote them descriptions of the opera house where elegant women in frayed, prewar clothing threaded diamonds through their chignons and adorned worn velvet capes with clusters of pearls, garnets, rubies. She wandered the museums and galleries of Rome, avoiding the blank areas on the walls where precious paintings had disappeared. They had been mysteriously "borrowed" by the Germans or loaned by Mussolini to his friend Hitler and were now victims of the postwar maelstrom of displaced persons, displaced paintings, razed towns, and vanished villages.

She wrote to Eleanor of the wonders of Florence and sent Aaron a tan portfolio of tooled Florentine leather for his new notebooks and papers. "See," all this told those at home, "I'm all right. I'm traveling and doing things, shopping and going to the theater. It's fun. I'm having fun."

She wondered if she fooled them and suspected sadly that she did not. Still, they all had their own busy lives, particularly with Aaron safely home. She reflected again on how wonderful it had been that the news of Aaron's safety coincided with that long wrenching letter from Joe Stevenson, the letter that she carried still in her leather bag, worn and frayed from reading and rereading. The news about Aaron had offset that crippling emptiness, filled the strange vacancy left by the loss of the knowledge that she loved and was loved.

That letter, those tissue sheets which Joe had filled in the darkness of a Belsen night, left her with an unjustified sense of betrayal—all the more bitter because she knew such betrayal to be unjust, irrational. Still, whatever Joe's reasons—and they were good reasons, she acknowledged finally, in the exhaustion of examined grief—he was gone and would not be back. She was alone for the first time in her life. She wandered the Bennington apartment where his presence hovered in the unfinished paperback mystery with his place still marked, the outline of a tube of oil paint on the cherry wood table they had refinished together, the odd items of clothing he had neglected to ship back to California—and why had he shipped anything to California, she wondered for the first time. He must have known even then, in a secret part of him, that their time had not come, would not come. She wanted to flee their apartment; she no longer wanted to live in Vermont and walk alone the paths they had walked together.

Eleanor Greenstein had been understanding and regretful when Rebecca told her of her decision to leave.

"But you have made some plans, I hope," the older woman said. "I know how it is, Rebecca, to begin again. Have some sort of a blueprint for the future in mind." And she hugged Leah's daughter, who had in these brief years filled the place of her own lost child whose young impatient life had been seared into death by the flames she still saw in her dreams.

Rebecca had had a blueprint for her future. In the darkness of a long night when she had wept with such passion that tears had failed her, she had envisioned her future with luminous clarity and made her decision. With it, a strange deadly calm had settled over her and subdued her passionate misery. It was, after all, quite simple. She would go home and marry Joshua Ellenberg. When she formulated the idea, it seemed to her logical, as inevitable as the last piece of a complicated jigsaw puzzle sliding effortlessly into place.

She thought then of the way Joshua had protected her as a child, guided her through her adolescence, comforted her through the years of Aaron's disappearance, and shielded her even as she rejected him on that wintry day when they stood together beneath a snowy bower. He would shield and comfort her again. He would take care of her. He would make a great deal of money and she would live within the shelter of his love and his protection. They would have children and a large home. Somewhere in that house there would be a small studio where she could toy with her painting and drawing. All this she foresaw clearly, even to the skylight in the studio and the russet carpeting on a phantom staircase.

She fell asleep then, cradled in the sweet calm she had known as a child when Joshua led her out of the Eldridge Street living room, crowded with boarders and visitors, to her small trundle bed, where he told her stories and fashioned toys for her from the mountain of rags he called his "merchandise." That was what she wanted now, in this season of loss, to once again be Joshua's Becca, his baby, his love.

She knew a good deal about Joshua's war. That first cheerful, irreverent letter had been followed by others which she had answered in a similar vein, writing with sisterly fondness. Joshua had fought along the Rhine and during the last days of that fierce assault a grenade had exploded in his hand, shattering every bone and pulverizing the flesh of his palm into shreds of blackened blood-laced meat.

"Nothing the docs could do with such ruined merchandise except get rid of it," Joshua had written. She knew then that his right hand had been amputated. In an English hospital he had been fitted with a prosthetic hand and although he insisted he was as good as new it was clear that his war was over. Leah had written

Rebecca that Joshua would soon be demobilized and sent home. Rebecca had decided to be in New York for his arrival. Her life in Vermont was over and her life with Joshua would begin.

She stood beside his parents at the west side dock waiting for the troopship to disgorge its cargo of returning soldiers. Near her, a young blonde woman lifted a hefty two-year-old who waved a small American flag and screamed "Daddy! Daddy!"

The woman wanly returned Rebecca's smile at the staccato shrill shouts.

"He's never met his dad. I was pregnant when Frank was shipped out and Frank Jr. here arrived when his daddy was fighting in Sicily."

Older children clung to their parents and grandparents and searched the crowd of disembarking soldiers with gazes both hopeful and apprehensive. An American Legion band played "Praise the Lord and Pass the Ammunition," "Over There," and "The Caisons Go Rolling Along" in rapid succession. Then as the first soldiers walked down the gangplank they broke into a rousing rendition of "God Bless America." Someone began singing and soon hundreds of voices filled the air. The small boy who had never seen his father waved his flag wildly and sang "Daddy, daddy, daddy," in tune to the music.

His song of summons was answered by a tall, smiling sergeant who loped toward them, expertly balancing himself on crutches.

"Frank, oh Frank!" the blonde woman called, tears streaking her face, her voice melting with gladness. Her arms went around the soldier who embraced her and the child together while his empty trouser leg flapped in the wind.

Rebecca turned away, her heart sinking, and searched the wave of khaki-clad men who surged toward the waiting crowds.

"There he is," she called to Sarah Ellenberg. "There's our Josh!"

And there he was, taller and leaner than she remembered, his crew-cut, sand-colored hair bleached to a new brightness by the oceanic sun. She tried not to look at his hand but was impelled to and when she hugged him her lips, in penance for the hurt he had suffered on her behalf, touched the hard black leather fingers that gripped her shoulder.

"Mom! Dad! Becca! Hey, this is great. I never expected you to be here, Becca baby."

"And I expected you to be the first GI down the gangplank, you operator. What slowed you down?"

"Blame her—my precious baggage slowed me down."

The young woman in the trim gray uniform of the British Nursing Corps was so tiny that Rebecca had not noticed her as she stood patiently at Joshua's side. Her military cap sat pertly on a crop of auburn hair and her small face was dotted with freckles.

"She outranks me, so be careful," Joshua said. "Mom, Dad, Becca, say hello to the biggest Ellenberg coup yet—my cockney bride, Sherry Goldstein Ellenberg, formerly of Bournemouth. She had the great good fortune of being in the right place at the right time—she was right there when they fitted me with this little beauty." He shook his prosthetic hand and hugged his wife, who blushed and hid her face in his uniform.

"Oh, my darling girl, my darling boy, my children. *Kinderlach*." Sarah Ellenberg engulfed the girl in a tearful embrace and Rebecca's own eyes were filled with tears as she bent forward and gave Joshua's wife a welcoming kiss.

"Sure I'm still an operator, Becca. Didn't I arrange to get my wife assigned to my own troopship? Do you know anyone else who had a trans-Atlantic honeymoon on the taxpayers' expense in this war?"

"Joshua can do anything," Sherry said and looked up at him, her amber eyes alight with love.

"We know that," Sam Ellenberg said proudly. He took his son's artificial hand in his own and put an arm around his new daughter-in-law.

Rebecca trailed along behind them, Sherry's kit bag over her shoulder. In her bedroom that night, she confronted both her regret and her relief at Joshua's marriage. She stared into the darkness and wondered now what she would do with the days and years of her life.

It was Aaron, months later, who provided her with an answer. His arrival home had been quieter than Joshua's and his attitude more subdued. He told them briefly, without detail, of his experiences in a Prisoner of War camp near Trieste. His status had confused his captors. He was an American Jew in British uniform fighting with a Palestinian brigade. Perhaps they had seized on such irregularities to claim an exemption from the stipulations of the Geneva convention and had not listed his name on standard Prisoner of War rosters. Still, they had not treated him badly. He was very thin because there had been very little food and there was still a scarcity of food in Europe. Men who are at war have no time for farming. But, oddly, there had been an excellent library in the prison camp, established by the Red Cross, and Aaron had spent the term of his imprisonment reading. It was then that he had decided to study law.

"This world isn't going to be changed by wars or revolutions," he told his family as they sat down together to their first Thanksgiving dinner of the new peace. "There's work to be done and I want to be part of it."

"I'm going to be a lawyer too," Michael echoed and they all laughed. Clearly, if Aaron decided to become a deep-sea diver, Michael would follow his brother into the aquatic depths.

Leah looked around that table with quiet joy. They were all there—her sons and daughter, Joshua and his petite wife who listened attentively to every word he uttered and smiled adoringly up at him, Mr. and Mrs. Schreiber, grown old and frail but finally possessed of a sad, accepting serenity. Their son was long dead and they knew now that their old friend Frederic Heinemann, the brave German who had introduced them to the Goldfeders, had perished in the concentration camp at Matthausen. But Hitler had been defeated, a heavy justice had been won, and they had been in their small way instrumental in its achievement. Their work was done. Fragile Mrs. Schreiber cut Michael an extra-large slice of the *apfelkuchen* she had baked for dessert. He was a growing boy. He needed sweets and nourishment. How like her son he looked. She coaxed the boy, who had become the grandson she would never have, to eat yet another piece.

Bonnie Cosgrove and her children were there but Peter Cosgrove had been buried in the American cemetery at Ardennes, one of the first casualties of that bloody battle. On a gold chain around her neck Bonnie wore the Purple Heart he had been awarded posthumously and her small son played with his dead father's medal.

Mollie and Seymour dominated the far end of the table flanked by pretty Annie, who was proudly pregnant now and awaiting the return of her husband who had been assigned to the occupying troops in Japan. Now that he was to become a grandfather and suffered from high-blood pressure and an incipient ulcer, fleshy, florid Seymour had at last abandoned the blonde models who had shared his bed for so many years. There were no more urgent out-of-town trips, no imperative overnight conferences in the city. He and Mollie served on their temple board, went to B'nai B'rith brunches, and held cocktail parties for the Joint Distribution Committee. Now he motioned everyone to silence as Annie told them of a letter she had received from her husband, describing a flight over Hiroshima. Again and again he had written of the waste, the charred desolation.

"It was very terrible," David said sadly, "but there was no other way."

That was what Jeffrey Coleman had told him during a brief visit some weeks after that day in early August when a great mushroom cloud of destruction rose over a devastated Japanese metropolis. Jeffrey's work at Los Alamos had been related to the development of the atomic bomb and it occurred to David that if, years before, his therapeutic effort with the talented young science student had been unsuccessful, Jeffrey would not be the brilliant physicist whose work had contributed to the development of the bomb that ended the war. They were all inexorably linked together in this endless chain of history, he thought, and gently smoothed the hair of Bonnie's youngest child, golden-blonde like her father's. Sorrowfully he thought of his friend Peter Cosgrove, his academic mentor, cut down by war in the fields of France which he had hiked so joyously in his student days.

David's eyes were watchful as Leah's head inclined toward Aaron and she spoke softly to him. The young man nodded and he and Leah rose from the table, murmured excuses, and left the room. Minutes later, as the family lingered over dessert and coffee, they heard the rear door softly close and through the diamond-paned French windows that lined the dining room, they saw mother and son disappear into the garden, heading for the small stone gazebo whose marble floor trapped a silver pool of wintry sunlight. Leah wore her dark-blue woolen cape, the hood pulled up. Within the heavy cowl her face was strangely pale but her gaze, turned on Aaron, was firm and her eyes glittered with determination. Aaron wore an old tan cardigan, a remnant of his high school days, two buttons still missing, lost on a day when he had rescued Lisa Frawley from a bramble bush along a north county path. But he had grown so thin that the sleeves of the sweater fluttered like loose woolen wings in the gentle wind and he shivered against the crisp autumnal chill.

"Are you cold?" Leah asked.

"I think I'm cold all the time now," he said. "Dad says it's slight anemia. He's pretty sure it'll pass once I gain back the weight and get generally recharged. Probably iron pills will help. I'm going to see Dad's friend Dr. Adler next week for a general checkup."

"I'm glad," she said. "This is a new beginning."

"Yes. Yes, it is."

"Aaron, I want us to have a new beginning too."

"Yes."

He fixed his eye on a vagrant prism of sunlight that flashed across a fallen maple leaf, the band of liquid gold balanced on the brittle scarlet surface. He waited for her to go on, his heart tight, thinking that he had waited a long time for this moment, for the words that would tell him at last what he had always longed to know.

They sat on the stone bench and Leah scattered some crumbs she had brought with her. Two hesitant sparrows, who had lingered too long in the north, flew in, hastily plucked up the minuscule morsels, and soared back onto the apple tree. They perched among the barren branches, fragile-winged sentinels balanced on a low-hung bough.

"I always loved that tree," Aaron said. "It's funny. I never had much feeling for this house. Maybe I was too old when we finally moved here. But in the prison camp when I thought of home I sometimes visualized the apartment on Eldridge Street, sometimes our house in Brighton Beach. If I thought of Scarsdale—of this house—at all, I thought only of that apple tree. I remembered the curve of its trunk and the way the heavy blossoms weighed down those new young branches. I would think of the way you and Becca used to sketch out here and of the long shadow of the tree in the first days of fall."

"Yes. Trees become a part of you as nothing else does. When I think of Russia, I too think of a particular tree—a Lombardy tree that stood in your grandparents' garden. Its smallest leaves were shaped like stars. Their small veins were yellow, as though the sun had left drops of golden light within them. Your father Yaakov—and I, we often sat beneath that tree and talked—and sang—and laughed. I loved that tree until—" Leah's voice faltered and she bent to pluck up a late-blooming wild rose, flowering on the bush that had somehow threaded its way through the stone lacework of the gazebo's wall. Her hood flew off and Aaron saw the small wings of silver that crested her black hair.

"Until—"

His voice prodded her on, gentle but insistent. She had come out here today to grant him a legacy long denied. He would have it; he must have it.

"Until—" he said again.

Her fingers smoothed the silver strands and his heart turned with a prescient grief.

"Until the very last day I lived in that house. Your father and grandparents were away. I was alone, up in the attic. Suddenly there were flames. The house next door was on fire—children were crying."

She spoke softly, as though her voice might disturb the rhythm of the remembered weeping, the staccato crackling of burning wood, the stertorous sputtering of flame against stone, the odors of singed fabric and molten metal.

"I ran out—hurrying toward the children. But I got only as far as the tree, the Lombardy tree. A man came across the fields. I saw his red hair and thought that it was your father. I ran to him. God help me—I ran to him!"

She buried her face in her hands and on their leafless bough the sparrows chirped mournfully. Aaron touched her shoulder, knowing now what she would tell him, wanting her to stop and knowing that she would not, that she could not.

"I fought him. Ran from him. Around and around the Lombardy tree. But I could not escape him. I knew it and he knew it. He caught me at last. That night I managed to reach Odessa—my brother Moshe's house. There I learned that your father had been killed. And a few weeks later I knew that I was pregnant."

"And you were never sure of who my father was," he said with a strange calm, understanding at last those moments when he had caught her studying his face, hovering over his boyhood bed.

"I was never sure. And how wrong I was to have let it matter. I should have loved you no matter who your father was. You were my son. And I did love you, Aaron—in some ways more than I loved your brother and sister. But that day stood between us. We lived together, you and I, in the shadow of that Lombardy tree, in the reflection of those terrible flames, of that terrible afternoon. Until the day of your bar mitzvah."

"My bar mitzvah?"

He remembered anew the smell of the salt sea in the small synagogue, David's eyes bright with pride, a baby Michael resting on Leah's shoulder, and his own voice trembling through the prophetic reading and then cracking with embarrassing suddenness—breaking into the timbre of manhood.

"Your voice," she said. "It became your father's voice, Yaakov's own tenor. There was no doubt. I was free of the wondering, of the uncertainty. But by then it was too late. We had lost so much."

"It's not too late."

Aaron's voice broke. He knelt beside Leah, his head on her lap, and she passed her fingers through the thick copper clusters of his hair that shimmered beneath the wetness of her own tears, which fell freely now. She raised his head and saw that he wept too, openly, as a strong man weeps. Long unshed tears coursed down his lean cheeks and she pressed her mouth to his face and tasted the bitter salinity of his sorrow.

"Can you ever forgive me, Aaron?" she asked.

He did not answer and she did not question his silence.

They rose then and he held her in a gentle embrace. Slowly, arms entwined, they walked across the long dark-velvet shadow of the apple tree and back to the house where lamps glowed in golden brightness against the drifting shadows of the gathering dusk.

*

"And what about you, Becca? What are you going to do now?" Aaron asked his sister as they walked down the Bronx River

Parkway together later that week. It was a time of decisions, of new beginnings, of soft luminous hope after the dark frightening years of the war. Aaron was beginning law school. Joshua Ellenberg, with Seymour's investment and blessing, was beginning his own business. Leah would work only part-time at S. Hart now. She had begun to do serious painting, and a studio was under construction at the back of the house. Only Rebecca remained in limbo, caught between a vanished love and a wistful yearning for a future that would link adventure with meaning.

"I don't know. I don't seem to have an urgent calling," she said, kicking at a pile of maple leaves, remembering a distant day when Joe had threaded them lazily through her hair as they lay naked in an isolated Vermont meadow, shivering deliciously as the fall wind caressed their intertwined bare bodies. Briefly then she hated Joe for leaving her and loved him for having loved her.

"Do you know what I'd do if I were you? I'd take a trip to Palestine. I'd do it now myself but I feel that I've wasted so much time—that I'm years behind. Finally, I feel that I'm really ready to study, to work toward what I want to be. But over in North Africa, I listened to our cousin Yaakov and the other Palestinians talk about the country. If I hadn't focused on the law, if I weren't sure of what I wanted to do, of what I should do, I'd hop a boat for Palestine tomorrow. Maybe I will do it in a couple of years. But right now, I know where I've been and I know where I'm going."

Rebecca envied him that peaceful certainty. "Palestine?" she said and thought of Joe's letter, of his description of the Belsen children bound for that sun-parched strip of territory where an elusive freedom waited. Palestine. Why not? She would meet her mother's brother, the legendary Moshe, and her cousins. She had seen photographs of the stark hills of Galilee and had thought then of sketching trips through that forbidding landscape. And of course she could stop in Italy en route and visit the museums. Yes, of course, she would go to Palestine.

And so she had traveled through a war-ravaged Italy and come at last to the dreamy port of Bari to await a ship for Haifa. She hurried now, along the winding ancient streets, to the hilltop post office. These might be the last letters she would mail from Italy. A ship for Haifa was due in port within a few days, and a new excitement at the thought of the journey dispersed the loneliness she had felt in this town where the aroma of rising dough mingled with the fragrance of a thousand flowers.

She posted her letters quickly and dashed off a picture postcard to Joshua and Sherry Ellenberg.

"Perhaps, Signorina Goldfeder, I can offer you a stamp for your postcard," a man's soft voice said. She looked up in irritation, prepared to ignore the clumsy attempt to pick her up. But then she remembered that the man had used her name and she hesitated.

"How do you know that I am Signorina Goldfeder?" she asked and studied him with her frank artist's gaze.

He was a tall man in his middle twenties and his thick hair was almost the same shade as his deeply bronzed skin—skin which had a leathery texture, as though sun and wind had burned their way onto and through his body. From that lean bronzed face glinted gray eyes, sleek as silk, and a thin slit of mouth betrayed startling white teeth. He wore khaki slacks and a blue nylon shirt open at the neck, the standard uniform that year for student tourists and seamen at liberty.

"I bring you greetings from your Uncle Moshe and cousin Yaakov on Kibbutz Beth HaCochav. Your cousin knew that you would be here. My name is Yehuda Arnon."

"And my aunt—does she too send her regards?" Rebecca asked warily.

"Your aunt—the good Henia—yes, she too sends regards. Have I passed the test?" He smiled at her in amusement. "May we go now to the square and have a cold coffee? I am very thirsty." He pasted a stamp on her postcard, his eyes sliding over the name.

"Ellenberg. There is an Ellenberg family on our kibbutz."

"A cousin of my friend's. His family and mine came from the same town in Russia." Joshua. Her friend and nearly-brother. Her protector and almost-husband. How lucky they had all been that Joshua had met and married Sherry. She dismissed the thought too quickly, not wanting to remember how she had almost surrendered her life.

"All right then. Let us go to a café. But I hope you don't mind if I have a *gelato* instead of coffee. If there's anything I hate worse than *ersatz* coffee, it's cold *ersatz* coffee."

He laughed.

"In Palestine the coffee of the Bari cafés would be considered manna from heaven," he said. "But of course you may have whatever you wish." He paused then and searched her face. "And I would not be very surprised if that is not what you have always had—whatever you wished."

She did not answer, reading an odd contempt in his tone, and they walked down the hill in silence and remained silent even after he had given their order to the waiter. It was the siesta hour and they sat alone in the deserted café and watched the high afternoon sun sweep in a golden arc across the deep-blue waters of the Adriatic Sea.

"Your uncle Moshe thought that perhaps you might help us with a small endeavor here in Bari," he said, when at last the waiter, annoyed at being disturbed during the siesta hour, had slammed down the coffee and *gelato* and disappeared into the shadows of the café.

"Us? Who would that be?" she asked. She heard the hostility in her voice and wondered what it was about this tall, self-assured stranger that provoked her annoyance.

"*Us*. Ah yes, who are *we*? Simply Jews concerned about other Jews. Specifically today, here in this port, about Jewish children. Survivors of the death camp at Oswiecim in Poland. Auschwitz, as the Germans called it. They are here in Bari, these orphaned survivors, and we want to get them to Palestine. Ah yes, I used that mysterious *we* yet again. That we includes your family, myself, and practically every Jew in Palestine. We work here in Europe through an organization which we call *Bericha*—the Hebrew word for flight. And the Jews of Europe are in flight, my dear Miss Goldfeder. They are in flight from memories of death and near-death, from the countries of their birth which now reject them, from the camps for displaced persons that remind them of the camps which consumed their mothers and fathers, their brothers and sisters. They flee their own fears, their nighttime terror and their daytime memory. And in all the wide world there is only one place which can give them refuge—Palestine."

He took a long sip of the coffee and looked out toward the harbor, marking the progress of a V-formation of gulls gliding toward a parapet of rocks. She saw how the color rose high beneath the deep bronze of his skin and how his eyes glistened with that dangerous brightness she had seen long ago in Gregory Liebowitz's eyes when he spoke fervently of a new society, of a world reborn. Her father had remarked dryly then, "Idealism has a strange effect on the adrenal glands." Poor Gregory, dead of dysentery in Ethiopia, never to know either the brave new world of which he had dreamed or the weary recovery of the old world he had so disparaged.

"But Jews are being admitted into Palestine," she said.

Only that morning the Paris *Tribune* had carried a front-page picture of a group of Jews disembarking from a British naval vessel at Haifa port in which a smiling British sailor carried a Jewish child ashore.

"Yes. The British make good propaganda. I too read this morning's paper. But surely you know that the British have a very strict quota system—a White Paper, which allows only a few Jews into Palestine. They are more concerned about placating their sources of oil than with Jewish lives. They run a blockade against immigrant ships and if the ships are caught, the passengers are sent back to the Europe of their nightmares or to detention camps on

Cyprus. Our organization helps to get the Jews to ports on the Mediterranean and then we try to smuggle them into Palestine. Illegal immigration, the British call it, and we call it Aliyah Beth. But you must know something of this—your family has been involved in it for many years."

He looked searchingly at her and she turned away, not wanting his eyes to capture and thus command her own.

She knew, of course, about her Uncle Moshe's work but she had thought about it, when she thought about it at all, as a part of the war. Her own life had absorbed her and the problems of the Jews of Europe were pitiable but remote. She was not visiting Palestine out of any deep ideological conviction but because her relatives were there, because it had seemed a logical place to go, because in a way she too was in flight. Flight. *Bericha*. She did, after all, have something in common with the man who sat across the table from her, his smooth gray eyes staring openly, contemptuously at her American clothing, her oversized new leather bag, the smooth skin of her bare, sunburned arms.

"But why have you come to me? What can I do?" She asked the question reluctantly. She did not, in fact, want to do anything. She wanted to board her ship, select a deck chair, and lie in the sun, not thinking, not remembering.

"Whatever I tell you is in strictest confidence. Whether or not you decide to help us, you must never speak of what I say to you today. Is that agreed? Please, I am not being dramatic but it is necessary that we understand this." He leaned closer to her and suddenly put his arm around her, bent his head laughingly toward her, kissed her on the lips, and spooned some *gelato* from her dish into his mouth.

She looked at him in amazement and then saw the shadows across the sunny cobblestones of the piazza. Two men in business suits stood on the church steps and watched them. She too laughed lightly then, took the spoon from him, and playfully fed him, knowing that her heart was beating too fast and a pool of sweat had formed between her breasts. The men crossed the square and as they passed, she heard them speaking softly in English.

"You did that very well," he said admiringly and she blushed.

"I'm an international intrigue film addict. You know—Ingrid Bergman, Lilli Palmer. Who were those men?"

"Probably British intelligence agents. They're swarming over all the Mediterranean ports trying to get a line on *Bericha* and *Mosad* people. *Mosad* is a kind of network intelligence operation for the Jewish community in Palestine over in Europe. They'll ask about us, but my guess is we'll be described as an itinerant seaman type trying to pick up a naive American tourist."

"I don't think I like the 'naive' part," she said and realized that she was beginning to enjoy herself.

"All right. A pretty American tourist. You are pretty, you know." He offered this not as a compliment but as a dry observation, a professional assessment, and she stiffened.

"All right. What do you think I can do? I am, after all, 'naive.'"

He bent forward, speaking so softly that she had to strain to catch his words.

"There are ten children hidden here in Bari. We call them the Auschwitz infants. They are the children of Jews who were gassed at Auschwitz. They survived because they were hidden in an underground tunnel in one of the women's barracks. One of these children, Shlomo, was born in the camp, delivered by the women, hidden by them, and saved by them and the other children. The children watched, from that underground tunnel, as one by one their mothers were taken off to die. They were alone, in what the Germans thought was an empty building, for two weeks, sharing among themselves the small amount of food and water the last survivor had been able to get to them. You can imagine how they are traumatized, terrified, by the thought of another camp—whether it be a displaced persons' camp in Europe or a detainment camp in Cyprus. They cannot again endure barbed wire and bunks and searchlights. We cannot risk putting them on an illegal ship which may be taken by the British. The British have, so far, seized every other ship which we have sent. These children are special. For them we have arranged identity papers and travel documents saying that they are Dutch orphans en route to a mission school in Nazareth. Through our good friend Father Joseph, at such a school, we have even managed to get school uniforms for them. We have arranged for their passage on the ship which you now await. But they must have an adult with them to supervise and chaperone. This is the rule of the steamship company. The *Mosad* agent, the girl who was to do this, has been detained at the Belgian border. We ask you to take her place."

Rebecca did not reply but looked out toward the rock parapet where the gulls strutted now, their heads arched upward above their slender elegant necks.

"You know that I have an American passport," she said at last. "It is unlikely that an American with the distinctly Jewish name of Rebecca Goldfeder will pass as the supervisor of a mission group."

"Yes. We thought of that. But then such a person might well be a Jew who has converted to Christianity, and I happen to have here such a certificate of baptism in the name of Rebecca Goldfeder as well as a set of credentials from the Mission of Saint Paul. This is, of course, a missionary school and missionaries convert. You are one of their successes, diligently continuing the good work. Your documents, I assure you, are exemplary. They were manufactured by the same man who produced the children's papers with the cooperation of our good Christian friends in Nazareth. Yoselle was a master printer in Hamburg in the days when Jews were allowed to be master printers in Hamburg, before it was feared that they would contaminate the reading matter of Aryans. I assure you all his documents are impeccable." He smiled and patted the battered portfolio which he kept close by his side.

"I see. And if I do not agree to do this? What will happen to the children?"

"We will discuss that after you meet these children. Please. You will come to see our Auschwitz infants?" There was a naked plea in his voice.

"Yes," she said, knowing that she could not say no.

The children, he told her, were staying at the home of Dr. Rafael Sarfadi, a Jewish professor of semantics at the University of Bari. His home was an ancient villa, nestled into a low hillside that overlooked the port. Signora Sarfadi, a tall, elegant woman who wore a gold linen dress, greeted them as though they were casual guests for tea. She stood in the open doorway and thanked Yehuda for the flowers he carried and kissed him on the cheek. Rebecca wondered at this until she glanced across the street and saw the two Englishmen, in their too-proper business suits, looking out toward the ocean.

"The more we display the less they will think we conceal," Yehuda said softly when he followed her gaze.

They walked after Signora Sarfadi through the archways leading to the enormous rooms of the ancient mansion. The polished tile floors were covered with Persian carpets of intricate rich design and the black mahogany furniture smelled of lemon oil. Fresh flowers stood in tall crystal vases and Rebecca thought of Leah and the garden flowers she cut each spring and summer morning. Her mother and Signora Sarfadi would understand each other. In each room through which they passed, there was a framed photo of a young man with dreamy liquid eyes. The last door led to a small utility room and Signora Sarfadi pushed aside a clumsy floor-polishing machine and pressed the corner of the wall against which it had leaned. Rebecca gasped as it slid open to reveal a narrow staircase. They descended it single-file until they reached a dimly lit basement room littered with small cots, toys, and children's clothing. As she first entered, Rebecca thought that the room was empty. A heavy quiet hovered in the air and there was no discernible movement. But then she saw the children's eyes.

Ten pairs of eyes, bright with fear and speculation, focused on her. The luminous, too-wise orbs, belonging to the ten children who squatted on the floor in the middle of the room, stared at her as though they would pierce her soul. The smallest child was perhaps four and the oldest eleven or twelve. They sat absolutely still, without a flicker of movement, a rustle of sound. They were all small masters of silence and immobility, their survival credentials earned in that underground tunnel where the slightest noise, the smallest motion of one, might have meant death for all.

"It's all right. She is a friend," Yehuda said softly to them in Yiddish and they breathed an almost uniform sign of relief, whispered to each other, and began to move about.

The oldest girl, whose dark hair was caught in chubby clumps at each side of her very round head, began to straighten the room like a flustered housewife surprised by an unexpected guest. As she picked up toys and clothing, she scolded two of the smaller girls who were pulling at the same book and picked up the smallest boy who had suddenly and inexplicably begun to cry. She spoke to him softly in a language Rebecca did not recognize and Yehuda translated a sentence which she spoke to Rebecca.

"Katia, that is the little mother of the group—she is already eleven years old—said to tell you that it is not that small Shlomo does not like you. He cries when he sees any stranger."

"And why not?" Rebecca thought. Small Shlomo then would be the child born in Auschwitz, his mother's pregnancy and his birth the precious secret of the women inmates who had delivered him and shielded him, a responsibility which the children had assumed when the last adults had left them, to fall beneath the showers of gas and be incinerated in the ovens that set the skies afire night and day. Rebecca turned to Signora Sarfadi, suddenly unable to meet the children's eyes.

"It is wonderful that you have such a place for them to hide."

"It is not an accident, Signorina. Jews have hidden themselves in this room for generations. This house was built by my husband's ancestors in the days of the Inquisition. It was here the Jewish women came to light Sabbath candles and say their prayers. Here men performed secret circumcisions and bar mitzvahs and met in forbidden prayer quorums. We had almost forgotten this room when the agents of *Bericha* and the *Mosad* contacted us. Now we hide Jewish children here, so that the British will not know they are near the Mediterranean. Do you think that ever a time will come for our people when this room will have no use?"

The sad defeat in her tone revealed her answer. She clearly did not think so. She might dress in gold linen and fill her tall crystal vases with fresh flowers, but she was Jewish and she was vulnerable. In the heavy gold locket that she wore around her neck there was surely a picture of the dead dreamy-eyed young man whose portrait populated the many rooms of her lovely home. Rebecca was certain that he was dead. One did not keep so many pictures of the living in polished metal frames.

Signora Sarfadi bent to take Shlomo from Katia's arms. The child fingered the locket until at last she loosed the chain and watched patiently as he stopped crying and searched for a way to open the gleaming oval.

A small girl, her blonde hair combed into a single braid down her back, approached Rebecca shyly. Her name was Mindell, Rebecca saw, from the small identity disk she and all the children wore about their necks.

"*Shain*. Pretty," she said, pointing to Rebecca's leather bag.

Rebecca held it out to her and the girl gently stroked the soft new leather. Watching her, Rebecca thought of all the things, the natural legacy of childhood that had been denied Mindell, whose small fingers hesitantly, lovingly fondled the magic newness of the bag—the tenderness of a mother's touch, the right to run and laugh, the strong embrace of a father's arms, the breathless excitement of ripping the wrapping off a present and holding something crinkling with newness, bought only for sweet pleasure. Was Mindell also to be denied, then, safe passage to the one place in the world where warmth and protection awaited her—the one place in the world which these children, so long homeless, could call home? Rebecca took the bag from Mindell and reached into it, extracting a small coin case of the same soft leather. She held it out to the child.

"A present. For you," she said softly.

Mindell took the purse, caressed it with her hands, and held it to her cheek.

"*Danke*—thank you," she said and tears like drops of liquid crystal stood in her blue eyes. She put her arms around Rebecca's neck and shyly placed her mouth against Rebecca's cheek—a hesitant, half-remembered gesture. Once, somewhere, in another life, where children played and parents laughed to see them, someone had kissed her and the memory fluttered slowly back. Confused, delighted, she darted away with her treasure to a corner of the room, where the other children clustered about her.

Rebecca's own eyes burned with unshed tears. She looked up to see Yehuda standing near her.

"She needs more than a small purse," he said dryly and she grew hot with a sudden swift rage. Who was he to judge and condemn her? He had no right, just as he had had no right to confront her with this challenge, with this absurd charge. But why assume that she would turn away from that which he undertook? She would surprise him, abrogate his arrogance. She needed no persuasive arguments from him, no idealistic injunctions, no resurrection of latent guilt. Her decision had been made when the child's lips had touched her cheek.

She looked coldly at him, copying the distant removed stare that was Leah's shield against a world that had so often demanded too much of her. She felt, at that moment, her mother's blood pulsing in her veins, her father's tenacious spirit surging through her. Quietly, firmly, in a voice that echoed the voices of her childhood, she spoke.

"We must make our plans. The ship leaves in three days; there is not much time. I will accompany the children, of course."

"Of course," said Signora Sarfadi, and her hand rested briefly on Rebecca's shoulder.

Three days later, Rebecca waited with the children for the boarding call of the *San Giovanni,* which would stop at ports of call on Rhodes, Cyprus, and Haifa. She wore a plain white blouse, dark blazer, pleated gray skirt, and oxfords. Her luxuriant dark hair was twisted into a severe bun and her eyes were protected by gold-rimmed glasses which Signora Sarfadi had produced with a knowing smile.

"If they look too closely at your eyes, they will never believe you to be a schoolmistress," she had said.

The children, neatly outfitted in their uniforms—the girls in gray serge dresses with starched white collars and the boys in suits of the same durable cheerless fabric, all bearing the insignia of the Mission of Saint Paul—stood quietly in an orderly line. Katia had combed everyone's hair and helped Rebecca to tuck shirts in and pull socks up. The port dispatcher, who had for days seen Rebecca in her sandals and bright skirts and blouses, raised his eyes in amusement at her sudden transformation but said nothing, an eloquent wink telegraphing his sympathy and complicity. The two British agents were also at the dock and as the line moved forward, one of them called after her with harsh urgency.

"Signorina. One moment please!"

Her heart stopped and she clutched her hands to conceal their trembling. But when she turned to him, her glance displayed only annoyance and condescension. She was a busy woman with ten children in her charge. Why was she being distracted?

"Excuse me, but you dropped your gloves."

"How very kind of you," she said with indifferent courtesy. She took the white gloves from him and they moved on through passport control, where her passport and the children's travel documents were duly examined and stamped. She felt nervous although Yehuda had assured her that at this point there was no need for apprehension.

"No one gives a damn if Jews leave a country. They just don't want them to enter," he had said in that dry bitter tone she had come to dread.

And then at last they were aboard the ship, watching the sunbeams skip across the waves as the children began the final lap of their very long voyage.

When the children were asleep that night, she came on deck, feeling the need to sit alone. The sea wind licked her face while she stared up at the star-filled night. She loosened her hair and put the glasses on her lap. She realized then, as she watched the moon weave its way in and out of a gossamer net of clouds, that she had not thought once of Joe Stevenson since the moment she first saw the children in their basement fortress.

"Are you enjoying the crossing?" a familiar voice asked and she looked up, startled and confused.

Yehuda Arnon stood in front of her, a lit cigarette in his mouth, his eyes on the dark fierce waves.

"I didn't know you were going to be on board," she said.

"You didn't think I would let you sail alone, did you?" he retorted but did not wait for her answer. As suddenly as he had appeared, he turned and walked down the deck. She watched until the ember of his cigarette faded into the darkness and wondered whether he had sailed with them because he was not certain he could rely on her or whether his presence was meant to reassure her. Either way, she was annoyed: annoyed that he was on board, and equally annoyed that he had walked off and left her to look at the stars alone.

She was very busy the next day, caught between comforting small Shlomo, who suffered from a bout of seasickness, and entertaining the children during the brief stop at Rhodes. She sat on deck with them playing the games she had long ago taught her brother Michael, using motions in place of words because Katia was the only child who understood even rudimentary English. She began also to teach them the first lines of a song which long ago

Lisa Frawley had taught her, laughing and encouraging them as they struggled to sing in a language not their own. Again and again they stumbled over the words.

> Jesus loves me, this I know,
> Because the Bible tells me so.

"Zo," they all pronounced it and struggled to attain the sibilant *s*.

Yehuda, strolling past them, glanced quizzically at her but she ignored him and began a clapping game.

A total exhaustion overcame her that night when she relaxed at last on her deck chair, comfortable in the knowledge that the children were all asleep at last in their berths. She did not look up at the star-encrusted skies but closed her eyes and surrendered to the rocking of the rhythmic waves.

She sensed his presence even before he spoke, and opened her eyes.

"A difficult day." He leaned against the rail, the cigarette unlit between his lips. Such narrow lips, she noted, set above a strong square chin.

"Yes." She knew that he could not approach her during the course of the day. One British agent was a passenger and doubtless members of the crew were in the pay of the British. Here he was probably known as a Palestinian Jew and a *Bericha* agent. He could not jeopardize the children by approaching them and she knew it was irrational to resent him for that diligently maintained distance.

"You were very good with little Shlomo."

"I have a young brother who went through a difficult time during the war when our older brother was missing in action in North Africa. Shlomo reminds me of Michael."

She knew with shame but without regret why she had offered this information to Yehuda Arnon. He saw her, she knew, as a spoiled American girl who had neither suffered nor endured any difficulty. She was telling him that the war had affected her too—she too had spent sleepless nights worrying over the fate of someone she loved, she too had known fear and uncertainty. And loss. She shivered suddenly and wished, in her weariness, for Joe Stevenson's arms to embrace her, for Joshua Ellenberg to envelop her within a blanket. But they were gone and far away, absorbed in their own worlds, their own lives. She had only herself to rely on. She closed her eyes and heard Yehuda's steps retreat down the deck. Minutes later a warm rough blanket was draped over her shoulders and she felt strong hands tuck it firmly about her body.

"That's better," Yehuda said. "That is the way. My daughter also likes to be snuggled this way."

His daughter, He was married then. What was the wife of such an arrogant, contemptuous man like? She wondered too how old his daughter was, and if he had other children. She fell into a light sleep then and when she awoke he was gone. Yet she knew he had watched over her as she slept because of the small hill of cigarette ash where he had stood, leaning against the rail.

There was foul weather the next two days, as the ocean became a glasslike expanse of white water, shattered into angry dark-blue fissures by a violent westbound wind. The children wept and she was relieved to see them at last surrender into childish misery, almost glad when Katia clung to her for comfort and Mindell, her secret favorite, perched on her lap to play with her purse. She did not go on deck that night or the next and she wondered if Yehuda had waited for her. She imagined him leaning against the rail, sending small sad wisps of cigarette smoke out across the waves.

Early on the fourth morning they docked at Haifa and she felt a rush of excitement as she stood on board and stared out at the busy port. There were signs everywhere, screaming their dock-side messages in Hebrew, English, and Arabic. Dark-skinned dock workers shifted cargo and British soldiers in khaki shorts and shirts patrolled the port. Trucks with Hebrew lettering on them were lined up and sunburned young men in shorts and sweat-stained undershirts heaved enormous sacks of produce, here and there sending onions or tomatoes skittling into the dirt. She looked northward, where the city of shops and villas climbed the graceful slopes of Mount Carmel. This then was Palestine.

Behind her the children, her Auschwitz infants, dressed in their uniforms, their hair combed and faces very clean, stood quietly. For them, this was only another test to be endured, another border to be crossed. They knew the rules and stood so still, so quiet, that she feared their unchildlike quiescence itself would betray them. Just ahead of them, moving swiftly toward passport control, she saw the British agent. He stopped at the desk, showed his identity card to the official, and bent forward, speaking rapidly, gesturing toward them. Rebecca's palms grew damp and her heart ricocheted in urgent irregular beat. They would not, after all, be admitted. She could not brazen it through. She looked at the children and saw that mute anguished plea in their eyes, the plea that had pierced her heart in Signora Sarfadi's basement. She could not fail them. On deck Yehuda looked down at them. He lifted his hand slightly, an almost imperceptible gesture, a sign of trust. A new strength came to her and she turned confidently to the children.

Smiling, she began to sing.

Jesus loves me, this I know,
Because the Bible tells me so.

Katia's clear sweet voice picked up the song and then, with awkward accent but brave tremulous tone, all the children sang as they reached the desk of the passport control officer.

She held out her passport and the children's papers to him and they continued singing as he looked carefully through the papers.

"Can you hurry please?" she said imperiously. "The children are very tired and I should like to get them to the mission in Nazareth as soon as possible. We have been traveling for a very long time."

"These children are all en route to the mission?" he asked.

"As you read and as you see." She might have been her mother, responding with annoyance to a delinquent supplier, or Eleanor

Greenstein, impatiently answering the questions of a novice buyer. She had had good teachers and learned her lessons well.

The British immigration officer that day was a young man with a soft blond moustache named Guy Wilkes who attended early services each Sunday and was the father of two blonde, rosy-cheeked little girls whom he missed terribly. He smiled at the group of singing children because the hymn was a favorite of his and had been mastered by his eldest daughter just before he left for this "rotten Mideast posting." Mindell, who at nine was mistress of a portfolio of survival secrets, smiled shyly back at him, closed her eyes demurely, and softly sang another chorus. Guy Wilkes turned reluctantly to the task at hand.

"You are Rebecca Goldfeder and you are chaperoning these children who are en route to the Mission of Saint Paul in Nazareth?" he asked.

She nodded.

"You are a convert then, I take it."

"Saint Paul himself was a convert," she replied with just a hint of admonishment. "I'd be very grateful if you could expedite the processing of these papers." She leaned forward as though to take him into her confidence. "The children are exhausted."

He glanced up and saw Mindell, leaning wearily against the wall. He leafed through the set of papers and sighed.

"It does create a difficulty when there are no legitimate papers."

"But these are emergency documents issued by the Church. They are legitimate. The children must not be penalized because they were orphaned in the war and their papers lost."

"Of course not." He thought of his two little daughters, peacefully playing now in an apple orchard in Surrey. They were duly registered in his own slender navy-blue passport. He looked at the blonde child who so resembled his own Phoebe and then at the scowling intelligence agent who stood watching him. The trouble with the Investigative Division was that they saw an illegal immigrant in every new arrival. They took themselves too bloody seriously, those blokes. Also, their salaries and travel allowances far exceeded his. Mindell gave him another shy smile and he reached for his entry stamp. One by one he called off the children's names, stamped their documents, and waved them on through the gate. He stamped Rebecca's passport and handed it back to her, flushed with his own beneficent diligence.

"Take good care of the little ones, Madame. Good luck in the Lord's land."

"Thank you." She smiled graciously at him, wanting in fact to throw her arms around his neck and kiss him, to thank him for this gift he would never know he had given.

And then they were on the dock where a yellow bus marked "Mission of Saint Paul" was waiting. A tall priest held out his hand to her and they helped the children onto the bus while two men in monk's garb went to collect their baggage. Finally they were moving, rolling away from the dockside area, then out of the busy city streets clogged with oversized American cars and huge blue-and-yellow buses, and through the low, gentle hills of the lower Galilee. The tall priest suddenly burst into song—Hebrew song.

"Haveinu shalom aleichem," he and the two monks sang, and when they turned to the children their faces, stained to the color of sun and earth, radiated warmth and welcome, victory and relief.

"Haveinu shalom aleichem—we bring peace and welcome unto you..." Their voices rose joyously and she too sang and was surprised to feel a single tear trace its way slowly down her cheek. Then the children's voices took up the song, stumbling over the words in the language that would one day be their own, but was as yet unlearned. Katia held Shlomo on her lap and clapped his hands together.

"We're in *Aretz,"* she told the child. "Look. See. We're home."

They looked out the windows at the roads lined with great cypresses and the fields through which tender green shoots of corn and oats kissed their way, emerging from the rick dark earth. In the meadows blood-red anemones tangled with vines of pale-pink cyclamens. Their fragrance enveloped the children who had lived for so long beneath the earth, smelling only the stink of death and the sickly scent of danger. Crying, laughing, singing, they breathed deep as the bus, unfollowed, they saw with relief, rumbled through the gates of Kibbutz Beth HaCochav, where the priest ripped off his cassock to reveal his work shirt and trousers and the monks discarded their robes and cowls and stood before them in kibbutz shorts. Jubilantly, they lifted the children out of the bus and into the arms of the waiting men and women. Again, the song of welcome arose, sung now by the children of the kibbutz who surrounded the new arrivals and hung garlands of flowers about their necks.

Rebecca was the last to descend and she stood on the steps of the bus uncertainly.

Shlomo and another child grew frightened at the wild explosion of joy and began to cry. A tall, motherly looking woman bent to comfort them. She wiped their tears and gave each a large sugar cookie, taken from the pocket of the apron that covered her overalls. Within that same pocket, Rebecca knew, there would also be a length of string for an impromptu game of cat's cradle, one or two crayons, and perhaps a small scissors. Like Sarah Ellenberg, she belonged to the army of women who carry with them, always, small weapons against a child's tears.

She looked up at Rebecca and her face lit up.

"Rivkale—you must be Leah's Rivka," she cried and embraced the girl. "I'm your aunt Henia. Ah—I would have known you anywhere with that hair and those eyes. You are your mother's daughter. Moshe—Moshe! Come and meet your niece."

They surrounded Rebecca—the tall, soft-eyed man who was her mother's brother and shared her father's gentle calm, her cousin Yaakov and his bride Baila, her other cousins and the men and women who had known both Leah and David in Russia. There were questions and kisses, tentative embraces and great bearlike hugs of delight. They welcomed her and were proud of her. The story of how the children had sung their way into the country traveled from person to person and they shook their heads admiringly and said with pride, "What a bluff, what *chutzpah*!"

They had lunch in the huge communal dining hall, and then Henia and Moshe led her to a quiet room where Henia turned down the bed and drew the shutters against the bright afternoon sunlight.

"You must get some rest," her aunt said and kissed Rebecca on the forehead. "You are a very brave girl. Now sleep. Later we will talk again."

Alone in that simple room, Rebecca went to the window and looked out at a slender cypress that sent a pyramid of shade across the sun-dappled lawn. In the distance she saw a man walking slowly, a small girl astride his shoulders, a boy, naked except for his bright blue bloomers and a sun hat, clutching his hand. It was Yehuda, his face relaxed into a softness she had not seen before.

He had two children then, a boy and girl, and both of them had inherited his earth-colored hair. She wondered which of the kibbutz women she had seen in that flurry of welcoming excitement was his wife. The little girl laughed loudly and Yehuda swung her high above his head. Rebecca watched them for a moment, then closed the shutter tightly, washed her face, and stretched out across the bed, tumbling swiftly into a heavy sleep.

When she awoke the room was pitch-dark and she looked at her watch and saw that she had slept away her first afternoon in Palestine. She went to the window and opened the shutter. Beneath the cypress, Yehuda stood, dressed now in a light-colored shirt, the ember of his cigarette glowing like a fiery jewel suspended against the velvet darkness. A sense of puzzlement, teasing and sensuous, suffused her. She had known, somehow, that he would be there, just as she knew he would be gone when she emerged from the room.

She dressed quickly and went out. He was not there. She stood briefly on the steps and breathed in the sweet heavy scent of newly green oranges, mingling with the bitter-sweet aroma of ripening citrons. How cool the nights in Palestine were, how sweet the air, how large the stars. Across the path she saw the brightly lit communal dining room and heard the singing. "*Haveinu shalom aleichem*—we bring you peace and welcome." She too sang as she hurried across the wet grass toward the warmth and light.

17

On the last day of 1947, tiny Sherry Ellenberg, after a long and lusty labor during which Joshua, in a nervous frenzy, bought and sold shares in a new future called television, gave birth to twins. The boy and girl were named Scott and Lisa and their bright tomorrows were toasted in the Goldfeders' living room in champagne passed by a uniformed maid.

"I remember when Rebecca was born we drank *shnaps* from jelly jars," Sarah Ellenberg recalled with wistful regret.

The years of poverty, the crowded rooms, so cold in the winter and so stifling in the summer, the bare floors and sagging secondhand couches and beds, the tureens of watered-down chicken soup which she and Leah and Mollie had fed their armies of boarders, were remembered with wry fondness now. They were safe at last. They had emerged from the shadows of want and worry into the full sunlight of earned ease and prosperity. It was pleasant now, to stroke the delicate stems of Leah's fine Baccarat champagne glasses, to sip the cold smooth wine and think of the coarse thick jars and the harsh strong liquor of distant threatening days. Those early years in America had been filtered through frayed screens of memory, achieving in retrospect a sweet softness that diluted their stern reality.

Recently, their former boarder Masha had visited them, her skin darkened by the California sun and thickened by age, her body draped in soft satin and furs, jewels sparkling and heavy on the taut neck that had once bent hour after hour over needlework. She passed Seymour color photos of her children and he in turn offered a snapshot of his infant grandson.

"How I miss those old days, when we were all one family," she said and the wistfulness had been real.

Leah smiled, wondering if among Masha's memories of togetherness, she included fragments of those nights before Mollie's arrival when she and Seymour had danced together in the crowded parlor or disappeared behind the closed doors of a bedroom. Now, portly grandfather and prosperous matron, they passed their color photos, sweet testimony of their survival and their success.

Masha showed them pictures of her terraced California villa and her shimmering swimming pool, and they admired them as they mourned together the lost days of Eldridge Street where the hallways had smelled of urine and the front-room air had been thick with the scent of too many bodies and noisy with the sounds of too many voices.

Lisa and Scott Ellenberg were toasted also in Cambridge, Massachusetts, where Aaron Goldfeder and Kate Reznikoff, a slight blonde girl from New Orleans who sat next to him in Torts at the Harvard Law School, were celebrating the New Year by painting Kate's Brattle Street apartment.

"Is Joshua a close friend?" Kate asked. Aaron's network of family and friends fascinated her. Her own family had lived in the South since the Revolution, regarding their move to New Orleans from Atlanta, after the Civil War, as "recent." Her father served as a surrogate court judge, occupying the seat that his father and grandfather had held before him. Each year, during the Mardi Gras season, Kate's family took a Caribbean cruise, quietly absenting themselves from the city which did not allow Jews to participate in its most famous festival. They never discussed the exclusion and were, instead, very pleased to point out the stained-glass windows in the synagogue which had been donated by Christian members of the bar in memory of Kate's grandparents. Aaron was the first traveler from the world of immigrant American Jews whom Kate had met and she prodded him again and again to tell her tales of his father's evening studies, of his mother's early days in the sweatshop, of his own tenement life. She absorbed them with odd fascination, an almost bittersweet jealousy, and basked in their telling and retelling, as visitors from a cold clime cling to the sun of warmer worlds.

Aaron obliged her, glad to have something to share with the fragile blonde girl whose soft drawling voice belied her keen legal mind, her ability to pierce each question at its heart and pluck from it a nugget of knowledge. Kate was the first girl since Lisa Frawley, of whom he still sometimes dreamed, to send his blood rushing faster and fill his body with the pleasant ache of tender desire.

"Joshua's almost like a brother. His family boarded with us when we lived on the east side and they came from the same town in Russia as my parents. I used to think that he was in love with my sister, Rebecca, and that probably they would marry."

"Your sister who's in Palestine now?" Kate asked, although she knew the answer.

Her own married sisters lived in Charleston and Atlanta and it seemed somehow appropriate to her that Aaron's sister was living on a kibbutz while her own soft-voiced siblings met their friends for bridge, instructed their staffs, and combed their young children's shining hair.

"Do you think your sister is happy in Palestine, Aaron?" she asked.

"I think so. Come on, let's be happy here." His arms went around her and his tongue, insistent and knowing, sweetly licked her lips until they parted and her body weakened beneath his touch, and trembled in submission.

*

News of the babies' arrival was cabled to Rebecca in Palestine and reached her on Beth HaCochav where she had remained after arriving there with the children. She lingered there from week to week, uncertain of her plans, unwilling to leave. Sporadically, she took sketching trips through the Galilee, worked in the irrigation ditches, and, when she was called upon, participated in the landing operations of illegal immigrants that took place in the dead of night. The weeks and months drifted by and she stayed on, vaguely aware that she was waiting for something to happen but not knowing what it was she anticipated. Often in the evening, she walked through a gentle incline where the rich dark grapes that were sold to the vintners of Rishon LeZion grew on vines that twined themselves through a fragile network of arbors. The early darkness fused its way through the drapery of leaf and fruit and she relished the strange melancholy that engulfed her when the last thread of light was swallowed and she stood alone in the blackness that smelled of humous earth and sweet grape.

She read the cable, smiled at the thought of Joshua as a father of not one, but two screaming infants, and placed it in a drawer. Still smiling, she turned back to plaiting Mindell's thick blond braids.

"There. Now you're ready for the party," she said at last. "Aren't you coming to the party?" Mindell asked. "You'll have to change."

She looked critically at Rebecca's soiled work pants, the heavy black knit sweater which had once belonged to Yaakov, and the high boots, still caked with crusts of mud from the irrigation ditches.

"Oh, Rivka, I wish you hadn't cut your hair. It was so pretty."

Rebecca touched the sleek cap of dark hair which encircled her head and smiled.

"No. I am not going to the party because I must work tonight. And I'm glad I cut my hair even if you're not. After all, it wasn't you who had to get up at five in the morning and wash it in ice-cold water."

She hugged Mindell and remembered the day Henia had cut her hair and the sense of lightness and freedom she had felt as the silken black sheaves slid to the ground beside her.

Rebecca Goldfeder, the Scarsdale schoolgirl, her parents' doll, her lover's playmate, cavorting across tennis courts, rushing through Vermont woods, had had time to brush and dress her hair, to luxuriate in its smooth fall down her naked back after a long leisurely bath, to twist it into coronet and topknot. But Rivka, Yaakov's cousin, transitory kibbutz worker and itinerant agent in illegal immigration, could not spare the time for such luxurious frivolity. Besides, her long black hair had made her too easily recognizable and remembered. Walking down the streets of Haifa one day, not long after her arrival with the Auschwitz children, she had been stopped by a British agent.

"You got away with it once, Miss Goldfeder," he said, his lips pursed in a thin ugly line of anger. "But next time we'll recognize you, we'll be ready for you."

But he had not recognized her a week later because a kibbutz hat covered her shorn hair and when she stopped him and asked him for a match, he lit her cigarette and walked on without pausing. It was that daring of Rebecca's, that instinct for innovation, which impressed the leaders of *Bericha,* who assigned her to operations of special risk.

Yehuda had glanced at the new haircut through hooded lids.

"Ah—a new haircut and thus a new Miss Goldfeder, I dare say," he said, his silken gray eyes roving insolently over her. She was suddenly conscious of the fact that Baila's blue shirt was too small for her, pulling tightly across her breasts, and realized, too, that it was stained dark with sweat beneath her armpits. She had worked in the banana fields that morning, shrouding the young fruit in lengths of blue plastic against an early frost.

"Perhaps you too ought to get a haircut, Yehuda," she replied curtly. "Perhaps the new Yehuda Arnon will be a pleasanter Yehuda Arnon."

She walked quickly away, her heels kicking up small clouds of red dust.

"Rebecca!" he called after her, but she did not turn and he did not follow her.

That night at dinner Yaakov told her Yehuda had sailed for another *Bericha* mission in Europe and she wondered if he had called after her to say good-bye. Beneath the grape arbor that night, she wept softly and wondered why it was that she and Yehuda seemed always to be moving in opposite directions. They lay in wait for each other endlessly and then drifted stealthily away, as though fearful of encounter. She felt his eyes upon her as she walked into the communal dining room, but when she had laden her tray and searched for a place to eat, his seat was empty. Often, late at night, she glimpsed him standing beneath the umbrella of the cypress tree opposite her door, but when she emerged into the night he was gone, leaving only a small mound of cigarette butts behind him. Late in the afternoon, she waited for him as he came back from the fields but always dashed away moments before he passed her. It was as though they were playing an elaborate game of hide and seek, interchanging the roles of pursuer and quarry.

He was in Europe still, this New Year's Eve, when the cold Galilee wind whipped the kibbutz and small kerosene fires burned in every room. It would be bitter cold in the Mediterranean ports and on the clumsy, ancient ships which carried the illegals. Sighing, she bundled Mindell into a heavy sweater and sent her off to the party.

"But if you're back early enough, you'll come to the party, won't you?" the child asked.

"Of course," Rebecca assured her and watched Mindell run through the cold to the brightly lit dining room.

She marveled again at the swiftness with which Mindell, Katia, Shlomo, and the other children had adjusted to their new lives, had reclaimed their shattered childhoods and learned to dance and play, to shout out loud, to laugh with joy and scream with anger. Within months they were unrecognizable from the other children of the kibbutz, except for isolated moments when one or another of them drifted suddenly into a mysterious tenebrous silence, filled with grim memories of those subterranean years when they hid from death but could not escape the screams and entreaties of the dying. Shadowy figures of vanished parents, half-remembered siblings, would glide through their dreams, and the child who had gone to sleep smiling and happy wakened in the night terrified by desperate grief. Still, the children grew better and Rebecca hoped she would come back early enough tonight to see "her" children at the first New Year they would usher in in freedom and joy.

"Rebecca—Rivkala—are you there? Henia sent over an extra sweater for you. It will be bitter cold at the sea tonight. I've given Yaakov one as well. He's manning the radio."

Baila strode into the room and tossed Rebecca a heavy hooded blue sweater.

"Yes, I know. I've been listening to the weather reports. The cold doesn't bother me particularly but the wind velocity does. If the winds are as strong as they say, the longboats will have a terrible time rowing inland. Some of the illegals may have to swim for shore."

She shivered, remembering the night only three weeks before when one of the longboats had taken water and the entire boatload of immigrants had been forced to take to the sea. One old man among them had carried a small Torah which he refused to release, and he held it aloft in one hand as he was pulled ashore through the raging surf. It had been his dead, already stiffening body that they loaded into the waiting truck, but the Torah, encased in its worn red velvet coverlet, was barely damp. Moshe Abrahami, who had cradled the old man's body in his arms, built an ark for it, polishing and sanding the wood until it gleamed with a golden smoothness.

"That old man—for a moment—a split second—I thought that he was my father, your grandfather," he told Rebecca. He rubbed fiercely at the wood and a cloud of golden dust floated above his fingers.

There had been no news of Rebecca's grandparents since the opening of the Russian front; the letters sent from the United States and Palestine were returned to Moshe, Leah, and Mollie marked "Addressee Unknown." The village of their birth had vanished and they saw their lost mother and father in the faces of weary bearded man, in the frightened eyes of careworn women.

"Perhaps the wind will let up," Baila said, looking through the window where the cypress tree bent and swayed in vectorial arcs.

"There are many children on this ship—the most important cargo of all." She smiled and touched her abdomen, proudly tumid now. Baila's first child would be born at winter's end.

"How do you know?" Rebecca asked.

"*Bericha* had a communication from Yehuda."

"Is he on the ship?" She kept her tone casual but felt her blood pulse more quickly and the electric tingling of her palms.

"I wouldn't think so. He was to act as liaison for arranging another ship in a month's time. We've got to get as many people in before the British pull out, because after that we'll be too busy fighting the Arabs to launch any immigration operation."

"I know," Rebecca replied.

It was impossible to live in Palestine and not know. From the moment the United Nations had voted to partition Palestine, only a month before, illegal immigration operations had been intensified. The British would leave the country in the spring and there was little doubt that the Arabs would launch an invasion then. The immigrants smuggled in now were to be fighters for Israel in six months' time. They were en route from one war to another, these grim survivors of death who even now held no guarantee of life.

"You don't like Yehuda, do you?" Baila asked, leaning back on Rebecca's bed and watching her husband's American cousin pack a waterproof kit bag of first-aid supplies.

"I don't know. And I don't know how Yehuda feels about me. Ever since that first day in Italy I've had the feeling that he saw me as a spoiled American kid who always had her own way. Now I think he sees me as someone grabbing an adventure. I don't think it occurs to him that I can be as serious, as involved in all this as he is."

Rebecca slapped a small flask of brandy into her bag. She did not drink brandy, but on their last rescue operation Yehuda had had to swim to shore carrying a small child, and when he sat beside her on the truck heading back to the kibbutz, his body was riveted with violent shivers. She had passed him the flask then and watched as his limbs slowly quieted under the liquor's warmth.

"You are wrong, Rivka. You would have to be blind to watch you with the children and not know how deeply you feel for them. Yehuda sees that," Baila said.

"Do you know that when I sailed with the children, it was the first time in my life that I had done anything for anyone else. It was the first time anyone had ever expected me to do anything for anyone but myself. Yehuda kept waiting for me to say no. And then he kept waiting for me to fail. Now, I don't know how he feels about me. But I do know that I'm tired of proving myself to him." Her voice rang with an anger she had not known she harbored and her hand trembled imperceptibly as she pulled on an extra pair of socks.

"Be gentler. He's had a hard time, our Yehuda."

"Baila—what happened to his wife?"

The question Rebecca had wanted to ask for months floated on the waves of that new sudden anger, an anger that she now recognized had gathered through the lonely months, the strange silences and stranger avoidances. The kibbutz was like a small town where gossip flourished and privacy was virtually nonexistent. Since her arrival in the summer, Rebecca had learned about divorces and affairs, distant scandals and current flirtations.

She knew that Margalit, married now to Noah, had lived for years in the same room as tall Reuven who managed the carp pond. She knew that the small blond Yardeni twins were the children of a Tel Aviv restaurateur who had lived briefly with a kibbutz girl. There was a former kibbutz member in New York who had absconded years before with funds earmarked for agricultural equipment. She knew of two couples who casually and cheerfully switched partners. But she knew nothing of Yehuda Arnon's wife, the woman who was the mother of the small boy and girl who walked with him each evening. The net of silence, the strange secrecy, was puzzling in Beth HaCochav where knowledge as well as property was communally shared. Knowledge of everyone, with the strange exception of Yehuda Arnon.

She had asked her question but Baila remained silent, her fingers toying with the edges of the blanket. "I myself am new to the kibbutz," she said evasively.

"Yes. But you know."

"I know what I've heard."

"And what have you heard?"

Baila sighed and looked through the window. A group of children walked through the gentle twilight, hand in hand, on their way to the party. As they walked, they sang a song popular that year, when their country hovered at the edge of history, balanced precariously between war and peace.

> The days drift past,
> The year ends,
> But the melody, the melody always remains…

"I have heard that Danielle looks very much like her mother—Yehuda's wife, Miriam—except that Miriam had blonde hair. She was very beautiful, they say, so beautiful that when she walked down the streets in Haifa, the men stopped their work to look at her."

Rebecca's heart twisted in an unfamiliar pang which she recognized, with annoyed surprise, to be jealousy. She was jealous of a woman she had never known.

"Miriam came with her parents in the early thirties from Czechoslovakia and grew up here on Beth HaCochav. Yehuda was born here. They grew up together, working and studying, and were married here. Danielle was born in the first year of the war in Europe and Noam three years later. Yehuda was already working in the *Mosad*, going back and forth to Europe, helping to smuggle Jews out. In those days he worked against both the Germans and the British. *Mosad* desperately needed an agent in Czechoslovakia who could pass as a Gentile, who knew the language. Miriam seemed the natural choice. Yehuda was against it but she fought for the assignment. The kibbutz could take care of the children and they say she could no longer bear to be without Yehuda. Those who knew them say that when they walked together it was as though only one person moved. They spoke little because they read each other's thoughts. They had grown up, you see, like brother and sister and had become lovers. They were each an extension of the other."

"Like you and Yaakov," Rebecca said.

"No. Between Yaakov and me there is a great love but he is a child of Palestine and there are things that happened to me in Hungary and in Belsen which he will never know about—which he must never know about. But there was nothing in their lives which Miriam and Yehuda did not share."

"I see," Rebecca said, remembering back to the childhood she had shared with Joshua and the special, dangerous closeness it had created. Joshua, so newly a father. Twins. Of course, twins. Two for the price of one. Clever Joshua. She smiled and turned back, to Baila who continued talking, her eyes fixed on the windblown cypress tree.

"Miriam won out in the end, of course. A British plane dropped her behind the lines in Czechoslovakia. Ah, the brave British. Even while they were impounding illegal ships and sending Jewish immigrants back to Europe, they had no objection to using Jewish agents. Well, Miriam operated out of Prague for months. She was a successful agent. Her looks and the language made it easy for her to pass. But in the end it was her own beauty that betrayed her. She was on her way to a country rendezvous with Yehuda, and a German officer who had been flirting with her trailed her to the spot. Yehuda was hiding in the brush but he saw the officer run toward her and watched her struggle. He rushed out and the German pulled his gun. Miriam ran between the bullet and her husband. It pierced her forehead and she died instantly. Yehuda strangled the German officer with his bare hands and hid both the bodies. Miriam's he concealed in a cave covered over by a thicket of blackberries where they had often met. Her body, we think, was never found. But Yehuda blamed himself then, and does still, I think, for Miriam's death. And there are those who also blame him, who feel he was not "professional." Miriam's parents, the old couple who sit always alone, blame him still, I know. That is why she is never spoken of, here on Beth HaCochav. And that is why the *Mosad* will not let husbands and wives or lovers work together. They are a danger to each other. If Miriam had not been Yehuda's wife, she might be alive today."

Baila, who seldom smoked, lit a cigarette and offered one to Rebecca. They sat in silence and thought of the beautiful young mother lying dead in a land no longer her own, a victim of her own love, her own courage. Rebecca felt a heavy grief for the lovely Miriam and a strange solidarity with her. She began to understand, now, Yehuda's brooding silences, his silent vigils beneath the cypress tree, his long waits and sudden disappearances. There was a necessity for the distance he had established between them, and she wondered if that distance could ever be bridged. Her father, the specialist in emotional pain, whose sad eyes so often reflected the anguish he had absorbed through long hours of listening, had told her once that there were hurts which could not be healed. Survival did not mean recovery. She longed suddenly, to lean on her father's shoulder, to hear his gentle voice. Perhaps, after all, she should go home. Impatiently, she snuffed her cigarette out.

"Thank you for telling me," she said to Baila and kissed her cousin's wife who sat now with her hands across her stomach, as though to protect that unborn life within her from the dangers which haunted her dreams and memories. Outside the truck, painted black, its headlights blinded, honked impatiently. Rebecca seized her kit bag, covered her hair with a wool cap, and hurried out. In the clear silent night, the bells of a nearby Galilean mission church tolled their last count of the year. Soon, in distant cities, women in soft gowns and men in evening dress would lift their glasses and toast the new year of 1948. Rebecca Goldfeder, too, thought of the months ahead as she huddled in the corner of the pitch-dark truck between two swollen yellow life rafts, and rolled down an unpaved coastal road to an ancient Crusader port where a battered Greek freighter flying a Panamanian flag listed from side to side in the cold darkness.

The truck trundled to a stop in a small cove and Rebecca sniffed the fresh sea air, heard the waves crash wildly against the sloping promontory which shielded them from sight. She and the others pulled on their high boots and rain gear, working in silence, preserving their concentration for the task that awaited them.

"It's a cold night for an operation," one man said, climbing down from the truck.

"Yes. But a good one. No stars. No moon. And the British getting drunker by the minute, celebrating their last New Year's Eve in Palestine."

They stood outside the truck ready to move, shifting their booted feet across the sand congealed by the cold into a gritty hardness. They peered across the water, searching for a flicker of light, but sheer darkness confronted them. From the interior of the truck they heard Yaakov speaking softly, insistently, into the microphone, but they knew from his repeated questions that there was no answer.

"Perhaps they didn't get through the blockade," someone said softly.

No one replied, but the air was heavy with their fear.

Two gulls, soaring in concentric circles across a cliff, hooted wildly at each other and from across the water came the mournful call of a third gull. The wind blew in keening sobs through the tall dune grass and a small jackal scurried out from beneath a brush pine and streaked off into the darkness.

"Hello. Shalom. Answer me. Are you there? Hello. Shalom. Answer. Signal." A note of desperation had crept into Yaakov's firm tone.

How many children were there on that boat? Rebecca wondered, and thought of her Auschwitz infants. Would these other unknown children, waiting out there on dark water, ever play with Mindell and Katia and Shlomo? Would they ever walk through gentle evening mist singing softly like Yehuda's small daughter Danielle? She thought of her brother Michael, reading while sprawled across the living room rug, his father reading in one chair, his mother in another, bent over her sketch pad. Wasn't that the natural legacy of any child—to sit in a circle of light, surrounded by warmth and love? A violent wind shrieked above them and lifted loose branches, which fell in dull thuds against the compacted sand.

Yaakov emerged from the truck, his hand raw with cold, twisting his fingers.

"There's no reply. Either their radio is out or they didn't make it through the blockade. The British are using power boats now. I'm afraid if I keep trying the British will trace our signal. We'll wait another hour and head back."

He mounted the promontory and looked across the inlet. Someone lit a cigarette and its tiny red glow pierced the thick darkness.

"Put it out, damn it. The British might be patrolling this beach."

Like a tiny phosphorescent insect, the lit cigarette sailed through the air onto the sand. Rebecca searched the expanse of darkness across the rolling waves, thinking of the nights she had stared from her window and glimpsed the glowing embers of Yehuda's cigarettes. Suddenly she saw an almost infinitesimal light across the cove, flickering on and off, staying lit for a long moment and then again extinguishing itself.

"Yaakov, look to the left," she called.

He took out his binoculars and focused in the direction to which she pointed.

"Yes. That's them. It must be them. They're using code. Let me read them."

Their hearts stood still as the light sparked on and off, growing weaker, then stronger, signaling the location of the ship, then repeating the message and waiting as Yaakov flashed an acknowledgment and a read-back, using the emergency safari light they carried in the truck.

They moved quickly now, with practiced efficiency. Two by two, they unloaded the lifeboats, spread the blankets in readiness in the back of the truck, unlashed the lengths of rope.

Rebecca was aboard the first lifeboat and she clutched the rubber side as it was shoved off into the crashing surf. Icy water settled in pools beneath her feet, traveling down over the tops of her boots. A sudden wind whipped her face and the spray was salty against her tongue. The light rubber raft moved easily now, soaring atop the waves, responding to the strong pull of the oarsmen.

"There they are!"

A lantern flickered and they saw another boat approaching them, launched from the immigrant ship. She tossed a rope to it and it was caught by a sailor. The boats were pulled alongside each other and one by one the children, small shivering bundles of fear, cloaked in layers of sweaters, were passed from boat to boat. The children did not make a sound but Rebecca whispered softly to each as her arms went about them, and passing them to the kibbutz member behind her, she saw the tears frozen in their eyes and how their small mouths twisted to subdue the screams of fear.

The rubber boat listed dangerously. Swiftly, they distributed the weight of their human cargo and rowed back to shore, the lengths of rope in readiness to be cast out again when they approached the surf. There the waiting kibbutz members lurched forward, seized the hemp, and pulled the boat to shore. Again the children were passed hand over hand into the waiting truck, where warm blankets and thermoses of soup were waiting.

"Two more trips, I think," Yaakov whispered to her and she nodded and climbed back into the rubber raft to repeat the operation. In the darkness they passed the other yellow boat and heard the soft sobs of a very young child, muted cries, not of fear, but of agonized desolation.

The next boatload was simpler to manage because the illegal immigrants were mostly adults and adolescents who maneuvered from boat to boat easily. But the wind had changed and they knew that they were lucky there would be only one more trip out.

By the third journey Rebecca's clothing was soaked and stiff with sea water and her fingers struggled numbly for life within her gloves. The tiny craft jostled its way over waves that veered skyward with sudden wild spurts, showering them with icy pellets of spray. At last they pulled alongside the longboat and she saw, with sinking heart, that this group of passengers consisted of very old men and women, and children so ill that they lay in immobile heaps. The rubber raft lurched dangerously, bobbing drunkenly between the waves. One by one, the immigrants were transferred. A bearded old man, the sea spray like glinting jeweled moisture against the whiteness of his long beard, murmured the Psalms in unfaltering sequence.

"A song of degrees. Out of the depths have I cried unto Thee O Lord. Lord, hear my voice: let thine ears be attentive to the voice of my supplications..."

"Amen." A woman's frail voice threaded the darkness with ancient acquiescence.

"Amen," Rebecca heard herself say as she gently took a small boy swathed in blankets into her arms and settled him on a tarpaulin in the corner of the boat, which sagged suddenly.

"That's it. We can't take any more."

"One more. One more small boy," a voice called from the longboat.

"We're overloaded now."

"One more."

She looked toward shore. The other boat was being dragged up onto the beach and the truck's lights were flashing on and off and on again. It was the danger signal. They would have to leave within minutes. There would be no other boat to pick up one more small boy.

"All right."

She leaned forward and the sailor, holding a rope in one hand and a blanketed bundle of child life in the other, leaned across toward her. An enormous wave crested suddenly and dizzying hills of foam peaked between them in wildly mobile aqueous mountains. The impact of the wave sent the sailor reeling backward. The child was knocked out of his grasp and there was a sharp splash as the small body hit the turbulent waters.

"Rebecca, no! You'll never make it," the oarsman called but she was already over the side of the boat, her arms reaching desperately for the child who bobbed lightly above the water like a piece of aimless jetsam. She gripped him and swam toward the boat, gasping for air, feeling the harshness of the salt water against the membranes of her lungs, strangling her breath. The yellow rubber wall of the boat seemed enormously high and the child's weight dragged her down. She could not make it herself, much less hoist him up with her. The old man's voice, still intoning the Psalms, floated above the rushing waters. A song of degrees, Lord, a song of degrees.

"Hang on, Rebecca. Another minute. I'm behind you."

She recognized the voice and was fired with renewed energy. She strengthened her grip on the boy, clutched his limp body, and treaded water, breathing with anguished care. Yehuda flashed through the wilderness of crashing waves and took the child from her.

"Okay. You scramble up there. Gideon is directly above you. Grab his arm and I'll pass the boy up."

Blindly, she followed his directions, felt Gideon's fingers pull at her wrists, then hold her body as she lowered herself painfully over the side and took the child from Yehuda, heaving him with a wild spurt of strength onto the rubber floor of the boat, which veered dangerously from side to side. Then they were moving through the crashing white waters, to be pulled at last to safety in the surf and then to the waiting trucks on shore, their motors already grumbling. A British patrol had been sighted and they sped from the cove without looking back to the beach where a child's wool hat on a hillock of sand was the only sign that they had been there pulling life out of the sea.

As they rumbled along the dark stretch of coastal road, the brandy seared her body and she listened again to the old man as he continued to chant the words of David. "I will give thanks in the great congregation. I will praise Thee among much people."

"Where is Yehuda?" she asked Yaakov suddenly, as though waking from a sleep. She had thought him beside her, felt his breath against her neck, but had awakened from that half-coma of exhaustion to find it was her cousin who sat close by her, watching her anxiously.

"He went back to the ship. He sails back to Bari with them. Why?"

"No reason."

She watched the small lights of the houses that lined the pitch-dark road, feeling a strange vacuity, an odd elusive sense of betrayal. Later that night, after the excitement of their arrival had subsided, she stood alone in her room and looked at the slender cypress. She knew, with quiet certainty, that she must leave Beth HaCochav. She had been waiting too long for something that would not, could not, happen. In Jerusalem, they said, the noon light turned the ancient stones the color of gold-dusted cyclamens. She fell asleep, wondering how such a color could be created on her palette. Perhaps in Jerusalem she would learn.

18

Aaron awoke early that spring morning and remained motionless in the half-darkness, watching a vagrant slat of sunshine streak through the Venetian blind and onto Kate's bare shoulder. The soft golden glow matched her hair, matted damply now about her head, one small ringlet nestled against her cheek. Sometime during the night he had heard the shower running and knew that Kate had crept out of bed and was standing beneath the steaming water, her eyes closed and her head tilted upward, allowing the droplets to slip slowly down her body. Once, wakened and finding her gone, Aaron had watched her briefly from the bathroom doorway but had gone back to bed before she saw him. Sweet, wet Katie, he had thought sleepily then and now he lightly touched her damp curl and reached over to the night table and switched on the small bedside radio.

> There was a boy, a very strange enchanted boy,
> A little shy and sad of eye,
> But very wise was he…

A man's voice, pitched to an uneasy softness, crooned the lyric, and Kate stirred reluctantly into wakefulness.

"Come on, Aaron. It's too early for 'Nature Boy.' Let me sleep."

But she lifted her arms and the sunlight danced between her small, perfect breasts. He laughed and thrust his head against the gliding patch of golden light that danced across her skin. He felt it warm against his head, felt her long fingers lifting one strand of his hair, then another, hiding the sun and releasing it as though the liquid rays were casual playthings.

"Now your hair is amber. No. Now it's russet—the color of fall pears and leaves. Watch—when the sunlight jumps you're going to turn copper, like the bottoms of your mother's pots. Aaron, do you think our children will have your hair? Do you think we'll have children? Do you think we could be Goldfeder and Goldfeder, Esq.? Oh, Aaron."

"Shut up," he said and slid her down, leaving the vagrant light to waft across the empty pillow as his hands slid across her body, his lips burying themselves against the soft golden tufts of hair that peaked below the gentle mound of her stomach. His red hair nestled into the curve of her shoulders, his body rose and fell in steady urgent rhythm, and when the full light of morning pierced the slatted blind, his full love thrust forward within her and he lay back, sweetly spent, and fingered the curl on her cheek, damp now with his own sweat.

The radio played on and they lay in each other's arms, listening to the announcer's insouciant voice tell them that President Truman had just returned to the White House after a weekend in Missouri, Senator Robert Taft had condemned the Marshall Plan for aid to Europe, milk prices were up, bread prices were down. Locally, Representative John F. Kennedy would speak that afternoon in Harvard Commons. On the international scene, in Tel Aviv, the interim Jewish government was preparing to issue the declaration of the independence that would declare it the State of Israel. Drifting back to sleep against Kate's shoulder, Aaron dimly remembered now, that that was why he had awakened so early that morning. He had wanted to hear just that announcement. Rebecca would be coming home soon, then. Yaakov would insist that she leave before war broke out and he could not imagine his laughing impetuous sister, for whom life had been a series of enthusiastic triumphs, lingering in a land at war. Perhaps when Rebecca came, he and Kate might marry. He looked down at the small blonde girl who lay beside him. Her eyes were closed and her pale gold lashes were wet with secret tears. Sweet Katie, he thought and kissed her eyes, licking the mysterious salt on her cheek. Sweet Kate, who wept in the depths of love, who lived slightly apart from others, hovering on the edges of their lives, grasping at the tales of their childhoods. He understood that strange apartness of hers, remembering with tenacious clarity the days and nights of his boyhood when he had hovered in doorways and peered through darkened windows. Poor sweet Kate, he thought, and his heart was mysteriously heavy for the young woman beside him and the vanished boy he had been.

*

In New York City that same afternoon, Leah and David strode up Park Avenue from Grand Central Station on their way to Charles Ferguson's new art gallery on Fifty-seventh Street, where several of Leah's paintings were included in an exhibition. As always, when he walked with Leah, David was conscious of the admiring glances of passersby, who looked back at his tall dark-haired wife, dressed in a navy-blue cape suit of her own design. A silk scarf with geometric patterns screened in shades of deep purple and pale blue fluttered at her neck. The design was taken from one of Leah's large graphics, and Joshua Ellenberg's company had manufactured scarves and blouses in that pattern and others of Leah's creation.

"Do you know what I'm thinking of doing?" Joshua had asked her the last time he had visited her studio, where his watchful eye scanned her recent work. "I'm thinking of taking your designs for a whole line of linens—tablecloths, sheets, draperies—why not?"

He slapped the black leather fingers of his prosthetic hand against his thigh for emphasis and picked up a small painting in red and gold tempera.

"Wouldn't you want to sit down to a Thanksgiving table set with this kind of cloth? Listen—I'm telling you America is moving on. It's had it with white sheets and cloths. Look to the future with J. Ellenberg. Hey, let me write that down for my ad man."

Leah had smiled up at the tall young man in the well-cut Italian suit, his bulging leather portfolio always at hand, seeing him again as the tiny gamin-faced merchant scurrying down crowded east side streets. Joshua was cultivating a moustache now, as sleek as his thick pomaded hair, and his name appeared frequently on the pages of *Women's Wear Daily*. "Enterprising Joshua Ellenberg, offshoot of internationally famous S. Hart Inc., keeps an attentive finger on fashion's pulse" "Could the mysterious L. G. who signs Joshua Ellenberg's fabulous new fabric collection be Leah Goldfeder, whose stunning, innovative designs put S. Hart Inc. on the fashion map?"

Little Joshua, her children's playmate, now father, husband, entrepreneur, en route to becoming a fashion tycoon, urging his shy petite wife from an attached house in Queens to a split level in Great Neck, moving farther and farther from the teeming streets of his boyhood. Leah had sold Joshua several of her designs, smiling to think that people would be stretching to sleep against the patterns she created in the redwood and glass studio behind their home.

David, as always, moved too quickly for her down the crowded avenue, and she hurried now to keep up with him. It was as though the habit of rushing had been grafted onto his nature so that he seldom slowed his pace, fearful of losing precious minutes as he rushed from the hospital to his consulting room. The years spent dashing from his grueling factory job to his evening studies had established a life pattern which he could not break although he knew with precise, professional detachment that he must. Too often now, his breath came in short frenzied gasps and a sudden arrhythmic escalation of his heartbeat left him weak and worried. But still he walked too fast, climbed steps two at a time, and answered the telephone on its first demanding ring. He left Leah several paces behind him now and waited for her at the entry of Waldorf-Astoria, looking upward at the flag flying over the facade of the great hotel.

It was the custom of the Waldorf to fly the flag of the country of a visiting head of state. Only the week before David had attended a psychiatric conference at the hotel when de Gaulle was visiting, and had seen the French tricolor sway in the young springtime breeze. But the flag that fluttered easily and gracefully in the wind today was one the Waldorf had never flown before. A little breathless still, he waited for Leah to catch up to him and clasped her gloved hand.

"Look," he said, "we are watching history."

Above them the white satin banner, with the blue star of David stitched between two slashes of matching blue, fluttered in the sun-tinged air. Leah stared up at it, remembering the first time she had seen the banner of Jewish independence in the Zionist meeting room in Odessa. She thought of the whirling horas of her youth, of the passionate discussions of agricultural settlements, a philosophy of collectivism, of her brother Moshe astride a podium, Henia learning to use a rifle, of Yaakov lying dead in an Odessa street. She remembered the fierce wind that had blown the day Moshe and Henia sailed for Palestine almost two decades earlier and she thought of the young men of her village who had died of malaria in the swamps of the Huleh. It had all led to this day, to this reading of a document of independence in a Tel Aviv museum.

"May fifteenth," Leah said. "A Jewish state at last. And Weizmann is here in New York. A flag is flying for the head of a Jewish state. Oh, David, what does it mean? Will Rebecca be all right? And Moshe and Yaakov and the new baby? David, a Jewish state. Does it mean another war?" Gladness and grief mingled in her voice, and he gripped her arm in the familiar posture of comforter and protector to the woman who had become his wife because of shared grief and loss. His voice took on the soothing cadence he had discovered years ago in that Odessa park.

"Rebecca will be all right. Probably she's planning now to come home. And your brother's family has survived so much that they will survive this too. Come, we must hurry. Charles will be waiting for you at the gallery."

They took a cab the rest of the way, sitting like frightened children against the cracked leather seats. Now, again, they would listen to news broadcasts on the hour, mount a war map of Palestine in their book-lined study, move the small pins from battlefield to battlefield, hear the phone ring with beating heart and sweating palms. A sudden sharp pain seared David's chest, paralyzed his arms, and he was glad that Leah was content to sit quietly without talking. By the time they reached Fifty-seventh Street the pain had disappeared, but he promised himself that as soon as he had time he would go for a checkup. It was just fatigue, but still it would not hurt to have it checked. Next week, perhaps when his appointment schedule was lighter, after he had written up his lecture for the Psychoanalytic Institute. He dismissed it then and followed Leah into the gallery where Charles Ferguson stood lost in thought before the largest painting Leah had ever done, one which had absorbed her for almost a year. *Lost in Flames* she had called it, and the large canvas was alive with tongues of fire through which scorched black silhouetted figures danced, some leaping forward, some gliding slowly back toward fiery devastation.

"Perhaps I should feel jealous," David thought with the peculiar clinical objectivity he brought to his own life.

He read the inscription, feeling sadness and loss coupled with a strange gratitude. "In Memory of Eli Feinstein, So Good and Brave," the small brass plaque read. His wife's lover had been good and brave, David acknowledged, and pressed Leah's hand to his lips. How fortunate they had been, he and Leah, who had married seeking only solace and yet had journeyed through the years to love.

"David," Leah said, "Charles has been asking about the children."

"Well," he said, "Aaron is at the Harvard Law School. Michael is studying hard and Rebecca seems to be quite involved in her painting. She's studying at the Bezalel Art Academy in Palestine. No, not Palestine. I stand corrected. Today, Rebecca is in Israel."

A sudden spray of sunlight tossed a rainbow across the soft white breast of a sculpture in alabaster of a mother and child and he moved closer, as though to listen for a wordless cry.

*

Rebecca awakened early that first morning of statehood, after a night spent dancing in the streets. It seemed as though all of Jewish Jerusalem had converged in Zion Square to hear the rasping voice of David Ben Gurion, via radio from Tel Aviv, read out the Declaration of Independence. Rebecca trembled as she heard the white-haired grocer's son from Poland call for peace and dedication. Loudspeakers boomed his words into the square.

"We extend our hand in peace and neighborliness to all the neighboring states and their peoples and invite them to cooperate with the independent Jewish nation for the common good of all. The State of Israel is prepared to make its contribution to the progress of the Middle East as a whole.... With trust in Almighty God we set our hand to this Declaration at this session of the Provisional State Council on the soil of the Homeland in the City of Tel Aviv, on this Sabbath Eve..."

The silence which had prevailed during the reading was broken by a sudden shout of joy, by a wild hora in which the dancers whirled in an ancient dervish dance of celebration. Accordionists played feverishly. Kiosk owners threw open their stands and passed drinks and food to the singing, dancing crowds. No money changed hands in Jewish Jerusalem that day. The dancing crowd parted for a Haganah half-track and a young officer in battle dress saluted them with a bottle of orange soda.

"Save your strength, *chaverim,*" he called. "Tomorrow we fight."

Now that tomorrow was here, and Rebecca watched as the pale-gold Jerusalem light streaked through the high-arched windows of her room on the Saint George Road in the Musrara quarter of Jerusalem. The muted sounds of early morning floated on the gold-tinged air with reassuring familiarity. From the Damascus Gate she heard the ululating call of the muezzin summoning the faithful to worship, the ancient summons resounding from a public address system and wafting above the matins murmured by the monks in the compound of Notre Dame. It mingled with the muttered Sabbath prayers of the aged Hasidic rabbi's followers who met in a prayer quorum two houses away.

In the hallway just outside her door, Rebecca's Arab landlady, Nimra Halby, was sloshing down the marble floor with a huge rag attached to a stick and soaked in water and disinfectant in a battered aluminum bucket optimistically marked, "Property of His Majesty's Government."

"I doubt that King George misses it," Danni Friedman, a fellow boarder who studied medicine on Mt. Scopus, remarked one day.

On the street below, mules drawing small carts moved at a steady pace, pausing at strategic points so that the vendors might advertise their products in proud insistent calls. Rebecca waited for the matutinal threnody, the summons to seize cucumbers that would tempt Allah Himself, tomatoes which were the jewels of the vine, melons the color of sunlight. She was proud that she now knew the words for the produce in both Hebrew and Arabic and occasionally engineered a small purchase of her own, using words instead of pantomime. But this morning the carts did not pause and it seemed to Rebecca, listening carefully now, that they rolled across the cobblestone road at a more rapid pace than usual. She went to the window and looked down into the street, suddenly conscious of a new sound, punctuating the muezzin's call and the monks' chant. A staccato of gunfire, distant enough to take on the sound of muted irregular drumbeats, issued from the direction of the Rawdah School, and it was toward that sound that the laden carts were moving.

On this Sabbath morning, they did not carry pyramids of tender green cucumbers or mounds of lacy lettuce but were packed with sacks of clothing and household goods, battered chairs and mattresses. On one, an ancient wooden ice chest, moisture still dripping from its opening, had been trussed with frayed rope. Small children, their eyes wide with fear but glinting with an adventure they did not comprehend, rode atop their household goods, clutching odd treasures. One boy held his shoeshine kit while his elder sister clutched a ragged one-armed doll in one hand and balanced a live infant in the other, crooning to both as her father led the cart and her mother walked behind, two goats, one white and one black, trailing her on a leash.

The strange procession moved steadily toward Suleiman Road, one cart pulling to the side when a copper tray careened off it and clattered across the cobblestones of Saint George Road. A man, his black-and-white checked kaffiyeh askew, hurried to retrieve it while his wife, in her festive purple robe, carrying an infant, waited for him, tears streaming unheeded down her cheeks.

There was a knock at Rebecca's door and she turned from the window and opened it, hoping that Nimra Halby had brought her coffee as she often did. But this morning Rebecca's landlady was dressed to go out, her long black gown covered with a shawl of the sheerest blue mohair, which she pulled over her hair.

"I am going now, Geveret Rebecca," she said. "There is coffee in the *finjan* on the stove—also some good goat cheese and *pita*. Please finish it. It will grow stale. The floors are all cleaned and the garbage is out. I have a great deal of lamb in the ice chest. Please, if I am not back by tomorrow and it is possible, add another block of ice." The Arab woman spoke in the clipped Mandate English shared by both the Jewish and Arab residents of Palestine, who had been educated by the British and employed in their civil service network.

"But where are you going? And why are you going?" Rebecca asked.

She liked her landlady. In the months she had lived in the large stone house an intimacy had developed between them, an instinctive understanding peculiar to women who have been used always to the support of men and are living without them. Nimra Halby was a widow who spoke softly to the shade of her dead husband, asking his advice about monies to be sent to her daughter who lived with relations in Lebanon, and transfers of documents to her sons studying medicine and architecture in Paris.

"It is better for a girl who speaks English and can read and write to live in Beirut," Nimra had told Rebecca. "There she will have the opportunities you have had to make her life her own. Here, in Palestine, it could not happen."

"But what am I doing with that life which is my own?" Rebecca had wondered then, thinking wistfully of Beth HaCochav where each day had been purposefully linked to the next, where she had heard Mindell's laughter, shared the warmth of her uncle's family, and been involved in important, exciting work. She thought, too, of the starlit nights when she had watched from the window and seen Yehuda standing in the shadowed tent of the cypress tree, looking through the darkness to the room that was her own. Here in Jerusalem she was alone except for the students she worked with at the studio and the boarders in Nimra Halby's house.

But within that aloneness, within that guarded quiet she had imposed upon herself, she felt a slow magic evolve. Her work was taking form. The seeds of talent which Charles Ferguson had observed so many years before, the talent that had sent her into Joe Stevenson's studio, was slowly taking form and growing. She worked in broad brush strokes now, taking a long time over the colors of her palette, her lips pursed like a cautious pedantic cook, as she added a modicum of gold to a splash of pink oil and produced the delicate, elusive rhodochrosite shade of a Jerusalem sunset on a winter's day.

"Soon, I think, you will begin to see people with your brush," her instructor told her. He was a tall bearded man who had walked across Russia four decades earlier and arrived in Jerusalem with a handful of sable brushes and three canvases sewn into the lining of his quilted jacket. One of these canvases hung now in the Museum of Modern Art in New York, another in the Tate Gallery in London, and a third in the Bezalel Museum, just below the art studio where he both worked and taught.

Rebecca had, in fact, begun to think of painting Nimra Halby, seeing in the Arab woman's face the lines of strength mingling with a soft sadness, in her eyes the reflection of a shared struggle. Nimra Halby had worked hard to make this strong stone house her own and to maintain it. She had forded her neighbors' and relatives' disapproval by taking a job in the British civil service and moving painfully up the administrative ladder by dint of perseverance and talent. She had had the courage to send her children off in search of better lives. She reminded Rebecca of her mother and she often thought of how well Leah and Nimra would understand each other—strong women both, who had seized the reins of their own lives.

"Why am I going?" Nimra Halby answered her boarder with barely concealed impatience. "Are you not living in Jerusalem? Don't you see what is happening in the city? Listen carefully. Perhaps you will hear the Jews near Notre Dame telling the Arabs to leave Musrara."

She motioned to the tumultuous street below where now a parade of ancient American taxis followed the carts. Three chickens, their necks clutched by a boy's brown fingers, clawed the windows of an old Checker cab.

"Which Jews are asking you to leave your home, Nimra Halby?" Danni Friedman asked, moving across Rebecca's room to stand at the window with them.

The young medical student came from Degania Aleph, a kibbutz in the north, and during his three years in Jerusalem, Nimra Halby's home had been his own. Rebecca had seen the Arab woman carry trays of coffee and sweet cakes to Danni's room when he studied for exams, and she had heard her get up in the night and pour naphthalene fluid into the hot-water heater so that Danni might bathe when he returned from his hospital duties on

Mount Scopus. She remembered the grim April day, exactly one month earlier, when the convoy to Mount Scopus had been ambushed. Danni was to have traveled with the convoy and his Arab landlady had sat frozen by her radio, listening to reports of the dead and wounded, weeping, stopping only when she heard the sound of his key in the latch and he entered the room. He had missed the bus, he told them sheepishly, but had spent all those hours at the Shaare Tzedek Hospital working with the wounded. The Arab landlady and her Jewish student boarders wept with relief and toasted each other in vinegary arak, celebrating Danni's survival and their own.

This morning Danni did not wear his medical whites but was dressed in the khaki fatigues of his Haganah uniform. An enormous Colt revolver hung clumsily from the holster at his waist and although the day had not reached its full heat, circles of sweat stained his loose army shirt. Rebecca had not heard him leave that morning and it occurred to her that he had been out all night standing guard duty.

"The Jews who call upon you to leave Musrara are not members of the Haganah, or of the new Jewish government. They are from the Stern Gang, wild terrorists, and there aren't many of them. You know this. Stay here, Nimra Halby. Please. Do not turn yourself into a refugee. This house is your home. This city is your home. Stay."

The Arab woman remained at the window, her young Jewish boarders flanking her. The air vibrated with the static of a loudspeaker which no longer carried the chant of the muezzin. Arabic words, frenzied, passionate, tumbled over each other. The muted staccato sounds of gunfire were supplemented by the tumultuous crescendo of rockets spewing flame and noise.

"The damn Davidka," Danni muttered. "Misfiring half the time. Can you hear it?"

"And can you hear him? The spokesman of my people?" Nimra Halby asked and they stood quietly and listened to the impassioned Arab's plea.

"I hear him. He says to leave and tomorrow you will return to claim Tel Aviv," Danni said. He had learned Arabic from the goatherds of the Galilee, English from the Mandate police, and Hebrew from his grandfather who had cleared the first rocks from the fields of Degania.

"I don't want Tel Aviv," Nimra replied. "I want only my house built by my husband's father."

"Then stay in it," Danni pleaded. "Stay in it and nothing will happen to you. We will protect you."

"No. I cannot. But I will return. You will take care of the lamb?" she asked Rebecca.

Rebecca nodded.

"I will put fresh ice on it tomorrow if you are not back."

"Good." The Arab woman pulled her shawl around her head, draping it across her face. She drew herself up tall and her eyes narrowed. Slowly, without turning back to the young people who stood watching her, she left the room and they heard her walk softly down the stairs, heard the heavy door, carved of cedar, girdled in brass, slam behind her. Through the window, then, they followed her progress down the street, where she trailed long lines of Arabs who hurried by on foot, laden with packages and suitcases. Nimra Halby carried nothing but her large purse and did not once look back at the large stone house to which she had come as a bride and where she had borne her children.

"Oh God," Rebecca cried softly, shivering in her nightdress, her bare feet cold on the tile floor which Nimra Halby had so proudly shown her the day she rented the room.

"He won't help us today," Danni said grimly. "Today we fight for Jerusalem ourselves. Come, Rebecca. Get dressed. Have some coffee and come back with me to the emergency clinic at Saint Joseph's. You're a doctor's daughter. You know how to bandage a wound."

"My father's a psychiatrist," Rebecca said and she and Danni laughed with a sudden explosion of uncontained mirth, as though she had said something wildly funny. They laughed until tears came and they realized, by the wordless gaze that arrested their laughter as suddenly as it had begun, that it had only shielded the fear and sorrow they felt for the Arab woman in whose home they stood and whom they knew they would not see again.

"I had meant to paint her," Rebecca said in a small, almost aggrieved voice, as though angered by the wars that again and again upset her life. The promises of her laughing childhood had been broken and like a betrayed child she thought of all that had been denied her.

"This is not a time to paint." Danni's voice was harsh and she saw, for the first time, a scarlet crescent of blood across the sleeve of his shirt. She dressed swiftly then, and seized as many linens as she could carry from the carved cabinet where Nimra Halby had kept her sheets and pillow slips.

The Saint Joseph Convent School was nestled into a gentle hillside in one of those Jerusalem cul-de-sacs where the city is suddenly fenced off by a brace of tamarisks. Here, a self-contained community conducted an islandic existence, independent of the ancient city which surrounded it. Through the generations, young girls in uniforms had come to this enclave, with their book bags and writing tablets, heavy crucifixes suspended about their necks, and prostrated themselves before the east windows of the church, which looked out toward the Hill of Calvary, and studied geometry and home economics, irregular Latin verbs and the histories of Shakespeare.

But there were no students in the old classrooms today. The tenacious smell of chalk dust mingled with the odor of ethyl alcohol, the sweet cloying scent of morphine, and the stench of vomit. The corridors were crowded with stretchers and the air rang with the sounds of men weeping and moaning with pain. Above them, on the bulletin boards, brightly colored posters invited the convent students to take a botanical hike through the Judean hills, to join a bus tour of Crusader sites, to go on retreat at a monastery in Jericho. Relics of another life before Palestine had become a battlefield, some of the posters were now smeared with blood where the wounded had leaned against them.

"We've got all the casualties from the battle at Neve Yaakov," Danni said. "Thank God you thought to bring that linen."

"Are you here to work?" a Magen David Adom nurse called to Rebecca. "Good. We can use another pair of hands. Put this on." She tossed Rebecca an enormous white surgical coverall and watched approvingly as she struggled into it, glancing incuriously at the patch of dried blood on the shoulder. "Cover this corridor and the reception area, please. The water is in the chemistry lab but give only half-cup portions and then only if it's desperate. Dr. Joseph is operating in the chapel. I'm Nurse Rachel and Nurse Dalia is in the library."

She disappeared into the chapel and Rebecca stood still for a moment, remembering what Aaron had told her about the battlefield in Ethiopia.

"It happened like a slow-motion film. I moved through it as though it were happening to someone else. I didn't shoot. Someone else shot. My ears didn't hear the screaming of the wounded. That someone else, that slow-motion ghost who had taken over my body, heard it. Even Gregory, poor dead Gregory, he was 'someone else's' friend."

Standing in the makeshift hospital, her eyes riveted to a pool of blood, her ears filled with screams and the muffled sounds of shamed weeping, she understood what Aaron had meant. Grimly, she commanded the "someone else" who inhabited her body to move down the corridor, to rip sheets into bandages, to apply a compress to the bloodied forehead of the fourteen-year-old boy who still tightly grasped the grenade he had not had time to throw before a bullet shattered his kneecap.

She learned that morning not to look at faces but to concentrate on wounds. She had made the mistake of looking up into the familiar deep-blue eyes of a young man delirious with pain, blood running from his right hand. He had held his other hand out to her and in the dirt-encrusted palm were three mangled fingers belonging to the bloodied right hand. A grenade had severed them by the muscle from his palm but he had plucked up the scraps of tendon, flesh, and bone and hurried with them to the clinic. His hands were his life, Rebecca knew, because he was Amnon Harel, the artist whose easel stood next to hers in the Bezalel studio and whose subtle use of line and color reminded her of Joe Stevenson's work. She took the proffered fingers—the flesh soft and spongy against her own, one sharp knucklebone shimmering like milk-white ivory where the flesh had been scorched from it—found a glass of water and some salt, and plunged them into it. She had heard her father talk once about preserving severed flesh in a saline solution and she prayed that there was hope for saving Amnon's fingers, the fingers whose magic gift captured the Judean hills in pastel tones as soft and delicate as the morning breath of a sleeping child.

At another bedside she held a block of ice in place against the groin of a tall, red-bearded man whose Number 6 bus she had often ridden to the German colony. A volley of submachine gun bullets had pierced his trunk and although the blood was staunched he moaned and writhed on the narrow cot. She did not look at him until he was quiet, and she thought then that the ice must have anesthesized his pain so that he slept at last. She moved to adjust his blanket and saw his hand dangling, blue and motionless. She pressed her ear against his mouth but she had known from the moment that she saw the hand that he was dead. Almost angrily she pulled the blanket over his face and seized the block of ice, taking it to where a mother sat with her seventeen-year-old son, waiting for Dr. Joseph to amputate the boy's left leg, mangled into shreds of broken cartilage where an Arab half-track had ridden over it once and then shifted into reverse and ridden back across it to compound the crippling.

As the civilian volunteers and Haganah soldiers carried in the wounded, depositing them in every available inch of space, they brought the news of the battles raging throughout the city. Avram Uzielli's troops had captured the Allenby Barracks, securing the Greek Colony, the German Colony, and Bakka. Fighting was fierce in the Old City and casualties were high among both the Jews and the Arabs. The Palmach, the key commando unit of the Jewish army, had taken Latrun in a surprise victory.

The Palmach, Rebecca thought with a sudden surge of fear which did not interfere with her calm cutting away of the bloodied blouse of a young woman Haganah fighter, who had passed out with the pain but would not die of the wound. Both her cousin Yaakov and Yehuda were in the Palmach. Were they in Latrun? No, of course not. She dismissed the thought. Yehuda was still in Europe. He had been traveling back and forth on *Bericha* vessels since New Year's Eve. In a daring new plan, it was rumored that *Bericha* was now landing some vessels off the coast of the Lebanese port of Tyre, and the illegals were crossing into Israel by foot across the northern border. Yehuda, of course, would be the logical choice to run such an operation. She had not heard from him since the night they had swum through the icy waters of the inlet to the rubber raft together, and she accepted that silence as decision.

Sirens wailed ceaselessly in the streets outside and Nurse Dalia emptied a bowl of water which she had just used to cleanse the gaping neck wound of an Irgun fighter and poured it onto the floor, using it to mop up the mess of blood and vomit the wounded man had left. Nurse Rachel was in the chapel and Dalia told Rebecca that Dr. Joseph was operating now on her fiancé, who had been wounded in street combat.

"That was amazing presence of mind—preserving that boy's fingers in saline solution. Dr. Joseph was able to stitch them right on and he's fairly sure they'll be manipulable. Have you studied nursing?" Rachel asked.

"No. But my father is a doctor." Rebecca continued to rip up Nimra Halby's linen, some of it still bearing the faded markings of a well-known Amman department store. Nimra Halby, who had stayed up all night worrying about Danni, would not mind the use to which her dowry was being put.

"Where did you learn to keep your head in such a situation?" the nurse said admiringly and dashed off, a clean sponge in one hand, a bottle of iodine in the other, to swab the cheek of a child who had been carried into the clinic by an old rabbi. He was a small Arab boy, one of the army of young shoeshine entrepreneurs who lined Suleiman Road. He had been caught in crossfire and the white-bearded rabbi, his white Sabbath caftan red now with the boy's blood, had found him and carried him across the fiery half-mile to the convent clinic.

Where had the rabbi, the man of prayer and study, found the strength? Rebecca wondered, and thought of the day when Eleanor Greenstein had told her about Leah's actions during the Rosenblatt fire. Rebecca had not been able to conceive of her mother wrapping the burning bodies of young girls in bolts of cloth and hurling them through windows to safety. But now she began to understand these secret veins of strength. Her children too, in all probability, would find it difficult to believe that she, Rebecca, could dress wounds in a makeshift Jerusalem clinic, its floors slimy with blood, its air thick with the odors of putrefaction, the screams of the wounded and the dying. But what children was she thinking of? She chided herself bitterly for the thought. The children she would not have with Joe Stevenson or with Joshua Ellenberg or with Yehuda Arnon? She reproached herself for even now being absorbed in her own problems. Gently, she pressed a damp compress down against the dark curls of the little shoeshine boy and listened to the muted murmur of the old man's voice as he intoned the Psalms, shuffling from cot to cot, his pale old eyes awash with tears.

A new series of sirens rent the air, their shrill wail rising above the sputtering bullets, the explosive discharge of the Davidka cannon, the screaming of the wounded and the dying on both sides of the city.

"What the hell was that?"

Dr. Joseph emerged from the chapel, his mask askew, sweat pouring down his forehead. His apron was covered with blood so thick it formed wedges into which small white worms of entrails and striped scraps of muscles had embedded themselves. The internationally famous surgeon had flown home from a medical conference in South America in time for the battle of Jerusalem, and had been operating for almost six hours without a break, using the chapel benches as surgical tables, utilizing the light of flashlights held by nurses because the electricity at Saint Joseph's had failed. Nurse Rachel, the slender Yemenite girl who had assisted him for much of the day, stood against the door, her hands hanging loosely at her sides. It was the first time in many hours that the tiny nurse was not moving frantically about, wheeling postoperative patients out of the chapel, preparing others for surgery, monitoring the meager supplies of morphine, bandages, and plasma. But now she stood absolutely still as though a great weight had settled upon her and held her immobile against the supporting doorframe.

A strangely familiar vacuity filled her eyes, and Rebecca knew it for the look of dazed incredulity that veils the eyes of those who have sustained an enormous loss. Her mother's eyes had held that look when the news came that Aaron was missing in action and again when she learned that the Russian village of her parents had been razed and its inhabitants taken to a remote wood called Babi Yar. And once, too, in the distant days of Rebecca's childhood, Leah's eyes had held that terrible wounded stare—during the days after the fire, Rebecca remembered suddenly—the summer when she and her cousin Annie had worn blue cartwheel hats whose trailing ribbons they had often sucked on. She understood then, with sad certainty, that Rachel's fiancé had died behind the closed door of the chapel, and she moved toward the nurse and led her to an empty bench, holding the girl's cold fingers in her own while outside the horns of death and danger continued their wailing threnody.

Dr. Joseph peered through the window.

"There's an ambulance outside. Damn it, that's what it is. A Magen David Adorn ambulance. Probably it was on its way over here. I can see the driver's head against the wheel. Poor bastard got hit before he could draw up here. God only knows what wounded and how many are in the van. We've got to get out there and pull them in."

"There's crossfire from the Swedish School ricocheting down there. We're sure targets for Abou Gharbieh's men if we step out that door. We can't afford to lose you, Doctor, and we don't even know if there are any wounded in that van." Danni Friedman had come in from the field only minutes before. A bullet had grazed his forehead en route and his argument carried with it the grim authority of the battles he had fought that day.

"But we can't take the risk of leaving men out there, suffering, in danger." The man whose life was dedicated to healing pleaded with the young soldier who would one day take his place in the operating theater.

"It's too great a risk." Danni's voice was weary and firm.

He too looked out at the beleaguered ambulance and watched as a hand appeared in the rear window of the van and, like a ghostly disembodied appendage, scraped at the blood-spattered glass, then fell.

"You can spare me." Rachel stepped forth, her eyes still frozen but her voice firm. "I don't care about the danger."

She did not care about anything at that moment, they knew, but the sight of that weak, pleading hand haunted them and they did not argue with her.

"I'll go with you," Rebecca said, acting with the swift impetuosity that had always governed her life.

"All right then. Go. I'll cover you with my Bren. Dash for the back door of the ambulance, see what you've got, and get back in here with them if you can as quickly as possible," Danni said briskly.

"Better than that," Rebecca said. "I can make it to the driver's seat and back it up to the convent entrance." Before Danni could protest she jerked open the door and dashed across the road, sprinting to avoid the bullets that skittered off the cobblestones about her. Within seconds she had jumped into the battered ambulance and left the door swinging open. She shoved the body of the driver across the seat, gunned the motor, and heard with relief the engine's noisy response. She shifted into reverse and bent low over the wheel to avoid a new streak of snipers' bullets that pierced the windshield and settled with a dull thud in the cracked upholstery of the seat behind her, understanding how the driver had been killed. Without looking behind her, she moved the ambulance backward to the porticoed entry of the convent where Danni, Rachel, and Dr. Joseph stood in readiness. Then she scrambled into the rear of the vehicle, jerked open the door, and summoned all her strength to help Danni and the others move the half-dozen wounded men who lay there into the convent. The last man was unconscious and could not help to ease himself out as the others could. He lay face down, and she inched him forward patiently until Danni was able to grasp his shoulders and carry him, like an exhausted child, to safety in his arms.

She stumbled behind them, feeling her own tiredness settle across her whole being, but still she knelt for a moment beside the unconscious man. A cap shielded his face and she moved it so that he might breathe more easily. Her fingers trembled and then reached out with wondering tenderness to touch Yehuda Arnon's earth-colored hair, matted now with sweat and blood.

She was still by his side hours later when he awoke. It was quiet in the convent now. Dr. Joseph slept sitting up in the large chair where the Mother Superior held court. The old rabbi repeated the Psalms and the two nurses moved up and down through the corridors, their eyes watchful. Grief had at last banished shock from Rachel's eyes and Rebecca saw with relief that the little Yemenite nurse had released that grief into tears.

"It is very hard for her because they were childhood sweethearts, she and her fiancé, poor Gideon," Dalia whispered. "They grew up together in Yemen and their families are neighbors in Rosh HaAyin. Gideon was studying medicine and it was their dream to work together in a clinic in the Negev. He and Rachel were lovers and still they were like brother and sister."

"I know yet another story of lovers who were like brother and sister to each other," Rebecca said.

She looked across to Yehuda who had watched his wife, the woman who had been both his sister and his mistress, gunned down in a forest of Czechoslovakia. He stirred in his sleep and she wiped the film of sweat that had formed in the stubble of his unshaven chin. His wound was not serious. A bullet had grazed his head and Dr. Joseph had cleaned and dressed it without even using a drop of his precious morphine.

Yehuda opened his eyes now and her heart melted at the sight of their silken gray sheen.

"Rebecca. Is it really you? What are you doing here? Where am I? What's happened?"

"You're at the Magen David Adom station in Saint Joseph's Convent in Jerusalem. An ambulance brought you down from Latrun."

"But the ambulance was ambushed. I remember now—the driver was hit."

"No ambush. It was sniper fire just outside our door, but we got everyone in."

"Ah, good. You are always expert at getting everyone in, Rivka. What's the news?"

"Musrara is entirely in Jewish hands. We have no more news from Latrun. Was it very bad there, Yehuda? Was Yaakov there?"

"No, Yaakov is in the north. Yes, it was bad but it is bad everywhere. Still, here we are fighting with guns, not being gassed in showers or shot down in fields—or forests. Such a forest it was, too. Wild with vines and bushes. Sweet blackberries grew there. The brambles—they are sharp against our arms. Go carefully, Miriam. Don't let the thorns tear your stockings. Ah, look, your arm is scratched. Here, let me lick the blood. How I love your soft arms. Miriam, please, don't go into the clearing, there's a shadow there. I see him coming closer and closer, Miriam, no. Stay back!" His voice rose in a delirium of grief and confusion. He sat up, his face flushed with fever, his arms flailing wildly, his shoulders shaking with remembered misery.

Gently, like a mother soothing a child grappling with nightmares, Rebecca eased Yehuda down, tucked the thin blanket firmly about his trembling body, and patted his shaking shoulders until his hand came up and grasped her fingers in his own. She sat beside him then and even when his fingers relaxed their grip, she did not remove her hand. She did not remember falling asleep as she sat by his side, but hours later, when she awoke to the shimmering rose-gold light of a new Jerusalem morning, her hand was still in his. With a gentleness that matched her own, he pressed it to his lips and smiled up at her, his silken gray eyes caressing her face. The fever was gone. Yehuda seemed tranquil. Gone, too, was the terrible tension that had hovered between them. He looked up at her.

"Good morning, Rivka," he said. "Darling Rivka."

She wept then and did not care that he saw her tears. That night, a fresh white bandage on his forehead, he left to find his unit and some days later she began the journey back to Beth HaCochav.

*

One month later she stood between Mindell and Danielle in a field where blood-red anemones covered the coarse green meadow grass. The children pelted her with the crimson blossoms and she watched the linear shadows the tall grass carved in their slender sun-streaked limbs. The United Nations truce had been in effect for only two days and this was the first afternoon they had ventured any distance from the underground air-raid shelters. The two girls spotted a cluster of golden daffodils and dashed toward them, leaving Rebecca with the overflowing basket of anemones. She sank to her knees and braided the flowers the way her mother and her aunt Mollie had taught her, her fingers threading the stems together until she had fashioned a graceful wreath. "For me?"

His footsteps had been cushioned by the thick grasses and she had not heard him approach. She stood and held the flowers out toward him. He took them and placed them on her head, then cupped her chin in his hand and bent to kiss her lips. Where the bullet had grazed his forehead the broken skin took on a milky sheen, and she stood on her toes and touched the small scar with her lips. They stood quietly then, hand in hand, beneath the warm shower of golden sunlight and watched the children run toward them, their arms overflowing with the bright flowers of the field.

19

Weddings. Leah had dreamed of them through the night before Aaron's wedding. Clutching at the strands of memories, she lay quietly in bed and felt the damp, sultry breeze of New Orleans' Lake Pontchartrain waft across her naked body. Just outside her door was the murmuring of patois French as two chambermaids argued about whether *Madame and Monsieur le professeur* would want *café* in their room. They settled at last on setting the tray just outside the door and Leah gratefully leaned back. She pulled the sheet up over her, careful not to disturb David who slept heavily beside her, his warm rhythmic breath caressing and moistening her neck. She turned toward him and, with light fingers, touched his thick short beard so intricately threaded with silver; when he did not awaken she moved the sheet up, curving it to the contours of his body like a solicitous mother.

Weddings. In the luxury of matutinal silence, in this strange hotel room in a strange city, she thought of all the different weddings of her lifetime at which she had danced and wept. She remembered her own first marriage when she had been a girl bride, dressed in a peasant costume of her own design. Her long dark hair had been threaded with flowers and the blossoms drifted to the floor as she and Yaakov whirled joyously to the tunes of what had seemed like a hundred horas. And then only a year later she had been a widow and then a bride once more. A pregnant bride in a shapeless dress, she had stood joylessly beneath the wedding canopy, beside the man whose body she covered now with such care, her quiet David who had nurtured her love and his own with a magical patience, nourishing it from a seedling into the full fragrance that had belonged to them now for three decades.

Other marriage days filled her mind and she thought of the quiet sad Depression-day wedding of their little boarder Pearl, in the parlor of the Eldridge Street apartment, and then of the gracious springtime wedding of her niece, Annie Hart, in a Westchester garden, the groom wearing his uniform, his eyes clouded with thoughts of war and death even as he pledged himself to love and life. Pearl's son was a medical student now, her daughter a college senior, and Annie Hart had two fat babies and her uniformed groom wore a gray flannel suit and daily rode a commuter train from Stamford to a Madison Avenue office.

Weddings were, after all, only the beginning of the marriage, a fragile foundation of ritual and memory on which to build a shared life. Still, it pained her, even two years later, that she had not seen her daughter married but had to content herself with photographs of her Becca in a simple white dress and sandals, one hand holding a bouquet of wild flowers, the other linked to that of a tall man whose serious silken light eyes were lifted to a sun so bright that the photographed faces of the bride and her groom were brushed with its glow. There had been no time for Rebecca and Yehuda to wait for David and Leah to attend their wedding. They had seized their hour during the pause of a war, during a brief cease-fire, and on the October night that marked the end of their honeymoon week Yehuda had marched on Beersheva. Leah worried, then, that her own history would repeat itself in her daughter. It was an impossible war that they fought there, in the land where oranges grew golden and young trees shored up a shifting desert—a war of concentration-camp survivors, inadequately armed young men and women, even small children opposing well-equipped Arab armies. Would Rebecca, so newly a bride, coming at last into that legacy of happiness which had seemed her birthright but which had proven so elusive, become, as Leah had become, a young widow whose bridegroom wandered through shadowy dreams? But Yehuda had survived the war and he and Rebecca, with his two children and the small girl, Mindell, whom they had adopted, had joined a group of young people and set out to found a new kibbutz where the Red Sea licked at the sands of the desert.

"We wanted a new beginning," Rebecca had written and Leah remembered her daughter's words now. A new beginning was, after all, what all weddings were. Today was a new beginning for

Aaron and Katie, the slight blonde girl, Aaron's classmate, now his colleague and his bride. Katie, her daughter-in-law who would one day be the mother of her grandchildren. Leah smiled and David stirred lazily into wakefulness beside her, his hand reaching automatically upward to touch her face, to pull her lips down upon his own.

"Why the smile?" he asked. "It's too early in the morning to smile."

"My Aaron's wedding day," she said. "It's hard to believe. Soon I'll be a mother-in-law for the second time. No, it's not true. I'm too young."

She stretched luxuriously, arching her back and draping her long hair about her breasts. Wings of silver darted through her jet-black hair and laugh lines crinkled at her eyes but her skin was smooth and her body firm.

"Well, then, concentrate on Michael. Think of yourself as the mother of an adolescent," David said.

"Michael's been having a marvelous time. I'm glad Melanie, Katie's cousin, was able to come early so that he had some company. I rather imagine that Katie's family arranged that. They are such lovely people, I think. Don't you like the Reznikoffs, David?"

"Yes." But David's answer was too abrupt and he shifted position suddenly, his arms dropping from the cushion of Leah's outstretched body to his side as he often lay when he was thinking through a professional problem. Leah sometimes teased him about lying like that, marking the origin of that pose from David's own didactic analysis and the long hours he had spent lying on the couch in Dr. Simonsohn's office, struggling backward to frozen moments, immutable memories.

David frowned, trying vainly to remember the name of a young patient of whom Katie reminded him. A tall girl, a student at a professional school—perhaps a medical student. He had seen her only a few times and in the end had referred her to a colleague. But something about the way she had held her head, moved her hands as she talked, reminded him of the young woman Aaron was marrying. But her name and her history eluded him and he turned to Leah who was looking at him anxiously.

"What's the matter, David? You're upset about something. Something about the Reznikoffs? About Katie?"

She was alert now, all playfulness vanished. A quiet, barely perceptible danger signal had been sounded and she tensed toward it, her breasts suddenly hard as though flushed with milk for an infant who would not drink.

"A little," he said. "Nothing I can pinpoint. But sometimes I get a strange feeling about Aaron's Katie, a feeling that she is not quite with us—that she drifts in another world. Perhaps it's this way she has of disappearing suddenly. It's happened when she's visited us at home and last night when she was opening her gifts. Suddenly she wasn't there but it was her mother who was removing the wrappings, reading the cards, as though she were quite accustomed to picking up after Katie in that way."

"Perhaps she and Aaron went for a walk," Leah said remembering now that she too had looked about for Katie, wanting to ask her whether she liked the pattern on the sterling which Mollie and Seymour had sent.

"No. Aaron too was looking for her. I saw him on the terrace and then in the study. He looked concerned but not surprised." David frowned, as though a missing piece of a puzzle had presented itself to him but he was reluctant to fit it into place. "I got the feeling he too has become used to this sort of thing—sudden moods, sudden silences," he said at last.

"Well, everyone has their moods. Sometimes you have to forget you're a psychiatrist, David."

Leah jumped out of bed, feeling oddly relieved. David worried too much, read symptoms into everything. Katie was a lovely girl, brilliant and gentle, so loving to Aaron who had lost so much love. It was a beautiful day and it would be a lovely wedding.

David remained outstretched on the bed watching her, his arms again rigid at his sides. Leaves of light dappled Leah's bare shoulders and as he watched them he thought of how strangely bright Katie's eyes had been when she came quietly back into the room and settled herself between the mountains of gifts and the white hills of tissue paper in which they had been wrapped.

*

Michael Goldfeder changed his shirt twice that morning and settled finally for a white button-down collar broadcloth and an orange-and-black rep Princeton tie. He looked at himself for a long time in the mirror before phoning room service to have breakfast served on the small balcony with its filigreed black wrought iron railing that overlooked Baronne Street. He knew his mother and father expected him to eat with them, but he had been intrigued by the small balcony since their arrival at the Roosevelt Hotel earlier in the week and the idea of breakfasting out there alone made him feel cosmopolitan, debonair. It reaffirmed the feeling that had swelled in him last night when Katie's tiny cousin from Baton Rouge, a girl called Melanie because, as she told him with a shy smile, her mother had just loved Olivia de Havilland in *Gone With the Wind,* had pressed her body close to his as they danced in the Creole nightclub in the Vieux Carré section of the city.

"I haven't met many Northerners before," Melanie had said. "We all thought it was so wonderful of Katie to go north to law school. But wasn't it lucky that she did and met Aaron there. I think he's so handsome."

Michael felt a brief twinge of jealousy and glanced across the polished dance floor to the spot where Aaron and Katie moved slowly in time to the music, revolving in a single circle of rose-colored light, their bodies melding, Aaron's chin resting lightly on her soft golden head. But why did Katie always look so sad? Michael wondered, and lowered his own head so that his chin touched the crown of dark curls into which Melanie had twisted her hair, but the girl moved her head impatiently and then, as though to compensate, shifted her position, allowing her small soft breast to touch Michael's hand as they circled the floor.

"How old are you, Michael?" she asked in that soft slow voice, so like Katie's own.

"Nineteen," he replied, tacking on a year without conscience. He was after all almost nineteen, and many boys in his class at Princeton were nineteen.

"Oh dear. Do you think you'll be called up for this terrible Korea business?"

He had not thought about it really, although he had read the United Nations proceedings and President Truman's foreign policy statement. And of course his parents spoke of it, his father using the same pained, worrying tones in which he spoke of all war, all suffering.

"You would suppose that after Hitler they would have learned, we would have learned," David had said bitterly, slamming the paper down. "Think of it, Leah. This will be the fourth war of our lifetimes—the fourth war to touch our lives." His eyes found Michael who was bent over a physics text and he turned away.

"Perhaps there won't be a war," Leah replied, but Michael knew his mother did not believe her own words.

"There will be a war." David's voice was definite, resigned. "A shooting war in Korea and a war of words here with that maniac Senator McCarthy finding Communists under every bed, breeding hatred and fear. You know, Leah, when I decided to become an analyst I said to myself, 'Goldfeder, instead of cursing the darkness, light a few candles.' So I've lit my candles, hundreds of them, but see, they do not even pierce an inch of the darkness."

He sat quietly then and Michael saw him reach for the small bottle of pills he kept in his pocket. When Leah turned away David slipped a pill into his mouth and remained seated, his hands stretched across the newspaper, blotting out its messages of new death, new destruction, of subversive activity in the world of the arts and theater, of angry exchanges in the United Nations, which had been formed to cope with international anger.

"Oh, I might go over to Korea," Michael said now, in the dim nightclub, as he moved the girl's light body through the fluid bright circles of red and blue light that shimmered across the dance floor. "I'm in ROTC, you know." He held her closer, shutting out the memory of his father's face.

"I'll bet you look really neat in your uniform." She looked up at him admiringly, as though envisaging him in the garb of war, the sunlight sparkling on his epaulettes. Rhett Butler home from the fray. Jay Gatsby in his well-pressed lieutenant's uniform. She was a girl with a literary bent and her mother complained to her friends across the bridge table that Melanie was never without a book.

When Michael brought her home that night, to the large white house on the corner of Carondelet Street, where the Reznikoff family lived, he kissed her for a long hushed moment in the shadowed corner of the porch that smelled heavily of sweet fig blossoms and the tumid vines of wisteria that draped the garden. She touched his face with her soft hand that smelled of lemons and murmured into the darkness, "You're so handsome, Michael. Even handsomer than your brother. I think I'll go north to school too."

They had both laughed then and Michael remembered her words as he studied himself carefully in the mirror of his hotel room. He was tall and slender like Aaron, but he had inherited his mother's thick dark hair and his father's even features and light eyes. He moved with the easy grace of the natural athlete and spoke with the slow assurance that his words would be acknowledged by a pleasant rejoinder, a quick smile. People enjoyed agreeing with Michael. He was a lucky boy with the added asset of being aware of, and acknowledging, his luck. Everyone liked Michael Goldfeder and he was not ashamed to like himself.

"He is the happiest of our children," Michael had once heard his father tell his mother.

"Rebecca was always a happy child," Leah had protested.

"Ah, Rebecca was happy because she thought it her job, her duty to be happy. But Michael was born into it."

His father's words had puzzled Michael and he posited them away beneath memories among which he seldom furrowed—the memories of the years when Aaron had been missing in action and their lives centered about the war map in David's study and whispered phone conversations in Yiddish between his mother and his aunt Mollie; and then there was the year of the war in Israel when Leah had jumped to every ring of the telephone and kept a large picture of Rebecca in her studio.

But the tall, carefully dressed Michael, who ate his breakfast now on the sun-spattered balcony, did not want to think of nights of quiet weeping and the long days when minutes stretched like hours. Rebecca lived happily in Israel with her tall, somber-faced husband, peaceful at last among the rows of young green plants shooting their way upward through the desert sands, and painting in an exciting new primitive style, according to Charles Ferguson to whom she sent transparencies of her work. And Aaron was a practicing attorney, his copper-colored hair prematurely peppered with gray, about to be married to a golden-haired, slow-voiced girl whose head came up to his chin. And he, Michael, was pouring a cup of coffee and lacing it with thick cream as he watched the busy, colorful street beneath his balcony.

Street vendors passed beneath him, thrusting straw baskets laden with bright springtime fruit—orange-skinned persimmons and sweet purple figs—at leisurely parading passersby. A small soap-box orchestra stood on the corner of Baronne and South Rampart thrashing out metallic jazz beats against scrub boards and clanging pots and pans together. The city intrigued Michael and he thought back to their first day in New Orleans when Katie's parents had driven them through the Dryades market district and they had wandered about the stalls where small black boys and widely smiling coffee-colored women thrust bolts of colorful fabric and artfully crafted small wood figurines at them.

Katie had not joined them then, nor had she come on the other small tours that followed, pleading tiredness, an overcrowded schedule, but Melanie had told him that Katie seldom left the house on Carondelet Street when she came home for visits.

"Katie gets her moods, she does," Melanie had said and pulled Michael off to look at a group of small black boys who were imitating the song of the tall woman who wandered the marketplace selling blackberries. Melanie laughingly tossed them a few coins and the children ran off to buy "snowballs," scoops of slivered ice dyed the colors of the rainbow with sweet syrups.

David, too, had stayed at home after the first excursion. This was his first visit to the American South and his heart had sunk the first time he boarded a bus and saw how black passengers passed to the rear with lowered eyes. On Lafitte Square he had looked at the separate drinking fountains marked "Colored" and "White" and traveled back through the years to his own consulting room and heard again Jeffrey Coleman's tortured voice rising upward from the couch, speaking in remembered anguish of the ultimate agony of quotidian separation and humiliation.

"Don't you see," David had said that night to Leah and Michael, as they chatted about their purchases, "we are back in Odessa again. The Dryades market is the Jewish ghetto. We go as tourists to spy on misery. Colorful misery, yes, but still a disgrace to us, to our humanity. Pogroms, lynchings, whites and blacks, Aryans and *Untermenschen*—it all comes to the same thing. I do not wonder that Katie stays at home."

His father was right, Michael admitted, but still New Orleans had captivated him—the graceful transitions from French to English, the wrought-iron lacework balconies bordering homes where slow-moving ceiling fans could be seen through crenellated windows, the color and music of the winding streets. Beneath his own balcony now a procession of musicians wound their way, the largest group Michael had seen all week. The dancing black women who led them were dressed in skirts of shining fabrics and low-cut blouses the color of the flowers of high summer. They danced with each other and alone, their heels clicking, their bodies swaying rhythmically to the music. A saxophone rent the air with a sudden piercing note and as though on cue, voices shouted wildly in a surging song. But through the throbbing cacophony Michael heard a keening, a low sobbing moan. The music softened, grew almost susurrant, and then suddenly picked up pace, boomed out with wild gladness.

The waiter came in to clear the breakfast dishes and he too looked down to the street.

"What's happening?" Michael asked curiously. "Is it a holiday or something?"

"It's a funeral," the waiter replied, loading the tray. "A Bourbon Street jazz pianist died and this is his funeral walk-around. There's the widow now."

But Michael turned away and moved from the sunlight of the balcony into the shadows of his room. He did not want to look at a woman newly widowed on this bright morning of the day when his brother Aaron would take a bride.

*

Aaron too awakened early that morning although he had promised Katie he would try to sleep late, offering her the promise to appease the guilt she felt because she had kept him up so late the night before their wedding day. He lay in bed and listened to the sounds drifting up from the busy street below, registering the wild wail of a saxophone and then rich voices of men and women mingling in a song that sounded strangely like a lullaby. Gradually he made out the words.

> Sleep, sleep deeply,
> Rest now in Jesus' arms…

It was not a lullaby, then, but a dirge, and the thought disquieted him. He was relieved when the musicians moved on down the street and he could no longer hear them.

He had not slept enough, he knew, and he also knew that no more sleep would come. Fitfully he turned and looked at the telephone, but Katie would not be awake yet. She always slept with a peculiar lethean heaviness after what they called, with wry bitterness, a "scene." There were other words for it, he knew, and he knew too that his father could provide him with a clinical vocabulary that would clearly define those wild hours that tore at Katie's soul and at his own love for her. But he could not, would not, bring himself to speak to David or anyone else about it. If he defined those sudden stretches of silence, which were invariably followed by wild weeping and self-castigation when Katie thrust herself at him like an exhausted child and beat against his chest with wearied fists, he would have to acknowledge a disease, search out a cure. It was safer, easier, to dismiss those lost hours as "scenes" and to assure himself that the intervals between them grew longer and longer. Soon, perhaps, they would disappear entirely and the delicate golden-haired girl, whose steady gaze made him tremble with love and yearning, would live happily ever after like the fairy-tale prince and princess in the oversized book he had gazed at wondrously so long ago in the reading room of the East Broadway branch of the New York Public Library. He remembered, now, thinking that his mother resembled those dark-haired crowned beauties and he smiled at the sudden memory of how the sun had pierced those soot-encrusted windows as he read, settling into liquid golden pools on the battered oak table.

The phone rang and he reached for it and said hello, his voice still thick with dreamy memory.

"Aaron, did I wake you?" Katie's voice was shy, hesitant, as it always was on such a morning, after a night that had trembled with her sobs.

"No, darling. Of course not."

"Aaron, listen to me carefully. There is still time. If you don't want to go through with it, we can call the wedding off. It's happened before."

He thought of her sitting up in bed, her blonde curls caught up in a pale ribbon, her fragile face drained of color, her body tense with secret fears. There would be a small rose blush across her shoulder and he wished himself beside her now so that he could kiss away the flower on her skin. His sweet, sad Katie, his lovely bride.

"I love you Katie," he said in reply.

"I love you too, but still..." Her words trailed off like unstrung beads and were lost, scattered. She had had only enough strength to say it once and he was too weak with love and pity to seize her strength.

"At four then," she said and her voice shook. "Aaron. Love."

"At four." He did not say good-bye but listened for the click which was some moments in coming, and then he too gently replaced the receiver and leaned back against the pillows.

He wanted to marry Katie and had wanted to marry her since the day he had sat behind her in the huge lecture hall at the Harvard Law School and watched her small fine features absorbed in thought as her pencil absently curled a tendril of hair that looped its way about her ear. Her hair was the color of fine-spun gold and he had longed to touch it, thinking of its softness between his fingers. He had wanted to marry Katie even after the first "scene" which had occurred on a soft spring evening after a film at the Brattle Theatre. They had walked slowly through Harvard Square which was strangely deserted. The spring term was over and summer school had not yet begun. A lone guitarist stood on the corner and strummed the melancholy folk songs which had been so popular that gentle spring.

> I *hashé*—Come with me
> You are young and you are free.

They stopped to look at the new prints in the window of Sehoenhof's and in the plate-glass reflection he saw tears streaking down Katie's face. She made no move to wipe them away or explain them. They walked on, still silent, and they had not broken step.

When he put his arm across her shoulder she shook it off with a sudden violence that frightened him, but at the apartment the silent tears became wild sobs. Her white skin grew pink and mottled and she held still at last when he bathed her face with a damp cloth and held her close, although she pummeled him with clenched fists, her head butting fiercely against his shoulders. Still, with gentle strength he held her and when at last the sobs stopped, he caressed her gently, his fingers massaging hers into calm, as he listened with heavy heart to the words she shot at him—small verbal volleys of anguish that made his own eyes fill and his heart grow tumid with despair.

"You must leave me, Aaron. I'm no good. I can't help it. I can't get close. No one comes close to me. If you do, you'll be sorry. Please go, Aaron. Please, please, please."

But he had not gone, not then and not on any other night through the months and years that followed. Each "scene" became a strand in a net which was woven closer and closer, entangling him inextricably with the frail blonde girl for whom his heart yearned and his body ached.

Once she told him that during her junior year at Sophie Newcomb College, perhaps because of the pressure of exams, she had experienced a time so dark that she had sought refuge in a small hospital. She had stayed there for some weeks and remembered it now only as a place of patterned walks and stone benches, shadowed rooms and patient voices that gently but insistently pursued her, wrestled with her. She had left abruptly one afternoon, the darkness and exhaustion vanquished.

"But why didn't you stay?" Aaron asked.

"It wasn't necessary. And I wanted to study for the law boards," she answered.

She had an incredible mind, finely honed, retentive, capable of seizing a problem, approaching it from all dimensions, unearthing its core, and molding it at last into a skillful argument. She was a better law student than Aaron and he watched with pride and a twinge of envy as she stood in her powder-blue wool ballerina skirt and matching blouse and argued winning cases in the law school moot court. In their senior year she published an article in a leading law journal and even before she passed the bar, legal scholars in distant cities called her for opinions on the new civil rights legislation on which she had published a lengthy thesis called "Separate Is Not Equal."

But it was only during this wedding trip to her home in New Orleans (he had wanted to come before but she had objected, raised arguments, canceled plans) that he had begun to understand the punishing drive that kept her at the library bent over old decisions, new interpretations, pursuing small threads of law and rolling them into a skein that she would unravel at last to strangle a small injustice, to gain a tiny, an almost infinitesimal legal victory in the long and endless battle to which they had committed themselves.

She had driven with him only one morning through the city of her childhood and she watched with set face as he registered for the first time the reality of segregation. They had traveled, on that sultry day, out past the old Metairie Cemetery where the dead were buried aboveground in vaults so that they would not decompose too quickly in the rich muddied Louisiana earth when the river overflowed its banks. Wilted flowers strung with faded ribbons lay on the mottled marble stone and he had looked away and reminded himself that they were taking this road past death to get to the Harmony Club, the Jewish country club, where their marriage reception would be held.

"Can we swim there?" he asked.

She shook her head.

"The pool is closed. But I'll tell you what. We'll borrow some suits there and swim down at Pontchartrain Beach."

It was late afternoon when they reached the beach and the rose-colored sand was brushed with gold and hard beneath their feet. They swam in the clear water and watched two small sailboats, each with bright red sails, flirt with each other as they skimmed across the smooth water that mirrored the muted dying sunlight. At the far end of the beach there was a wall of sea-smooth rock and although the rest of the beach was deserted, a large group of swimmers congregated there. Aaron looked more closely and saw that all of them were black. Katie followed his gaze.

"Now you understand. In America's Southland we accomplish God's work for him and divide up nature between the coloreds and the whites. That's their share of sea and sun, over there by the seawall."

Her voice was brittle and she told him then about her nursemaid Eula, a black girl, who had taken care of small Katie from her birth. When Katie was six or seven Eula had taken her to the beach and sat on the sand while Katie and her sisters cavorted in the water. Then she had gone for a swim in the section of the beach near the seawall.

"I followed her. I was always following her. I loved Eula. She was the only one who hugged and kissed me when I was a little girl. My daddy was always busy and my mother was rushing off to her clubs and bridge games. Sometimes I used to think that they thought hugging, touching, was too Jewish. Maybe Jews had been kept out of the Mardi Gras because they hugged each other too much." She laughed harshly and continued. "You don't understand that, I know, Aaron, because in your family there's so much touching."

Aaron did not reply but he thought of the long nights of his own childhood when he had waited in the silent darkness for the touch of his mother's lips, the gentle pressure of her hands-thinking always that this was the night she would forgive him at last for the mysterious sin he could not remember committing.

"Anyway," Katie had continued, "I followed Eula over to where she was swimming. She was beautiful, all coffee-colored, and heir laugh sounded like bells on a quiet afternoon. She was laughing with some boys and I rushed toward her, splashing like mad, thinking I'd be in their game. Aaron, she acted as though I were a stranger. 'Get back you, girl,' she yelled at me. I felt as though she had hit me. And you know, she never hugged me again. Never."

Katie clutched herself then, as though caught by a sudden chill, and he wrapped the towel about her shoulders which trembled although the day was still warm.

The long familiar silence, which he had come to recognize and fear, began then, and persisted through the days that followed. And last night she had vanished from a party in the midst of unwrapping gifts and he found her at last walking in the garden, silent tears coursing down her cheeks. He had known then that they hovered at the edge of a "scene" and he was relieved when Michael and young Melanie left the Vieux Carré nightclub early, knowing that Katie was poised at the brink of whirling misery.

It had come and run its course as he held and soothed her and now on his wedding morning, he sank back, exhausted by his bride's aching sorrow. But she would not always be this way, he assured himself, and passed his hand over a scratch on his shoulder where her long nail had scraped at his flesh as he held her tight in his grasp. A fleck of dried blood came off on his finger and he looked at it closely, as though it held the secret to an urgent riddle, then flicked it away impatiently. Everything would be all right, he told himself. They would create a home together and the warmth of their love would seal them against those cold winds that raged against Katie's calm and dragged her down into a whirling vortex of darkness. They would have children, small boys and girls with hair that glittered like amber in the sunlight or shone pale gold in the haze of wintry light. They would work together in the shared quiet of book-lined rooms and dash after each other down country lanes.

His lips curved into a smile and his eyes closed. Slowly he drifted back to sleep and did not hear the last bleat of a mournful saxophone as the funeral procession wound its way across Baronne Street to the Cemetery of Saint Vincent de Paul on the other side of town.

*

The wedding party that gathered that afternoon at the Touro Synagogue on Saint Charles Avenue was a large one and as the guests entered they blinked sharply, caught by the flash of the photographer from the *Picayune-Times*. The marriage of Judge Elias Reznikoff's lawyer daughter to the son of the designer and painter Leah Goldfeder and the New York psychoanalyst Dr. David Goldfeder was no small event in New Orleans. The society page would forgive their Jewishness, even utilize it as an exotic dimension to a clearly brilliant match.

Mollie and Seymour Hart arrived in the limousine they had hired for their stay in New Orleans and smiled beamingly into the camera. They were used to being photographed; their pictures were taken regularly at art auctions for various charities, Hadassah donor luncheons, Israel Bond kick-off dinners. Mollie cut the pictures from the newspapers and maintained a current montage in a gilt frame in their living room, showing them proudly to visitors. Seymour had retired and S. Hart Inc. was run now by his son Jakie, a pleasant plump young man who had developed a paunch and an ulcer although he was still in his early thirties. It was Jakie now who phoned his fashionably thin wife in Woodmere to tell her he was staying over in the city to entertain a buyer, to catch up on work, to meet with designers. But he would not prolong his extracurricular activities as long as Seymour had, David predicted. By forty-five Jake would be content to stay at home and watch television and dream about slender, smooth-skinned models who had glided in and out of his office and joined him in double beds at the Plaza and the Waldorf and on long weekends in Puerto Rico. It was difficult to look at Jakie and remember the frightened boy, newly arrived from Russia, who had not dared to go out into Eldridge Street without clutching Aaron's hand. But then, David reflected, within all the adults assembled in the gray-yellow brick synagogue there lurked the vanished children whose small voices still echoed back across the dangerous terrain of distant days and years.

Leah looked across the room to the corner where Katie stood between her parents. How beautiful the girl looked, but so pale and weary. Violet shadows stretched from below her eyes to her high ivory-shaded cheekbones, almost matching the spray of delicate gentians that rested on her white Bible. Her wedding dress, layered swathes of tulle and delicate lacework, time-faded into an eggshell color, had belonged to her grandmother who had been married in this very synagogue a century before.

Leah marveled at the luxury of heirlooms, of the miracle of a family remaining for an entire century in one place. Her own family had wandered throughout their generations, her grandparents fleeing the pogroms of Hungary to come to Poland, her own parents in turn seeking what they had thought would be greater protection in Russia, and finally she and Mollie emigrating to America and Moshe, her brother, to Palestine. What had happened to the beautiful wedding dress brought from Moscow for Mollie's marriage to the shy rabbinical student Seymour Hart had been in that other lost life? She smiled bitterly. She did not know the fate of her own parents, her relatives and friends, yet wondered about a vanished bridal gown. Still, David had told her once, such trivia provided people with their greatest emotional protection. How much simpler it is to worry over the number of miles one gets to the gallon than to think of the fate of a relative ill with cancer, or of swiftly passing years, or alienated, alienating children. It was simpler to worry over a wedding dress than to ponder the fate of her parents, the gentle Talmudic scholar and his gentler wife, whom she had last seen standing together in the half-light of a prewar dawn, their hands clutching the wooden porch railing of the house that had been her childhood home.

Such ghosts would never haunt Aaron and Katie, children of the American dream. True, Katie was often moody, abstracted, but that would pass when she had children. And she wanted children, Leah knew, because Katie had told her so herself. A large family, she had said—think of it, a row of children all with hair the color of burnished copper.

Leah and David stood together beneath the bower of flowers as the rabbi intoned the nuptial blessings. They turned to each other as Aaron's strong voice rang out in the ancient vow and he slipped a narrow gold band on Katie's finger. "Behold, with this ring you are consecrated unto me, according to the laws of Moses and of Israel."

Leah clutched David's hand.

"At last," she whispered. "Aaron is safely married."

But David did not reply. He had remembered, suddenly, the name of the patient whom Katie so powerfully brought to mind. Marilyn Turner had been her name. She had shared Katie's smile and soft voice, her powerful intellectual tenacity. She was involved in cancer research, haunted by her father's death during her childhood of a carcinoma of the colon. One afternoon, a week after the publication of a brilliant paper, she had gone up to the roof of her apartment house to sunbathe; still holding the blanket she had brought with her, she stepped out on the roof's edge and plummeted to the street below. David remembered the story well now, too well.

"*Mazel tov, mazel tov*, good luck!" Seymour Hart hugged David, his breath heavy with whiskey and tobacco.

"Yes. Thank you. *Mazel tov*. Good luck," he said and hurried to kiss his new daughter-in-law, feeling a strange compulsion, as though the touch of his lips might somehow keep her from danger.

20

Although his gallery did not open until the afternoon, it was Charles Ferguson's habit to arrive early, attend to clerical duties, read through catalogues and art journals, and slowly walk through the large, thickly carpeted room to look at his collection with as much interest as though he were seeing his paintings and sculptures for the first time. He then stepped out onto the street where he studied his display window, making a note to shift a particular painting from one location to another or to place a plant between a large sculpture and a small group of serial graphics. But on this particular spring morning he surveyed his window with pleasure, pleased with the two paintings displayed on twin easels. One was of an enormous butterfly, the winged creature poised on the stark canvas and given life in bright free strokes of gold and orange. The other was a primitive painting in bright acrylic colors showing a group of young farmers bending over rows of seedlings which seemed to dance out of the ground. The signatures on both paintings read "Goldfeder," and Charles dabbed fussily at a spot on the plate glass' and reflected proudly that he was probably the only gallery on Madison Avenue displaying the work of both a mother and a daughter. "Mr. Ferguson?"

He had not heard the quiet step of the small ferret-faced man who stole up beside him, an envelope in his hand. The man wore an overcoat although the day was warm, and spots of lint glinted whitely on his badly pressed pants.

"You are Mr. Charles Ferguson?" he asked and Charles braced himself for his usual speech to salesmen and unsolicited artist's agents.

"Yes, I'm Charles Ferguson, but I'm afraid I have a crowded schedule today. I've no time for appointments."

"I don't want an appointment," the little man said. "I just want you to take this."

He shoved the outstretched envelope into the gallery owner's hand and disappeared into the hurrying crowd of shoppers.

Charles looked at it in surprise, then opened it and withdrew a single sheet of paper. It was the stationery of the United States Senate and it informed him in terse legal phraseology that he was required to appear as a witness in the federal building on Church Street in a week's time. He read it again and felt an arrow of fear pierce his heart with sudden pain. Only the night before he had been at a party and watched a well-known writer down drink after drink. The writer, someone explained to Charles, who had never seen the man drink before, had been called as a witness that afternoon. Before the Committee. There was no need to explain which committee, and Charles had left the party early and had not bothered to read the newspaper that night.

He read the subpoena in his hand again, searched through his wallet for a card, and then went inside and closed the door of his office. He dialed the number slowly and when the phone was answered, he hesitated for a moment as though unsure of whom he had been calling. It was with an effort, in an old man's voice, that he at last said, "Mr. Aaron Goldfeder. Charles Ferguson calling." He doodled on the pad beside his desk, fashioned a drawing of dancing flames, then crushed it with a nervous fist. "Aaron, how are you?" he said into the phone. "I'm sorry to bother you, but the thing is I've received a subpoena. To appear before the Committee. I know you're busy but..."

An hour later, he was downtown in the small law office which Aaron Goldfeder shared with his wife, Katie. The newspaper rested on a table but he did not look down at the picture of the Senator from Wisconsin who brandished a pointed pencil as though it were a lethal weapon.

*

David Goldfeder, seated in an uptown office, did glance at the morning paper as his old friend, Dr. Sydney Adler, settled himself behind the polished mahogany desk, shuffled the papers in front of him, picked up a ringing phone to offer a curt monosyllabic reply, and fumbled with a cigar wrapper.

"So David, how is life treating you?" the portly internist asked. "Is Leah well? And the children?"

David took a long puff on his pipe. Syd Adler was procrastinating too much, spending too much time on small talk. He had spent a quarter of an hour locating an irrelevant X ray taken at least three years ago. The news must be bad. Well, he could always wait for bad news. He blew a smoke ring, watched it wreathe its way around Syd's head, and told him of the success of Aaron's law practice, of Michael's record at Princeton. Syd was bald now, a small halo of gray hair fringing his forehead. David remembered sitting in back of Syd in a pathology laboratory and watching his friend's too-long hair curl about his shirt collar. None of them could afford the time or the money for a barber in those days when they struggled together through medical school. Well, they had the time and money now but Syd had lost his hair. David smiled.

"And what do you hear from Tom Boder?" Syd asked.

The news must be really bad, David thought, if Syd was dredging up classmates neither of them had thought about for years. He shrugged and looked pointedly at his watch.

"I have a patient due in about forty-five minutes," he said.

"Don't worry. At least your patients don't die if you're late. Your daughter's still living on that kibbutz. She hasn't made you a grandfather yet?"

"Well, there are two children from her husband's first marriage and a little girl they adopted. I expect they'll have their own soon."

He did not tell Syd that Rebecca had miscarried twice and he worried about her although her letters remained cheerful and optimistic. The new young kibbutz in the Negev heartland was flourishing and their last season had been a good one with a bumper crop of avocadoes. Avocadoes. David had never even seen an avocado before he was forty and now his daughter cultivated them in the sands of a distant desert. Rebecca's painting too was satisfying. She had at last developed her own bright primitive technique, accomplished with layers of heavy acrylic paints. Her paintings were displayed in Paris and London, and often, on his way home, he walked past Charles Ferguson's gallery for the joy of his daughter's work and his wife's, displayed in the same window. Yes. Rebecca was settled and happy. He was glad he could say that about at least one of his children.

"What about Peter Cosgrove's widow?" Syd continued, his eyes raking over the report he held in his hand. "That pretty woman. A friend of your wife's, wasn't she?"

"Yes. Bonnie. Bonnie remarried. A surgeon from Atlanta. In fact, she and her family were at my son Aaron's wedding two years ago. Everyone looking very well."

"Well, Aaron certainly picked himself a pretty wife. And a brilliant one."

The comment surprised David. Syd had not come to Aaron's wedding and he could not remember introducing him to Katie on any other occasion.

"You've met Katie?" he asked.

"Oh yes. A few months ago. When you sent her to me. I must tell you I was a bit annoyed about your sending her to me for that kind of information, David. Your sources are as good as mine. Still, I imagine you wanted an objective referral. At least, that's what she said. In any case I gave her the name of Dr. Hernandez in San Juan. A good solid man. And I assume there's been no problem as I haven't heard from her since."

"No. No problem." Why had Katie lied to Syd Adler, he wondered, but knew that he would not ask her.

David allowed his pipe to go out, remembering now that Katie had flown to Puerto Rico alone for a weekend holiday some months earlier. She had been tired and Aaron was too involved in a case to join her. She just wanted a weekend in the sun, she had said in the soft quiet voice which generally meant she would have her own way. She had returned with the same pallor she wore when she left.

But of course there was very little sunlight in Dr. Hernandez's maternity clinic, a small cluster of pastel-colored buildings not far from the beach where more babies were aborted than born. Angrily, David tapped his pipe on the desk, shaking the dead ashes into Syd Adler's large ceramic ashtray.

"All right, Syd," he said. "Enough small talk. What's the situation?"

"What's the situation? You tell me. You're a doctor. You're fifty-nine years old. A busy man with a superactive schedule, working twelve, thirteen hours a day at a sedentary job that demands absolute concentration. Your younger years were stressful, exhausting, and not spectacular for their concentration on nutrition, exercise, and rest. You've also undergone a terrific strain—given the combination of your war work and Aaron's situation. The heart, my friend, as we both learned, is made of muscle, not cast iron. You've been overworking it. Tightness in the chest, constriction in the arm. You recognized the symptoms before you got here," Syd Adler replied in the same dry tones David had heard him use earlier when he had answered a call from his son asking for an advance on his allowance which had been refused.

"The symptoms I knew. But not the extent of the damage," he said. "What did the electrocardiogram show?"

"Not much. No damage. Minimal strain. As far as your heart is concerned, if you act like a normal human being you'll live to be an incontinent old man boring too many grandchildren. But you've got to curtail your schedule. Work less. Play more. Take up golf maybe."

"Golf!" David snorted.

"All right. Not golf. Travel. The only time your condition could become dangerous is if you undergo a severe strain. You have a prescription and I'll depend upon you to use it properly. But you have to make some changes, create a break.

"Take a trip to Israel. Visit Rebecca and her family. You've never even met her husband, David."

"Yes. We would have gone long before this but Leah cannot leave her sister now. She wants to be with Mollie until the end."

Sydney nodded. He was Mollie Hart's doctor and it was he who two years earlier had diagnosed the tumor which had lodged itself in the cheerful plump woman's abdomen as a malignant carcinoma. There had been immediate surgery but he had not needed the pathologist's report to tell him that the insidious cancer had metastasized and invaded both liver and kidney. The infinitesimal cells of death burgeoned wildly on the soft masses of flesh and tissue and would not be subdued by the surgeon's knife or the blinding rays of the cobalt machine. For two years now, the cancerous cells had spread, feeding like molecular maggots on Mollie's flesh, weighing her down with a pain so heavy she could not sustain it. Confined to her bed, she relied more and more on massive injections of Demerol and for months she had lived in a shadowy, airborne world, speaking the Yiddish of her childhood, remembering distant days, vanished years. Through this clearing in her wilderness of pain, she called alternately for her mother and her son and cried out to an absent Shimon, asking why he did not send for her. She too wanted to go to America, the *goldene medine*—the land of riches and plenty. The days of her dying were passed in the distant time of longing and loneliness. Leah visited her sister almost every day, carrying fresh flowers which Mollie never noticed, answering plaintive questions in a firm calm voice although her eyes were often hot with tears and her fingers trembled so that the pen-and-ink sketches she made of the dying woman wept and wavered their way across the crisp white paper of her pad.

"Still, David," Seymour continued, "you must think about rearranging your schedule. You're a doctor. I don't have to spell the prognosis out to you if you continue to work at the crazy pace you think is normal."

"I consider myself warned," David said seriously. "I will try to lighten my patient load and I promise that when we can, Leah and I will go to Israel and spend several months doing nothing but getting to know our daughter again."

"Fair enough," the internist said. "Take care, David. And send my regards to your beautiful daughter-in-law. Tell her I'd much rather refer her to a good obstetrician than to Hernandez's clinic."

"I'll do that, Syd," David replied. He had never referred her to Syd Adler although she had often heard his friend's name mentioned in their home. He could not confront Aaron's wife with his knowledge of her lies, which he knew to be symptomatic of an illness. She was burdened by an emotional neoplasm which, like Mollie's terrible cancer, multiplied and swelled, threatening that marriage so bravely begun in the brightness of the Louisiana summer. The disease had always been there, David knew and had known it for years, but now it was spreading with dangerous momentum and he, the doctor, was paralyzed by that knowledge and by his love for the tall red-headed young man whom he had raised as his own son.

*

"Joshua Ellenberg, please." Aaron frowned again at the paper he held in his hand and listened to the rapid succession of clicks until a young woman's voice said with forbidding officiousness, "Mr. Ellenberg's office. Who's calling please?"

"Aaron Goldfeder," he replied and imagined his boyhood friend behind that enormous teak desk, swiveling about in a huge blue leather contour chair, the exact shade of the thick blue carpet that lined his office, which looked more like an elaborate suburban living room than a place of business. Aaron's own office was small and austere, as was Katie's in the adjoining room, but then a civil rights practice was not the most lucrative and, as Katie pointed out, she spend most of her time in law libraries or in Washington and Aaron had never been comfortable in luxurious surroundings.

"Aaron, how are you?" Joshua came on the phone at once. Any call from the Goldfeder family was immediately accepted.

"Good. Can we have lunch today, Joshua? It's important," Aaron said.

"I'm scheduled to have lunch with a buyer from I. Magnin. He's flown in especially."

"It's important," Aaron repeated.

"All right. One o'clock here."

An hour later the two friends were seated across from each other in Joshua's private dining room overlooking the East River. Through the window they watched the progress of a small tugboat which bobbed up and down on aqueous hillocks of foam. It occurred to Aaron that the luxurious room in which they sat was only blocks away from the Eldridge Street apartment where they had spent their shared boyhood.

"All right, Aaron. What's so important?" Joshua pushed away his unfinished tuna salad plate and poured more coffee for both of them.

"Charles Ferguson's been subpoenaed by the Committee. I met with him this morning. Shortly afterward I received a call from Vermont. Eleanor Greenstein's been called as well. I don't have to tell you what an ugly business the Committee can be." Aaron's tone was heavy and he took out a cigarette although he seldom smoked.

"Charles and Eleanor. Hmm. The only thing they have in common really is your mother," Joshua said thoughtfully.

"Exactly. They both knew her during the same period. The Committee's been going after creative people with a vengeance. Theater people. Writers. Katie's been representing some of them in Washington. I guess they're launching an invasion on the art world now."

"Leah hasn't been subpoenaed?"

"No, not yet."

"I see."

"I want to know as much as possible about those years, Joshua. The years my mother worked at Rosenblatts. That abortive union business. The fire."

"Aaron, I was a kid then. Ten, maybe eleven years old. I was an errand boy. What could I know?" Joshua protested.

"Joshua, I know you and I know you well enough to be sure that as a kid of eleven you knew as much about what was going on as any grownup. And what you didn't know then you've probably learned or surmised since. I've got to have that information if I'm to give Charles and Eleanor any kind of representation and if I'm to help my mother. She's the one they'll get to next, I'm sure," Aaron said.

"All right. You may not like all of it but I'll tell you what I know." Joshua leaned back in his chair and the fingers of his good hand stroked the wrist to which his black leather prothesis was strapped. It had begun to ache as it always did when something unnerved him, upset him.

An hour later Aaron walked out of Joshua Ellenberg Enterprises carrying a small black book filled with names and dates. He remembered Eli Feinstein's name now and he remembered, too, that long hot summer decades past when the ghost of polio roamed the streets of the lower east side and he and Rebecca and Aaron had been sent to the mountains for the summer. That fiery summer had ended in the flames that consumed Rosenblatts. Now those same flames reached across the years and threatened to consume the lives they had labored for so strenuously. Somehow he would have to protect his mother, Aaron knew. Somehow. He reached into his pocket and withdrew the subpoena Charles Ferguson had received that morning. He had two weeks in which to work.

21

The white stone federal building on Church Street was not air-conditioned and the windows in the hearing room on the third floor could not be opened. The room had been painted that winter, and congealed scabs of oily olive-green paint sealed the windows and resisted the mallet thrusts of the sweating workmen who struggled with them. The cloying odor of paint hung over the cavernous chamber in an odiferous veil, and when fans were brought in the moving air wafted the ugly smell from one side of the room to the other and lifted small clouds of dust from forgotten corners.

Aaron and Katie Goldfeder had arrived early, and as they spread their papers on a large golden oak conference table, a nervous cleaning woman circled them with a damp mop.

"The witch hunters from Washington see Communists in dust motes," Aaron muttered. "She'd better be careful or she'll be subpoenaed as part of an environmental conspiracy engineered by the Kremlin."

"Hmmm. Maybe if I defended her she'd come in and do the apartment," Katie replied. "Well, here it all is. I think it will work, Aaron."

She handed him a stapled sheath of mimeographed papers with a top sheet that read "The Rosenblatt Experience." He glanced at it and slowly leafed through it although he knew its contents as well as Katie did. For the last two weeks, since the day Charles Ferguson had sat before him, the subpoena twisted in his hand, he had lived and breathed life at Rosenblatts, the factory whose name was still synonymous with avarice and exploitation, fire and death. He had flown to Atlanta and met with his mother's friend Bonnie, who still wept when she thought of that day. Bonnie had opened a large candy box and shown him news clippings, yellowed photographs, a scrap of pink organdy, its charred edges crumbling to ashes beneath his touch.

"It was the dress I wore that day. I had just finished it. It was the first dress I ever designed and made. They took me home wrapped in a bolt of cloth. Leah had used that cloth to beat out the flames on my dress and this scrap is all that was left of the dress itself. The girl who worked the machine next to me—Goldie was her name and she was to be married that week—the flames caught the hem of her dress, her hair, she was a torch of fire that ran and danced until she fell to the ground. I'll never forget it, never."

The prosperous Atlanta matron sat on the terrace of her home in bright sunshine and shivered in remembered terror. She gave him the box of mementos and made him promise that he would call her as a witness if he needed her.

"There is nothing that I would not do for your mother," Bonnie said. "Leah gave me my life."

He had traveled upstate to a small farming community and visited the chubby grandmother who had been the tiny factory girl, Philomena Visconti. Philomena too had her collection of clippings which included obituaries in the Italian newspapers of her father, Salvatore Visconti, who had worked closely with Eli Feinstein and died with him in the wilderness of flames.

"They were men who saw the bad and worked for the good," Philomena told him. "They wanted to change things, not the whole world, but the bad things in their world. Instead those things killed them. My father was forty-six and his friend Eli Feinstein was not even forty. They called him a saint, my father's friend Eli, and even though he was Jewish, in every church on the east side they lit candles for him and said Novenas. Such a man who believed in good and work and love. I remember him well and of course I remember your mother. Your beautiful mother."

Aaron spent hours in the library of the I.L.G.W.U, building. He read reports of the fledgling union which had been in formation at Rosenblatts and he read of Arnold Rosenblatt's angry determined resistance. "Communist instigators, subversives," the manufacturer had declared.

"He was ahead of his time," Aaron muttered and doggedly continued to copy the material. Arnold Rosenblatt would have found a good home in Washington, where former friends nervously crossed the street to avoid talking to each other and the word "subversive" was whispered nervously at coffee counters and in library stacks.

In the union library he also found a small pamphlet by Eli Feinstein, a naive political treatise quoting Debs and Marx, Dubinsky and Weber. The Committee would have a ball with it, Aaron thought, and photostated it carefully.

He returned from the union library to his office that day and found his father standing in front of his window.

"Joshua tells me you are interested in the time of the Rosenblatt fire," David said. "Perhaps I can help you. Come. Let's go for a walk."

They strolled along the esplanade by the river and sat at last on a bench. The river breeze moistened their faces and they both took off their jackets and loosened their ties.

"I like this place," David said. "When our ship, the one we came to this country on, approached New York harbor, I went out on deck and looked across to the shore. A man wearing a white straw hat leaned on the railing and he looked over to the ship, I don't know if he saw us clearly but he lifted his hat and waved it. We were welcomed. I took it as an omen, a good omen."

"You've had a good life here," Aaron said, but the statement was suspended like a question between them.

"Yes. But complicated. And perhaps the most complicated time was the time you are so interested in now. The years your mother worked at Rosenblatts when she knew Eli Feinstein. You know now that they loved each other."

Aaron nodded.

"He was a fine man. A remarkable man. I have some things here that may help you. I went after the fire to his room. There were no relatives and your mother had been the person closest to him but she was sick with grief. So I went to do what I could. I saved his records of the union, some speeches, the minutes of the meetings. From them you can see how innocent, how Utopian his dreams were. You have the financial records there too. People making five, six dollars a week, gave fifty cents of it to a strike fund, a milk fund. Also, I saved the eulogies from his funeral. You may need perhaps quotations from Stephen Wise, David Dubinsky." David passed a frayed manila portfolio to his son and continued to stare out across the water. A small scow trundled by and plowed up furrows of foam and a man on board leaned forward and studied the harbor.

"Dad," Aaron said. "You knew everything and you didn't mind?"

"I minded. It tore me apart. But your mother and I did not marry because of love. It was her right, then, to find love. She found it with Eli Feinstein. She had protected herself, since her first husband's death, with a barricade of grief and it was Feinstein, not me, who penetrated that barricade, who brought your mother to life again. I cannot say what would have happened if he had not died in the fire. Sometimes, God help me, I was glad of that fire, of the man's death. I'm not a saint, Aaron. But he did die and he had freed her for love again. That love found my own. We've had a good life, Aaron, and we've tried to give you and your brother and sister good lives. Now, Joshua tells me, you try in turn to give us something." David smiled, touched his son's shoulder.

"I didn't want you to be hurt," Aaron said.

David had left then, walking very slowly, his face lifted to the gentle river wind, and Aaron had taken the portfolio back to his office where he and Katie had studied its contents far into the night. In the end they integrated much of it into the report and attached the eulogies as Appendices.

He fingered the report now and glanced at the door. The room was slowly filling. Lawyers for the Committee were taking their seats at the long conference table, assembling their notebooks, hissing nervously into the small microphones. But it was the small section reserved for the press which interested Aaron, and he watched as the first group of reporters filed in and let out a sigh of relief. Each reporter carried a copy of "The Rosenblatt Experience."

"They have it," he whispered to Katie.

"Of course. I told you we could rely on Joe Abramson to make sure the press would get it. And they're reading it already."

Charles Ferguson slipped into the seat next to Aaron, shook his hand hurriedly. The older man's palm was wet and his knees shook beneath the table.

"You're sure the Senator won't be here?" he asked Aaron.

"I'm sure. This is just a fishing trip, Charles. A preliminary hearing. The Senator won't touch you until he knows he can make some waves. He's sent these jokers up to see if anything is jumping." He waved toward the table and looked curiously at two of the young lawyers who sat there, studying a single document. He knew one of them well. Danny Cole had been in his year at the law school and he had been a good student with one major fault. He had always looked for shortcuts. Well, he had found a shortcut to power but it was too bad, too damn bad. Aaron didn't have too much sympathy to waste on Danny Cole, who had been known, in his time, to cheat at chess.

It was Danny Cole who began the questioning as soon as Charles Ferguson was sworn in. It took him a few minutes to establish that Charles was an art dealer who had taught for years at the Irvington Settlement House. "Of course, during those years Mr. Ferguson had taught many artists who rose to national prominence. Did any particular name come to mind?" It was a calm, unhurried question. Danny Cole glanced out the window, fingered his tie, smiled reassuringly at Charles.

"No particular name," Charles said and the word "name" itself made people glance at each other and look away. Each day for months, afternoon headlines had screamed about one Hollywood writer who had "named names" and another who had steadfastly refused to "name names." America had a new vocabulary and old words had taken on chimerical meanings. It was David who had observed wryly that people were no longer "friends" but "acquaintances."

"What about the well-known designer and painter, Leah Goldfeder. Isn't it true that she studied with you?"

"Yes. She was my student until she went to work."

"Ah. Until she went to work at a place called Rosenblatts?" Danny consulted his notebook and when he looked up Aaron was standing.

"Counselor, it's very opportune that you mention the name Rosenblatts. When my client told me he had been summoned here it occurred to me that you might have some interest in that particular period in his life. I therefore prepared some material which might spare you and this committee a good deal of time."

He stepped forward with the stack of reports and noticed that Danny Cole had begun to sweat. His hair was damp and rings of dark blue had formed beneath the arms of his light jacket.

"I think you are out of order, Mr. Goldfeder," he said.

"Oh? Then I apologize. But since some members of the press have somehow obtained this report I thought it might be efficacious for the Committee to study it."

The members of the press were now rustling the pages of the report and two men had already left the room. Others were making rapid pencil notes. Danny Cole glanced nervously at his colleagues and cleared his throat. An older attorney leaned forward.

"I think, Mr. Cole, that this panel should have access to any material which has somehow made its way to the press. It was very kind of Mr. Goldfeder to prepare copies for us as well. If you please, Mr. Goldfeder."

Aaron nodded and handed the pile of reports to a court messenger to distribute to the men at the conference table. He sat down beside Katie, who had not looked up from her pad.

"They will recess," she said in a low voice, "until this afternoon. Then they will adjourn."

Danny Cole coughed.

"We will recess this hearing until three o'clock this afternoon to give this panel an opportunity to peruse this, uh, report," he said.

There was a low murmur in the room and a shuffling of chairs.

"Congratulations, Goldfeder. It looks like you've made them cut bait," a smiling reporter from the newspaper PM said. "You'd better get extra help at your gallery, Mr. Ferguson. You're going to be swamped."

Charles Ferguson looked at Aaron in surprise.

"What happened here? What have you done?" he asked.

"It was all Katie's idea," Aaron said. "She'll explain."

"Actually another lawyer had the idea a while ago. A woman writer was called before the Committee and it was known that they would try to get her to give the names of people she had known in various committees, forums. Her lawyer prepared a press release saying that she was perfectly prepared to discuss her own activities and affiliations but would not discuss anyone else. Because the press already had the statement, the Committee was left with very little wind in their sails. They couldn't pretend to great surprise at her intransigence. In the end they excused her. It occurred to me that the same thing would work here. It we furnished the press with all the information on Rosenblatts and the sort of man Eli Feinstein was, the work of the union, it would tear away all the suppressed hints of scandal and leftist operations. The committee specializes in the veiled allusion, but we gave the press whole cloth. If a lawyer says 'Isn't it true that Arnold Rosenblatt felt that the union Leah and Feinstein were involved in was subversive and Communistic?' the implication is that it was. But if we give them background material on Rosenblatt and on the people involved, they're foiled. There's danger in rumor and hint, but documented evidence and corroborated statements can overturn that sort of thing." Katie snapped the lock on her briefcase. "*I* won't stay for this afternoon, Aaron. You don't need me."

"But don't you want to stay?" Aaron asked.

"I'm very tired."

"I know."

Katie had worked day and night on this report since the afternoon he had arrived home from Joshua's office and discussed the situation with her. She had conceived of the idea and written the documentation. It had been Katie who found Joe Abramson, a public relations man with years of courthouse experience, who had taken over the job of contacting the press. Now the days and nights of work had left their mark. Dark circles curled beneath her eyes and her white skin had the fragile, translucent look of a sand-thin seashell.

"Go home," he said softly and put his hand on hers. Her upturned palm was ice-cold to his touch. He watched as she walked to the door, then turned away, a heavy sadness dragging down the elation he had felt moments before.

Katie was right, of course. The hearing reconvened after lunch and was almost immediately adjourned. The afternoon papers were already on the street and the second page of PM carried an ancient photograph of Eli Feinstein with the caption UNSUNG HERO OF EARLY ORGANIZED LABOR. An enterprising Post reporter had already been to see Philomena and obtained a snapshot of her father, and Charles Ferguson had had a call from the *Times* asking if they could photograph Leah Goldfeder's large painting *Lost in Flames*. Eleanor Greenstein had received a call from Washington quashing her subpoena.

Aaron held a brief, spontaneous news conference on the steps of the federal building.

"Mr. Goldfeder," a reporter asked, "how do you interpret what happened here today?"

"I think today we proved again what my parents and others knew when they came to this country. We proved that in America the truth counts for more than the implication and that the people will not stand by and allow the country to be taken over by sneers and smears, allegations and insinuation," he said and was surprised at the sudden quiet that greeted his words. Then someone clapped and soon the small group of reporters had put down their pencils and offered Aaron a very rare tribute—the applause of newsmen.

At the bottom of the steps, Michael waited for him.

"Hey, Aaron, everything over already?" he asked.

"We're adjourned. Hey, what are you doing here? I thought you were supposed to be holed up in the Halls of Nassau studying for your graduate record exams."

"Yeah. Well, I got a ride in and I thought I'd hear you give your argument. Only I thought you'd be giving it in a hearing room, not on the steps." Michael grinned. He had just noticed that he was taller than his brother and the knowledge pleased him.

"Well, you missed that but I can still buy you a drink. Come on. We'll celebrate," Aaron said and threw his arm over Michael's shoulder. It was Katie he had thought to celebrate with and he thought ruefully of the reservations he had made at the small French restaurant on Sixty-ninth street. Well, he would cancel them and he would not make such reservations again in a hurry. Still, he was being unfair. She was tired, exhausted. Poor Katie. The two words clicked together like magnetic marbles in his mind, and he took Michael's arm and hurried him across the street.

It was only when they were seated at a corner table in the small, dimly lit bar, which had lost its luncheon crowd and not yet filled up with its after-work drinkers, that Aaron turned to his brother.

"Okay, Mike," he said. "What brought you into New York?"

"I told you. One of the guys was driving in so I thought I'd grab the ride, listen to you defend the republic, and run up to see Aunt Mollie. Mom wrote and asked me to try to work in a visit. How is she?" Michael fingered his drink but his eyes did not meet Aaron's.

"Not good," Aaron said shortly. "Not good at all. Katie and I were there over the weekend. We thought we'd take Uncle Seymour out for a ride but he wouldn't leave the house. It's funny, after all those years he spent running around—screwing every model at S. Hart, flying to Miami for nonexistent dress shows—now he won't leave Mollie's side even though half the time she doesn't recognize him. When she does she calls him Shimon and he calls her Malcha. It's hard to believe after all those years listening to them scream that their names were Mollie and Seymour. But I guess you're too young to remember those days. Listen, Mike, let's have a drink and then you tell me what you're really doing here. It's hard to believe that you came down to be the dutiful nephew."

He stared hard at his brother, so suddenly become a man. Since Michael's childhood Aaron had known instinctively when something was troubling the younger boy. They shared an electric rapport although a dozen years separated them in age. More and more Aaron felt Michael to be his contemporary, sharing his feelings, understanding with peculiar precosity situations complex and undefined. Often, during the two years of his marriage, when he thought of talking to someone about Katie, it had occurred to him that he might drive to Princeton and talk to Michael. He regretted, at those times, the promise he'd given Katie years before, that he would never discuss her with his father. But Michael, after all, was so young. It would have been unfair to burden him with problems he might not even comprehend and in the end Aaron had talked to no one.

Their drinks had arrived and Michael stirred his rum Collins with a red plastic swizzle stick and took a long sip before he spoke.

"The thing of it is, I'm not sure I want to take the graduate record exams. I'm not sure I want to go to M.I.T. for graduate work at all. At least not now. Maybe in a couple of years, but not now. After."

"After what?" Aaron put a finger into his bourbon and licked the drink like a small child. Bourbon was not his drink. It was

Katie's, but she had so taken over his life and thoughts that often in restaurants he ordered dishes that she preferred, bought his shirts in the tones of pale blue that she favored, chose films that she wanted to see, books that she had mentioned reading.

"After the army. I want to go to Korea, Aaron. I'm sorry I let everyone talk me out of it two years ago. I should have served then."

"And now you've missed it all," Aaron said dryly.

He took a long drink and the bourbon seared his throat.

"You know, Michael, war's not much fun. The only souvenirs you get are stray bullets where you don't need them. That is, if you're lucky enough to stay alive. You wouldn't remember my friend Gregory Liebowitz. We were going to change the world together. Bring in a new era of freedom. It was the year of the people and Mother Bloor smiled down on all of us. We were going to take from the rich, give to the poor. Wipe out starvation and unemployment. People said things like that back in the thirties and they even believed them. And Gregory, the poor bastard, said them loudest of all. Now, of course, Uncle Joe McCarthy sits in Washington calling people like that dangerous to democracy. Dangerous. Naive, maybe, simplistic, yes, but God, they weren't dangerous. The only thing Gregory ever was a threat to was himself. But he put on battle fatigues and went to Ethiopia to keep the world safe for democracy. He died there. Of diarrhea. You don't even get a Purple Heart for diarrhea, Mike." The bitterness in his own tone shocked him and he ordered another drink. It had been years since he thought of Gregory, of the long weeks in Ethiopia, of the small boy who had carried his father's head in his arms.

"I remember Gregory, I think," Michael said. "Look, Aaron, you're talking to me as though I'm some kind of a kid. I'm twenty-one. I'm graduating from college. My whole life I've been the kid, the little boy. No one seems to have noticed that somehow I grew up. I'm not Leah and David's little boy any more. Rebecca wasn't much older than me when she went to Europe and then to Palestine.

When she fought in the War for Independence. But me—I've spent my whole life in Scarsdale and Princeton and now everyone expects me to finish up with a stretch in the libraries and laboratories of exotic Cambridge. Wow!"

Impatiently he downed his drink and coughed as the liquor briefly choked him.

"The world's blowing up around us, with that McCarthy circus in Washington and the crazy 'military action' in Korea, and I'm supposed to drink coffee in Harvard Square." He stared glumly out the window and saw with satisfaction that it had begun to rain. It was a late spring drizzle and the tiny droplets were shot with dancing prisms as they fell.

"What do you want to do with your life, Mike?" Aaron asked quietly.

"You mean eventually, finally? All right. I do want to get that advanced degree at M.I.T. I want to be an engineer. A designing engineer. I'm good at it and I like it and I think I'll be able to do important work, useful work."

Aaron smiled. None of them had been immune, after all. All three Goldfeder children had caught David's fever for "useful" work, for small assaults on enormous problems, for the kindling of tiny flames against an ever-widening darkness.

"Right now I want to do something different, something exciting. That's why I thought of Korea. It's not war, I'm looking for, Aaron, you know me better than that." Michael looked up and met his brother's eyes. He had never noticed before that Aaron's thick auburn-colored brows were slivered with silver.

"All right. I can understand that. But I think you can find what you're looking for without putting on a uniform and going to oversee an artificial peace on an artificial parallel. I like Ike too, but I don't think he knows what he's going to do in Korea. Southeast Asia is a big can of worms. We've opened it up but we don't know where to go fishing with it. You don't want to be part of an army that isn't even sure it's an army. You can get a deferment. You don't want to become a lieutenant just because that little twirp Melanie thinks uniforms are cute," Aaron said.

"Stop picking on Melanie. We're just friends. Anyway, she's Katie's cousin and she's a lot like Katie."

"She's nothing like Katie," Aaron said with a harshness that surprised them both. In appeasement, he ordered another round of drinks and held his glass apologetically up to his brother. "If I were you, Aaron, I'd think about heading for the Middle East. For Israel. You could spend some time with Rebecca. Tour the country. Maybe even spend a year working on a kibbutz in a border area. At least you won't be wearing a uniform and you won't be carrying a gun unless you have to."

"Israel," Michael repeated. "That's a thought. It's funny. I just read an article in an engineering journal by a scientist who teaches at the Technion in Haifa. They're doing a lot of interesting bridge suspension work there. I was thinking that I wouldn't mind seeing their setup. And God, I've missed Becca. I can't imagine her a little kibbutz woman. Maybe you've got something, Aaron. It's an idea. A real idea. Thanks."

He grinned in embarrassment at his brother who thought wistfully that in a different year he might have reached across the table and ruffled Michael's hair. But they were men now and met for drinks in a dimly lit bar.

"Sure," he said. "And Mike—I didn't mean to put you down."

He looked down. His glass was empty. He did not want another drink and he did not want to go home.

"Well, I'd better take off if I'm going to see Aunt Mollie and grab my ride back. See you, Aaron."

They gripped hands and Michael was out the door. Aaron watched him streak by, a tall thin young man whose black-and-orange scarf dangled over his shoulder. The rain had stopped and the street shimmered wetly in the beginning darkness. Aaron paid the bill and checked his attaché case. He had three copies of "The Rosenblatt Experience" for their files. It had been a long day and quite suddenly he was in a hurry to get home. Perhaps it would be different tonight. Perhaps.

22

Mollie Hart died on a fall morning and although those who mourned her stood in a circle of liquid sunlight that formed about the dark earth of her freshly dug grave, they shivered as a stray wind breathed out the warning of winter. Newly yellowed leaves gleamed on the tall elms that lined the cemetery lanes, and overhead a lonesome line of birds streaked darkly through the gray-blue sky, winging their way southward. Mollie's children, Jakie and Annie, huddled together, their families beside them, arms touching, fingers intertwined, but Seymour Hart stood alone. He swayed from side to side as he intoned the Kaddish, the prayer for the dead. His body trembled with each word and he moved in the remembered pattern of the days of his boyhood when those who worshiped with him in the small Russian prayer house released their bodies to the winds of prayer. His voice rose and fell in melodious chant and his children stared at him as though he had become a stranger to them. When he stepped forward toward the grave into which the light coffin that held Mollie's withered body had been lowered, tears streaked his face. He clenched a handful of earth, felt it grit beneath his fingernails, and dropped it at last onto the pale fragrant wood. He shivered violently at the sound of its soft thud and did not look to see how the clump of earth shattered into small black grains that wept their way across the rough, unvarnished surface of the plain pine coffin.

Leah and David moved forward together but it was a flower, a golden autumn zinnia from her own garden that Leah allowed to flutter down, while David bent and gently placed within the grave a smooth stone which he had carried in his pocket for weeks.

Annie and her husband, Jakie and his wife, approached together and the young women pressed their faces against the rough fabric of their husbands' jackets and did not look as their own earth offerings drifted down. But Aaron Goldfeder came forth alone and used a small spade to place the first shovelful of ground covering on the naked coffin. A small pebble, caught in the humous dirt, echoed sharply against the light wood. It was a lonely sound and he moved back, his face burning suddenly at the awareness of his own aloneness at this place of death and farewell, where couples moved together, supporting each other with touch and word. Only the widower stood alone and Aaron went to his uncle and put his arm around the quaking shoulders that had so often supported him, a sleepy small boy, mounting the steps of the Eldridge Street tenement or the Brighton Beach house. His uncle had smelled of tobacco and camphor and the wild-cherry cough drops that he bought in brown paper sacks and gave to small children for a treat. But today his uncle smelled of grief and loss and the mildewed pages of the ancient prayer book he carried with him.

"Katie wanted to be here but she didn't feel well," he told Seymour and wondered if his uncle believed him.

Katie had arrived home from Washington late the night before, so late in fact that they had not had a chance to discuss her appearance before the Committee. Still, she had awakened with him that morning and had watched, through heavy-lidded eyes, as he dressed.

"You have to come to Mollie's funeral with me. It will kill my family if you don't."

She had turned away, her cheek brushing the white pillowcase that matched her own snow-pale skin.

"You know I hate going to funerals."

The huge violet eyes had closed and her nose quivered as though the scent of death had seeped into the room. Her splayed fingers, clutching the blanket tightly, whitened and he saw that her nails were ragged and knew that she had bitten them on the plane.

"Poor Katie," he thought and wondered when it was that pity finally cancelled out love, that compassion negated passion. "Please," he said. "I'm not going."

Her voice had become querulous and he had not wanted an argument, knowing that when he argued with Katie at such times there could be neither gain nor satisfaction. His small victories turned into desperate defeats as she wept wildly or stared at him with wide empty eyes, abandoned to a depression that would hold her prisoner for days.

"It's all right. Don't go," he had said, straining to keep his voice even, his tone unaccusing.

And so he stood alone now beside his uncle, his arm on the older man's shoulders, which grew still beneath his touch.

"Yes. I know. Leah told me. She's a good girl, your Katie," Seymour said. "So pretty. My Mollie was a pretty girl too. In Russia sometimes, when we were first married, before the children came, we went on picnics. Sandwiches of Sabbath bread, hard-boiled eggs, and cold borscht we took. Mollie made necklaces from flowers. For her and for me. In the long grass, we took off our shoes and wore our necklaces. From a red flower she made them. The 'Blood of Russia' we called it. Do you remember the flower we called the 'Blood of Russia'?" he asked Leah, as she came up to him, David's hand on her arm.

"Yes. I remember it. A small red flower with a black heart. Mollie and my mother used it to make dyes and Shaindel—do you remember her, Seymour? Shaindel, the herb healer—she used the dark heart for poultices."

"Shaindel. Of course, I remember her. She gave Malcha talcum powder made from wild lilacs for a wedding present. So much she gave her that Malcha still had left when she came to America. On Eldridge Street, when Malcha took a bath, the whole house smelled like the meadowlands of Mother Russia. Do you remember, Leah?"

"I remember."

In front of them, the gravediggers, tall gaunt men in earth-caked work clothes, tossed heaps of black earth into the gaping grave. Just behind them a woman sobbed, her grief escaping her in a sudden muffled moan. Aaron turned and recognized the woman as the young bookkeeper who had been their boarder. Pearl, her name was, he recalled, and Mollie had done all the baking for her wedding. He remembered now the golden mountains of sesame-seed cakes gilded with honey and the way Mollie's face had grown red in the heat of the kitchen and how small patches of flour clung to her arms, dotted her nose. Tears stung his eyes as he thought of how she had suddenly bent from her work to hug him, to tuck a scrap of the raw sweet dough he had loved into his mouth, leaving streaks of flour on his dark serge jacket. It was for such small things that dead were mourned and remembered—for the sweet lingering fragrance of lilac talcum, for the taste of honey and the rich redness of dark-hearted scarlet flowers that grew between tall blades of grass on vanished landscapes. He thought of the pallor of Katie's naked shoulders in the dim light of early evening and the red flower that blushed beneath her skin in moments of pain and passion.

Leah tucked her arm through Seymour's and slowly they walked away from the grave. They did not look back. The funeral was over and now their mourning would begin.

Aaron and David waited for Jakie and Annie and their families to follow and then they too turned. The gravediggers continued their work, but there was no sound as the soft earth mounted and covered the coffin. As the last of the mourners moved away, one of the workmen began to sing a mournful Puccini aria in a tenor that was startlingly rich and clear.

"I am sorry that Michael isn't here. He loved Mollie very much," David said.

"Yes. And I think he was her favorite," Aaron replied.

"That may be. She was here for his birth and throughout your mother's pregnancy. And because Michael's birth—the very fact of his birth—meant the end of a bad time for your mother," David said gently.

"I know." There was calm acceptance in Aaron's voice. He had never begrudged Michael his special status in the family. For him too, Michael's birth had been the end of a bad time, of the season of his mother's sadness, her long silences and searching stare. "Still, it was the best thing for him to begin traveling right after graduation. He was so damn restless. And Rebecca wrote that he was in great spirits when he got to Israel. Went off on a hiking trip straight away. Good old Mike. All that energy." A note of wistfulness had stolen into Aaron's voice and David looked at him thoughtfully.

"Michael's not all that much younger than you. Less than a dozen years. You're a young man, Aaron. You're up to a hiking trip in the Galilee."

"Am I?" Aaron laughed harshly. "Some mornings I don't think I'm up to tying my shoelaces."

A squirrel scurried across the narrow cemetery lane and stopped briefly at their feet, its small furry body trembling, its eyes bright with fear. They too stopped and walked on only when the small animal streaked by. They were careful men, considerate of terror.

David waited for his son to continue talking but Aaron was silent. The crisp, newly fallen leaves crackled beneath their feet and just ahead of them Annie cried out suddenly and bent to lift her small daughter in her arms. Her mother had died and left her and the day would come when she would die and leave the small blonde child whose hair fell about her plump pink cheeks. She hugged the child too tightly and the little girl wailed shrilly but Annie clutched her even closer, fending off her own mortality with her daughter's writhing body. Aaron stared at his cousin and wondered what it was like to hold a child who was flesh of one's flesh, whose breath and blood would commingle with his own. Again he was intensely aware of his solitude, his aloneness.

"Aaron," David continued, his voice soft, hesitant, as though the words he spoke were of such fragility that a harsher tone would shatter them. "I have never before spoken to you of Katie, of your marriage, because I sensed that you did not want me to. And because I felt that you would come to me if I could help. I thought perhaps that things would get better but I have seen that that has not happened. But now I can no longer remain silent. You have heard me speak of the tyranny of the sick. It is not the fault of sick people that they are ill. Their illness is not their fault, but it affects everyone around them. Katie's illness—and I know that she is ill—has hurt you. I cannot, I will not talk to you about Katie, but how can I watch what happens to you without speaking? If I were an oncologist and saw you developing symptoms of cancer, would I remain silent? And so I cannot be quiet now. You must protect yourself, my son, and I, if I can, must help you."

"I don't see how you can help me, Dad," Aaron said and David felt a bitter relief that no denial was offered but that at least the illness and the danger were acknowledged.

"Katie will not seek help?" he asked. "Not from me. But I could refer her. There are excellent therapists. Gifted analysts."

"I've tried to get her to see someone. God, how I've tried. But she won't go. She's afraid—it sounds wild—but she's afraid any treatment will somehow impair her intellectually," Aaron replied, his voice leaden with despair.

"It is a common fear, you know, among talented people. Artists, writers. People who work with their minds as Katie does. But not insurmountable. If you can persuade her to see someone."

"I can't," Aaron said shortly. "What else can I do?"

"Can I talk to her, perhaps?"

"No. I've already betrayed a promise by speaking to you at all."

"I see."

They walked in silence for a few minutes, pausing to allow Seymour and Leah to pass them. Leah took a handkerchief from her purse and gently wiped Seymour's eyes, as though he were a small boy. Her face was set in the lines David knew so well, the mask of strength that contained her sorrow. Only in the darkness of the night when she moved toward him, her arms seeking his body, would the tears come and release her grief. He yearned suddenly for the night, for the pressure of her weight against his, for the wet heat of her sorrow against his bare chest. He turned to Aaron.

"Have you thought of traveling—a vacation, a rest? Both of you have been working so hard. You know, your mother and I plan now to go to Israel. An ocean crossing. Two weeks of sea and sky. Perhaps if you joined us, there would be an opportunity for Katie and myself to speak. We have never been together for any sustained time. I have the feeling that something good might come of it. Will you think about it, Aaron?"

He was relieved when Aaron nodded.

"I'll try, Dad. I'll speak to her tonight."

They walked swiftly now, anxious to reach their car, to drive through the cemetery gates and speed northward to the large house where bowls of fall flowers stood on gleaming dark wood tables and the smell of fresh coffee, of newly baked cakes, banished the vegetal odor of earth freshly dug to receive the burden of death.

*

It was late when Aaron left his parents' Scarsdale home, where Leah, Jakie, Annie, and Seymour would observe the week of mourning. He drove slowly down the East River Drive and looked down at the lights that flickered in the watery darkness. A small ship stood stationary in the distant bay and he wondered if a young man leaned against its rail and searched for a sign of welcome among the low-burning harbor lights, remembering the young David who had caught sight of an unknown man on an unknown shore waving a white straw hat—a careless gesture of welcome and freedom. David's words of that afternoon echoed comfortingly in his mind and he felt a brief surge of optimism. Others had suffered as Katie did, had sought help, found relief. They were not alone.

He hoped now that Katie would be home when he arrived and he pressed down on the accelerator and felt the salt breath of the river wind against his cheek. Tonight would be different, he assured himself, and fought back the memories of the many nights that he had let himself into the darkened apartment to find Katie, still wearing her hat and coat, lying rigidly across their bed, frozen into the posture of misery.

Through recent months, as the pressure of work had increased, her moods had grown more and more parallactic. Each day their office was bombarded with new and urgent calls. Men and women, distinguished in their fields, trembled with fear, broke into sweats at an unexpected knock, and reached for their telephones. Frantically, they called the few lawyers who would confront the accusers and force them to give substance to the shadows of inference which paralyzed their victims and forced friends to deny each other, colleagues to pass on the street without speaking.

Katie and Aaron struggled with a calendar crowded with such cases, and Katie's quiet voice, laced with the disarming sweet accent of the South, was listened to attentively in hearing rooms where men's pasts were probed and, too often, their futures destroyed. More and more often, as hysteria rose, she proved her point by using what she referred to bitterly as a public relations gimmick, rather than a legal argument. She planted press releases or ferreted out the photograph of the young son of a Hollywood actor accused of belonging to a union which was purported to be a Communist front. She introduced the photograph as Exhibit A, established the identity of the subject and the fact that he had been killed on Guadalcanal.

"Does a Communist whose philosophy has been programmed by the Kremlin send his nineteen-year-old son off to die for democracy?" she asked in the soft, reasonable tone her opponents had come to fear, and she read a letter in which the actor encouraged his boy to do his best "for the greatest country on God's earth." It did not hurt her case that the letter, found in the dead soldier's pocket, was flecked with the dark blood of death.

But still the cases continued to pile up. One day when Aaron was visiting in Scarsdale, David had stared at a newspaper that reported the jailing of a prominent writer on charges of contempt of Congress for refusing to answer questions about colleagues. He had sighed deeply, his fingers reaching for the bottle of pills which he kept always in his pocket.

"It reminds me of Russia before the Revolution," he said. "Do you remember, Leah? The sudden arrests, the fear, the Czar's police?"

"And since the Revolution? Has anything changed? Ah yes, the Czar's police are now the people's police," she replied bitterly.

Through the years, since the war's end, letters had trickled in from their few surviving friends and relatives. Affidavits were requested and Seymour and David sent them at once and then again there was silence. Letters went unanswered and were returned undelivered. Occasionally Moshe would write to tell them of the arrival of an acquaintance in Israel—sad, bleak reports of broken people living out their broken lives.

Katie and Aaron worked with fierce intensity. She traveled back and forth from Washington, spent long nights in the law library. But still, with increasing frequency, she would arrive home at night and stare blindly into the silence until the tears came, then the sobs, then the steady stream of recriminations. She had not argued well enough. She was not doing enough. No, she was doing too much. No one helped her. Everyone conspired against her. No one cared. Aaron did not love her. She wanted to have a baby. Why didn't she have a baby?

The questions, repeated again and again, had taken on the wail of an accusation, a susurrant lament, that haunted him even during their quiet times. Why wasn't Katie pregnant? Was it his fault? The teasing doubt thrust itself at him when his body was intertwined with hers and they made love with the desperate urgency of those who had little time and feared unnamed dangers. Too often, then, he surrendered, feeling himself hopeless and helpless, as his penis shriveled within her and they withdrew and turned from each other, locked in their separate miseries.

"You don't love me," she would say, tossing the words into the silent darkness, shooting them out like small incendiary pellets, ignited to scorch them both with anguish.

"I love you." But his tone was dead and he thought of how heavy a burden was the love she demanded. He could not sustain it.

Still, tonight he felt new hope. He had the feeling that Mollie's death had ended one chapter and begun another and he sped home with a sense of urgency.

*

"Katie?"

The apartment was dark but she was or had been home because the mail was neatly stacked on the dining room table. He riffled through it quickly, thinking that they must be on every mailing list in America. He tossed aside the urgent requests from the Committee for a Sane Nuclear Policy, the Emergency Civil Liberties Union, the NAACP Legal Defense Fund, and quickly and eagerly read a letter from Rebecca. Her desert kibbutz had just completed the building of a communal dining hall and now, as they ate, they looked out on the gentle ocher-colored slopes of the Edomite Mountains. It was very hot but their swimming pool would be finished in a few months' time.

She hoped Aaron and Katie planned a trip to Israel. She looked forward to meeting Katie and of course Yehuda and their children, Danielle, Noam, and Mindell, wanted to know their aunt and uncle.

Aaron smiled at the thought of gay, carefree Rebecca mothering a family of three, working in the fields and on construction projects, and finding time for her own painting which an *Art News* critic had recently called "a revolutionary approach to primitive perception." Still, he was pleased with her letter and pleased too that it had arrived that day. It was an omen of a kind and he held it in his hand and went into the bedroom to find Katie.

She was stretched out on the bed as he had feared she would be, still wearing her pale-blue coat with the small matching pillbox hat askew on her soft golden curls. Her deep-blue eyes were rimmed with violet circles of fatigue and she stared vacantly up at the ceiling. She had not even bothered to peel off her white gloves which were covered with soot from the Washington journey and her fingers were listlessly intertwined.

Often when Aaron found her like this, he grew angry, almost repelled by what he had come to think of as her selfishness, her emotional sloth. The tyranny of the sick, David had said, and David had been right. Again and again Aaron rebuked himself for such feelings, arguing, with a reasonableness that he did not feel, that Katie could not help herself, but more often his argument was defeated by irritation and anger and he would leave the bedroom, slamming the door sharply. But tonight he sank down beside her on the bed, took her in his arms, removed her small hat—a doll's hat, really—and gently ran his fingers through her soft hair.

"I'm sorry I wasn't at Mollie's funeral," she said softly. "Was it terrible?"

"You know. Seymour took it very hard. And Jakie and Annie too. But my mother was strong. So strong." He thought of his mother, tall and erect at the graveside, and remembered how her black suit had fit too loosely, its jacket billowing about her narrow frame. She had lost weight during her sister's long illness.

"I'm sure she was. Where does Leah get her strength, her control? God, I wish she'd share her secret with me."

"And you? How did it go with you yesterday?"

"You didn't see the papers? Of course not. That was big time. The Senator himself. Holy Joe. He spits when he talks. A little-known fact vital to the archives of civil liberties. All his creepy aides keep handkerchiefs handy to wipe up the saliva."

"They ought to use them to hold their noses. The stench must be awful."

"It is. The Senator called General Marshall himself an instrument of the Soviet conspiracy. That ought to please Ike."

"Give him enough rope and he'll hang himself. But how did you do?"

He hated the dry bitterness of her tone and stroked her hair Rebecca's letter still between his fingers. Perhaps he and Katie should visit Israel, eat in the shadow of rose-colored mountains swim beneath a desert sky, while the sickness that infected their marriage was burned to cinders by the scorching desert sun.

"Oh, I won a motion for adjournment and heard the Senator mumble something about how women lawyers ought to stay home and take shit out of diapers instead of bringing it into court. I almost told him that I'd prefer doing that to wiping his spit off my face."

"Katie, Katie." He smiled, stroked her neck, and felt her body relax beneath his touch.

"Oh, Aaron, I'm so tired." The tension in her voice had melted and he saw, without surprise, the familiar tears, twin lambent droplets, course slowly down her pale cheeks.

"Of course you are." He pressed her to him. "What we need, what we both need, is a vacation. A long vacation."

"What kind of vacation?" she asked, her voice limpid, dreamy.

She peeled off her gloves, let them drop to the floor in small flags of defeat. She unbuttoned her coat and slipped out of it but remained supine on the bed. She wore a white silk blouse and blue skirt that matched her coat. He unbuttoned the blouse and cupped her breast in his hand, gently fondling the nipple, feeling it grow taut and hard beneath his fingers.

"My mother and father are planning a trip to Israel. If we join them it will be a real family reunion—our first in years. Michael and Rebecca are there—all of us would be together. My uncle Moshe, my aunt Henia, and my cousins. I haven't seen my cousin Yaakov since we were together in Ethiopia. We wouldn't have to go straight to Israel. Perhaps a few weeks in Greece. Or in Italy."

She sat up abruptly and pushed his hand away. Small fiery patches dotted her cheeks and her eyes were bright—not with tears but with a surging febrile rage.

"You're talking about weeks and months. A stopover in Greece. A few weeks in Italy. What world are you living in, Aaron? Have you any idea of what my calendar is like—the number of cases, the number of appearances? This isn't exactly the season for family reunions!"

"Come off it, Katie." His anger matched her own now. "My calendar's just as crowded and there isn't a case on it that I couldn't farm out to another lawyer. The same is true for you. The world of civil liberties doesn't rest on the shoulders of Aaron and Katie Goldfeder."

"You know damn well there aren't enough lawyers who handle these cases the way we do. I've got to take care of them, Aaron. I've promised the clients. I've promised myself. There's so much to do, so much to fight. We can't live thinking only of ourselves the way my parents and sisters do. We've got our jobs to do. We've got to make the world right."

Her small fists pummeled the bed and he saw, through the sheer silk of her blouse, the small flower of rage flash into bloody blossom on her shoulder.

"Katie, Katie." He repeated her name soothingly, his voice taking on the tone his aunt Mollie had used as an aural panacea through their childhood. Aaron, Aaron. Becca, Becca. Jakey, Jakey. The simple repetition had soothed and smoothed. Mollie, Mollie, he thought and heard again the thud of earth upon her coffin. "We can't make the world right by ourselves. You know that. We have to think of our lives, of our future, of a family."

He walked across the room and looked out the window. In the apartment across the way a mother slowly undressed a small girl. She peeled off one sock and then the other. He saw the child's toes wiggle pinkly and the woman bend to kiss them. Quickly he drew the blinds, strangely pained by the glimpsed intimacy.

"But I haven't got a family. I want a baby. Don't give me vacations. Give me a baby!"

She hugged her shoulder and drew her knees up to her chest. Her pale skin was mottled and her body shook as her sobs broke forth in heaving gulps, tears and spittle wetly veiling her face. A wave of fatigue and revulsion broke over him and he turned away so that she would not see the sudden anger that flashed across his face. But he could not silence the words that rushed to his lips.

"Goddamn it! I can't go through this crap again. I have to be in court early tomorrow. I'll get some sleep downtown."

He was drained of patience and of pity. Tonight had not been different and tomorrow night would not be different. Their love, their lives, would drown in the torrents of her tears and her terror. She would not help herself and he could not help her. Rebecca's letter fell from his hand as he fumbled through the bureau drawers for a change of clothes. He packed swiftly and waited briefly in the hall for her to call out to him. When she did not, he slammed the door behind him. He was down the hall and at the elevator when at last she moaned, in the piteous tones of a small child frightened by a sudden incomprehensible darkness, "Aaron, I'm so scared. Aaron."

There was no answer and she fell back against the pillow into a heavy lethereal sleep that embraced her like a weary lover.

*

The bedroom was streaked with the gray light of a rain-ridden dawn when Katie awoke, and she sat up abruptly and looked about the room as though seeing it for the first time. She stared at the shadowy outlines of their furnishings—at the desk piled high with books, the bureau on which their silver-framed marriage portrait rested (the sunlight cleaving Aaron's face in two, severing the smile he turned down to her own serious gaze), the armchair in which he spent long evenings reading, his lean form radiant in the soft light of the reading lamp. They seemed to her unfamiliar objects and she struggled toward a memory of how they had been acquired—relieved when she recalled the day they had found the large mahogany desk at a Vermont antique auction. Always on such mornings she searched for such scraps of reality to root her firmly in the new and dreaded day. She shivered in the morning chill and saw, with vague surprise, that she still wore her skirt and blouse and had slept without troubling to slide beneath the blankets. She remembered then what had happened the night before and in the morning stillness she heard again her own words, Aaron's fierce reply. She remembered the slamming of the door as he left and she knew with grievous certainty that when he left a dangerous border had been crossed. It was the first time that he had turned from her during such a time of darkness, the first time that he had not tried to calm and cajole her out of the desperate arguments born of her despair. But if he had left her once, he would leave her again. And in the harsh light of a new morning, she did not blame him, she could not blame him.

Slowly she eased herself up, stripped off her clothes, and left them in a careless pile on the floor. In the bathroom she allowed the water to run until threads of steam clouded the mirror and then she stood for a long time beneath the hot spray of the shower as though its heat might scald away her misery. Very slowly she washed herself, using the lemon-shaped soap her mother sent her each month from the Dryades market so that her skin always breathed the fragrance shared by her mother and sisters as they sat beneath the fig trees in their gardens, played endless games of cards, and talked in the soft, unhurried accents of ease and acceptance. She washed her hair too, using Aaron's shampoo, and when she stepped out of the shower she wrapped herself in his white terrycloth robe which smelled lightly of his body and wiped her cheek dry with the belt, relishing its roughness against her skin. She pressed his robe tighter, sniffed a tendril of her hair that smelled of him, of the dark damp hours of their love, of his body close upon her own. She called the office but there was no answer. Probably he had gone out to breakfast or perhaps over to Joshua Ellenberg's lavish suite of offices to shower and shave, to breakfast on the china dishes which Joshua had had engraved with his monogram.

"Aaron, I'm sorry," she said aloud to the empty room, rehearsing a speech to be delivered at a distant hour when lights were dimmed and soft music played in soothing, narcotizing segues. But this time soft lights, soft words, would not be enough, she knew. They had entered a new time which would require new words, new actions.

She stooped to pick up her soiled clothing and found Rebecca's letter, a tissue-thin green sheet of paper, lying on the floor. She read it through and thought of how simple life was for this unknown sister-in-law, for Leah's daughter who had inherited Leah's strength, her gifts and sense of purpose. Rebecca worked on a dining hall and it was built. She helped with the planting of a crop and it was harvested. She stood with brush and palette before an easel and a painting evolved. She did not work with amorphous words, struggling with abstract concepts, excising small nuggets of reason from a heavy lodestone of law. She did not yearn to be a mother, then abort the small life that struggled within her womb. Lucky Rebecca. Poor Katie and poor Aaron. Poor, poor Aaron.

In the kitchen she made herself breakfast, carefully measuring out cereal and milk, boiling an egg, brewing coffee, waiting patiently for the golden toast to soar up from the stainless-steel depths of the toaster. The domestic routine soothed her and she felt a new calm, a new control. But when she had set the food neatly on the table before her, she could not eat. A nausea gripped her and she remembered that she had barely eaten the previous day. She managed to down her juice and half a cup of coffee and went into the bedroom to lie down. The phone rang and she did not reach for it but allowed herself to drift into a half-sleep.

When she awoke her body was coated with a damp veil of sweat and her hand swung wildly toward the silent telephone. She knew that she had missed an urgent call and the loss was profound, irrevocable. Again a wave of nausea coursed over her and she ran to the bathroom and vomited up the juice and coffee which she had forced herself to drink.

A small vial of yellow-jacketed pills stood in the medicine chest, given to her by Dr. Hernandez as he checked her for the last time before she left Puerto Rico. "Nembutal," the pharmacist's label read, and the cadence of the word soothed her. It was the only comfort the doctor had offered her during that long weekend of silence and pain. He did not believe in abortions, he had told her, as his rubber-gloved finger probed her womb and found the shielded embryo huddled within it. Abortions were an affront to his religion. She too did not believe in abortions. They were an affront to her desire. Yet together, in the sterile white room, with the hot Caribbean sun piercing the shaded window, a seabird screaming wildly from across the nearby beach, they had become partners in this act which they mutually disavowed. Perhaps a ghostly Dr. Hernandez had performed the abortion just as a ghostly Katie Goldfeder had undergone it.

From a safe distance, her real self had watched her strange penumbric twin make the arrangements, get the name of the Puerto Rican doctor from her father-in-law's friend, and juggle bank accounts so that Aaron, inveterately careless about money, would not notice the $1,000 shortage. Her real self had frowned in disappointment, offered arguments, even wept as the plane carried her through skies of brilliant blue in which families of careless clouds chased each other. But her real self had been defeated and had fashioned that defeat into a shadowy memory which had lost both shape and substance so that she often, with exquisite ease, forgot she had ever journeyed to Puerto Rico and cursed her husband because no life came to her womb, choosing at that moment to forget the life that had been destroyed within it.

Still, the pills were real and remembered and she gulped down several of them, not remembering Dr. Hernandez's instructions. They would calm her, he said, not meeting her eyes. She was to take them if she felt upset. They had both been in a hurry and anxious to leave each other. He was going to Mass and she was catching a plane. He had not said how many to take. One more or less could not make a difference, she thought, and swallowed yet another. Nembutal. What a nice name. She felt better already.

She dressed carefully, putting on a blue silk shirtwaist that Aaron especially liked. Her hair was dry and she brushed it into a cloud of gold that circled her small face. With trembling fingers she pressed pale powder on the circlets of violet beneath her eyes and outlined her lips in creamy pink. She would go to the office and see Aaron. Neither of them had a court appearance that day. She would tell him that she had thought about it and wanted the vacation in Israel. And then she would see David and her father-in-law would give her the name of a psychiatrist who would help her. She had no secrets from Aaron's father, she knew. His wise, sad eyes had long ago fixed on her with knowledge, pierced the soft membrane of charm, and searched out the darkness of her true self. What he did not know for certain, he had guessed. He did not like her but for Aaron's sake he would help her. She would begin treatment as soon as they returned from Israel. She saw everything with startling clarity now. Aaron was right. Other lawyers could handle their cases. The only important thing was that no more doors be slammed between them.

The pills were taking effect and she regretted now not using them before. A new calm propelled her, organized her thoughts, motivated her movements. How simple everything seemed, how organized and orderly. The unmade bed briefly troubled her and she smoothed the covers, puffed up the pillow. A stranger had slept there in fitful sleep, an unknown ghostly Katie who would soon be vanquished. Tonight the real Katie would sleep there with Aaron; she would thread her fingers through his copper-colored hair, move to the rhythm of his love, sob not with grief but with gladness as her body arched beneath his, and they would begin again. Yet again.

Swiftly she left the apartment and in the lobby she was startled to see that the rain still streaked steadily down.

"A cab, Mrs. Goldfeder?" the doorman asked.

She wore no raincoat, carried no umbrella, but she shook her head. The rain was so clean, so soothing. She and Aaron had loved to walk in the rain through the Harvard Yard and return to towel each other dry in their small apartment where a wood fire glowed radiantly against their naked bodies.

"I'll walk," she said happily. Aaron's hair had matched the firelight. She remembered that.

She did not hear the doorman's protest, the neighbor who called after her. How light and cleansed she felt as the rain drifted about her. Years dropped away, unnamed burdens drifted off. The chimerical pills floated about in her bloodstream, magically cushioning harsh nerve endings. She carried neither purse nor attaché case, only Rebecca's letter like a lucky talisman pinched between her fingers. She floated down the street, a small golden-haired woman in a blue silk dress that soon shimmered wetly and clung to her body, exactly matching the bright blueness of her eyes.

She did not notice the passersby who stared after her nor the traffic light on the corner of Fifth Avenue and Twelfth Street that went from red to green with startling speed. The rain whispered to her and she followed its rhythmic voice, its steady stroke, and walked calmly into the street. She never saw the speeding taxi, its windshield blinded by the rapid swirls of water, that streaked toward her, swerved but could not avoid her. With silent impact the tons of metal met her flesh, struck her small bright figure, tossed it briefly skyward and then onto the sleek black asphalt where it lay in startled death. Its bright-blue eyes were open in astonishment and one blue-sleeved arm neatly, gracefully spread across a soft breast sadly spattered with mud and blood. A woman wept and the cab driver vomited. A very young policeman found the green air letter from Israel and went to search for a telephone.

Sheets of rain, harsh unremitting savage floods of autumnal grief, fell the next day as once again the family gathered at the cemetery, to bury Katie. It was a small funeral and the mourners stood beneath black umbrellas, their faces pale with shock. Again

Aaron Goldfeder stood alone in black suit and hat, a clear plastic cape draped over his shoulders. On its surface, the rain tapped out a message of grief and loss, waste and yearning, time past, time lost. He stepped forward when the rabbi motioned to him and in a quiet voice he intoned the prayer for the dead. Unlike his uncle Seymour, he stood erect and held his body still.

The earth that he picked up to drop into the open grave congealed into mud within his hand and fell too swiftly onto the rain-dampened wood.

"Poor Katie, sweet Katie, wet Katie," he thought, the words weeping their way through his mind.

He saw his golden-haired wife emerge from the shower, her body still red with the pressure of his own. He saw her slender form slide through the waters of Pontchartrain and remembered the small fire that glowed orange and gold in their Cambridge apartment and how he had so often rubbed her dry after a laughing dash through the rain, delighting in her soft white skin that glowed golden in the firelight.

Around him, at the open grave site, others moved forward to deposit their offerings of earth—her parents who had never understood Katie in life and did not comprehend her in death, her sisters, dazed and bewildered, smelling of the lemon-scented soap which Katie too had used, whose fragrance had wafted toward him, battling the odor of disinfectant and formaldehyde, when he bent to identify her poor broken body as it lay on a slab in the morgue.

Her family left the cemetery swiftly, the rain whipping their backs as the wind shifted. The stale odor of repeated grief filled the hired car from the funeral home which he shared with his parents. Katie's family, grief and accusation in their eyes, rode behind him. They would return to New Orleans for the week of mourning.

"They blame me," he said and was relieved when his father did not argue with him.

"Only because they do not know whom to blame," David replied gently. He was an expert on grief, a skilled practitioner in the mystic fields of guilt and anger. His very skill sickened him now. He wanted only to take Aaron's head and hold it gently in his own hands, to pass his fingers across the young man's wounded eyes.

"They're right to blame me. All she wanted was a child. And I couldn't give it to her. I couldn't give it to her."

David stared ahead. It was the moment to tell Aaron about Katie's trip to Puerto Rico, to relieve his guilt but compound his sorrow. An accident, a taxi speeding down a rain-dark street—that could be absorbed, accepted. But this other death, for which an appointment had been made, a check written, a skillful web of deceit woven—with such a death Aaron could never become reconciled. Still, he had to be told.

"Aaron." Leah's voice was firm and her husband and son bent to catch her words. "Surely you could have given her a child." Quietly as the car sped northward, she told her son about the infant born to Lisa Frawley as he fought in North Africa, the boy child conceived in the sheltering shadows of trees and strangled at birth in the cord of sustenance.

Aaron leaned back. The knowledge shocked and subdued him. Vagrant griefs tossed about in his thoughts, became entangled and hammered at his heart. Tears came at last and he wept as the car moved out of the city, and Leah and David, their eyes meeting in sadness and sympathy, sat in patient painful vigil and watched their son's broad shoulders shake, his body break with sobs, as he submitted at last to his love and to his sorrow.

Home
1956
23

The blonde girl, her thick hair caught in a single braid, nestled the tiny goat within her arms, lifted a bottle, and pressed the pink rubber nipple into the quivering creature's mouth. The young kid closed its eyes and sucked the blue-white liquid with surprising strength. When the bottle was empty, its small rough tongue darted out to lick up the few drops that dribbled about its mouth and it moaned softly, pressing its body against the girl's small breast.

"Ah, you're still thirsty, Mushi, and I don't want to go back for more water. Can you wait? They'll be here any minute."

She stood and peered down the narrow black ribbon of asphalt highway that wove its way through the oceans of drifting golden sand. There had been no highway six years ago when they arrived at the site chosen for their new kibbutz, Shaarei HaNegev—Gateway to the Southland.

"You see," Yehuda had said, when the new highway opened, "Moses performed a miracle when he parted the Red Sea, but we perform a modern miracle: We have parted the desert."

Mindell looked across at the desert which was both their adversary and their comfort. She loved the endless expanse, broken only by the stunted growth of tamarisk and pink-flowered cactus; she loved the hot gem-like glitter of the sands in the bright sunlight of high noon. It banished the years of darkness in the tunnel beneath a barracks, the closeness of other small bodies pressed against her own, the wail of a siren and the echoing bark of harsh voices in the language of hate.

"Still waiting, Mindell?"

Her sister Danielle came toward her and Mindell saw with relief that Danielle carried a canteen. Mushi would have another drink after all.

"They should be here any minute if they left Beersheva right after breakfast. What's *Ima* doing?" she asked.

"Still nursing the baby. What an appetite. I think he's greedier than Mushi. And he's only a week old."

Danielle carefully unscrewed her canteen and poured the water into the bottle, flinching when a drop fell to the earth and was swallowed by the sand. The sisters shared the desert dweller's reverence for water and both of them had lived through months of drought when the kibbutz posted stern notices, rationing the flushing of toilets, the usage of showers. They remembered the time, only a year before, when the *fedayeen* had sabotaged the pipeline and the flow of water had ceased entirely. They had had to use the emergency cistern then, measuring out liters in pale blue plastic jugs, saving as much water as they could for their own livestock and that of the bedouins, who carried their smallest goats and lambs and led young camels, delicately balanced on stock-thin legs, to the drinking troughs which the kibbutz set up.

"But the bedouins are Arabs too. Why would the *fedayeen* want to hurt their own people?" Mindell had asked then, and Yehuda had pressed his hand against the small white scar on his forehead.

"You ask a reasonable question, Mindell, but you know that hate is an enemy of reason. It is another one of your good questions that I cannot answer."

She loved Yehuda for that honesty, for not answering, for acknowledging his own bewilderment in the face of hers. She asked too many questions, she knew. Again and again, she asked why her parents—her real parents, the slender fair-haired woman whom she remembered only for a bright pink dress and a picture hat to match and the man with the small moustache who wore a gold watch on a long chain about his waist—had had to die in the low, windowless dark red brick building that stood in a grassy corner of the town of terror they called Oswiecim and the Germans called Auschwitz. Yehuda offered no answers and Rebecca—the second mother of her life—spoke softly of grief and loss, of love and acceptance. She did not understand Rebecca's words but took comfort from the soft voice, the light touch of her hands. Mindell offered the same words to Danielle who was, after all, a year younger than she was, who had never been out of Israel, who did not understand terror and darkness, the screams of sirens and the staccato message of handguns. Danielle, too, asked such questions because she too lived with the ghostly memory of a mother who had gone away and never returned. But the new baby, the infant born to Rebecca and Yehuda, the small bundle of cooing flesh they had named Yaakov, would never ask such questions. His mother would never stand beneath a spigot that spewed forth gaseous death or be shot in a forest clearing created for lovers' trysts. This new baby, their brother, had natural parents, and today grandparents—real grandparents—were coming all the way from America.

Grandparents and a new uncle, she remembered belatedly and hoped their uncle Aaron would be as much fun as their uncle Michael was. Michael had spent several weeks on the kibbutz and he was hiking up north now but he too would return tomorrow for Yaakov's circumcision ceremony. Of course, they had been warned that Uncle Aaron might be a little sad because his wife had died recently, had been run over by a taxicab on a rainy New York street. It seemed to Mindell a mild, almost normal, way to die and she hoped her mother's brother would not drag his sadness behind him in a cloud that shadowed their joy. Oh well, if he did she would make him laugh, would thrust Mushi's face into his ear. No one would remain sad when Mushi's warm tongue tickled them.

Mindell was good at making people laugh. She had had enough of darkness and sorrow, of silent weeping and anguished keening. She laughed to block out the sounds of fear, the small gasps of misery, the sudden shriek of terror. Sometimes when she laughed too loudly, she saw Yehuda and Rebecca look swiftly at each other, pain and helplessness locked in their gaze. The new baby, little

Yaakov, would have the gift of quiet laughter, of small soft sounds of merriment. Lucky Yaakov, she thought, and hoped that Rebecca would let her hold him that afternoon and show him off to their American family.

"Mindell, does it hurt the baby?" Danielle asked.

"Does what hurt the baby?"

"You know. The cutting. The circumcision."

"Just a little, I think. A very little." But she herself was not reassured and she caressed Mushi and told herself that she would not watch the rabbi, she would turn her eyes out toward the desert, toward the bright clouds of dancing sands.

"When do you think they'll get here?" Danielle asked.

"Soon. They said before lunch and it's after lunch already."

"Maybe they knew we were having that horrid leftover stew and wanted to miss it. Chana thinks she's cooking food for cold German winters. Someone should tell her that we live in the Negev."

"What do you think they'll be like, Danielle?"

"Oh, nice. *Ima* says her mother, Grandma Leah, is beautiful. Tall and black-haired. Like a queen, she said. She's an artist too."

"It's strange to have a grandfather and grandmother you've never seen," Danielle said.

"It's stranger to have parents you don't remember," Mindell replied and was surprised at the quiet sadness in her own voice. It had been a long time since she thought of the woman in the bright pink dress and the man whose golden watch chain had sometimes scratched her cheek when he lifted her high above his head.

"Here they come. There's the car. Hurry, let's tell them!"

They ran off, their cheeks flushed with excitement, sandals fluttering, clouds of sand rising behind them, too shy suddenly to remain at the side of the road and greet the parents and brother of the young woman they loved so fiercely, whom they called *Ima* because she had become a mother to them and now, at last, had given them a brother.

*

Leah leaned forward, wiped the sand from the window of the huge old American taxi that had carried them southward from Beersheba, and watched the retreating figures of the two girls. The only other sign of life they had seen in the past hour had been a slender gazelle that leapt swiftly from behind a hillock of sand, glanced about, its liquid dark eyes wary with wisdom, and flashed across the rose-red desert floor into an outgrowth of smoke-colored rocks. Their driver, a jovial, moustachioed man named Danni who alternately sang, told jokes, and filled them with ecological and archeological information about the passing landscape, stopped the taxi until the animal vanished.

"A Bible beast," he said. "They don't like the sounds of cars and motors. Frightens them to death. And in the Negev life is precious, we've got to protect it."

They understood Danni's concern about protecting life because they had noticed, when he rolled up his sleeves at the kiosk in Mitzpeh Rimon, the small row of blue numbers etched into his arm. Anyone who had hovered so close to death understood the preciousness of life.

On the seat beside them Aaron slept, and Leah and David spoke softly, knowing how little sleep he had had during their ocean voyage and the few days in the country. On shipboard, David, awakening at night with sudden tightness constricting his chest, pain flashing through his arm, would stealthily take a pill and go up on deck into the quiet darkness and allow the movement of the sea to cradle him into calm. It was then that he would see Aaron leaning against the rail, watching the waves, and the terrible sorrow he read in his son's hunched shoulders moved him to a pity he could not reveal to Aaron. He was grateful then that it had not been necessary for him to tell Aaron about the abortion and he remained concealed in the shadows, nursing his secret pain as Aaron nursed his.

Leah, too, would waken in the silvery light of dawn and hear Aaron pacing in his stateroom next door. She heard him speak aloud one night, when the light washed through their porthole and the air sparkled with dancing argentous motes. At the sound of Aaron's voice she turned her head to the wall, unwilling to eavesdrop on her son's misery. He would recover from Katie's death, she knew, and remembered with muted sadness the days and nights of her own grief, of her own yearnings for death. Her grief had passed as his would, and she searched for words to offer him but knew that, after all, there was nothing she could say.

"Are we almost there, Danni?" she asked softly.

"We are there, *Geveret*," Danni replied. "Those two girls who ran away like my frightened gazelles were probably young members of the kibbutz. We turn in now to Shaarei HaNegev."

Skillfully he veered off on a small fork of road lined with acacia trees swaying gently in the breeze that breathed against their faces like slow gusts of air thrusting forth from an open oven.

Just beyond them a row of neatly whitewashed bungalows gleamed whitely against air that shimmered with the golden light of the low-hanging midday sun. Small plots of grass bordered each house and flame-colored flowers nestled in the soft patches of shadow at the brightly painted doorways. A family shared an army blanket spread on a lawn of coarse desert grass, its greenery parched and yellowed. The father, a tall young man with a long blond beard and thick blond hair, read aloud to a small girl while the mother, a tiny Yemenite woman, diapered a kicking baby who writhed upward and chortled loudly. A boy and a girl, hands linked, rode down the path on battered bicycles and veered off to opposite sides of the road to allow the Goldfeders' taxi to pass.

"Shalom!" they called and waved.

"Shalom," David replied from the open window and Aaron smiled and waved.

In the distance they saw the gentle slopes of the ocher-colored Edomite mountains and they knew that farther south the blue waters of the Gulf of Aqabah licked the shores of the desert kingdom that was Israel's southland. David felt a new pride in his daughter and her family who had carved a home for themselves in this harsh and beautiful place, who had set down grass amid swirling sands and built small homes with bravely painted doors, and coaxed life and nurture from a land abandoned to death.

The taxi stopped in front of a large white building bordered by a porch built beneath a concrete awning. A group of young people sat around a radio and listened in concentrated silence to a news broadcast.

"Ah, they are waiting to hear whether the *fedayeen* who made the attack on the jeep near Dimona have been caught," Danni said. "The stupid bastards, those *fedayeen*. What does it do for them? They provoke, we retaliate, they provoke again. Ach!" He spat into his hands and wiped them on his large handkerchief. "Well, we are arrived at the dining hall of Shaarei HaNegev and just in time, too. This is the hour of real heat and I am going to try this swimming pool the kibbutz boasts so much about."

They emerged from the taxi and felt the full impact of the desert day. Here the air was tumid with the golden stillness of a thick, impenetrable heat. The sand on which they stood burned against the soles of their shoes and they moved swiftly, almost fearfully, into the sweetness of the shaded porch.

"Who here is Yehuda Arnon?" Danni called. "I have brought with me his wife's American family."

"Ah yes. For the brith," a girl who had been passing out the glasses of lemonade said, and David recognized the impeccable Oxford accent although the girl was barefoot and her blue work pants and halter were streaked with paint. "Yehuda!" she called. "Your Rivka's family is here."

The door opened and Rebecca's husband, the father of their grandchild, came out. Leah and David smiled at the tall young man who looked exactly as Rebecca had described him. Silver hair flecked his temples, his narrow features were sharply chiseled, and his gray eyes, so light and silken-smooth, were startling against his bronzed skin.

He was like the swift and gentle gazelle, Leah thought, and moved toward him, her arms outstretched.

"Yehuda," she said. "Thank you for making me a grandmother."

"And I thank you for giving me my wife," he replied and his strong arms encircled her, his lips dryly brushed her cheek. He shook hands gravely with David and Aaron and they were all pleasantly conscious of the fact that they had liked each other at once without awkwardness or embarrassment.

"I will take you now to Rivka and the baby," he said and Leah felt a tremor of nervousness.

It had been six years since they waved good-bye to Rebecca as she sailed for Italy. Six years in Rebecca's life and the life of their family. Children had been born and loved ones had died. Mollie. Sarah Ellenberg. The tiny fragile Schreibers. They had danced at weddings and wept at funerals. Michael had grown to manhood and Aaron had suffered loss. Rebecca had fought a war, become a wife and mother. So much had happened, perhaps too much. They had become unraveled, had lost the thread of each other's lives.

She followed Yehuda too slowly as he led the way to a small white house, but suddenly the stillness of the air was pierced by an infant's wail and all doubt was banished. Leah rushed forward and thrust open the door to the room where Becca sat, the sunlight splayed across her thick black hair, an infant held to her breast. It was their Becca of the laughing mouth, with a new softness in her large dark eyes that filled with tears as her parents moved toward her.

Yehuda held the baby as Leah and Rebecca clung to each other. He smiled as Aaron and David joined them, entangling each other in a knot of embraces, laughing and crying, asking questions but never waiting for answers.

That night they sat about the gas heater in Rebecca and Yehuda's small bungalow and talked softly of the years that had passed. The desert night had turned swiftly and startlingly cold, and they huddled over the blue flame that danced erratically in the grate and bathed their faces in its fiery glow. Rebecca laughed when they told her how orthodox Seymour Hart had become. Since Mollie's death he had reverted to the customs of his youth, went to synagogue twice a day and argued vociferously with his son about closing the business on Saturdays. She was pleased when they told her that Eleanor Greenstein had married a Bennington professor, and she looked admiringly at a sample table napkin on which Leah's bright floral patterns would be embossed under Joshua Ellenberg's imprint later that year. Had they heard, she asked, that Joe Stevenson had had a successful show in Paris, that he had married a ceramicist who had lived only miles from his California home?

Mindell and Danielle sat quietly on the floor, listening wide-eyed to tales of people they had never seen, stories of places with names they found difficult to pronounce. The English was difficult for them to follow but they listened attentively, an avid audience at a rare performance, fearful of missing a nuance, a cadence. They were children for whom personal history was a luxury and they clung to each name and incident, ferreting away the stories that belonged to Rebecca's girlhood, seizing them as an adoptive legacy.

In a corner of the room Aaron and Yehuda's son, Noam, fashioned paper planes out of old copies of the *Jerusalem Post*. Aaron read the headlines as he made intricate folds.

"It's hard to think of our Josh as a corporate magnate," Rebecca said after Leah had described Joshua's office high above the East River, the factories all over the country that were his subsidiaries. "But then that's what he always wanted."

"Yes. Ellenberg Industries are much bigger than S. Hart ever was. But they share the same history. Both of them were launched by your mother's designs," David said and smiled proudly at Leah.

"We were lucky. Very lucky," Leah said, fingers finding David's.

But a stillness followed her words. Not all of them had been lucky. They did not look at Aaron who bent to his work, showing Noam a new way of folding the tail wing. He paused, as Noam tried, and read an item in the half-crumbled newspaper.

"It says here there was an ambush at Mitzpeh Rimon. That's where we stopped today, not far from here. Have you had any difficulty with the *fedayeen?*"

"There isn't a settlement in the south that hasn't had some difficulty," Yehuda answered, and they noticed for the first time the rifle that rested in a corner of the room. "These are unsettled times. The Arabs aren't ready for a war. They've had only six years to figure out what happened in the War for Independence. But they don't want us to feel that we're free to live in peace in what they still consider their lands. So they resort to these border raids. The *fedayeen* dash across, kill some livestock, set fire to a few buildings. If they can, they kill a settler, a soldier, a child. It is a war of nerves. But we are ready for them."

He walked across the room and took the rifle, flipping open the cartridge case, running his hand across its carefully cleaned and oiled butt.

The room in which they sat was lined with bookshelves. Rebecca's paintings, celebrating the varied colors of the Negev, the miracle of young grass, a single sheath of wheat trembling in the wind, hung in simple frames against the whitewashed walls. Bright woven pillows were tossed on the couch and the children's games stood on a low wicker table with an FM radio from which soft music flowed. It was a room designed for a family who delighted in life, in the joy of words, in the richness of color and the gentle sound of music. Yet within it, a man stood and checked his rifle while through the window they saw the roving beam of a searchlight, penetrating the secrets of the night, warning them that danger hovered close, that they could not, must not, assume security.

Leah shivered suddenly and took the sweater Rebecca handed her.

"Well, it's an advantage at least to struggle against danger that you can see," Aaron said and they did not know if he was thinking of his own distant war in the mountain country of Africa, when the enemy was concealed in jungle foliage and lurched forward from the cover of caves, or his more recent combat with the ghosts that had haunted and finally killed poor Katie.

"Too often we cannot see the dangers," Yehuda replied. "I had a friend, a man named Amos who lived on Kibbutz Yotvata, right near Eilat. It was his turn to serve as night watchman and he was making his rounds when he heard an animal bleating, as though in pain. It is a hard thing for a farmer to ignore the moans of an animal and so he followed the sounds. A young camel, its leg broken, lay just outside the settlement gate. The watchman forgot for a minute that he was a soldier as well as a farmer. He went out the gate and set his rifle down while his fingers probed the poor thing's broken bone. Within that minute he was shot in the back and his head was severed to be carried back and displayed in a camp of the *fedayeen*. They found his headless corpse in the morning, covered with desert maggots. He was a good man. I fought with him in Jerusalem and later in Beersheba. Once Rebecca and I went to Yotvata because he gave a small recital. He was a cellist. He never saw his enemy and later it was learned that the young camel's leg had been shattered by a bullet. So now when Amos's four year-old son grows to be bar mitzvah, he will say Kaddish for his father who was too good a farmer to be a cautious soldier."

They were silent and David looked at the children, at Mindell and Danielle and Noam, who had listened without shock and horror to their father's story. His colleagues at learned conferences would protest that such tales traumatized, created anxious fears, nocturnal terrors. But his son-in-law, heir to a new wisdom, knew that his children must be prepared, educated into vigilance, trained to strength. He was relieved that Rebecca's husband was not afraid to confront the truth.

"But don't you think that the Triparate Declaration will stop the *fedayeen* raids?" Aaron asked.

He referred to an agreement signed by France, Britain, and the United States, guaranteeing that the borders of Israel and its neighbors be secure and warning that punitive action would follow any infringement.

Yehuda shrugged.

"The Triparate Declaration's been in effect for four years now and for four years the *fedayeen* have ignored it and France, Britain, and the United States have ignored the *fedayeen*. Perhaps when Britain sees the dangers to Suez, it will make a move, but no one will move forward to protect Jewish lives. We must wait until the Canal or oil move the big powers to action. Meanwhile we must look to our own protection because the worst is not behind us. It is ahead of us. This Nasser makes us look back at Farouk as though he were a saint." His voice was grave but not frightened, and Danielle and Noam moved toward him like young tropistic plants, seeking the warmth of his outstretched arm, the shelter of his firm, lean body.

"Enough. No more talk of war. Tomorrow we have a celebration. Yaakov's circumcision and three kibbutz weddings," Rebecca said.

"I hope Michael will be here in time."

Leah looked worriedly out the window. Sheaves of stars were stretched across the vast desert skies but she saw only its impenetrable blackness and heard the keenings of a distant jackal, the slash of a sudden wind against the date-palm leaves. The stories had unnerved her, had quickened forgotten fears. She wanted to be done with danger, free of the fear of violence, but outside this bright room where her family gathered, chilly winds blew and unknown strangers moved stealthily across the shifting sands.

"Oh, Michael will probably drive down with the lorry from Beth HaCochav," Yehuda said. "That was his plan. They must have left the Galilee this morning and probably they stopped over in Beersheva. They'll reach here at midday, about the same time we expect the rabbi to arrive."

"The rabbi's going to be pretty busy," Noam said. "Chana's had the kitchen ovens going since early this morning. Cakes and cookies and puddings."

"I'm not worried about having enough to eat, but where will everyone sleep?" Rebecca wondered.

"That will take care of itself," Yehuda assured her. "You know when we were teen-agers we hitchhiked through the country. There were fewer houses then, fewer settlements. Yet wherever we went, beds were found. We slept on porches and balconies, and sometimes people would insist that we take their bedrooms and they themselves would sleep outside on sleeping bags."

There was a wistfulness in his voice for those long-lost nights of his youth, and Leah saw Rebecca turn away, her eyes bright with pain. It was with his first wife, Miriam, that the silken-eyed Yehudah had shared the sleeping bags and beds in unknown rooms and beneath star-studded skies. Old loves encroached on new ones; pain and pleasure, anguish and ardor commingled. Rebecca would have to learn how to assimilate the old and the new, to pluck the pain from loss and to treasure moments in muted memory—just as Leah had.

"What I am really worried about," Yehuda continued, keeping his voice low because Danielle had fallen asleep, her head resting on his shoulder, "is security. If the *fedayeen* know there is a celebration here they will consider it a great triumph, a victory, to launch a raid."

"But how would they ever know?" Mindell asked.

"Maybe by smelling Chana's cooking," Noam offered.

"Now we are being silly. It must be time to go to bed."

They rose and said good night. Yehuda, still holding the sleeping Danielle whom he would carry back to the children's house, bent to kiss Leah, the mother-in-law whom he had met that morning and recognized at once. David held Rebecca close and felt with joy the full maternal body, smelling faintly of milk, of the woman who had grown from his small laughing daughter, his American princess, to mother the motherless and capture beauty across stretches of canvas. He was proud of her and proud too of his tall sons. They would struggle, his gentle, thoughtful boys, but they would triumph.

Aaron stood across the room and David glimpsed a new softness in his son's eyes. Aaron would sleep well that night, he knew, and he wondered if he himself would find sleep, already conscious of the familiar pain which inched across his chest and shot with deadly accuracy into his arms. But Syd Adler had been right. The pains came more infrequently now and frightened him less. And the pills were immediately efficacious. He hurried toward them and Leah complained, as they crossed from Rebecca's bungalow to their own, that he walked too quickly across the unfamiliar terrain.

*

The rabbi, a plump young man whose short bronze beard curled gently and whose embroidered skullcap wobbled uneasily on his thick hair, arrived just before midday, driving a yellow Studebaker caked with desert dust and overflowing with pomegranates and melons, baskets of new spring tomatoes, tiny cucumbers with prickly spines. The various kibbutzim he had visited on his swing through the *aravah,* the southernmost part of the Negev, sent gifts to their neighbors, and he distributed them with a shy smile and replaced a bushel of northern oranges with a basket of bright-green scallions. A rifle was slung across the crates and his blue-velvet prayer-shawl bag rested on it. He wore khaki shorts and a work shirt, but he changed into baggy gray slacks to perform the first of the marriages on the soft parched grass of the lawn.

The wedding canopy was a prayer shawl stretched on poles of fresh-cut palm wood and fringed with streamers of braided flowers. The brides wore simple dresses of thin white fabric and carried small bouquets of hardy desert flowers—the pale-white bud of the tamarisk, the pink-and-white meadow saffron, fragile spears of lavender, and rich purple wild irises that grow between moon-colored mounds of sand. The kibbutz children had collected the bridal bouquets and Leah had met Mindell and Danielle in the pale opal light of morning, their arms laden with flowers. She smiled at her adopted granddaughters' bright faces and sniffed their burdens of sweetness. The fears of the previous night vanished and she walked between them into the communal dining hall and ate an enormous breakfast of salad, cheeses, and herring, feeling hungrier than she had felt for months.

The second bridegroom shattered a white wrapped glass beneath his foot and the shouts of "*Mazal tov!*—Good luck!" rang out as the lorry from Beth HaCochav drove up. The visitors from the north poured out, adding their shouted good wishes to those that already filled the air.

Leah watched her brother Moshe stride toward her and felt again the shock of recognition she had experienced when he and Henia met their boat at Haifa harbor. More than three decades had passed since she said good-bye to her brother at the Odessa port. Newly widowed, newly wedded, she had watched him begin his journey, dry-eyed because those were the years during which she refused to surrender to tears. Now at another dock-side they had greeted each other and the years dropped as easily as petals fall from a fragile flower. With her hair and his both graying, he a grandfather and she a grandmother, both of them orphaned by the flames of hell that had consumed the town of their birth, their only sister buried, the children grown, she allowed herself the luxury of sorrow and wept against the breast of her brother, distant but always close. The familiar rapport rushed back and their words flowed as easily and swiftly as their tears.

Moshe, the first out of the lorry, hugged her now and then Michael whirled her around in a small dance of welcome. Yaakov and Baila and their children—three small boys dressed only in royal-blue bloomers and bright red kibbutz hats—poured out, and Henia, always calm and controlled, her face wreathed in lines of contentment, followed her grandchildren.

The family, arms wrapped about each other as though to fend off new partings, new separations, joined the other members of the kibbutz to witness the third and last wedding to be performed that day. The groom was a grave-eyed boy who stood beside his bride in khaki shorts and an open shirt, his sandaled feet shifting nervously. The bride had made her dress out of the gauzy white fabric which the bedouins use for their kaffiyehs. The bright sun shone through the sheer fabric and the girl's skin glinted golden beneath it. Her fingers lightly touched her shy groom's hand and when she turned, Leah saw that her face had the sweet innocent quality of a young child. She lifted it to her new husband as a young bud rises to the warmth of the sunlight, and Leah's heart turned.

Her brother walked up to her.

"Come, Leah. Walk with me a bit. The circumcision ceremony will not be for another half-hour and I want to see the avocado fields," he said.

An accordionist struck up a gay hora and as they walked the music trailed behind them, one tune leading to another.

"Do you remember that one?" Moshe asked. "We used to dance to it in the Zionist clubhouse in Odessa."

"I remember," she said.

She looked at her brother who had been a slender boy with their father's narrow build and delicate features. He was a muscular man, his skin stained a golden brown. His thick hair was gray and he walked with the purposeful stride of a man who has little patience for leisure but moves swiftly from one task to another.

"It was an age ago. So many things have happened," he said.

"Yes. Do you remember those days in Odessa—right after Yaakov's death? You asked me then to come to Palestine with you."

"Yes. But you don't regret going to America, do you? You did such wonderful things there. The designing. The painting. And your life with David and the children has been good."

Moshe studied his sister's face. The daring of the young girl he had known had evolved into the strength of the woman. His sister stood tall and straight, her dark eyes large and quiet. She wore her dark hair today in a coronet of braids, just as she had worn it when she had been a bride, as young as the golden-skinned girl who had stood that day beneath the marriage canopy. Bands of silver ran through its dark thickness and he had noticed, too, the network of fine lines about her wide-set eyes.

The brother and sister stood now at the edge of a field where young plants grew in hopeful, fragile rows of green, shivering beneath the rhythmic silvery caress of the streams of water splayed forth by a revolving sprinkler. Prisms of color danced in the crystal spray and tiny rivulets ran through the hoed fields, turning the loose sands into fertile, sustaining earth.

"I should like to paint this field. This field and the stretch of desert beyond," Leah said. A canvas stirred to life in her mind and she wondered if she could buy brushes and paints in Beersheba.

Her brother did not reply. A patient man, he waited for an answer to his question.

"No," she said at last. "We each had our separate journeys to make, Moshe. And we traveled forth to life—to new and different lives. What I regret is that we left so many behind to death. But that we could not help. No one can tell anyone else which roads to travel. Even our children we cannot tell. They must find their own ways, make their own journeys."

She stooped and plucked up a clump of hard-packed earth in which loose grains of sand were trapped. She passed it to her brother, and as he took it the loose sand drifted to the ground and was lifted and carried away by a gentle desert breeze. They smiled and walked quickly back to join the others.

*

An ancient acacia tree grew just beyond the bungalow where Rebecca and Yehuda lived, and its mushroom-shaped crest, brown-leaved and thorn-entwined, cast a circle of shade onto the pebbled ground below. Here a long table had been set up and covered with a thick white cloth of heavy linen. A small pillow covered with an embroidered pillow slip had been placed on it and just above it a small blue amulet dangled from one branch of the acacia tree and a bright red ribbon had been tied to another. A polished silver wine goblet stood on the table, and Leah was startled when she recognized it as her father's. Moshe followed her gaze.

"Yes. He gave it to me the morning that we sailed. And now we use it at the circumcision of his great-grandson," Moshe said, and put his hand on his sister's shoulder. All journeys have their landmarks and she confronted this one with a commingling of joy and anguish.

They heard the infant's lusty cry and Rebecca and Yehuda moved toward the table just behind the rabbi. Baila held the baby, smiled, and handed him to Aaron, who took the infant and walked toward the chair, following the rabbi's mimed directions. The white pillow was placed on Aaron's lap and he put the infant on it, his large freckled hands handling the small bundle of writhing flesh with surprising ease, with a natural gentleness. The rabbi lifted a scalpel that glinted in the sunlight and the infant blinked at the sudden silvery brightness. The prayer was intoned and the guests took up the words of the rabbi in fluent unison.

"Blessed art Thou O Lord our God, king of the universe, who had made us holy through His commandments and commanded us about circumcision."

The scalpel flashed and the blue amulet danced in a shifting breeze. A scarlet drop of blood fell on the snowy whiteness of the pillow slip as the foreskin was severed from the tiny penis.

The baby wailed piteously and a sponge of cotton soaked with ed wine was pressed against his lips. Hungrily he sucked and miled, the pain forgotten, the wine sweet and anesthesizing, and e lay quietly as the bandage was applied.

In the circlet of shade, Rebecca and Yehuda held hands and oftly repeated another blessing after the rabbi.

"Blessed art Thou O Lord our God who has sustained us in life nto this day," they said.

Leah looked at Aaron, her own firstborn, who held the child till, grateful that he had served as godfather to the infant who bore is father's name. A cycle had been completed and new generations vould begin new journeys. She moved to stand beside David and laced her hand within his.

*

A small pain awakened David later, deep into the night, after he long afternoon and evening of feasting and dancing, of song and alk, was at last over. In the darkness he spoke to it as though it vere an old adversary for whom he had formed a reluctant ondness.

"You're back again, are you?" he said. "Coming less and less often, though. Well, I'll soon take care of you."

Moving slowly, glad of the moon-streaked darkness, he found is pills and the glass of water he had learned to keep at his edside. Well, he had invited this attack, he knew, by the wild lancing of the evening, but still he did not regret it. The music whirled through his head again and he thought of how his body ad moved easily, the steps of the dances easily remembered, as he lanced to the happy tunes of his youth.

He smiled as he remembered the feel of the firmness of Leah's flesh beneath his hands as he whirled her around the coarse wood floor of the kibbutz social hall. She slept heavily beside him now, her mouth slowly open, curved into a smile as though she too remembered the dancing and the joy. Her bare arm was flung across the pillow and gently he eased it down, kissed the soft white flesh of her forearm, and covered it with a blanket.

The pill, as always, had stimulated him to a wakefulness which he knew he would not overcome, but the pain, blessedly, was gone. He thought of reading but was afraid the light would waken Leah. He would take a walk instead, he decided, and dressed quickly and quietly, putting on his warmest sweater and jacket against the chill of the desert night.

Outside the air was brisk and stars filled the sky, a myriad of silver flowers which clustered here and ranged there against the soft blackness. He looked up at the argentous overgrowth and found the familiar constellations, the Orion family outlined against the velvety sky, trembling so close to him that he felt his face must be bathed in the metallic light that shimmered through the night.

He walked on and passed the small bungalow of the couple wed that afternoon. A lamp glowed softly in their window and as he passed he saw the naked form of the young bridegroom, carefully holding a glass of water, his fingers cupped about it as though it were a precious offering. Rebecca's small house was dark and David wondered how many brothers and sisters would join the infant Yaakov in the years to come, how many grandchildren he would welcome. Still, it did not matter. He had this day held his first infant grandson close. He walked on, shivering beneath a new and harsher chill. The slight breeze that wafted over him was ice edged, reminding him of the cold night air of the Russian forest of his boyhood. He trembled suddenly, overcome by cold and by memory. He would go back to the room where Leah slept, to seek out the familiar contours of her warmth and feel her breath sweet against his neck. Now pain had gone and a sweet fatigue replaced it.

He quickened his steps, but as he passed the pink stucco children's house, a slender figure slipped out of the shadows. He paused, thinking it was the watchman, and as he stood there the man touched a window, struggled with it briefly and when it did not yield, stole over to another. Now David clearly saw the moving figure's white headdress, the flash of polished blue metal in his hand.

"Stop!" David called and hurried over to the building.

The stranger wheeled about and David saw the milk white fear in the Arab's eyes, the tight terrified set of his lips. He saw the hand move upward and the blue metal flash in the silvery starlight. A shot shattered the silence of the night and David's body exploded with heat and pain but he moved forward and shouted again, "Stop! Stop, I say!" He did not recognize his own voice but cursed it for its softness.

Lights flashed on, doors opened, and men with rifles and guns dashed across the compound, shouting orders with fierce staccato efficiency. David fell then, his face sinking into the softness of the blanket of desert grass. The pain washed over him and then with blessed swiftness, vanished. Briefly, his fingers opened and closed and opened again.

He was dead when she reached him, when she bent over his body and covered it with hot, unbelieving tears. She took his hand, the palm outstretched as though searching for her absent touch, and pressed it to her mouth, biting at the flesh, scraping her face with her husband's lifeless fingers.

"No, David," she protested wildly. "No. No. No!"

He was not dead. He could not be dead. They had traveled too far together to be separated like this.

It was Mindell and Danielle who moved forward at last, shivering in their long white nightdresses, their soft eyes bright with new grief. Gently, each took one of Leah's hands and led her away from David's lifeless body to the bungalow where dim lights burned against the danger and the darkness of the night.

Russia
1956
Epilogue

Fall arrives early in Russia. Its warning chill begins even before the last crops of summer are harvested and the leaves turn gold and russet while the flowers of late summer bloom with a desperate brightness. The workers in the communal fields wear heavy jackets in the cold light of dawn, shed them as the sun slowly rises, and put them on again only hours later when the sun's brief life wanes and its harsh gold pales against the sky that turns so swiftly from blue to gray.

The tall woman who sat in the rear seat of the Intourist car, which traveled slowly north along the road that parallels the Sea of Azov, wore a hooded cape of thick blue wool. The driver, swiveling slightly in his seat, had noticed that her shoes and bag were of the soft American leather his own wife yearned for. But when she spoke to him, to advise him of a runoff where the sea road cut into a forest clearing lined with dwarf pines, she spoke in a clear but oddly accented Russian. She carried an American passport, he knew, having checked it routinely at the Odessa hotel when he picked her up. Leah Goldfeder. It was not a Russian name but he had gone to school with a boy whose name was similar—Goldenkrantz or Goldenberg. A Jewish boy, he knew, having once seen his identity card where the line which calls for nationality had been marked "Jew." Perhaps this woman too was Jewish. He had heard that once many Jews had lived in this part of Russia where the sea air penetrated the green thickness of forest lands. It was, after all, beautiful country.

He drove slowly, enjoying the ride, enjoying the luxury of having only one passenger with whom he could talk in his own language when usually his touring car was full of foreigners and he struggled to explain his country in languages painfully learned and painfully used.

As the day grew warmer the woman removed her hood. Her long hair was pulled softly back from her face and nestled into a loose bun at the nape of her neck. Waves of white rippled through her hair and when he caught sight of her face in his rear-view mirror he saw that she was older than he had thought, close to sixty perhaps, and very beautiful. She had a rare face, the sort of strong face which was denied prettiness in girlhood but became proud with beauty in age. He saw that a small half-dimple lurked at one corner of her mouth which was just a bit too wide.

She leaned forward in her seat, her eyes raking the road. Once she asked him to stop and he waited as she knelt in a meadow, thick with long wild grass and varicolored flowers. She gathered up long-stemmed yellow buttercups and bright-red flowers from whose dark hearts wiry black tendrils sprang.

"Just north of Osipenko," she said, "there is a small village. I am looking for a farm just outside of it."

"Osipenko." The name stirred no memory and he pulled over and reached for his map. It was marked but a note recorded that the town had been razed some years back because a new road had been built through it.

"The town is no longer there," he said, and she sighed.

She had not really expected the town to be there. The week before she had visited the site of the village of her birth and that village too had not been there. Fields of silver-green alfalfa grew where once small wooden houses had stood, behind rough planks spread to create a road through encroaching mud. Only one very old man remembered that once there had been a village there, a tiny town of *Zhids—Jews*. What had happened to them? He did not know. He did not remember. He smoked a long curving pipe of the sort her father had smoked, its bowl carved of ivory. Wistful blue strands of smoke wept about his mouth and he watched them rise in the sunlight as though they might contain the answers to the rgent questions this strange woman asked. The *Zhids* had gone uring the war, during the days of shooting and the nights of fire. ıe had turned away then, and the old man was briefly bitter ecause she did not thank him, but later a woman had told him that ıe American lady had been crying.

Leah leaned back against the seat of the car, her fingers deftly ıoving among the flowers. Perhaps, after all, she should have llowed Aaron or Michael to travel with her from Israel. They had ıanted to come, had argued and insisted. But she had remained rm and Moshe had advised them to let her do as she wished. She ad wanted to return to this land where her journey had begun, to ıe fields bright with wild flowers and the city by the sea from hich she and David had gone forth to their new lives.

It was a journey which David would have wanted her to make, he knew, a journey which they had vaguely planned to make ɔgether. Instead he lay buried in the first grave to be dug in the mall cemetery the young kibbutz had reserved for its dead. Small hildren, his own grandchildren and others, would come to his rave each year and place tiny pebbles of tribute on the headstone, nowing that the man buried there had died protecting the lives of leeping children. Already the American doctor, the visiting randfather, had become a kibbutz myth. And Leah too would ome, with Aaron and Michael and the families that would be born ɔ them in turn. Through the years they would journey again and gain to visit their dead, to see how Rebecca's children grew, how he sand turned to earth and how the newly planted date palms ently brushed the sky.

But to Russia she had journeyed alone, yet she was not alone. Gentle ghosts traveled at her side, memories both harsh and sweet vhispered to her through long silences.

"Now, Madame," the driver said. "We are just north of)sipenko and there are no farms here."

"Ah, but once there were," she said, too softly for him to hear She raised her voice. "But this is the road I want. Drive very slowly now."

She opened the window and leaned out, her eyes marking a passing bramble bush, looking hard at a hedge where chinaberries would sparkle in a month's time, her hands still busy with the flowers on her lap.

"Here. Stop here," she said at last.

She got out of the car and walked toward a tree, a Lombardy tree, bent so low with age that the leaves on its lowest branche trailed across the twig-littered ground. The tree had a wide trunk and she knelt before it, touching its bark, rising to move about it in a slow circle. It was midday now and the sun, at its strongest, broke forth among the leaves. She leaned against the tree, her fine white skin dappled by sunlight and leafy shadow.

The driver followed her eyes as she gazed northward. Yes, once a house had stood there. He saw the single broken gray cinder block that must have been a foundation stone. But she, the tall woman in the dark blue cape, seemed to see the house itself. As he watched she slowly loosened her hair, shook it free of the confining pins, and allowed it to flow about her shoulders—a cascade of thick black hai through which white waves dipped in gentle strokes. Briefly, she seemed to dance, moving slowly in the steps of a mysterious secre rhythm as young girls sometimes do when they are alone and unseen. He turned away and went to smoke a cigarette on the other side of the car.

After some minutes she joined him, her hair once more replaced in its soft neat bun, her face set again in the comfortable lines of accepting age.

"We can start back now," she said. "Perhaps we will reach Odessa in time for a late lunch."

As they neared the city, she leaned forward.

"Do you have a daughter?" she asked.

He nodded.

"Perhaps she would like this."

She handed him a wreath of woven flowers, of the tall buttercups entwined with the dark-hearted red blossoms which, he remembered now, were sometimes called "The Blood of Russia." He thanked her and she leaned back. She had reached journey's end and had no need for souvenirs.

Lightning Source UK Ltd.
Milton Keynes UK
UKOW03f0809120417
298943UK00003B/72/P

9 781611 878